E. Everett-Gre

In Taunton Town

E. Everett-Green

In Taunton Town

1st Edition | ISBN: 978-3-75235-264-1

Place of Publication: Frankfurt am Main, Germany

Year of Publication: 2020

Outlook Verlag GmbH, Germany.

IN TAUNTON
TOWN

By

E. EVERETT-GREEN

CHAPTER I.

THE SNOWE FAMILY.

I certainly never thought when I was young that I should live to write a book! Scarce do I know how it betides that I have the courage to make so bold, now that I am well stricken in years, and that my hair has grown grey. To be sure (if I may say so without laying myself open to the charge of boasting, a thing abhorrent to me), I have always been reckoned something of a scholar, notwithstanding that I was born a farmer's son, and that my father would have been proud could he but have set his name on paper, as men of his station begin to do now-a-days, and think little of it. But times have changed since I was a boy—perhaps for the better, perhaps for the worse; who knows? Anyhow, there is more of learning in the world, for sure, though whether more of honesty let others be the judge!

And now, how and when am I to begin my tale?

Sitting over the fire and recalling stirring scenes of bygone days, it seems simple enough to record in writing my memories of those times when we good folks of the West Country thought we had found a deliverer who would break from the neck of England the yoke of the hated Papist tyranny which was being laid upon us (at least so we all feared and believed) by one whose name is yet spoken in these parts with a curse. But when one sits to a table with quill and ink-horn beside one, then it does not appear so simple a task; and inasmuch as I have no skill in such matters as the writing of chronicles, I must e'en go to work my own fashion, and if that fashion be a poor one, must ask pardon of all such as may have the patience or complaisance to read my poor story.

Well, then, it seems that the first thing to do is to state who I am, and how it came about that I was so mixed up with that brief period of history which has left such indelible marks in the hearts of the people of our fair West Country. The former is quickly and easily explained; the latter will be unfolded as this narrative proceeds.

My father was one Joseph Snowe, a farmer of some substance, and the eldest of three brothers. He was a man of some importance, being the owner of Five Gable Farm at Shorthorne; and Shorthorne—as I suppose all men know—lies midway betwixt Taunton and Bridgewater, two notable fair towns of our fertile and pleasant county of Somerset.

There was an old saw spoken anent the Snowe family which said that the men thereof who were not farmers and tillers of the soil were brewers of malt liquor and the keepers of hostelries. Nor would it become me to deny with too much eagerness the truth of this saying, seeing that I myself have been master of an inn these many years, and that I have brothers who both till the soil and sell and make malt liquor.

But to return to my father and his two brothers. Five Gable Farm had belonged to the Snowes as far back as we cared to ask questions. It had passed from father to son for many generations; and since I was the youngest of six brothers, there seemed little likelihood of its passing to alien hands for many a day to come.

My father's name was Joseph—as became the eldest of the house; for Joseph was a great name in the Snowe family. Next to him came Uncle John, of whom I shall have much to say in these pages; and last of the three, Uncle Robert, who was a good deal younger than the other pair, two sisters having been born in between.

Now Uncle John was a big man, as big as father himself, with a loud voice and a right jovial manner. I doubt not that he found this jovial address a great source of income to him; for he kept the inn of the Three Cups in gay Taunton Town, and travellers who paused at his door to ask the way or quaff a cup of mead on horseback seldom rode onwards after having had speech of mine host—unless much pressed for time—but dismounted to taste the good cheer of the house, and more often than not remained until the morrow beneath the friendly shelter of the roof-tree. I was to learn all about this in good sooth, as will shortly be made clear to all.

Uncle Robert had followed the example of Uncle John, or had perhaps been guided in his choice by the old adage of which I have spoken; for he too became master of an inn in Bridgewater, by name the Cross Keys. It was not such a flourishing or important house as the Three Cups in Taunton, nevertheless it was a comfortable and well-liked place of rest; and the name of Snowe went far in the district as a warranty for good cheer and fair charges.

Now it will readily be seen that it was a great matter of advantage to my father to have two brothers within easy distance of the farm, both in the inn-keeping line of business. All our spare produce was sent to one inn or the other, bought readily at fair prices, and often bespoken for months beforehand. We prided ourselves on the breed of our sheep, the quality of our beef, the excellence of our smoked hams; and the fame of all these things made us well known both in Taunton and in Bridgewater, so that private persons from the neighbourhood would come craving of mother to spare them of our produce, and these earnings of hers came in the course of a year to a tidy little sum of money.

But I must not wander on in this fashion, or I shall scarce get my story told as I have promised. And to pave the way for the tale I am to tell, I must needs talk for a while about myself, even though this may savour somewhat of self-conceit and vanity. Not that I have any cause to be vain of my outward man, as I will incontinently show, for I have been malformed and somewhat of a hunchback all my life; and if the word I have used is somewhat too strong, at least it is the one I most often heard employed towards me when first I mixed with other lads in Taunton Town. And I may not deny that I had and always have had a stoop of the neck, and that one of my shoulders is higher than the other, whilst my stature has always been notably less than that of any of the men of my name and race.

Now this would be very surprising in a family noted for its tall and comely sons and daughters, had it not been for the lamentable fact that in my tender infancy I was overlooked by a witch, or in some sort bewitched, so that from that day forward I began to grow crooked, and never attained the grace or stature which my brothers and sisters inherited as a natural right.

And this misfortune befell me in this wise.

I was but a babe in arms, I think I was nigh upon a year old, and as fine and comely a child (so at least my mother will have it) as one need wish to see. She had been out to visit a neighbour, and was returning across the moor as the dusk was drawing on; and as ill-luck would have it, her way led her close to the hut where there lived a witch, who went by the name of Mother Whale —though whether this were truly her name, or whether witches have rightly any names at all, I have not knowledge to say. Be that as it may, Mother Whale was so called by all the country side; and young maids resorted to her to have their fortunes told, whilst the village swains who dared as much would purchase from her small bottles in which she had brewed love potions to win them their sweethearts, or magic draughts to make them strong in feats of courage or skill. She had worked many notable cures on cattle and pigs, as well as on human beings, by her charms and simples, and was held in much repute. Nevertheless men feared her not a little also, because that she was without doubt possessed of the evil eye; and when she chose to overlook a man or his possessions, as sure as the sun shone in the sky some grievous harm would happen to him or to them, as had been proved times without number—so all the folks of the place said.

My mother felt a great fear when she found herself nigh to this lonely hut so near the day's end, for she had an idea that witches who were fairly friendly and well disposed by day became full of evil purposes at night (which may or may not be true—I pass no opinion on the matter), and she was hurrying by in a great fright, when suddenly the form of the old woman rose from the very ground at her feet.

I have heard my mother tell the story many and many a time; and she always maintains that there was nothing to conceal the old woman—not so much as a mound or a tuft of grass—and that she must have sprung out of the bowels of the earth, for there she suddenly was, standing full in front of her; and my mother being already somewhat scared, fell now into such a terrible fright that she dropped me upon a heap of sharp-pointed stones close by (when I ask her if the old woman might not have been concealed behind this heap of stones, she always grows irritable, and tells me not to cavil at her words), and fled for her very life. But inasmuch as the power of a mother's love is a notable thing, and will run many a risk sooner than leave a helpless babe in peril, so it befell that my mother turned back after a while, and even dared to go boldly up to the very hut itself in search of her offspring.

The door of the hut stood open as she approached, and by the light of the turf fire she could see what passed within, and a sight was revealed to her which made her heart stand still and curdled the very blood in her veins. For the old woman had actually got me laid across her lap, and was rubbing my back, which was sorely cut and bruised by the stones, with some preparation of her own; and when my mother appeared to claim her child, she looked her over with a glance which made the poor creature shake in her shoes, and chid her severely for dropping a tender babe and fleeing without so much as a backward glance.

My mother declares that from that day forward she always knew that harm would come of it; that the witch had overlooked either her or me. And in truth from that time I grew puny and peaked, and when I began to walk (which was not till long after a child should do so) it was easy to see that something was wrong with me. All the place knew that I had been bewitched, and held Mother Whale responsible, and respected and feared her the more for it; but for my part I often wonder whether it was not the fall upon the stones, for Mother Whale was always very good to me, and in my lonely childhood I found in her one of my chiefest friends.

For my childhood was lonely. I could not work on the farm like my brothers. I was sickly and weak until I grew to be ten or twelve years old. My back would ache for almost nothing, and I was so little use that I was always pushed on one side, or bidden to run indoors out of the way. My sisters were kind to me, and would find me little light household tasks; but the manhood in me revolted from doing "woman's work," and I suppose that is why I became what the neighbours used to call a scholar,—which convinced them almost more than anything else that I had indeed been bewitched.

I could write a long history of the joys opened out before me when once I had mastered the mysteries of reading, and could cull from the row of ancient books upon the shelf in the parlour the treasures they contained. But this would be but tedious reading for others. The Bible was in itself a perfect storehouse of information, and my mother encouraged me to read it, thinking that it might prove an antidote to the poison of witchcraft which she always believed was working within me. And there were certain godly pamphlets written by persecuted men of past days, showing forth the evils of Popery, and claiming for men the rights which Protestants have since won for themselves: these I was permitted and encouraged to read, and also "Fox's Book of Martyrs," which had a gruesome fascination for me, the more so as it was illustrated with many a horrid picture of some martyr enduring punishment or death. I was brought up in the fervent conviction that all Papists would like to serve us good Protestants as these martyrs were being served in my pictures; and not unnaturally I grew up with a pious horror of the very name of Popery, and shivered from head to foot when I heard whispers of the Popish inclinations of the King, and the unconcealed Popery of the Duke of York, who was like to be his successor—unless, indeed, the Duke of Monmouth should turn out to be the King's legitimate son, when all danger of a Papist on the throne would cease at once.

Without therefore pausing to speak of the other books in which I delighted more than in all these godly writings put together—to wit, the immortal dramas of the great bard William Shakespeare, and that marvellous conception of Mr. John Milton's, "Paradise Lost"—I will pursue the theme just suggested, that of the Protestant Succession, as men began to call it, meaning the hopes and aspirations of the people of the country, that if the King died without issue by his Queen, some way might be found for placing the Duke of Monmouth upon the throne instead of the dark Duke of York, whom men both feared and hated.

Now it is needless to say much respecting the parentage of the Duke of Monmouth, for all the world knows that he was the son of Lucy Walters, a woman of whom little good can be written, and that the King was always supposed to be his father, and indeed gave to him a father's affection; so much so that men hoped he would seek to pass an Act of Parliament excluding the Duke of York from the succession, on account of his religion, and appointing the Duke of Monmouth to succeed him.

This hope was the more fervent in the minds of the people because there were many who declared that the Duke was born in lawful wedlock, and that there was in existence a black box containing all the needful proofs of this fact. We in the West Country believed in that black box almost as in an article of faith, and every news-letter that came to Taunton Town was eagerly opened and scanned in hopes of finding in it some precious hint with regard to this matter.

But my own interest in the handsome and dashing young Duke was of a more personal and particular nature than could have been the case simply from reading books and leaflets and pamphlets, or even from hearing through our uncles on their visits the talk of the towns.

And it came about in this wise.

I have said before that I was but a puny and sickly child, and that until I grew to be ten years old I had but little health. This was indeed my melancholy condition; for in addition to my crooked spine and lack of muscle, I suffered from time to time from that obscure and painful malady which used to be known as "King's Evil," and which was not to be cured by any leech or physician, but only by the touch of the King's hand, or the hand of his lawful successor. Some indeed declared that a seventh son could sometimes cure it by touching; but though I was taken more than once to such, I received no good from the touch. It was the seventh son of a seventh son in whom the power was said to lie, and some held that it lay also in the hand of a man who had been hanged; but my mother would never let me try that touch, and so I went on enduring the evil until the day of which I am about to write.

I had an aunt in the town of Ilminster, one Betsy Marwell by name, my mother's sister, and a widow of some substance. She having heard of me and my malady, sent one day when I was about ten years old, and bid my mother let me pay a visit to her, for that she knew a great collector of herbs and simples who had had wonderful success in curing all manner of maladies that baffled the skill of the leeches; and she would keep me in her house and doctor me with his preparations, and send me home, she fondly hoped, in better and sounder health than I had when I came.

I remember well even now that first visit I ever paid away from my own home, and the excitements of dwelling in a town, and of sitting at table in a parlour with a carpet laid down in the middle, and eating with a fork instead of a wooden spoon as I had always done at home. I remember the grave face and the long beard of the man who came to look at me, and who bid me take many baths with sundry simples thrown in, and use certain ointments of his preparation, and who said that in time I should be sound and whole again.

I abode with my aunt two whole months, and it was during that time that the wonderful thing happened to me of which I am now about to write.

I had not been long at Ilminster before the whole town was thrown into joyful excitement by the news that the Duke of Monmouth was about to make a progress through the county, staying in the houses of such of the gentry as had accommodation sufficient to receive him and his suite, and allowing himself to be seen by the people, and approached by all who desired it. I soon heard that the house of Mr. Speke—White Lackington by name—was to be one of the places visited. I knew Mr. Speke by name right well—he and his son-in-law, Mr. Trenchard, being looked upon in our county as men of great virtue, and stanch to the Protestant cause, as in very truth they were, and suffered for it much; and I knew by this time that White Lackington House was but the distance of a mile or so from Ilminster, and I thought it would go hard but that I would make shift to see the Duke when he was there, if I were still with my aunt.

Indeed when the time drew near there was no difficulty about this, for all the world was agog about the Duke, and preparations were being made to admit all those who desired to see him to the park of White Lackington upon a certain day; whilst my aunt Betsy was as eager as any to see the hero, and before the day arrived she drew me to her side and spoke to me very earnestly.

First she examined my wounds, and shook her head over them. To be sure they were better than when I came to her, and some were fast disappearing; but she was not satisfied with the progress I had made, and she said to me with grave emphasis,—

"Dicon"—my name, I should say, was Richard, but I was never called anything but Dicon for many a long year of my life—"Dicon, to-morrow, if by any hap you can make shift to do so, get near to his Grace the Duke, and pray of him to lay his hand upon you and touch you for the King's Evil. If he be, as I hold him, the rightful son of our gracious King, his touch will be a cure for you such as none other can help you to. If you can only make shift

8

yourself to touch him in the throng, it will perchance be enough. But let not this chance slip unused. Providence, it may be, hath sent it. Let the people but know him for the true heir to the throne, and not all the Dukes of York ever yet born shall keep him from his own when the right time comes!"

Whereby it may be seen that my aunt was a woman of spirit, as indeed she proved herself to be in days to come.

Upon the morrow we, in common with half the good folks of Ilminster, set forth for White Lackington to see the Duke at our ease. He had ridden into Ilminster the previous day, to attend divine service in the church; but although I had been well-nigh squeezed to death in the press, I had not succeeded in obtaining so much as a sight of him. But to-day there would be no such crowding and crushing. The wide park land gave space for us to move at ease, and all would be able to look upon the face of one whom they loved, perhaps with scarce sufficient cause.

How we huzzahed and shouted, and tossed our caps into the air, when the party from the great house moved across the sunny gardens and came toward us! For my part, I had a most excellent view, for I climbed into the fork of the huge chestnut tree which is one of the notable objects of interest at White Lackington, and from my perch up there I beheld the Duke, was able to scan his handsome features, to see the smiles that lighted his face, and almost to hear the gracious words he addressed to the people who crowded round him as he moved.

Fortune favoured me that day; for as the throng about him increased, the Duke took up his position beneath the great chestnut tree, and I was able to command a fine view of everything that went on.

I was greatly charmed by the gracious manner of the Duke, by his kindness to all who approached, and by the friendly way in which he addressed even the humblest who succeeded in reaching him. I was wondering whether my courage would permit me to drop myself suddenly at his feet and ask the boon my aunt had desired, when my way was paved in a curious fashion. A woman suddenly forced her way through the crowd, threw herself on her knees before the Duke, touched his hand, and as suddenly disappeared in the throng, before the Duke had time to speak a single word or ask the meaning of her approach.

"Marry, but that is Elizabeth Parcet," said one of those who stood by; "the poor soul suffers terribly from the King's Evil. Doubtless she has touched your Grace with a view to cure herself of her malady."

Now hearing those words, and marking the look upon the Duke's face, I tarried no longer, but without pausing to think what I was doing or what I should say, I hastily let myself down from my exalted position, and fell on my knees before the Duke.

"Touch me, even me also, your Grace!" I cried, clasping my hands together. "I too am a sufferer from that dread malady, and I would fain be made whole."

Immediately I felt a hand laid kindly upon me, and my face and hands were touched by long white fingers such as I had seldom seen in all my life before.

"There, boy," said a kindly voice which I knew to be the Duke's. "May thy wish be given thee, and thyself healed of thy malady."

Bowing and blushing, overcome with confusion now that the thing was done, I made my way out of the crowd, scarce daring to utter the words of fervent thanks which rose to my lips.

As I went home in triumph that day, I knew within myself that I was healed, and so I told my aunt and the kind old man who had given me his simples and herbs, and who listened to my eager tale with a smile on his lips.

"Ay, lad; ay, lad," he said, nodding his head till his long beard waved to and fro, "I doubt not that thou wilt be cured. Yet cease not for a while to use my ointment and simples. They cannot harm thee, and may give thee strength and health yet."

I promised I would do so, and I kept my word, for that our father had always bidden us do. But it was the touch of the Duke's hand that cured me of my malady; that I never doubted at that time, since within a week of receiving it all my wounds were healed, and at once I began to gain such strength and power and vigour as I had not known since the day of my accident. Herbs and simples may have a value of their own—I would not take upon myself to deny it; but I was cured of the King's Evil by other means than that, and went to my home rejoicing when the time came that I had no further need for my good aunt's care or skill.

She shed many tears at parting with me, and bid me not forget her, and come and see her again some day. This I promised I would do when occasion served, and I kept my word, as this tale will show. But we little guessed how and under what circumstances the next visit would be paid, nor how large a part the gay young Duke who had touched me for my cure would play in my future life.

At home I was received with wonder and joy. Of course my parents knew nothing of my adventure at White Lackington, for we did not write letters to absent friends, as men are beginning to do now. But when seated at the well-spread supper-table I told them of what had befallen me, they listened with open eyes and mouths agape, and my father, bringing his hand heavily down upon the table, cried,—

"That settles the question. The black box could do no more. The Duke of Monmouth is our rightful King. Hurrah for the Protestant Duke! Down with the Papists and with the Popish Duke of York!"

And we all echoed these words with acclamation. Our hearts were from that day forward centred in the Duke.

All this happened in the year 1680, when I was just ten years of age.

CHAPTER II.

MY CAREER IS SETTLED.

Of the next two years of my life I need say little. They passed in a fashion that to me was pleasant and easy enough.

I have before explained that I had been a sickly child, and was on this account spared from those duties about the farm which were required of my brothers; and I have said something with regard to my acquirements in the matter of reading, which were then somewhat more rare than they are like to become as time goes on. My father had a small library of books which had been bequeathed to him by a distant kinsman, who could have known but little of his tastes, and in these books I revelled with a delight past the power of expression. Whilst at my aunt Betsy's house in Ilminster, I had also acquired the rudiments of the art of writing and the casting up of accounts and the keeping of books; and when I returned home, I had no mind to let these things slip from my memory.

Nor was there any need for this, since my father showed no disposition to make use of me upon the farm, having indeed the full belief that I had been bewitched, and that I should bring him ill-luck with the beasts if I went amongst them.

Nor was the belief in my possession of unlawful powers lessened by an incident which I will forthwith relate, although, truth to tell, I cannot explain it, nor do I think it to be any proof that there is aught amiss with me, or ever was. I believe that dumb beasts may be governed by motives of caprice, even as human beings are, and that they can take likes and dislikes and act upon them as stubbornly as their masters.

My father was a breeder and owner of forest ponies, and once in the year they were collected from the moors, where they used to run wild during a great part of the year. The foals were branded, the numbers of the yearlings and two-year-olds counted, and such amongst the rest as were old enough and strong enough for work were taken up and broken in, and sold in the neighbourhood at the various fairs to such as were wanting the like.

Now it chanced that one of the ponies thus driven in and kept for breaking, soon after my return from Ilminster, was a particularly handsome animal. He had a coat as black as the raven's wing, and eyes as large and soft as those of a deer; when he galloped round and round the field in which he was placed, he seemed scarce to touch the ground, and his pace was such that none could come anigh him save by artfulness or coaxing. And he would not suffer so much as a halter to be put upon him, but tossed his head and was off like a lightning flash, and cared not whom he overthrew and maimed as he wrested himself away; so that two of our men had been sorely hurt by him, and the rest began to say that handsome as he was, and valuable as he would prove could we but get the mastery over him, yet he had plainly been bewitched, and was possessed of a devil of malice and wickedness, and to try to tame him would be but labour thrown away. In good sooth, before long people came so to fear him that my father had perforce to say reluctantly that he was past breaking, and must either be sent back to the moor to run wild all his days, or be shot to rid him of the evil fiend within.

Now when I heard them talk thus I was grieved to the heart, for I greatly admired the beautiful creature, and had more than once stolen into the field when none else had been by, and had coaxed him to come and eat out of my hand, sometimes giving him a bit of bread or a morsel of sugar that I had reserved from mine own breakfast or midday meal, and which he came to look for now as his right. He would rub his nose upon my shoulder, and seemed to like the feel of my hands caressing his ears and his neck. It seemed to me that I could even make shift to put a halter upon him if I tried; but I had never dared to do so hitherto, lest they should say I was spoiling him—it being always thought that I knew nothing of the ways of beasts or how to manage them.

Nevertheless it was allowed by all that I could ride. Not being gifted with the strength of the others for walking, I had been suffered to ride one of the forest ponies from the time I was little more than an infant. I could ride barebacked across country without a qualm of fear, and I had little doubt that if once I could make a spring and place myself upon the back of this unruly pony, I should be able to master him forthwith.

Well, to make a long story short, and to avoid the appearance of praising myself, I will only say that when all others had given him up, I went to the refractory colt and used my methods upon him. There was no magic in these;

that I will swear if need be. But I made the creature fond of me by gentle caresses and endearing words, and when I was sure of his affection I was able to do what I would with him. He scarcely resented the halter when it was put upon him; and though the first time he felt the bit between his teeth he tossed his head and his eyes grew red and angry, yet a few kind words and caresses reconciled him even to this; and he made no plunge or unruly demonstration when I gently clambered upon his back for the first time, talking all the while and praising him for his docility. I think he looked upon it as another form of caress, and he held his tail and head high as he set to trot with his burden around the field, his long elastic stride seeming to scorn the earth he trod on, and sending thrills of delight through his rider; for methought it was like the action of one of those winged steeds from Ph[oe]bus' chariot, of which I had read in one of my books.

Erelong Blackbird—for so I came to call him from his colour and his easy pace, which always made me think of flying—would carry me whithersoever I wished, and would follow me about the farm like a dog. I always looked to him myself within the stable, feeding him with my own hands, and bringing him water in the pail from the clearest spring. Indeed not one of the men cared to approach him, even though he was presently cured of his trick of giving a sly kick to any who passed by. But there was a look in his eye (so at least they said; I never saw it) which bespoke the devil within; and some of the men looked askance even at me, and would whisper, when they saw me tending and caressing my favourite, that it was plain there was a pair of us. Even my father did not quite like it, though he made me a present of Blackbird, and was always rather proud of the conquest I had made.

Certainly the possession of this light-footed steed all mine own (and he would suffer none else to mount him even when he had grown tame within stable walls, so that I had the exclusive use of him and all his great strength) added not a little to my happiness and health during the two years which followed my visit to Ilminster. With my books and some food in a wallet at my back, I would start off with the first freshness of the morning, and ride to one of those favourite solitary haunts of which Blackbird and I came to have many. Then turning him loose—for he would always come at a call or a whistle, and indeed seldom strayed far away, having come to guard me almost as a dog guards his master—I would set to study might and main at those arts of caligraphy and calculation which I was so wishful to acquire. Moreover, I would also declaim aloud from one of my books, reading out the words loud, and striving to give each its due weight and meaning, as my aunt Betsy had taught me to do when she made me read to her. And never was boy happier than I all through the long days of summer and the mild sunshiny ones of spring and autumn. I was so hardy by this time that only severe cold drove me within doors; and there was always a warm corner in the ingle nook where I could sit at ease. As for my sisters, when they had time to do so, they were glad enough for me to read to them out of my immortal Shakespeare, explaining as well as I could the meaning of all I read, and awakening by degrees within them so great a respect for my learning that I found myself at last in the way of being quite famous in our parish.

This fame of mine gained for me another advantage, which was the interest taken in me by our parson, who came sometimes to overlook my self-imposed tasks, and who of his own accord taught me the axioms and some of the lore of Euclid, and set my brain all in a ferment to puzzle out the propositions in the little brown volume he lent me. I never, however, became a mathematician of any note, since these studies were destined to be speedily interrupted; but much of the last winter spent at home was given to the scrawling of lines and circles upon the hearth-stone with a fragment of charcoal, and my brain certainly grew in those days, and I was conscious of a widening of my mental horizon such as it is impossible to explain in words.

But soon a great change came into my life.

It was a beautiful mild day in May. I had been out with Blackbird as usual, and riding homewards in time for the supper, I saw our uncle John from Taunton standing in the yard with father.

Our uncle John was a favourite with us all, and I was well pleased to see him. He had always news to tell of what was going on in the world, and I had begun to desire to know more of this than was possible in our quiet life upon the farm. So I threw myself off Blackbird's back with haste and ran up with my greeting.

"Hey, Dicon lad, but thou hast mended wonderful for the better since I saw thee last!" cried Uncle John. "We shall make a man of thee yet, I take it, hunchback or no. What has come to thee, lad?"

"I was touched for the King's Evil by our gracious Duke," I answered with enthusiasm, "and since I have been whole from that malady, I have grown in strength and soundness every way. Tell me of the Duke, mine uncle. Where is he? what does he? and how goes it with him? Will he be King after his father? When will the black box be opened and the truth anent him be brought to light?"

My uncle smiled as though he knew more than he would say, but he put his finger to his lips as if to impose caution.

"Hist, boy, it is not well to wear the heart always on the sleeve. The days we live in are something too full of peril. There be wheels within wheels and plots within plots of which we simple country folks know little. Walk warily, and wait till the right moment comes; that is what men in these days have to do."

I was disappointed at the caution of the answer; nevertheless my uncle did tell us something of the movements of the Duke during the past year. He had made another "progress" through Cheshire and the more northern portion of the kingdom, and this progress had been very jealously regarded by the court party. The Duke of York was always the enemy of Monmouth, as was perhaps natural, and the King, who loved them both, had often an evil time of it between them. Sometimes Monmouth seemed in the ascendant, sometimes his black-browed uncle; and the plots and machinations of scheming courtiers and ambitious statesmen were without end. I grew bewildered even trying to follow Uncle John's talk about all these fine nobles, whose names I scarcely knew. But when he pulled out from his capacious pocket two or three old "news-letters," as they were then called, and asked if I could read them, I soon became absorbed in the contents to the exclusion of all besides; for anything new to read was as an elixir to me. And when our father and uncle were smoking their pipes, and mother and the girls washing up and putting away, I began reading loud to them the most interesting bits of news that I could find, quite unaware that Uncle John had ceased to talk with father, and was staring at me open-eyed.

At last he broke into speech.

"By the Lord Harry," he exclaimed (a favourite expletive of his), "the boy reads like a parson! Where did he learn it all?"

"He has always been a scholar," answered mother, with some pride; "that is what I say to them that pity his crooked back. He has a better head than the best of them. He will be a fine scholar in time.—Dicon, go get thy writing-book, and show thine uncle what thou canst do."

Aunt Betsy had given me a neat book full of blank paper, and I had taken pains to write my best themes and most lengthy calculations and cipherings into it. I showed it to my uncle with some pride; and as he turned the leaves I saw him look astonished, impressed, and almost triumphant, and I wondered not a little what could be in his mind.

"Why, boy," he cried, looking up at me at last, "canst add up rows of figures like that, and bring the right total at the end?"

"I trow I can, uncle," I replied with some confidence; for by this time I knew that I could trust myself to get the right answer however long the sum might be. "Set me down a sum and I will show you. I can reckon in my head too, and I seldom make an error."

Well, not to be tedious in telling all this—for I find it hard to know just how much to say and how much to leave unsaid in this history—it appeared at length that our uncle's inn in Taunton was becoming so well patronized by all sorts and conditions of men, that he knew not how to find time to keep his books as well as to entertain his guests; and since neither his wife nor his daughter had any skill with the pen, he was looking about him for somebody whom he could trust to relieve him of those laborious duties of book-keeping which he had hitherto managed to overtake himself, though at the cost of much time and labour.

Seeing my aptitude at figures, and hearing my fluency at reading aloud, he had been seized with the idea that I should be valuable to him.

Many and many a time had he wanted the weekly news-letter read aloud to his customers and guests in an evening; but there was no one with skill enough to make it intelligible thus read. He could read to himself, but had no courage to declaim it to others. Then if only he could have my pen at command during the evening, he could enter easily and rapidly into his books the outgoings of the day, and have bills made out when need was without trouble to himself. Like many men of his class, he had a marvellous memory for figures, and could keep a whole day's reckoning in his head without effort; but the trouble of writing it down afterwards was great, and to be spared that labour he would give much.

Then he was proud that any nephew of his should possess such talents as I did, and he roundly declared to my father that it would be a sin and a shame to keep such a boy at a farm, where he could learn nothing but what he could teach himself. In Taunton there was a free school to which he would send me by day, to learn all I could there with boys of my own age; whilst in the evening I should aid him with his books, and read the news-letter to such as desired to hear it, or amuse the guests of the better sort by declaiming to them some of those scenes from Shakespeare or Milton which I had now by heart, and which my mother made me recite to my uncle to show how clever I was.

It may well be guessed how excited I was whilst this matter was being discussed over my head. Of course no question was asked of me as to my own disposition in the matter. It was a thing for my father and mother to decide as they would; and when my mother argued my lack of health and strength of body, my uncle laughed at her, and said I was full strong enough for him; whilst my father remarked that schooling for a few years would be a grand thing for me, since I should never make a farmer, lived I all my life on the farm, but that in Taunton Town I might rise by my wits to some post such as that of clerk, or schoolmaster, or even parson, and it might be a fine thing for me in the end.

Uncle John was very liberal in his offer to my parents. He said he would feed and clothe me, give me a groat from time to time for myself, and send me regularly to school for the first year at least, and probably for two years, till I had learned as much as was needful, and then they would see what my future career should be. Uncle John had no son to succeed him in the business, only a daughter, who was likely to wed a son of Mr. Hucker the serge-maker, and that son was more like to take to serge-making than to inn-keeping. A hint was given that if I did well and grew to be a help and comfort to my uncle, I might look even to be his successor in the business. Certainly that would be a grand opening for one who had always been looked upon as likely to do badly in life; and before the talk had lasted an hour, it was settled, to my great satisfaction, that I was to return with my uncle to Taunton, and remain in his house as an inmate for at least three years.

How eagerly I made my few simple preparations for leaving home; and how I counted the hours until I and my uncle were to start off for his home in the town! Ever since my stay in Ilminster I had greatly desired a town life. I loved my home in a fashion, but it did not satisfy the cravings of my nature. I felt shut up and out of reach of news there. I missed the heart-beat of a great nation, of which I had been dimly conscious when at my aunt's house during the excitement of the Duke's progress, when so many stirring matters had been discussed daily. I was sure that stirring times were coming upon us. I gathered it from my uncle's words, as well as from certain statements made in the news-letter which I had read. I was conscious that there were things of great moment going on in the world of which we country folk knew nothing. I wanted to know more—to be in the thick of the tumult and the strife. Little knew I how fully my aspirations would be fulfilled during my residence in Taunton, and how fearful would be the scenes upon which I was destined to look in days to come!

I was up with the lark upon the following morning; and whilst I was attending to Blackbird and diligently grooming off from his sleek sides the last remnants of his winter coat, my uncle came in at the door and stood looking at me with an air of approval.

"So you know how to groom a horse as well as how to read a book?" he said. "That is a pretty pony you have there. I never saw a better made animal. He will be a fine fellow to go, I take it; and a rare weight-carrier, if my eye does not deceive me. How old is he?"

"Five this spring, and he can go like the wind. He's been broken these two years; but he will not let any ride him save me. Uncle, may I take him with me to Taunton? If he goes not with me, he must be turned loose to forget all his breaking, and be a wild thing again; for he will not suffer any rider on his back save me only."

Uncle John made me tell all the story of Blackbird's refractory youth and of my success with him, and at the end gave a cordial assent to my request to take my favourite with me.

"To be sure, boy, to be sure. You will want something to ride even in the town. There is many an errand I shall send you now which I have had to do myself hitherto. You know something of fat beasts and milch cows, I take it, else you are scarce your father's son; and if you know not how to drive a bargain yet, Uncle John will soon teach you!"

At that we both laughed, and I felt already as though raised to man's estate by being thus addressed by my uncle.

The taking of Blackbird to Taunton Town made my departure from home a matter of much less regret to me; for the distance being less than seven miles, and Blackbird making nothing of my weight or of that distance, I could when occasion served pay ready visits to my father's house, notwithstanding the fact that the road was in evil plight, as was the fashion with roads then (a matter which time has seen considerably amended, and may amend even more as coaches seem to grow more and more in favour), and highwaymen made travelling ofttimes dangerous, even for such as owned but small worldly wealth.

How well I remember our start on that bright May morning! Blackbird seemed to partake of my joy, and held his head proudly, whisked his long tail to and fro, and arched his neck and looked so proud and gay withal that my uncle kept regarding him with approving eyes, and more than once remarked, "Thou shouldst teach him to turn a lady's palfrey, nephew Dicon, and he would put a pretty penny in thy pocket!"

But I thought I preferred the feel of my eager steed between my knees to any gold in my purse. Blackbird and I had been comrades and friends too long for the thought of parting with him to have any attractions for me. I patted his glossy neck, and was glad his exclusive preference for me would brook no other rider. As we galloped across the moorland that day, making wide circuits from the road in our exuberance of spirit, and returning to join my uncle's sober roadster when we had had our fill of motion and fresh air, he would give an approving nod and say, "Fine pony that; and you know how to ride, boy. When you go a-wooing it had better be on horseback. Pity one can't sell the steed! he would fetch a pretty price. We'll see, we'll see! Maybe he will learn sense in the air of a town."

I had once spent a night at my uncle John's inn, on the occasion of my journey to Ilminster. Although living so near to Taunton as we did, I had never been in the way of going thither. My mother loved not towns and their ways; and though I had liberty to scour the country round at will on Blackbird, I was always bidden to keep to the open country, and never to extend my excursions to either of the towns within reach of us. So that after we had passed Volis Cross and descended the hill, the country was almost strange to me, and I eagerly demanded the name of every house and hamlet we passed, until my attention was completely absorbed by our entrance into Taunton itself.

That fine town, which will always be the queen of towns to me, was looking its best and gayest upon that brilliant May evening. The clocks were chiming six as we rode across the bridge into North Street, and it seemed to me that there must be something going on; for the town was plainly *en fête*—the streets decked with garlands, and the people saluting each other with the gayest of gay greetings, as though all hearts were in tune for merriment.

"What is it? what does it mean?" I asked of my uncle; and he looked surprised at the question as he replied,—

"Why, boy, dost live so nigh to Taunton and not know that to-morrow is the eleventh day of May?"

I certainly knew that, for I had a calendar of mine own, and studied it with care; but why Taunton should be so joyful on that account I did not know, and my puzzled face said as much.

"Why, boy," he said again, "thee such a scholar and not to know how the good folks of Taunton suffered and starved when holding the town for the Parliament against that villain Goring, who sought to win it back to its allegiance to a traitor King? Hast never read that page of history, nor how it was relieved on the eleventh day of May? Well, that is why we keep the day with garlands and songs and rejoicings, as thou wilt see to-morrow. Marry, they say that the King likes it not well, and our Mayor looks sourly on our sports, and threatens us with penalties if we are thus disloyal to the monarchy. But the people will e'en go their own way. The King has done his part to gain their ill-will, as doubtless thou wilt learn in good time. Where are our stately walls that once held at bay the thousands of a false King's troops? Where are many of the noble buildings and commodious houses which once adorned the Eastreech and East Street? He has worked his will on them. He has destroyed and ravaged at pleasure. But the mind and the heart and the will of the citizens are not his. If he takes away our charter (which he did, though we have it again now), he wins not the love of the people. We give him loyal and liege service, but we do not give him love and trust."

My uncle's face was rather grim as he spoke thus, and I understood that I had come to a place where the divine right of kings, in which I had believed until now, was not greatly regarded. The story of the nation had not formed one of my studies. I knew little enough of the events of the past century, albeit my father had lived through the great civil war, and had seen some fighting, though holding aloof from it himself. I had not thought much of anything save the position of the Duke of Monmouth, and the hope that he would one day be King. As I rode through the streets of Taunton and saw the decorations being put up for the morrow, I felt indeed that a new life was opening before me, and that I was now to learn many things which hitherto had been but names to me.

CHAPTER III.

MY NEW HOME.

"The eleventh of May was a joyful day,
    When Taunton got relief;
Which turned our sorrow into joy,
    And eased us of our grief.

"The Taunton men were valiant then
    In keeping of the town,
While many of those who were our foes
    Lay gasping on the ground.

"When Colonel Massey, of the same,
    Did understand aright,
He, like a man of courage bold,
    Prepared himself to fight.

"With that our soldiers one and all
    Cast up their caps, and cried,
'What need we fear what man can do,
    Since God is on our side?'

"Long time did Goring lie encamped
    Against fair Taunton Town;
He made a vow to starve us out,
    And batter our castle down.

"Within our castle did remain
   (A garrison so strong)
Those likely lads which did unto
   Our Parliament belong.

"Before daylight appeared in view,
   The news to them was come
That Goring and his cursèd crew
   Were all dispersed and gone.

"But who can tell what joy was there,
   And what content of mind
Was put into the hearts of those
   Who'd been so long confined?

"Our bread was fourteenpence per pound,
   And all things sold full dear;
Which made our soldiers make short meals
   And pinch themselves full near.

"Our beer was eighteenpence per quart
   (As for a truth was told),
And butter eighteenpence per pound
   To Christians there was sold.

"The Cavaliers dispersed with fear,
   And forced were to run,
On the eleventh of May, by break of day,
   Ere rising of the sun."

It was with the words of this song, chanted by a number of voices in the street below, that I was awakened upon the first morning of my residence in my new home.

I had slept profoundly, despite the excitements of my arrival; and when I awoke suddenly, roused by the sound of this unfamiliar chant, it took me some moments to recollect where I was, and to convince myself that I was not dreaming still. The moment that memory returned to me I sprang out of bed, and putting my head out of the open window, tried to obtain a view of the singers below.

But this I was unable to do, as I might have known had I taken pains to consider. My room was high up in the quaint old inn, which even in my youth was accounted an old house. It looked upon the court-yard behind, where the stables lay, and where hostlers were already passing to and fro. I remembered well that I had observed this last night, and that I had also remarked with satisfaction how my window was provided with a little wooden balcony, of which the house had many. It was in an angle of the building above the stables, and not in the main block of the house where the guests were lodged. Near at hand, and at right angles, rose the walls of another house, which I could see was not a part of the inn. It did not look so old, and it was more like a gentleman's private residence, I thought. All the windows were close curtained, and I could not gather anything as to the character of its inhabitants. It seemed passing strange to me then that houses should be thus locked together; and I was calculating with what ease I could make shift by the aid of a water-pipe to get in at the window of this house were it left open, and possess myself of anything the room contained, when the sound of an impatient neigh from the yard below warned me that time was getting on, and that Blackbird was probably still unfed (for I had warned the men not to go to him at first, save in my presence), and that he was asking for his breakfast as plainly as though he could utter human speech.

I, too, was in a great hurry to be up and doing, and to see some of the wonders of the town of which I was in future to be a resident. In a few moments I was dressed (words of the song below still floating up to me clearly enough, and getting fixed in my memory, as all words with rhyme and rhythm have a trick of doing), and was ready to try to find my way down the curious stairways and along the intricate passages I had traversed last night under the guidance of my cousin Meg. It was not so easy as I expected, but as yet nobody in that part of the house was stirring. It was still very early, for all that the sun was shining brightly; and I had Blackbird fed, and was ready and eager to be out in the streets before there was any sign of my uncle or aunt to be seen.

However, my impatience was too great to be stayed by any thought of a rebuke later, and plunging under the archway which led from the street to the yard, I found myself in the open space where East Street and Fore Street join, and looked about me with a lively curiosity, wondering where I should go and what I should do.

The singers were no longer in sight; they had passed on, and the wide streets were almost empty. But as I stood looking admiringly about me, a boy of about my own age came swinging along with a parcel under his arm, whistling the very tune I had heard set to the words I have just quoted.

I looked curiously at him, and he returned my glance with interest. No doubt he was familiar with most of the faces of the towns-folk in these parts, and wondered who I was. Perhaps my crooked back attracted his notice, but I did not think of that then, and noting that he half paused as though not unwilling to speak, I wished him good-morning, and he returned the salutation.

There was something so bright and friendly in his smile as he did so that I found courage to say, "Are you going somewhere? May I go with you?"

"Why, yes, if you like," he answered readily. "I am going to my work. I am apprenticed to Master Simpson of High Street. If you know aught of Taunton, doubtless you have heard of him."

"But I do not. I only came hither yester-e'en with mine uncle. I am nephew to John Snowe of the Three Cups yonder. I am to dwell with him, and go to the Free School here. I would fain know all I can of Taunton Town. It is a right fair city. I like it well."

"And you have come on a good day!" cried my new friend, with brightening eyes. "To-night, so soon as the sun be down, we shall light a great bonfire in Paul's Fields, and all the town will be there to see. Ah! I would I had lived in the days when Taunton Town held for the Parliament against King Charles! But it may be even yet that we may some of us live to see fine doings and hard fighting; for if the King dies before his brother, and the Papist Duke of York sits upon the throne—"

The lad paused as if struck by the magnitude of the thought within him, and I glanced round to be sure we were not overheard, and asked with keen interest, "Well, and what then?"

"Why, then, methinks there would be hard blows struck for the rightful heir, the young Duke of Monmouth," answered the boy, with sparkling eyes. "All Taunton and the West Country would rise for him, as they rose for the rights of the nation against the King's father. The poltroons of London may lick the dust before a Papist usurper, but not we of the free West Country! We will know the reason why before we bow to a Papist, be he never so much the King's brother!"

The boldness of this boy astonished me greatly, and also his evident comprehension of the burning questions of the day, with which I myself was but imperfectly acquainted. My heart always warmed within me at any mention of the Duke of Monmouth, and I eagerly plunged into the story of my own miraculous cure at the hands of his Grace—a tale to which my companion listened with kindling eyes.

"Marry, but thou shalt come with me and tell it to my master!" he said, as I ended. "If proof were lacking, there it is; for none save a lawful King or his lawful heir can cure the King's Evil. There will be a ready welcome for thee at Master Simpson's. He is one that is bound heart and soul to the cause of the Duke."

"And what is thy name?" I asked, as I willingly allowed myself to be led whither my comrade would.

"Will Wiseman is my name, and I be apprenticed to Master Simpson, as I have said. I dwell beneath his roof; but yester-eve I visited my aunt in the North Street, and tarried with her till dawn. Thou sayest thou art nephew to Master Snowe of the Three Cups? He is a good man, one of our Capital Burgesses; and we take it he would be stanch to the good cause if the time should come for men to declare themselves."

I was considerably impressed by Will's way of talking. It was as though he were living in a world of which I knew almost nothing; as though he were looking forward to something definite and expected, whilst to me the future was absolutely blank and vague. I felt my ignorance so great that I did not know so much as how to frame questions; but I was saved the trouble of doing this partly from the eager talk of my companion, partly from our speedy arrival at our destination. For soon after we had passed the bend in High Street, where it turns sharp to the right toward Shuttern, Will paused before a door with a right goodly sign hanging above it; and after obtaining entrance, began quickly taking down the shutters, in which office I gave him what assistance I could, so that soon the bright light of morning was streaming into the interior of the shop.

So soon as this was the case I stood open-mouthed in admiration and wonder, for I had never seen so goodly a shop in all my life before. Master Simpson must be a man of much substance—so much I could see at a glance—and his wares were beautiful to the eye and delicate to the touch. There were bales of costly silk set in a mighty pyramid in one place; and cloths and lawns, and the good serge manufactured in Taunton Town, disposed with a simple eye to effect, in due order along shelves and in the large window. And besides all these things, there was an inner shop, visible through an archway, in which I saw a sight that made my mouth water; for there were shelves, guarded by wire doors, in which hundreds of books were arranged in tempting order— books new and books old—a sight that drew me like a magnet, so that I forgot Will and his work, forgot the strangeness of the house and my lack of manners, and went straight to the book-cases and began reading the names of the volumes one by one, speaking them half aloud without knowing it.

I was aroused by feeling a strong hand laid upon my shoulder, and by the sound of a friendly voice in my ear.

"Hey, but we have a scholar here, in good sooth! So thou art nephew to good Master Snowe, Will tells me; and hast been touched for King's Evil by our gracious Duke? Now, boy, tell me all about that, and how the cure was made, and I will give thee a book for thy pains; for it may be that this cure of thine shall be a notable thing in the annals of the day that be coming."

The speaker was plainly the master of the house and shop. He was soberly habited, as became his condition in life; but he had a strong face as well as a strong hand and voice, and I felt drawn towards him I scarce knew why, and told him my tale very gladly, with the story of my own brief and uneventful life to boot.

He listened with attention, nodding his head the while. Heaven forgive me if I did amiss. I had no thought to deceive him or others, but I spoke no word of the man of herbs and potions, nor of the ointments I had been using for my wounds ere ever the Duke's hand touched me. In good sooth, I had scarce ever thought of him and his simples since. Never for a moment did I believe that these had had anything to do with my cure. It is only long since, when I have heard from others how in nature there be such marvellous cures for human ills to be found by those who have skill and faith to seek them aright, that I have wondered if perchance it was the herb baths and ointments, and not the touch of the Duke's white hand, that made me whole and sound. But in those days no such thought ever came to me. I had well-nigh forgotten the kind old man with his long beard, and of him I spoke no word; only telling how weak and ill I was and had been from childhood, and how soon after I had besought the Duke to touch me I became sound and whole, and had no return of the Evil, which none but such a one as he could cure.

Master Simpson heard me with great satisfaction, and kept his word right generously, making me the proud and happy possessor of a small copy of "Æsop's Fables," with the Latin on one side of the page and the English on the other—a treasure that in those days was even more costly than it has become now, and which in spite of its shabby binding was looked upon as of exceeding worth.

"Thou hadst better learn the Latin tongue, an thou hast the chance at the Free School," said Master Simpson. "Learning is a grand thing, and will be a mighty power in the days to come. Learn all thou canst, boy, when thou art young. The time may come when thou wilt not have the leisure; make the most of that leisure now."

I was well disposed to carry out that sage advice, being greedy after knowledge, and I almost longed to run away then and there to study my book, and see if I could make out aught of the strange Latin words. Even the possession of such a book made me feel almost a scholar. But I could not refuse the invitation of Master Simpson to come and take breakfast with him, albeit my uncle and aunt might well be wondering what had become of me. But, as I reflected, the hostlers would tell him I had risen and gone abroad, and upon this festive holiday I did not think I should be chidden for my early walk.

Behind the shop was a pleasant parlour, and behind that again a kitchen, from whence a savoury odour proceeded. It gave one an appetite even to scent it, and I was nothing loath to follow the mercer into that same kitchen, where a goodly fire burned on the hearth, and a merry-faced young maiden was flitting about setting trenchers on the table, and humming a gay ditty the while. She made a reverence as we came in, and her father (for she was none other than the master's daughter) gave her a blessing; after which he turned him to a portly dame who was taking a steaming pot from the fire, and bid her good-morn, telling her my name and state, and how I was come to Taunton to make a scholar of myself.

From the likeness which showed itself between the pair before me, I felt assured that they must be brother and sister, as was indeed the case. Master Simpson was a widower, but his sister kept house for him, and played a mother's part to the young Eliza, who gave her almost a daughter's love. It was pleasant to see so much affection between those of a household, for at home, albeit we all loved each other well, it was not our fashion to show it; wherefore it seemed pretty to me to watch the sly caresses which Eliza would bestow upon her father, or the way in which Mistress Susan's glance softened when she addressed herself to the maid.

Will Wiseman and a young man who served in the shop, but who spoke no word and gave himself only to making a right royal meal, sat at table with us, though somewhat apart; and ever and anon Will would put in a word when his master turned to him with a question. He plainly heard and gave heed to everything that passed, with a keen intelligence that was shown in the glance of his eye and in the ready way in which his words came when he had occasion to speak. I took a great liking to Will from the first moment of our acquaintance, and everything I noted about him increased the good-will I bore him.

We had a merry meal, and I told the story of my cure yet once again that day. Lizzie's eyes brightened at the tale (Eliza was always called Lizzie both at home and abroad, since it appeared that there were many Elizas in the town, and confusion apt to arise), and she clasped her hands together and cried,—

"Faith, but Miss Blake will greatly rejoice to hear this! I will tell her forthwith, and I warrant me I shall be high in favour all the day for the same story. Good Dicon, thou wilt be a rare favourite in Taunton Town an thou dost uphold here the rights of our well-loved Duke!"

"Hist, lassie!" answered her father, yet smiling nevertheless. "It behoves us to talk with care even in Taunton Town. Let not such words be heard by the Rev. Mr. Axe, nor still less by Mr. Blewer. The Duke hath his foes as well as his friends within the town. We must not hurt a good cause by over-zeal ere the right moment comes."

Lizzie laughed, and asked with a pretty, saucy air who would trouble to take note of the words of such an obscure maiden as herself; and then she looked at the clock and sprang up, and said she must even go, or she should be late, and Miss Blake would chide. And I then learned that Miss Blake was the mistress of the school where this maiden went daily for instruction, and moreover that it stood adjoining my uncle's inn, and must indeed be the house I had been wondering about in looking from my windows on awakening this very morning.

So on understanding this much, I sprang up and asked leave to escort pretty Lizzie to her school; and soon we were walking along the garlanded streets, and she was telling me how greatly Miss Blake and Mrs. Musgrave loved the Duke, and how dear his cause was to the hearts of the people of Taunton. I also learned that Miss Blake and Mrs. Musgrave were two ladies of virtue and learning, and that they had each kept a school for girls in the beginning, but had now joined these two seminaries into one. Miss Blake took the younger maidens, and Mrs. Musgrave the elder ones; and my companion chattered so fast about her companions, telling me their names, ages, and accomplishments with such fluency, that I was quite bewildered; and the only item of information which I retained in my head was that there was one, Mary Mead, a youthful heiress, some years older than any of her companions, who had been educated by Mrs. Musgrave, and still remained in her charge, although since she was now of marriageable age it was likely that her condition in life would speedily be changed.

We parted the best of friends at the door of the seminary, where some other maidens were assembling, who looked curiously upon me as I took off my cap and made my best bow to them all. The door of the school was a few paces round the corner, and the house was of fine proportions. I well understood as I looked at it—Lizzie and her companions having now disappeared within—how it was that my room over our stable buildings approached so nigh to it. I felt a good deal of interest in the close vicinity of these bright-faced town maidens, who seemed so different from the country girls I had lived amongst hitherto. Not that I would disparage mine own sisters and their friends; but there were a brightness and ease of manner and readiness of wit amongst these damsels which dazzled and captivated me, and which I had never seen at home.

When I got back to the inn, I found breakfast well-nigh done; but I received no chiding for my absence, especially when I said whither I had been and with whom. Master Simpson was plainly a notable man of good repute in Taunton, and a friend of mine uncle's to boot. My uncle, too, was pleased at the gift of the book which I had received, arguing that Master Simpson must have thought well of my scholarship. I read him two or three of the fables; whereat he laughed not a little, and bid me hold myself in readiness to amuse his guests therewith on another occasion.

I was not to go to school till the following week, and to-day I had leave to wander whither I would, to see what I could and what I most desired, and enjoy the merry-making of the town.

My cousin Meg, a fine buxom lass of nigh upon twenty summers, was all agog to go with me; and I was proud enough to have such a companion. So after I had helped her with her dishes and so forth, being skilled in many feminine tasks through helping my mother at home when she and the girls were pressed, she donned her holiday gown and gayest hood—and well she became them both, as I failed not to tell her—and I put on my best clothes, which seemed to me fine enough even if somewhat lacking in the grace and fashion I saw in some of the towns-folk of the better sort; and forth we sallied to see the sights of the town, and to enjoy any revelry that might be going.

The best of the merry-making would be towards evening, when the shops would close, and the apprentices and shopmen be free to join; but even now there was plenty to see and to admire. The fine proportions of the streets and public buildings filled me with a great wonder; and when we dived down a passage past Huish's Almshouse, and came out in front of St. Mary's Church, I stood still and silent in speechless admiration, marvelling at its wondrous beauty and lofty dignity, and asking of myself whether St. Paul's itself in fair London town could be as goodly a sight.

It so chanced that service was going on, and nothing would serve me but that I must go in and hear what it was like. Meg was willing enough to gratify me: for from being bred a dissenter, like the majority of the towns-folk, she attended the services of the dissenting flock in Paul's Meeting Sunday by Sunday; and the offices of the Establishment, which she was wont to hear stigmatized as "Popish," were quite unfamiliar to her, and had therefore a certain fascination.

There were two clergymen taking part in the service; and when we were in the street again, Meg said to me (interrupting my raptures about the architectural beauties of the place),—

"He with the grey hair peeping from beneath his wig is Mr. Axe. He is much beloved in Taunton, although men say that he is an enemy to the Duke of Monmouth, and tells men freely that he can never be lawful King, but that if the King dies childless, as seems like, we must submit to see the Duke of York upon the throne—a thing which is abhorrent to the minds of many. Yet in spite of this he is loved and trusted. But the other, Mr. Blewer, is hated and feared. I scarce know why we all think so ill of him, but he hath a cruel face and an evil eye; and some say that he is the bitter foe of all who follow not the teachings of the Established Church, whilst there be others who call him a Papist at heart, and say that when the Duke of York is King (if ever such a day comes, which Heaven forbid!) he will show what manner of man he is, and evil will fall upon many in Taunton through him."

"He has a bad face and a cruel mouth," I answered, having studied his face with a sense of reluctant fascination for which I could not account as I knelt in the church. Could it have been that some presentiment of his cruelty stole over me even then? I know not how that may be, but I do know that though my hair is now grey, and though I have lived beyond the allotted span of man's days, I cannot even now think of that miscreant without a tingling of the blood in my veins such as I seldom experience for aught besides.

That day was a notable one in my life, although it seems like a dream now. I looked upon the outside of many a noble building—St. James's Church; Paul's Meeting, which I was to worship in for a time; the Castle; the Free School, which I was to know right well erelong; and the Almshouses, which had been erected by the charitable in bygone years for the benefit of the aged poor.

The town was all bedecked with flags and garlands, and the bands of singers went about chanting their ditties, receiving rewards from many of the richer and more prosperous of the towns-folk, as well as the humbler, who were all so devoted to the cause of what they termed "liberty and right."

In the evening there was a grand bonfire in Paul's Field, and another in Priory Fields at the other extremity of the town.

Will Wiseman and I joined forces, and rushed from one to the other, getting an excellent view of both; and we danced around the fire with the best of them, and hooted for the Duke of York and the Pope, and shouted for the King and the Duke of Monmouth, until at last we had no voice left wherewith to shout more. When the embers burned low, and the sheriff's officer came to bid the people disperse, we went reluctantly home with the crowd, talking in friendly whispers of the glorious days that perhaps were coming, when we should be able to show the metal of which we were made, and almost ready to wish for the excitements and horrors of another civil war, if only we might bear a share in its glory and its danger.

We had heard so many stories from the bystanders who did remember those days, that our blood was fired, and we ardently longed for a repetition of such exciting events.

Well, we were destined to see something of bloodshed before many years had passed over our heads, and one of us was to shed his blood—as he sincerely longed at that moment to do, but whether in the fashion that came about it is not for me to say here.

And so ended my first eventful day in Taunton Town.

CHAPTER IV.

MY NEW LIFE.

If I were to begin to set down in order all the many things that happened to me without and within the town of Taunton during the early days of my residence there, I should go far to fill a volume ere ever I had reached the matters of which it is my intention more particularly to speak.

So I must strive after all the brevity of a skilled master of the craft of penmanship and story-telling, and seek to skim the cream from the surface of events, without wearying the reader with overmuch detail.

Let me say, in the first place, that I was very happy in my new life. I was kindly treated by my relatives. I made myself useful to my uncle in many ways, and I was a favourite with his guests, who delighted to hear the news of the day read to them whilst they smoked their pipes at ease, and who were all ready to talk with me when the reading was over, one telling me one bit of public gossip, and another another, till my mind was quite a storehouse of information, and I was able to talk upon almost any subject with the air of one who knew something about it.

The reputation for cleverness and knowledge which I soon gained (though in good sooth it was less knowledge than a good memory that I possessed) gave me a small standing of mine own in the place, and I had quite a brisk little business erelong, in writing letters for those who could not do it for themselves, and getting them passed on by trusty hands, by means of some of the many visitors who passed to and fro between our town and other places. My uncle let me keep for myself all such moneys as I gained in this fashion, and so I was able to take home to my mother and sisters presents which made them open their eyes wide in amaze, on the occasions when I mounted Blackbird and rode over to my former home. I was looked upon now as a person of some importance; and although only a lad of thirteen summers, I felt as if I should soon arrive at man's estate.

I had something to suffer at the Free School from the gibes and the envy of the other boys, who liked not to be surpassed at their books by the "hunchback clown"—such was their name for me for a time—and who paid me many an ill turn and played off many a malicious trick, until at last they wearied of it, or I gradually grew into favour, I scarce knew which, and I was let alone to go mine own way. But in spite of all this I was happy in my school hours, for I was learning every day something new; and if the boys misliked me, the masters took good heed of me and favoured my thirst after knowledge, so that I was able to study with zeal and success, and to win the praise of Mr. Axe, who would come from time to time to hear the boys recite, or to ask them questions from Scripture or secular history, and who never left without a word of kindness for me.

I came to revere and love Mr. Axe right well. He was not truly the Vicar of beauteous St. Mary's Church. The Vicar, in very sooth, was one Mr. Hart, who was (so it was told me) also Canon of Bristol and Prebendary of Wells, so that he had but scant time to think of his duties here. Mr. Axe, however, supplied all that was lacking, and was greatly beloved by us—as much beloved as Mr. Blewer was mistrusted and feared: for we would cross the street to avoid coming within the radius of *his* basilisk glance; and I for one never saw him without the feeling that he would prove a cruel foe ere we had seen the last of him.

Now I had scarce been a month at my uncle's house before a great excitement befell us, and a great fear fell upon many of our towns-folk; for it was rumoured that this thing would lose the Duke of Monmouth his head, and that even if his life were spared he would have to fly the country, and be no more seen in this land.

And the reason for this rumour, which filled all Somersetshire with sorrow, was the discovery of a vile plot against the life of the King and that of the Duke of York, which wicked and slanderous tongues were eager to charge upon the virtuous and high-minded Duke of Monmouth.

Well do I remember the day when first the news of this infamous plot, which came to be called the Rye House Plot, reached the good citizens of Taunton.

It was upon a Sunday morning, and I, together with my uncle and aunt and his daughter Meg, had started forth for Paul's Meeting, which we always attended for morning service, when we noted that the people in the streets had an air of gravity and anxiety which was not usual, and that all seemed to be asking questions one of another, although none seemed to be ready with an answer.

Now generally we were the first to hear any news that might reach the town, because that travellers were wont to put up at the Three Cups rather than at the other hostelries, which were less beliked than our house. But to-day there had been none arrival, and my uncle stopped to ask the first acquaintance he encountered what was the meaning of the general discomposure.

Now it chanced that this acquaintance was none other than Heywood Dare —"Old Dare," as he was often called, less perhaps from his actual years than because he had a son who was also a notable man in his way, and who had a part to play in the days that were coming.

Now old Dare had a story of his own, and was a great man in Taunton. He was by trade a goldsmith, and a man of substance to boot; but it was not his wealth that had gained for him the repute in which he was held, but his courage and devotion to the cause of liberty and justice.

It was one of the grievances of the times that the King would not permit Parliament to sit sometimes for long years together. Men whispered that he received great sums of money from France, which enabled him to dispense with the summoning of his own loyal subjects to grant supplies. However that may be, the people were grieved and wroth that their assembly was not called and permitted to sit, as they claimed that it had the right to do; and petitions from townships were constantly sent up to his Majesty imploring him to call together his Parliament, until the King grew greatly incensed, issued proclamations forbidding the presentation of these petitions, and threatening with severe penalties those who went about "getting hands," as it was termed, to put to these documents. Indeed many barbarous severities had been put in practice against those who still strove to collect names for such papers; and curious enough were such documents when they were drawn up, for three-fourths of those who "set hand" to them could not write their names, but could only make a mark which was to stand instead of it.

Now some four years back Old Dare had got up a notable petition, and it had been signed or marked by half Taunton, and by Bridgewater and Ilminster and many another fair town. The sturdy old goldsmith pursued his way to London with it. It was his intention to deliver it to the King with his own hand; and this intention he carried out, meeting the King hard by the Houses of Parliament, and presenting his paper on bended knee. The King took it unsuspecting—for it was a bold man who would venture to place one of the abhorred petitions in the royal hands; but on unfolding it he became instantly aware of its nature, and turning sharply upon the offender, he asked him how he dared to do such a thing. "Sire," replied the intrepid goldsmith, "my name is Dare!" And forasmuch as there is always something noble in fearless courage, and that his Majesty is not without nobility of soul, no hurt was done to the bold petitioner, albeit no good that I ever heard of came from his petition.

Well then, to return to my present tale, it was Old Dare whom we encountered in the street to-day; and when my uncle asked what the coil was all about, he shook his head and answered,—

"I cannot say with knowledge; but a messenger rode post-haste to the house of the Mayor but now, and it was plain, by the stains of travel on him and his horse, that they had been hard pushed to reach the place. It is something of note, I take it, and something of evil, I fear." He lowered his voice and said in my uncle's ear (yet I heard every word, being very keen of hearing), "I fear me it will prove to be some plot to ruin the Duke and his Council of Six. It may be that they have been something rash and forward. I fear me we shall hear bad news ere the day is out."

I knew well what was meant by the Council of Six. The Duke of Monmouth had some faithful friends, lovers of liberty and constitutional rule—my Lord of Russell and Mr. Algernon Sydney being of the number—who met together often to discuss what might be done for a country beginning once again to groan beneath the yoke of an arbitrary exercise of the power of the Crown. Representations had been made to the King, it was said, to summon Parliament, and give to the people their lawful voice in the government; but this having proved of none avail, it had been whispered that these men had spoken of another Great Revolution, such as had cost the King's father his head; and of course such talk was accounted rank treason in those days, and was like to cost many a man his life.

Now we of the West Country in general, and of Taunton Town in particular, knew very well that if any rising or tumult took place, it would be like enough to be in our neighbourhood; and that, even if we kept ourselves tranquil, we might get the credit of being turbulent, and have our rights infringed, even if our charter were not taken from us, as it had been early in the King's reign, although restored seventeen years later. Also, we all of us pinned our chiefest hopes of constitutional government and the Protestant religion on the hoped-for succession of the Duke of Monmouth; and if he were to be implicated in a plot which should cost him liberty or life, our hopes would receive a crushing blow, and nothing lie before us but the succession of a bigoted Papist and a man of known cruelty and tyranny.

Small wonder was it, therefore, that our faces were grave, and that we all looked anxiously at our minister, Mr. Vincent, as he mounted the pulpit a little after the usual time, and looked seriously upon our upturned faces. He made no attempt at a regular sermon that day, but after giving thanks for the merciful preservation of his gracious Majesty the King from a recent and great danger, he proceeded to tell us that a plot had been laid against the King's life and that of the Duke of York, and how it was currently rumoured that the Duke of Monmouth and his friends were concerned in the matter.

Arrests had been made of certain persons, and the Duke had fled and hidden himself.

Mr. Vincent also told us, with great seriousness, that rumour had already been forward to declare that an insurrection had commenced, with Taunton as its centre; and counselled us, as we valued the peace of the realm and our own safety, to avoid any cause of offence, and to remain perfectly quiet and tranquil. The time might come in the future when it would be a righteous thing to rise up and strike a blow for the liberty and the faith of the country, but certainly that day had not yet come. The King upon the throne was the rightful one; his rule was on the whole fair and just. There was no quarrel with him. Nothing would so injure the righteous cause as a revolt against law and order; nothing would so greatly hurt the cause of the young Duke of Monmouth. We must show discretion and wisdom at this time, that none might have cause to look with suspicion upon us.

This wise counsel from one who was a pillar of strength amongst us was not without due effect. We looked at one another and resolved to abide by Mr. Vincent's counsel. We knew that our Mayor was a bitter enemy to all dissenters, and would fasten upon us an indictment of disaffection if we gave the smallest ground. Indeed he took instant action upon hearing of the plot, and called some bands of the militia into the town; and I verily believe that it was with his consent, if not at his instigation, that a deed was done in the town which made us who called ourselves dissenters tingle with rage and feel almost ready to raise the very tumult of which we were altogether innocent in fact.

Now the thing of which I speak was nothing less than the demolishing of the great chapel called Paul's Meeting, of which I have spoken, and in which hundreds of citizens met to worship Sunday by Sunday. And this thing was done, to the great shame of those concerned in it, just when the excitement which I have mentioned prevailed, notwithstanding that Mr. Vincent and Mr. Burgess, both of whom preached to us there, were godly men, and taught us submission to lawful rulers, and spoke no evil of dignitaries.

The first I knew of this was one evening just before our house generally closed for the night—it was summer then, and not dark till ten of the clock—when Will Wiseman came rushing into the yard, all bursting with excitement, and crying out to me in panting gasps,—

"Dicon, Dicon, come and see! come and see! They are pulling our meeting-house to pieces, and say they will make such a bonfire of our pews and pulpit as shall light to bed every dissenter in the county! Come and see! come and see! I would not go myself till I had told thee!"

Will Wiseman was certain to be in the forefront of everything; but I had no mind to be left behind. Forthwith we both rushed out from the yard, and soon the noise of a great tumult fell upon our ears. In the streets men were gathered together with dark faces and threatening mien, some talking angrily against the dissenters, who, it was declared, had been guilty of plotting against the King's life, but many more holding a stern silence and regarding their enemies with silent hostility; whilst hoarse cries and shouts rent the air, and grew louder and more distinct as we drew near to Paul's Meeting.

Once within sight of the building, we saw that it was lighted up from within; and unable to come near to the door for the surging mob around it, we climbed up to one of the windows and looked in.

What a sight it was! There were a hundred men inside, I should think, armed with hammers and saws and other tools and weapons; and these were all engaged in hammering, sawing, breaking down, and demolishing the whole of the woodwork in the chapel; and as fast as some pew, or great piece of panelling, or any large fragment of pulpit or gallery was broken off, other men would rush forward and drag it forth from the door, to carry it away into Paul's Fields, where it was plain that the great bonfire was to be made. And all the while they worked, they shouted out threats against their fellow-townsmen, calling out, "Down with all traitors! Down with the King's enemies! We will have nothing but the Church and the King!"

Yet many of the fellows now working like furies and shouting out these words had attended many a service in Paul's Meeting, and were friendly enough towards us, albeit perhaps not men of much personal godliness. But they were carried away by the excitement of the moment, and by the coward fear of getting into trouble with the Mayor should they show any lack of zeal. Men all over the kingdom were trembling just now in apprehension of arrest; for informers were going about the country, and many a lowly as well as many a noble and high personage was flung into prison on the most trivial charge. To join hands in reviling the dissenters and calling down blessings upon the King and the Church seemed the safest way of propitiating the authorities at such a moment; and this was what our towns-folk were now doing, by demolishing our chapel, and showing their zeal towards the Court party.

It was all very exciting; and though my heart and Will's swelled with indignation, we could not help watching till the whole of the building was stripped. Then we followed in the wake of the shouting crowd, and soon saw a great pillar of fire rising up from the midst of the assembled throng. As the great mountain of flame rose higher and higher, and waved its crown of smoke and sparks up to the roof of heaven as it seemed, the crowd yelled and shouted and danced around the pyre, bawling out every kind of folly that came into their heads; whilst outside the yelling ring, and a little distance away, stood the stern-faced men who had been wont to worship there, together with the ministers who had occupied the pulpit, and they looked on in silence, and gathered sometimes in groups together. Will Wiseman, who had the faculty of hearing what everybody said without seeming to listen, whispered to me, "They are saying that they will still meet for preaching and prayer whatever is done to their meeting-house."

And so indeed it proved, although the Mayor looked stern and dark, and sometimes uttered hints that sounded almost like a threat against "conventicles," as he termed them. Indeed he made himself so heartily misliked amongst the towns-folk, that but for the authority and protection bestowed by his office, I think some mischief would have been done him. But though a time of exceeding excitement prevailed for many weeks, there was no rising in the country; and by-and-by we were made glad by the tidings that there had been a reconciliation betwixt the Duke of Monmouth and the King, although Lord William Russell and Mr. Algernon Sydney ended their lives upon the scaffold.

Not that these men had any complicity in the murder plot against the King's life. They had souls far above the treachery and meanness of assassination. But the lesser and more villanous plot of minor conspirators was grafted upon the larger and wider-reaching intentions of these champions of liberty and of rule by constitutional rather than autocratic methods, and they were judged guilty of treason, and were doomed to death. Some said that the Duke of Monmouth had been led by promises of restoration to favour to bear witness against his friends. How that may be I will not say. At this time all Taunton was indignant at the aspersion cast upon the fair fame of the gallant young Duke, and the story was indignantly discredited, and by no one more hotly than by me. Now when my blood is cool, and I have grown wiser and have heard more of those days, I cannot be so sure of the innocence of the Duke as I felt then. Men are sorely tempted sometimes, and fall into sin almost ere they are aware of it. Human nature is weak, and a man may have many faults and many weaknesses and yet be the idol of the people for many a long day.

It was at this time that I grew better acquainted with several of the families in Taunton. I was in great request when the weekly news-letter came to my uncle's house—he had one of his own as well as that which was brought to the Mayor; for, as I have said, the Mayor was a bitter enemy to the dissenting portion of the towns-folk, and that was a very large section, as the well-filled building, Paul's Meeting, bore witness Sunday by Sunday.

Foremost amongst my friends I still reckoned Master Simpson and his family. Will Wiseman was my chosen comrade on all occasions, and Lizzie was the object of my boyish gallantry, and I continued to think her the prettiest and most charming maid in all Taunton Town.

But I must not omit to mention others who had a part to play in the drama that was slowly approaching. Of these I must mention the Herring family, father and mother, with three daughters, Anne, Susan, and Grace, all of whom attended Miss Blake's school; and Master John Hucker, a notable serge-maker, with his daughter Eliza; and the Hewling family, than which none other was more greatly beloved and esteemed in the whole of the town.

Mistress Hannah Hewling was mistress of this happy household. She was a spinster of some thirty years of age, and she played a mother's part to two virtuous and handsome young men, who were at the time of which I am now writing aged twenty and seventeen years respectively. This family had another home in London, where their parents lived, but owned this house property in Taunton, too, where these two brothers and their sister lived in the greatest amity and peace. The Hewlings were gentry, and people of substance, yet so friendly and kindly disposed towards their towns-folk that we all regarded them as friends. They would stop to speak a friendly word to any one of us in the street, and many were the evenings when they would invite some amongst us to their hospitable house. Sometimes there would be music to enliven us after supper—for Mistress Hannah played both harp and spinnet right sweetly, whilst Master Benjamin discoursed eloquent music on the flute, and Master William could draw strains from his violin that brought tears to the eyes of the listeners before they well knew it—or failing music, some one would read aloud from a godly book, or from some history of past days, and the elder members of the party would be invited to discuss the subject, whilst the rest of us listened in respectful silence, and framed our own opinions on what we heard.

It was in this way that I came to understand much of the questions of the day from the standpoint of those who believed the Duke of Monmouth to be the champion not of freedom and constitutional rule alone, but also of the Protestant religion. The things we read about the awful cruelty and treachery of those who were tainted by the curse of Popery often made our blood run cold within us; and when it became increasingly certain that the Duke of York was Papist up to the neck, and would throw off all disguise when once he ascended the throne, it was scarce to be marvelled at that we should fix our eyes upon one who might rise up to be a champion and deliverer, and save us from the oppression of a tyrant and bigot.

I was heart and soul with all men who held this view, but I noted often that my uncle would sit mute whilst such talk was going on, and that he was always slow to commit himself to any open opinion. And once when I had grown too excited to hold my peace any longer, and had openly spoken out some of the thoughts that were burning within me, he had taken me to task afterwards, not sternly indeed, but somewhat seriously, and had warned me that I had better learn the art of holding my tongue, and watching the turn of the tide before I launched my bark upon untried waters.

"But, uncle," I exclaimed eagerly, "surely you are for the Duke?"

"I am for the rightful King of the realm, whoever he be," was the cautious answer. "It is not given to us to choose our monarch. God sets Kings upon the throne, and bids us submit ourselves to the powers that be. That is my principle, and will be my practice; albeit I should greatly prefer to serve a King of the true faith."

I was puzzled by this way of stating the matter, for it was not after such cautious fashion that the greater part of our friends talked; but I began to note as time went by that my uncle was more cautious in many of his ways than were others, and that he made some small changes in his methods and habits.

After the Rye House Plot there was great excitement in the country, and greater efforts than ever were made to force men to attend public worship in the churches of the Establishment instead of in meeting-houses of their own. Many such meeting-houses and chapels were wrecked (like our own) in various places, and the flocks scattered, so that they could no longer hear their favourite doctrines preached by their favourite ministers, but must either absent themselves from public worship or go to church with the orthodox.

Now in St. Mary's Church there was held a grand service of thanksgiving for the safety of the King and the Duke of York, and the Mayor and Burgesses all attended in civic pomp. My uncle went, of course, in his capacity of one of the Capital Burgesses; but rather to our surprise, he desired that all of us should be present; and from that day forward he regularly attended the parish church, taking his wife and daughter and other members of his household. He gave as his reason for this, that it was right to obey the wishes of the ruling sovereign in so far as it was possible to do so without violation of the conscience, and that so long as good Mr. Axe filled the pulpit of St. Mary's, he could go and hear him with edification and pleasure.

I was quite of that opinion myself, used to the order and liturgy of the church, and finding the long extempore prayers at Paul's Meeting less to my liking than the collects set down in the prayer-book. I was glad to go to church; but I was a little puzzled by my uncle's sudden zeal for submission and orthodoxy. He said nothing that our friends could cavil at, and was hearty and warm towards them as ever; but he seemed to desire to be "all things to all men"—a line of conduct which I was far too young and hot-headed to understand the use of.

But I must not omit to mention, in dealing with my early experiences of Taunton, the school next door, and the two kindly gentlewomen who conducted it.

Meg had once been a scholar there, and kept very friendly relations with her mistresses. My aunt, too, was very kindly disposed towards them, and would often send me in with some small delicacy for their supper; and by-and-by I used to be admitted to the parlour where the ladies sat, and was sometimes bidden to take a seat and to tell them some of the gossip of the town. For these gentlewomen seldom stirred abroad themselves, and all their exercise was taken in the old garden behind the house, where the pupils walked or played for an hour in the middle of the day when the weather permitted. As I grew to be better acquainted with them, I was asked sometimes to read awhile whilst they plied their needles; and this reading became such a pleasure to them that by the time the first winter of my stay in Taunton arrived, I went in about once a week to read the news-letter after it had been exhausted at the inn, and to tell them all I had gleaned from travellers or from the talk of the towns-folk upon it.

It was these readings which introduced me first to the notice of fair Mistress Mary Mead, of whom I had heard upon the very first day of my sojourn in the town, but of whom I had had no thought till I was months afterwards brought into her presence.

And I think it behoves me here to explain somewhat of the history of fair Mistress Mary; for these pages will have a good deal to say of her, and it may be well that it should be fully understood what manner of person she was.

Her grandfather had been one of Cromwell's generals—a man stanch to the side of the Parliament; and he had fallen at the siege of Taunton, of which mention has been made. His son, Mistress Mary's father, had been enriched by the spoils of the Cavaliers in their misfortunes, and had amassed a considerable fortune. This daughter was his only child, and his wife, who was said to be of a noble royalist family, died in giving her birth. Sir Thomas Mead—for he had won his spurs of knighthood—died when his child was ten years old, leaving her to the guardianship of his friend the Earl of Lonsdale. Sir Thomas had trimmed his sails with the times, and had welcomed the King back from exile at the Restoration; but it was always supposed that he had not changed his views to any notable extent, and that his daughter had been brought up to glory in the doughty deeds of her grandsire, and to hate and abhor all undue exercise of royal prerogative, and all indications of Popery.

The girl had been brought up for convenience at the school where the better towns-folk sent their daughters, Sir Thomas not having yet learned to hold his head higher than the compeers of his father. When the child was left an orphan, Lord Lonsdale had summoned her to his house, and it was supposed that she would remain beneath her guardian's roof until she married; but some four years later she was suddenly sent back to the care of Miss Blake and Mrs. Musgrave, not exactly on the footing of the rest of the scholars, but to remain in their charge as a member of their household, and to observe the same secluded life as they did themselves.

Various surmises were afloat with regard to this sudden and unusual arrangement. Some declared that Mistress Mary's faithful attachment to her instructors (which was an admitted fact in all quarters) had led to this step, and that it was her own earnest pleadings which had caused her to be sent back. Others affirmed that her guardian was alarmed and displeased by her independence of mind and by her revolutionary tenets, and had sent her away in disgrace; but that theory was rather quashed by the improbability of Lord Lonsdale's choosing Miss Blake's school as the asylum for a refractory maiden, since both the heads of the establishment were known to be much of the same way of thinking. The third whisper was that Lord Lonsdale's son, the gallant and dashing Viscount Vere, had shown such unmistakable signs of falling in love with his father's ward, that Lord Lonsdale in a great fright (for he had other views of a more ambitious nature for his son) had sent Mary away in haste, choosing a place where she was known to have friends and to be happy, and hoping she would shortly relieve him of all embarrassment by selecting a husband for herself. But if this was the case, his choice of a place had hardly been a happy one; for Mistress Mary led a life of almost nun-like retirement, and had already been four years with her former mistresses without showing any signs of entering into bonds of wedlock.

I had heard all these tales and surmises respecting her before ever I was favoured by the sight of her fair sweet face and graceful form. But she came to be present often at the readings, and I learned to think her more exquisitely beautiful every time I saw her. There was a charm in the steady dark grey eyes, the delicate mobile features, and the easy grace of her every movement, which my poor pen has no power to describe. Her voice was low and sweet, the sweetest I have ever heard, and the rare laugh was like music. Surely had I been a man, and a comely and gallant one to boot, I should straightway have fallen in love with sweet Mistress Mary Mead. And I ceased to marvel at the stories of Viscount Vere; for even as a child she must have been passing fair, and how could he help loving what was so gracious and so good?

But I had no suspicion in those early days what I should be called upon to do for Mistress Mary Mead, nor how great a part I should play in her life's story.

CHAPTER V.

I GET AMONGST FINE FOLK.

I have been something remiss all this while in saying no word about my faithful four-footed friend Blackbird, who had accompanied me to Taunton, and who remained as constant in his attachment to me there as he had done at home, notwithstanding all the blandishments and the praise he received from the hostlers at the inn, and from the travellers and servants who chanced to note him in the stable. I could have sold him again and again for a good round sum had I been so minded, and had he not been so persistent in suffering none other rider than myself to mount him. Not that I was ever tempted to part with my comrade; for I was in no need of money, and I found continual pleasure in the journeys of exploration around Taunton which I made on Blackbird's back. I came in time to be well acquainted with the whole of the surrounding country; and very rich and beautiful country it was, as all men know who are acquainted with our "Queen of the West," the name given by Taunton men to their beloved city. And in due time the possession of Blackbird, and my reputation for riding, brought me employment of which I had never dreamed before.

I have spoken of beautiful Mistress Mary Mead, whom I came to regard with a great admiration and reverence. She was like a star in the firmament of my sky—far, far above me, and yet on whose loveliness I was ofttimes permitted to gaze, and who would sometimes give me a kindly smile or a gentle word of praise, which set all my pulses hammering and the blood tingling in my veins.

But there was better than this in store for me as the dark cold winter days passed by, and the spring sunshine began to coax forth the shy flowers in the meadows, and to woo the swelling buds to show their tender tints of green and gold.

Sweet Mistress Mary had been looking somewhat pale and fragile during the inclement winter, and when the first heat of coming spring filled the air, it seemed to make her languid rather than brisk; so the leech who was called in to see her said that she must take the air without the fatigue of walking, and, in fine, prescribed horse-exercise for her.

Now in mine uncle's stable was a fair grey palfrey which he had bought for her good looks, and which carried a lady as carefully and softly as it is given to steed to do. As soon then as I heard what was spoken anent Mistress Mary, I set to work to groom and tend Lady Jane (for so the palfrey was called by us) till her coat shone like satin, and all the long hair of winter was groomed away. Then I led her round to Mistress Mary to show her how fair a steed she was; and no sooner had she seen her than the wish to mount her and ride out into the open country lanes arose within her heart, and the blood mantled in her fair cheek, and already the medicine seemed like to work.

Now hanging upon Mistress Mary's hand, as she came to see Lady Jane, was a younger maiden whose face was well known to me by this time, and whose rank in life was equal to that of Mistress Mary, and much above that of those scholars of Miss Blake's who came to her from the town. Belike it was this that made these twain consort much together, as I heard from Lizzie that they did. The laughing maid with chestnut curls and dancing blue eyes was one Mistress Mary Bridges from Bishop's Hull, a goodly house lying west of Taunton about a mile away or something over. Mistress Mary was the only girl out of a fine family of boys. Perchance she was like to grow somewhat too much of a boy herself, for it was whispered that she could handle a carbine and shoot straight to the mark, and that she was as bold and fearless as a young lion; so it may be that for this same cause she was sent to Miss Blake's school, to be educated with Mistress Mary Mead, who was known for an accomplished and right gentle lady. During the inclement months of the winter, the younger Mistress Mary had dwelt beneath the roof of Miss Blake's house; but I had heard that with the approach of summer she would ride in and out on her palfrey. And the words that I heard her speak showed me that this was like enow to be true.

"Ah, Mary," she cried, with her rosy face all aglow, "now we will have right good times together, thou and I. We will go riding forth whither we will, when I have my pony in good John Snowe's stable. I will show thee mine own home, and all the beauteous glades and woods of which I have told thee. We will ride hither and thither, and be free as air! I have been but as a caged bird all these weeks. Now we will spread our wings and fare forth together and see the world. I will be Rosalind, and thou shalt be Celia! I will protect thee, and we will live the life of the forest together!" And she laughed so joyous a laugh that I could scarce forbear to join, albeit I knew my place, and strove to look unconcerned.

For a few days I heard no more of the matter, and then my uncle suddenly told me that he had promised I should attend the two Mistresses Mary three days in the week upon their rides, and that I must curtail my studies somewhat in order to be able to do this. Some attendant they must needs have, and to my great satisfaction and happiness I was told the Mistress Mary Mead herself had said that she would prefer Dicon Snowe to any other.

Now, although I say it, I think the maidens had made wise choice, for I doubt me if any other could so well have shown them the country round Taunton as

Blackbird and I. Moreover, knowing what would be wanted by the courageous and high-spirited ladies, I went out often early upon Lady Jane, and taught her the tricks of leaping, creeping through hedges, and overcoming obstacles that Blackbird was famous for; and since Mistress Mary Bridges' pony was as daring and eager as herself, there was little that we could not accomplish together when our minds were set upon it.

I knew my place, I hope, and I was careful to speak no word to my ladies save such as became their servant; but as we grew acquainted one with another, they would often draw me into their talk, in that way which the really high-born have no fear of doing, and discuss with me many matters in which I was more versed than they. And this I say without boasting of any learning; for what the ladies desired greatly to learn was news of those things that were going on in the world about them, of which little reached them, whilst I was always hearing stories from the travellers who passed by; and though some told one tale and some another, so that it was not easy to sift the grain of truth from the chaff of falsehood, yet one felt to know something as time went on, and I could tell my ladies many a tale which made them hang upon my lips as though I spoke words of magic charm.

And ever and again would our talk come back to the Duke of Monmouth, and the chance of his succeeding to the crown.

Mistress Mary Bridges came of a race that belonged to what men called the "Court party." At home she heard no good spoken of the Duke of Monmouth, and told us that her father had many times said with authority that there was no truth whatsoever in the story of the black box; that many men believed the Duke of Monmouth to be the son of Colonel Robert Sydney, and not of the King at all; that her father always declared him to be much more like "handsome Sydney," as he was called, than like the King; and that it would be vile sin and shame to England if any attempt were made to place upon the throne a man upon whose birth there rested such a stain and slur. His mother, as all the world knew, had been a vile woman, and the son was like to be little better than his mother. These things had young Mistress Mary heard her father say when he was speaking to his wife and others of this matter, and the daughter had been brought up to look upon the succession of the Duke as a silly fable, which would never come to aught save empty talk.

Her winter's residence in Taunton, however, had done something to shake this conviction. Her ardent and romantic nature had caught some of the fire of Mistress Mary Mead's silent but intense love and enthusiasm for the Duke; and when I told of my own adventure, spoke of his kindly ways to the people, his gentleness to me, and the miraculous cure he had worked upon me, she was still more shaken in her former beliefs, and looking from one to another of us would say meditatively,—

"Ah! I wonder which is the truth? I would fain believe him the King's lawful son. That treacherous black-browed Duke of York will be a terrible tyrant. I would it were any one else to succeed the King! But my father says we must never do evil that good may come; and to support an usurper would be that, even should he make the best King afterwards that the world has ever known!"

But then Mistress Mary Mead's soft eyes would light up with a glow of wondrous beauty, and she would say softly,—

"But he is no usurper; he is the lawful heir to the throne, and some day all men will know it! God will light for the righteous cause, and the truth will be made clear as the noonday. I know it, I know it! my heart tells it me!" And such a look would come into her face that all we could do was to gaze at her as though she had been an inspired prophetess; and the other Mary would throw her arms about her and cry,—

"Now, when thou lookest thus, I cannot but believe every word thou sayest. I could believe that the angels had revealed these things unto thee in vision."

And truly I could almost believe the same; for never saw I more perfect trust and confidence than in the lovely face of Mistress Mary, and I knew that she was one of those who would gladly lay down her life if need be in what she held to be a righteous cause.

Now, though I must not linger too long over the story of these pleasant rides, I must not omit to mention that more than once as we sallied forth into the lanes and woods we encountered a very gay and dashing young gallant, who (unless my fancy deceived me) looked long and earnestly at Mistress Mary, with a strange fixedness in his eyes, as though he saw something in her aspect that touched him nearly. And this thing happened more than once, till at last I began to wonder whether our comings and goings were marked and noted by this same gallant, and whether he put himself of set purpose in our path.

The first time or two when it happened I doubt if either of my ladies heeded the passing rider. But there came a day when we met him in a very straight and narrow way, and had to pass him in single file; and then it was that a strange thing happened. Young Mistress Mary had gone in front, and Mistress Mary Bridges followed her—I keeping, as behoved my position, somewhat in the rear. As Mistress Mary passed by this horseman, who had drawn rein and pulled his steed well-nigh into the hedge to let the ladies go by, I saw him put forth a hand and lay it for a moment on the neck of her palfrey, whilst I was certain that I heard these words pronounced in a very low tone, "Mary, sweetheart, hast thou forgotten me?"

I saw her start, and turn her head towards him who had thus addressed her; and albeit it was little of her face I could see, yet even that little had flushed, as I saw well, a vivid and beautiful crimson. She seemed to pause for a moment, as if without knowing it, and I think she spoke a soft word, though what it was I could not hear. But I saw his eyes lighten, and his hand seek hers for a moment, and again I heard him say as they passed each other by, "I will be faithful, I will be true."

Now all this greatly aroused and interested me; for Mistress Mary Mead was in very sooth the queen of my heart, and that she should be beloved by so fair and gallant a gentleman seemed to me most right and fitting. I knew not this dashing young lord (for such I rightly judged him to be), but I looked at him well as I passed by, and thought that his face was a right goodly and honest one, and that if any man deserved the love of my sweet lady, it would be one such as he. Methought he gave me a quick and earnest glance as he rode by, but he said no word, nor did he address either me or Mistress Mary when he met us on other occasions. Yet methinks there is a language of the eyes which is often more eloquent than that of the tongue, and I noted that the bloom returned with wondrous speed to Mistress Mary's pale cheeks, and that the languor and weakness from which she had been suffering grew less day by day.

The gay spring-tide flew by as upon wings, and the hot dry summer followed. There had been something of a drought the previous year, and again this summer there was great lack of rain, and some of the crops suffered, although others did well, and all men rejoiced in the brave sunshine and the way in which the hay was got in and the corn grew and ripened.

With these summer days, too, came the holidays at the schools. I had no more studies to prepare for my tutors and masters; nor had I any rides to take with my ladies, for Miss Blake's house was empty. Mistress Mary Mead had gone to spend the vacation with her friend at Bishop's Hull, and I might have felt my time hang heavy, missing their kindly notice of me, had it not been that another call was made upon my time, and one which brought me into contact with one in whom I had come to have a great interest.

I was standing idly in the court-yard one day, watching the comings and goings of various travellers, and exchanging a word now and again with one whom I knew, when all of a sudden I woke up to a sense of keen interest and excitement; for into the yard rode the gallant young gentleman whom we had so often encountered in our rides, and I at once went up and held his stirrup for him to dismount, asking him how we could serve him.

He looked hard at me, and I saw that he knew me instantly.

"Can I have speech with John Snowe?" he asked; and I at once said that my uncle was within, and would attend him in person. But he still remained standing beside his horse regarding me steadily; and before he moved away towards the inn, he remarked with would-be carelessness of manner, "I have not seen thee abroad of late with thy ladies."

"No, my lord," I answered—for I had made up my mind he could be nothing less—"the ladies be gone away for a while. They will not return till the summer has waned."

I thought he looked sorrowful, but he said no more, and turned towards the inn, bidding me hold his horse till his return, as he should not be long over his errand. I was curious to know what that errand could be, and to know the name and rank of the gallant gentleman. I was sure to find out that from mine uncle, who knew every one, high and low, in these parts; but my curiosity was gratified sooner than I looked for, for within five minutes I heard my uncle's voice calling to me to come in.

Leaving the horse with one of the hostlers, I ran to obey the summons, and found myself in the best parlour, where the stranger was half seated upon the table, tapping his riding-boot with his cane as he talked, my uncle standing respectfully before him, his cap in his hand. This confirmed my impressions as to the rank of the visitor; for my uncle by no means capped to every chance traveller, even of the better sort.

"This is the lad of whom your lordship has heard, Dicon Snowe, my brother's son," said my uncle as I appeared. "If he will suit your noble father's purpose, and if it be not for too long a time, we will make shift to spare him, albeit his place here will not be easy to fill."

"You shall not be the loser by it, good John," said the young gallant with a laugh; and I saw that his eyes lighted up with surprise at my entrance, and I thought that his face looked pleased.

He did not, however, speak openly to me, only giving me a friendly nod as he said something about "the morrow" to my uncle; and only when he was gone and we had seen him ride gaily past the windows did I venture to ask my kinsman, "Who is he? and wherefore has he come? What is it that he wants of me?"

"That is young Lord Vere—Viscount Vere, if you will—eldest son and heir to Lord Lonsdale of Court House, West Monkton. Doubtless you have been near the place sometimes when riding forth with the ladies."

"No," I answered, "Mistress Mary would never ride that way; but I have seen the house when I have been alone, albeit I knew not who lived in it. Is it not

Lord Lonsdale who is guardian to Mistress Mary Mead?"

"Ay; and some say his son was so smitten by her girlish charms, that to keep mischief from following she was sent to Miss Blake, and the Viscount to London and thence to foreign shores, whence he has but lately returned. But the business that brought him here was to obtain for his father, my Lord of Lonsdale, the assistance of a reader, who can beguile his leisure and write his despatches, whilst he recovers from an inflammation of the eyes which is keeping him a prisoner in his room. His secretary is away upon some mission, and his lordship has been doing all himself of late; but his eyes have suddenly become greatly inflamed and painful, so that he is unable to use them. It has been told him that I had here a youth who was an excellent reader and ready likewise with the pen, and he has sent to ask for him to be sent to Court House for a while. And so I must e'en make shift to spare thee, boy; for one must give favourable answer when a lord is the suer."

I gathered from what I had heard that it was something more than courtesy which prompted my uncle to part with me; but I was not disposed to fall foul of his motives, seeing that I was greatly the gainer thereby. For, like all young things, I was greedy of change, and thought that it would be a fine thing to belong for a time to my Lord of Lonsdale's household—to sit with him in his library and read to him and pen his despatches. I felt an inch taller as I went from my uncle's presence to make my simple preparations for leaving on the morrow. I had been not a little fascinated by the beauty and manly grace of the Viscount, and the thought that he was the secret lover of sweet Mistress Mary Mead gave him an added charm in my eyes. Perhaps I should be able to help those two to a happy termination to their courtship. Did not the mouse in the fable loose the bonds of the lion? And surely I might be able to do as much as that!

On the next morning I set forth in great spirits, riding Blackbird, and carrying a change of apparel in my saddlebag. I knew Court House well, for I had often seen its chimneys and gables from mine own home, from which it lay not so very far away by miles, but divided therefrom by a stretch of swampy land, so that there was no good way of approaching it. I did not even remember who lived there, though I must surely have heard. For until I came to dwell in Taunton, I took but small interest in the affairs of the neighbourhood, save those of the neighbours and friends amongst whom we lived.

But I was interested enough as I rode up and passed under the archway to the stables and inferior offices of the house and made known my errand there. I thought the men looked rather disdainfully at my crooked back and small stature, but whether they would have been rude or not I cannot say, for the

Viscount chanced to pass that way, sallying out to see to a favourite horse that was lame; and seeing me he nodded in his friendly fashion, and calling to an indoor servant, he bid him conduct me to the Earl without further ado.

So I was taken through one long passage and up a flight of stairs, and along yet another and a longer passage, and through a door into a hall of such vast and noble proportions that I would fain have lingered to look at it, only I was constrained to follow my guide, who turned down a long corridor lighted by tall narrow windows high up in the wall, and hung with many a fine picture the likes of which I had never seen before, until he paused at a massive door sunk in a niche in the wall, and almost immediately I found myself entering a room almost as large as a church, with windows filled with lozenges of stained glass bearing heraldic devices, and with cases of books the very sight of which made my mouth water and my fingers tingle in the longing desire to know what was within them.

At the far end of this room, beside a bureau heaped with books and papers, sat a stately gentleman, soberly but richly clad, and wearing over his eyes a shade to exclude the light. He held a paper-cutter like a dagger in his hands, with which he seemed to have been impatiently toying, and as soon as ever the servant had retired after explaining his errand, he pointed imperiously to a wooden chair near to the table, and said, "Sit there, Dicon Snowe, and read to me these letters one by one. Pause not unless I bid thee. And read thy best and clearest."

I obeyed in some fear and trembling, for I found it a very different thing to read out written matter to a lord from having to read the print of book or news-letter to my uncle's guests, or even to Miss Blake and Mrs. Musgrave. However, I knew that I should only do worse by letting myself think of this, and by getting frightened at my position; so I went to my task with what courage I could muster, and soon found the work so interesting that I forgot all about Lord Lonsdale's rank, and was as much at home in my task as though I had been in my uncle's parlour.

I may say without vanity that I pleased my master. I found this out by degrees as I pursued my avocations under his directions. There was always a good deal of reading and writing of despatches to be done in the mornings, and sometimes gentlemen would come in and talk with the Earl, whilst I sat silent over my task or waited idle for orders. I saw Sir William Portman frequently, the owner of Orchard Portman, and also of a fine timbered house in the town; and Sir Ralph Bridges, the father of Mistress Mary, came sometimes and talked long and earnestly with the Earl.

I could not hear a great deal of their talk from where I sat in my recess, and often I had writing to do which engrossed my attention; but I gathered that the health of the King was beginning to give anxiety to the Court, that the question of the succession was becoming an increasingly burning one, and that the power and influence of the Duke of Monmouth were steadily waning.

This was regarded as very satisfactory by the friends of the Earl, as I very well saw, although my own heart used to grow heavy within me as I heard their talk. The Duke was not in England now. He had fled to Holland, and was sometimes heard of there, sometimes in Brussels. It was said that he was planning a secret visit to England, to get speech with the King and seek to regain his favour. All believed the King to be greatly attached to him, and feared the result of a personal interview. But all were equally convinced that Charles would never pass over his brother and rightful heir, or seek to pass any measure putting Monmouth into the succession. These men of the Court Party seemed quite secure on this head; but the unpopularity of the Duke of York in the country, and the strange influence which Monmouth possessed over the hearts of the people, were sources of danger which they could not ignore. I heard the matter discussed in all its bearings, and felt every day to enter into a better understanding of the case; but all this did not shake my loyalty and love for the Duke one whit, though it opened my eyes to the knowledge that he would have a harder battle for his crown (thus I put it to myself) than I had hitherto believed.

In the after-part of the day I generally read other things to the Earl: history, poetry, learned writings of great men whose names I had never heard— nothing came amiss to Lord Lonsdale, who was a very learned man; and he was exceedingly kind in pausing from time to time to make some explanation which rendered the theme under discussion more intelligible to me. Of course I never paused to ask a question, but if he stopped to ask if I understood what I was reading (as he sometimes did), then I had to answer no, and he would give me a brief but masterly summary of the matter, and permit me then to ask a question if I did not understand. So I came to have a great love and reverence for the Earl, and to feel my mental horizon growing wider round me every day. I was well treated by the servants of the house, with whom I consorted at other times; and above all I began to feel an intense and growing admiration and love for young Lord Vere, who took much notice of me as the days went by, but of whom I will more fully speak in another chapter.

CHAPTER VI.

VISCOUNT VERE.

It may be that what I have now to relate will have something of a presumptuous sound, seeing that I was a lad of humble birth, and that my lord the Viscount was heir to a noble name and estate. Nevertheless truth is truth, be it never so strange, and there be laws of the heart which follow not the laws of custom and use. Nor was it anything strange that my heart should go forth to one so handsome, so noble, so kind of nature, so brave and gallant as the youthful Viscount, Lord Lonsdale's son; but it always seems passing strange to me when I think how he made of me a friend and comrade—me, a crook-backed lad of but fourteen years when first we became acquaint, the son of a farmer, and nephew to an inn-keeper—one who might never dare to speak such a word as "friendship" in connection with such an one as my Lord Vere. Yet so it turned out, and friends we became; and I may e'en write the word down without shame, albeit in all humility, since to this very day he speaks of me as friend, and loves to talk over with me those stirring adventures in which we both bore a part, as you shall hear.

How this strange friendship came about it now behoves me to relate.

I was, as I have explained, installed for a time in Lord Lonsdale's household, intrusted with the office of reading to him, and of writing such of his letters as he desired. My duties, however, did not occupy the whole of my time, and I had many hours of leisure to call mine own.

It was, I think, upon the third day of my stay, and I had found my way to the stables to look at Blackbird, and to ask whether it would be deemed right for me to take him out for exercise, when Lord Vere came into the yard, and seeing me there, cried out in his free and friendly fashion, "Well met, Dicon; let us ride forth together. I have somewhat to say to thee; and that pony of thine looks wild for a gallop."

So before a quarter of an hour had passed we were riding through the great gateway—I following in the wake of the Viscount, as was just and right, but feeling greatly honoured by being permitted thus to attend him.

I would fain describe my gallant young lord, only I fear that my poor pen lacks the skill to bring him before the eye of the reader. It is easy to speak of handsome, well-cut features, stamped with that high-bred look that is the birthright of so many of our noble families, of sunny blue eyes, delicately-arched brows, and a figure full of grace and power, and skilled in all martial exercises. But these words sound cold and poor, and do little towards conjuring up the picture of youthful grace and manhood that was presented in those days by young Lord Vere. There was a brightness about him which was like nothing so much as the golden halo round the head of a pictured saint. He seemed to carry sunshine and light with him. It shone in his eyes, it sparkled in his smile, it brought light and happiness to the faces of those with whom he spoke. I have lived long in the world now, and have seen many men and women whom I have had good cause to love, admire, and revere; but none amongst these has ever possessed that gracious and brilliant charm of the Viscount. Never have I felt my heart so stolen away and enslaved as it was by him. I know what the love is of man to maid, and how it makes all the world new, and makes a heaven of this earth; but even this love and glamour is not quite like that which filled my boyhood's heart when young Lord Vere rode beside me and made of me his friend. I always think when in Holy Writ I hear how the soul of David was knit unto the soul of Jonathan, and of how the love of Jonathan and David is spoken of as a love "passing the love of women," that I understand the import of these beautiful words better perhaps than other men may be able to do.

I felt the beginnings of this glamour as I rode after Lord Vere through the stately park and watched the sunlight playing in his golden curls and lighting up the bright tints of his riding coat and vest. The Viscount's hair was so thick and abundant, and curled with such a natural grace, that he wore no wig, like the greater part of the gentry in those days; and for my part I think that nothing could have so well become him as did his own bright hair, although I have heard envious gallants, who would fain have copied him an they had known how, sneer at his "maid's face" and floating love-locks.

We had scarce passed beyond the view of the house when Lord Vere reined in his horse and signed to me to come up beside him; and then with one quick glance round, as though to assure himself that there were none to overhear, he said in eager accents, "Dicon lad, I have wanted speech of thee for a purpose. I prithee tell me all thou knowest about sweet Mistress Mary Mead."

I was not greatly surprised at the question, albeit it had come somewhat soon and suddenly. Nor was I loath to speak of Mistress Mary; and I told my young lord all that I knew of her—how I was favoured sometimes to read to her with others in Miss Blake's parlour, and how I had been made her attendant since she had been bidden to take exercise on her palfrey with young Mistress Mary Bridges.

He listened eagerly, ever and anon putting some quick question anent her health or the fashion in which she occupied herself; and when I had told him all that I could, he looked thoughtful for a moment, and then said, "Boy, dost thou think her happy?"

Truth to tell, I had never seriously considered this question. Mistress Mary seemed to me as a thing apart, so greatly above my world that I did not judge of her as I should of others nearer to myself; but having had the thought suggested, I pondered awhile upon it, and then I answered,—

"Methinks, perhaps, that she is as one who feels a shadow resting upon her life. She is ofttimes pensive. She but seldom laughs, and her smile is sad as well as sweet. I could think of her as one who has some secret trouble which she is nursing; but I do not speak with knowledge, my lord, only as my heart prompts me, thinking of her and what I have noted when in her gentle presence."

Now although I could not doubt that the Viscount greatly loved Mistress Mary, yet methought his face lighted as if with joy to hear that she was ofttimes sad. And if at first I was surprised at this, I quickly began to understand better the reason for this joy.

He rode on for a few minutes in silence, one expression chasing another over his face; and at last looking earnestly at me, as though he would read my very soul, he said,—

"Dicon, I must speak to some one, else my heart will break for very impatience of these bonds of silence. Boy, I like thee. There is that in thy face which draws me to thee. Canst thou be discreet? canst thou keep a secret? and wilt thou be true to me if I tell thee more perhaps of myself than any man knoweth as yet?"

My heart bounded within me at these words. Already it was enslaved by the charm of this young noble. Even though I had been but three days in his father's house, I had heard nothing but praise of him, and had come already to regard him as a bright particular star. To be taken into his confidence was a favour so far above my merits and so far removed from anything I had dreamed, that I was bewildered with joy, and could only breathe forth a hearty and cordial promise that I would be true to the death, silent as the grave, and the very humble and devoted servant of the Viscount in any office in which he could employ me and in which I could serve him.

He looked at me smilingly as I blundered forth my clumsy asseverations, but I think he read in my eyes that I meant every word that I said; and when I had finished he held out his hand, and I placed mine within it, feeling lifted into another sphere by the very touch of those strong slim fingers.

"There, lad, that is the seal to our comradeship," he said, as he released my fingers with a strong pressure. "Now I must e'en speak to thee with some freedom; and yet, perchance, thou hast heard somewhat of this very matter. Has it ever been told thee that I love Mistress Mary as a man loves the maiden he would fain seek for his wife?"

"I have heard something of it, my lord," I answered; "albeit I think that none know rightly whether there be truth in the rumour or no."

"If men say that I love her as never woman was loved yet, they speak in very sooth no more than the truth," was the impetuous answer, and the young lord's face flushed with the generous ardour of his love, whilst his eyes kindled with such a light as methinks no maiden could resist; but after a brief moment the flush faded, and he smiled at his own vehemence, and said,—

"Nay, but I must not prate and rant like a hot-headed boy. I have reached man's estate, and as a man will I woo and win my fair lady. And thou, good Dicon, shalt help me to this, an thou wilt; for men have raised barriers betwixt us that be not easily broken down. Not only have they taken her away and placed her with those who would keep her from me, but they have taught her to think that her sweet love will injure me, and that to wed with her would be to do me grievous hurt."

"Is that so?" I asked, marvelling; and walking our horses at a foot's pace under the green trees, the Viscount told me all his tale.

"Truly I think that from very childhood we loved each other. Thou canst well guess how sweet a maid she was when she came to us, and how in my lonely boyhood she seemed to come like a creature of light and air; how we roved the woods and dells together, and played that we were king and queen of all the earth; and how we plighted our troth a thousand times, and never thought of life save as a thing to be shared together.

"I verily believe that, had my mother lived, she would have taken our part; for Mary was in sooth a daughter to her, and she loved her with a great and tender love. But she was taken away, and methinks the grief of that parting changed Mary from child to maiden at an early age. Be that as it may, when she was not yet fifteen years, and when I was but eighteen, I could refrain myself no longer, but told her fully and freely of my love; and she hid her sweet face upon my breast, and said that she had never known a thought or a wish save to be mine. And so we plighted our troth standing over my mother's grave, where it was that her tears had roused within me the resolve to speak at once and for ever, and to win for myself the right to chase those tears away. Our troth-plight was the more hallowed to both of us, I know, for that it was taken in that spot, amid so many memories of her who had been so infinitely dear to both."

The Viscount paused a moment and turned away his head; and I thought none the less highly of his manhood that the memory of his departed mother had brought tears to his eyes. For a moment he paused, and then he continued his tale, speaking in a graver tone, and with less of emotion.

"Having thus opened my heart to Mary, the time had come for me to speak to my father. I went to him without fear, and yet I was aware of some small misgiving in my heart. Not that I could see how he could, by any manner of means, find aught amiss with my choice; yet I remembered how he had from time to time spoken of my marriage, and had seemed to think that a daughter of our good friend Sir William Portman would prove to be the lady of my choice. Hitherto I had only smiled when he spoke thus, and had given the matter scarce another thought, having no intentions towards marriage till Mary should be older. But I remembered it as I approached the door of his room that day, and my heart sank somewhat within me."

"But surely, my lord, your noble father could not have aught but love for one so sweet as Mistress Mary?" I hazarded.

The Viscount slightly shook his head.

"Thou wilt find as thou growest in wisdom and in years, good Dicon, that a father may love a fair maid right well, and yet not desire her for his son's wife; and that he may care little for the lady he desires to call his daughter-in-law the whiles he is very eager to betroth her to his son. I was speedily to find that my father would hear not a word of my troth-plight to Mary. He strove first to laugh; and when I would not have the matter slighted, he grew stern and hard, told me that he had other projects for me, and that in these dangerous and perilous times—for they are more perilous than thou dost well know, Dicon, and are like to be more so should aught happen to the King—no man could walk too warily. He said he had chosen a wife for me out of the family of the Portmans, as, in sooth, I had half believed, and that Mary was no fit match for me. Some wealth she had, but her lineage was not equal to mine, and, child though she was, she was deeply tainted by the disloyalty and rebellious notions of her father. He had watched with pain the development of the germs of this evil, which had been fostered by those to whom her education had been intrusted, albeit at that time he had not known this. In short, he would have none of it. He would not listen to my pleading. He told me that I was but a boy, and knew not what was for mine own good; whilst she was a child, and would say yea to any swain who came a-wooing. And since I was unwilling thus to be treated, and asserted my manhood and my unchanging devotion in the finest phrases at my command, he took another line with me, and said that I must have a chance of seeing other maidens than my Mary; and, in fine, he told me to make ready to be sent to the King's Court, where it was full time that I presented myself, and where he intended to send me forthwith."

"Was not that good news, my lord?" I asked as he paused. "Surely your lordship must have desired to see the gay world of fashion and the person of the King's Majesty?"

"I wanted nothing so much then as to bask in the sunshine of Mary's bright eyes," answered Lord Vere quickly. "Nevertheless, if that might not be, and if it were needful to prove my constancy, I was willing to obey my father; and, indeed, I had no choice but to do as I was bid. Mary herself told me that I must submit myself to my father's will; and within a week I had bidden her farewell, vowing to be constant to her for ever, and quickly found myself in London, and welcomed at Court by many of my father's friends."

"And what is the life of the Court like, my lord?" I ventured to inquire; but the Viscount laughed and shook his head.

"Ask me that another time, good Dicon, and I will give thee thy fill of stories of its follies and pleasures and wickedness; but my thoughts are with my Mary to-day, and I will not sully her name nor her image by mingling with it any of these polluted memories. I was there some three months when my father came; and I heard then from him that Mary had been sent away from Court House to Miss Blake's, or rather to Mrs. Musgrave's care, in Taunton. My father said that a maid needed the care of women—which is doubtless true; and that, now my mother was dead, there was no one here to be a companion to her. I wrote her a letter when I was able to find a safe messenger; but she was long in replying, although I begged her to let me hear from her. And when she did write, it was to tell me that she would not hold me bound by any of the words I had spoken to her; that, since it would not be for my happiness or welfare to wed with her, she freely gave me up. She bid me do my father's will without thought of her; and albeit a spirit of gentle, sorrowful love breathed in every line of her letter, not a word of love did it contain, and I understood well that my father had made her believe it would injure my fortune to mate with her, and that she was striving to help me to forget, so that I might do that which was thought by others to forward my fortunes in the world."

"Ah! that was like her—that was like her!" I could not refrain from exclaiming. "That is what all who know her say of her—that she thinks always of others, never of herself. That is why all love her so much. They say of her ofttimes that she is like one of the holy angels, so full of goodness and purity."

Lord Vere's face kindled, as I soon found it always did at any praise of Mistress Mary; but he made no direct answer, only going on with his narrative.

"It was two years before I saw Court House again; but those years had served only to deepen my love for sweet Mary. Beside the image of her which I carried always in my heart, other women looked to me like 'painted Jezebels,' as I called them in my thoughts. I never saw one amongst them who stirred my heart or recalled in anywise the feelings with which I had regarded my Mary; and when I came back, I was resolved that I would rid her mind of those false notions which had been instilled into it by others. But, alas! I was something too impetuous and outspoken, and my father got wind of my intentions. What steps he took I know not, but Mary had left Taunton ere ever I was able to ride over to seek her. All I could learn was that she had been taken away for the sake of her health, and whither she had gone my father would not tell me. Kind in all else, he was inexorable about Mary, and soon I was so seriously beset to pay my addresses to Mistress Julia Portman, that I was glad to leave Court House once more, and travel abroad or pay visits at the Court; and only of late have I returned home, having arrived at man's estate and come into possession of the fortune bequeathed me by my mother, as fully bent as ever upon winning my Mary for my wife, albeit I have learned to go to work more warily now, and to use policy in my methods."

"And does my lord the Earl know that your heart is yet unchanged, my lord?" I asked eagerly.

"To him I have spoken no word," answered the Viscount gravely. "I trow he thinks my boyish freak forgotten. What he may have said to Mistress Mary, or to those who have charge of her, to keep her from me, I know not. That he still desires an alliance with the Portman family I cannot doubt, although Mistress Julia is now wed, and it is her younger sister Edith whose praises are from time to time sounded in my ears. But I have seen Mary. I have spoken to her, as thou, good Dicon, dost know. I have read in her sweet eyes that however she may strive to turn from me, yet her heart is mine as mine is hers. Her words may be few and cold, but her eyes speak eloquent language. Obstacles and difficulties may lie in our path; but I will overcome them in the strength of my love, and Mary shall be mine at last!"

As he spoke, my very heart went out to him in his generous, chivalrous love; and stretching out my hand and bringing it down upon his charger's neck in my eagerness, I cried,—

"O my lord, what maid could stand out against such love? And if I can do aught to help you, I am your very humble and devoted servant ever."

"Good lad, I believe thee," he answered warmly. "There is something in thy face which draws me to trust thee. I have watched thee oft when thou hast little known it: for when Mistress Mary rode forth I have seldom been far away, though not often have I dared to show myself. I read in thine eyes that thou didst love her. I knew that thou wert faithful and watchful. And now, tell me true, boy: is she, as my father would have me believe, one of those who look upon the young Duke of Monmouth as the coming saviour and deliverer of this nation? And would she look with aversion and displeasure upon one who (if indeed in days to come it comes to be a question of fighting) would be forced by duty and conviction to take up arms upon the other side?"

At that question I felt my face grow grave; for I knew right well how Mistress Mary's heart was with the Duke of Monmouth, and how she did indeed regard him as the coming deliverer of the nation, and the champion of the cause of true religion. Very deep in her heart were these matters buried. Very sacred in her eyes was the cause of him whom she often declared to be the embodiment of all that she held dear in matters appertaining to freedom of government and of faith. Could she indeed ally herself to one who was banded upon the other side? It would be a hard struggle betwixt love and duty—that at least I was sure of; and did she think also that her love would be hurtful to him to whom it was given, why, then, in very truth I thought that the scale would be turned against him.

The Viscount's face fell as I spoke to him of these matters, and told him of the assurance Mistress Mary felt, not only of the integrity of the Duke, but of his right to rule the kingdom as the legitimate son of the King; and I saw his face cloud over almost as if with impatience, as he answered sharply and decisively,—

"Why will people persist in believing a mischievous fable? If the King had a lawful son, he would be glad and thankful to proclaim him, and have done with the endless cabals and plots which are making his life a misery. Why, Dicon, there have been times when he must have been sorely tempted by his black brother's jealousy and spite, and by his love for the Duke, to proclaim him his lawful heir. But he has never done so; nay, more, when it has been almost offered to him—as it was to the great Eighth Harry—to appoint his own heir and make an end of these disastrous disputes as to the succession, he has never let himself be tempted to do this injustice to his brother. Honour has withheld him, though certainly were Monmouth his lawful son he would have acted very differently. Some say he is not the King's son at all, despite the affection between them. I tell you plainly, Dicon, that he is by no means the hero you good folk of the West Country imagine. He has many good qualities. He has distinguished himself in the Dutch wars by many acts of bravery; but he is tainted by the treachery of the Stuarts—for I will not deny that they are a treacherous race, though I am a loyal servant to the King. He is a bad husband to his virtuous Duchess. The vices of his mother are appearing in him; and though he is a stanch Protestant and a hater of Popery, yet he is not the saint and the deliverer you enthusiasts believe him. Have a care, Dicon, how you act if ever this comes to be a question of blows and of fighting; for the kingdom is *not* with the bastard Duke. We may not do ill that good may come, nor fight against our lawful King to set an usurper on the throne, be he never such a champion of liberty. What followed when Cromwell was ruler though not called King? A tyranny worse than the nation had ever groaned under in the King's time. The people had had their will then, and it ended in their sighing for their rightful King and bringing him back in triumph. And so it will be again if the Duke of Monmouth is ever foolish enough to try to claim the throne. I doubt me if he will ever succeed in winning it, but I am quite certain that he will never keep it; and there will be evil days then for those who take his part."

I listened with grave face and sinking heart to words which affected me more as coming from Lord Vere than they had done when spoken by his noble father and the other gentlemen. Somehow I had fancied that all young and generous souls would go out in love towards our idol the Duke, and to hear him spoken of by Lord Vere in such terms gave me a curious shock. I could not but tremble to think how Mistress Mary would take such words—she who had dreamed her dreams about the Duke till he became to her as the hero of some noble tale, as the stainless knight of romance going forth in the might of truth and righteousness to tread down all enemies with lofty courage and devotion.

Methought the Viscount would need all the charm of his grace and the attraction of their mutual love to approach Mistress Mary with such words on his lips and such thoughts in his heart; but after all, was not such love as theirs proof against all difference of opinion in outward matters? Only to Mistress Mary these things went deep, deep into her heart, and she could not regard them as mere externals.

This first ride and first talk were by no means the last; and before I left Court House (with a generous gratuity in my pocket, over and above the sum paid to my uncle) I felt that, despite the wide difference of our stations, I knew the heart of the Viscount as nobody in the world knew it, and that the word "friendship" between us was no mockery.

Heart and soul was I with him in his desire to win speech of Mistress Mary, and to plead his cause in person; and I took back with me a long letter written by Lord Vere, which I promised faithfully to deliver into her own hands, unseen by all the world, so soon as she should be returned and I could find a way of doing this discreetly.

CHAPTER VII.

A WINTER OF PLOTS.

I went back to my uncle's house with my head full of romantic stuff about lovers and love's dreams, and with every intention of working might and main to bring about the happiness of the two beings in whom these romantic notions centred—namely, the dashing young Viscount and sweet Mistress Mary Mead. Not only did I resolve to deliver the precious letter upon the first possible opportunity, but I also made up my mind to speak such glowing words of praise anent the writer thereof as should move the heart of any maiden, still more of one who I was very certain was predisposed to think kindly of him of whom I should thus speak. I was little versed in affairs of the heart; yet I had not read my Shakespeare so earnestly for nothing all these years, and I felt very sure that the heart of a young maid was not of adamant, and that the youthful wooing of which the Viscount had told me could not have failed to make an impression upon the tender and ardent imagination of Mistress Mary.

Nevertheless, in spite of all the eagerness on my part to set things in train for a happy consummation, I was destined to disappointment; for not only had Mistress Mary not returned to Miss Blake's house when I got back, but I speedily heard that she had accompanied her young namesake on a visit the latter was paying to some relatives in the adjoining county of Devon, and that she was not like to return to Taunton for some months to come. Moreover, I could not learn her exact whereabouts in Devonshire, only that it was at the other side of the county, and nigh to Cornwall. There was plainly no chance for me to pay her a flying visit on Blackbird. I should have to wait until she returned to her abode in the town. I shrewdly suspected that my Lord of Lonsdale had had somewhat to do with this journey of hers far away. Belike he had spoken to his friend Sir Ralph Bridges of his wish to keep his son from the fascinations of Mistress Mary, and this visit for her had been arranged between them.

Lord Vere was very sorrowful when he heard what had befallen, and declared it all part of a plot. But he was resolved that no machinations on the part of those about them should sunder him from his Mary, and made up his mind to wait in patience till she returned, and then see if he could not make shift by hook or by crook to get speech of her, and plead his cause in person. Meantime he hung much about Taunton, and improved his acquaintance with that city and with many of its inhabitants, making himself well beloved by all who saw him for his gay and winsome ways, and his gracious kindliness of demeanour to his inferiors. And doubtless this paved the way for what followed later.

I had not been home long before Will Wiseman sought me out, and with an air of secrecy and importance invited me to come when occasion served and visit him of an evening at Master Simpson's house.

"There be meetings twice or thrice in the week, Dicon," he whispered, with his finger on his lips. "Men say that the King cannot live long—that he has a mortal disease which is slowly consuming him. The friends of liberty are laying their plans, and are taking counsel together what it is best to do. They meet at Master Simpson's ofttimes, and if thou wilt come I will take care thou dost hear all that is said. Money is being got together, and men are secretly working amongst their fellows, so that at the right moment the whole county will rise as one man for the right. Come and hear for thyself; but not a word to thine uncle. He is too cautious a man to join with the friends of freedom. He desires to see how the issue will be decided ere he commits himself to take a side. That is not the stuff of which heroes are made." Will's eyes flashed with his enthusiasm; and I caught the spirit from him, and vowed I would come so soon as my duties would permit me.

What Will spoke of mine uncle was too true for me to resent. He was one of those who desired to embrace the winning side, whichever that side should be. I knew well that in his heart he favoured the cause of the Duke of Monmouth; but he was less sanguine than some of his towns-folk of the chances of the Duke's success, and he had no wish to imperil his life or his living by any unguarded movement that might cause him trouble later. He went steadily about his daily business, talking freely with all who came and went, but always professing that he had neither time nor knowledge to judge such matters. The making of kings was no business of his; all he strove after was to obey the laws of the land, and give his allegiance to the reigning sovereign.

By these methods he succeeded in keeping the confidence and liking of all men; for a pleasanter companion, and a more hearty man in his ways, it would be hard to find. If ever he heard me speak an unguarded word on great matters, he would smite me on the shoulder, and give me a kindly hint to guard my tongue, lest it should bring me into trouble, and urge me not to meddle with matters beyond my understanding. But I could not abide by such prudent counsel, and was all agog to hear what was the talk of Master Simpson's parlour, whither I repaired whenever I had the chance.

The men most frequently gathered together there for discussion and mutual encouragement as the winter drew on were the two Hewling brothers, of whom mention has been made, and who had wealth and leisure as well as good-will to expend in the cause; Master Herring and Master Hucker; a gentleman of the name of Sharpe, who was son to the Rev. Emmanuel Sharpe, who had once been Vicar of St. Mary Magdalen; and last, but not least, the two Dares, father and son, who always seemed of all present the most to incline to bold counsel and resolute action.

I should weary the reader were I to give too much in detail all that was planned and discussed at these meetings; but as the winter days drew on, and rumours from London spoke more certainly of the King's declining health, there was greater and greater desire amongst our friends to rouse in the minds of the people of the West Country a resolve to make a stand against Popery and unlawful tyranny. And I remember well how Heywood Dare stood forth one day and said that he would straightway go to Holland, find the Duke of Monmouth, and take counsel with him; whilst those who remained behind were to work ceaselessly in his interest here: so that when a blow was struck it might be a heavy and decisive one.

The Duke of Monmouth was now living at the Hague in a sort of honourable exile. The King had never ceased to regard him with affection; but the jealousies and dissensions of the Court, and the hostility of his own brother, had made him decree this thing for the sake of peace and quietness. It seemed to us that it should have been the Duke of York who ought to have been sent away; but unluckily we had no voice in the ruling of these matters. It was the Protestant Duke who had been forced to quit the country, and it certainly seemed an excellent thing to establish direct personal relations with him through the medium of Heywood Dare, a man of so much courage and devotion.

Those who worked amongst the people, sounding them and striving to kindle within their hearts an enthusiasm for the cause, reported favourably of the temper of the common people, but said that the gentry held aloof, and were not to be approached. The influence of the Earl of Lonsdale, Sir William Portman, and Sir Ralph Bridges was very great around Taunton, and all these gentlemen were loyal in their allegiance to what was termed the "Court party."

Sometimes I was called in and questioned about what I had heard at Court House of the matters appertaining to the Duke, and my reports were not favourable to our wishes. But I ventured once to hint that I thought perhaps the young lord, Viscount Vere, might be won over to our cause; and Mr. Benjamin Hewling was forthwith requested to seek him out and strive to sound him in the matter. For all those who knew most about the chances of such a struggle and the fortunes of war—should it ever come to a passage of arms—declared many times that we must have men of the better sort to lead and advise our recruits. Undisciplined soldiers would follow an experienced and gallant captain, when they would fall away in confusion and fear if they had no one above themselves to look to. I could well believe that there were hundreds who would follow the Viscount to danger and death, and fight to the very last gasp, who would turn tail and run like sheep had they only a plain townsman at their head.

How Mr. Benjamin Hewling fared on his mission I did not hear at once, but I thought in my heart that Lord Vere would scarce be adamant to a cause in which his Mary's heart was so bound up. He despised and hated the Duke of York—I knew that very well—albeit he declared his conviction of the necessity of supporting the rightful heir to the crown be he never so personally unbeloved. But if Mr. Benjamin, with his silver tongue and gentle ways, or Mistress Mary, with pleading glances and eloquent words, could make him see the matter differently, why, then, in him the good cause would have an able recruit; for my Lord Vere was skilled in every kind of martial exercise, had seen action abroad, and was of no small personal valour and gallantry.

I not unfrequently saw him in the streets arm in arm with Mr. Hewling, and I heard of him as being seen within their hospitable doors, whilst men spoke of the friendship which was growing up between him and the two brothers, of whom all men thought so well. That they were growing to be friends was evident enough, but whether the brothers Hewling would persuade him to look at public matters with their eyes was what none could say as yet.

Things were in this way at the approach of Christmas, and of that busy festive season which kept me so close at home that I could scarce stir abroad in search of amusement or information. There seemed to be nothing but coming and going from morning till night—the lack of rain, which still continued even during the winter, making the roads better for travellers, and the excited state of the country tending to make men restless and anxious for news.

But what excited me more than the rumours from London or the preparations for Christmas-tide was the return of Mistress Mary to Miss Blake's house just before the festive season came.

I did not know that she was back; for the school had broken up for the recess, and my informant Lizzie, who kept me conversant with what went on within those walls, had not heard anything of the matter when I was asked to come and read to the ladies, as I was in the way of doing from time to time. When therefore I entered the parlour, with my book beneath my arm and the most recent news-letter in my hand, who should be there, in her accustomed seat beside the fire, but Mistress Mary Mead, looking as sweet and lovely as ever, though perhaps a little pale; and seated beside her, with his hungry, cruel-looking eyes almost always fixed upon her face, was the Rev. Nicholas Blewer, the man whom above all others in Taunton Town I feared and hated.

How came he there? and how dared he sit beside Mistress Mary as though it were his right, and keep his evil eyes so constantly upon her face as he was doing now? I felt my blood boil in my veins as I saw him, and I should well have liked to take the knave by the throat and fling him out at the door. But instead I was forced to sit in my place and read to him as well as to the rest, and listen to his comments upon the news of the week—comments which, as I well saw, brought the flush of anger many times into Mistress Mary's cheek. For Mr. Blewer was a bitter enemy of those who held for liberty and the Duke; and it was whispered that at heart he was a Papist, and every whit as cruel as the Duke of York.

Now I trust that in thus speaking of Mr. Blewer it will not be thought that I would willingly speak evil of any man called to a holy office, or that I have any hatred towards the clergy of the Established Church of the land, for this is far from being the case. I hold that we owe them all reverence and honour, and, as these pages will show, I account Mr. Axe a great and noble man, albeit he took our contrary part in the struggle I am coming to. Yet inasmuch as there are black sheep in every flock, and as the cassock and surplice do not do away with a man's evil nature—nay, the very fact that a man of unbridled passions should blaspheme the name of God and the Holy Ghost by taking upon himself vows for which he is unfit, makes his office of necessity a mockery and a stumbling-block—so it always has seemed to me that if an ordained priest of God is untrue to his calling, he becomes a much worse man than if he had not mocked God by taking such vows into his lips. At least I can but say that Mr. Blewer always appeared to me to be an emissary of the Evil One disguised as a servant of God, and I am sure that Mistress Mary shrank from him as though he were indeed such an one.

It was a great matter of wonderment to me how he came to be in Miss Blake's parlour, for I was sure that neither she nor Mrs. Musgrave had any love for him. These ladies and their pupils (such as resided beneath their roof) attended service at St. Mary's Church, as it was considered right and proper to do, and Mr. Axe was revered and beloved by them. But why this evil-faced Mr. Blewer was admitted was a source of much perplexity to me, and my perplexity was turned to alarm when I perceived that upon rising to take his leave he saluted Mistress Mary's hand with a look which could not well be mistaken, and made as though he would have gone further and saluted her lips also had she not drawn herself away with a decision that was not to be mistaken.

I saw an ugly look spring into his eyes at that, and thought his smile more hideous than a frown would have been.

"Ah well, I must be patient, sweetheart," he said. "We shall learn to understand each other better in time."

Then, with a bow which included all the ladies, he retired, and I was almost astonished to see gentle Mistress Mary dash the hand that he had kissed against the marble mantel-shelf with such force that she must have bruised the tender skin.

"That odious man!" she cried, with unwonted heat. "Prithee, dear madam, have pity upon me, and let him come here no more."

"Dear Mary, I like him as little as thou," answered Miss Blake, with a shake of the head. "I know he is an evil creature. But what can I do, when your worthy guardian bids me give him access from time to time, that he may pay his addresses to you, and tells me that he does this with his approval and consent?"

I almost gasped at this, for I began to see that Mistress Mary was like to be made the victim of a plot which seemed vile and base to me, although I was certain that Lord Lonsdale had no idea of acting unjustly or cruelly. Doubtless he would think Mr. Blewer a suitable husband for his ward. No one knew aught against him, so far as I had ever heard, and he had some money, and came of a family as good as Mistress Mary's. To get her safely and quickly married would, of course, be the easiest way of keeping her out of the path of his son. I could not wonder at the turn matters had taken, and yet my heart felt hot within me as I thought of the Viscount and then recalled the cruel, wolfish face of Mr. Blewer.

That night, as I reached my room, I stepped out upon the balcony and eagerly scanned the windows of the house I had just quitted. Once or twice it had been my hap to see the fair face of Mistress Mary looking out from a window not very far away; and to-night fortune favoured me, for I had not been at my post more than a few minutes before a curtain was drawn aside and a gleam of light shone out. Then quickly a casement was flung open as if by an impatient hand, and Mistress Mary leaned out into the clear frosty night as though eager to inhale the fresh cold air. I thought I heard a sound break from her like a sob or a sigh. That she was in perplexity and trouble I could not doubt, and I longed with a longing that would brook no delay to go and comfort her.

I looked into the yard below. All was perfectly quiet and tranquil. I scanned all the windows of both houses, but no light shone from any save Mistress Mary's. I stood above her in my balcony, clasping the letter I had dashed in to fetch in my hand. The next minute I had hidden it in the breast of my doublet, and was swinging myself like a monkey from balcony and waterspout to balcony and waterspout, till my movements attracted her attention, and she gave a little cry of fear.

"Hist, mistress!" I cried in a low voice; "fear not. It is I—Dicon Snowe. I have somewhat to say to thee, and somewhat to give. Have no fear; I will reach thee without hurt."

For if my back was crooked, and my legs not of great service for long walks, I had a length and strength of arm that made amends for much, and such a transit as this was but child's play to me. I was soon upon the balcony outside the window by which she stood; but I came no further, knowing my place better than to intrude upon her.

"Mistress Mary," I said eagerly, "I have a letter for you from my lord the young Viscount Vere. I have had it these three months, but never have seen you to deliver it. I sware to him I would not let it leave my hands till I could place it in yours. Take it and read it; and if there be any answer, I will make shift to deliver that. For I love my lord as much as he deserves to be loved by high and low; and since I know his heart is bound up in love for you, I would fain carry him good tidings."

It was perhaps overbold of me to speak so, but my heart seemed burning within me; and although Mistress Mary's cheek glowed and she turned away with her letter, yet I saw the soft light which had come into her eyes, and I knew that her heart was not cold to him, however she might have schooled herself to think she must thwart his love.

She read her letter from end to end whilst I stood and watched her, though since she discreetly turned her back to me I could not see its effect upon her. Nevertheless, when she turned round I was sure there were tears upon her cheek, and I did not think that they were tears of sorrow.

"O Dicon," she said, coming forward towards me with the confidence that a sister might show to a brother, "Lord Vere says he has told all the story to thee. What must I say? What must I do when there be so many things against it, and it will hurt him so with his father if I let him have his way?"

"Methinks, lady, it will hurt him the more if you be cruel to him," I answered eagerly; "for his very heart is bound up in this matter, and he has been faithful all these years."

"I know it, I know it! How can I doubt it, and how could I help loving him, when he was suffered to be all the world to me in days of yore? But a maid may not always wed as her heart prompts, and I would suffer untold woe myself sooner than hurt him. And it has been said to me that it would hurt him grievously if I were to wed with him; and in very truth there be many and grievous barriers betwixt us," and she sighed heavily, whilst a cloud came over her face.

I guessed of what she was thinking, and that it was the different view they took of the coming strife, and I knew not how to reassure her here; but I ventured to remark,—

"But Mr. Blewer hates the cause of the Duke and of freedom as my lord the Viscount never would. Sure it were better to marry a noble foe than one so cruel and false!"

"Marry Mr. Blewer!" cried Mistress Mary, with a vehemence I scarce believed her capable of; "sooner would I die than do that! Nay, come what will, none shall coerce me there. I can live and die a maid, if Heaven so will it, but I will never wed with yon bad man!"

Right glad was I to hear her speak with such spirit and resolve; for we of the stronger sex are always half afraid that women may be cajoled or coerced into anything if only the persecution be determined enough. Yet I could not get her to intrust me with a letter to Lord Vere, nor yet with a direct message; only when I said that I would tell him what had passed betwixt us twain, she did not say me nay.

I had no rest till I had got speech of the Viscount and had told him all that had passed. His brow darkened ominously as he heard of Mr. Blewer, and of his own father's support of such a suit.

"He had better have a care how he goads me," I heard him mutter through his shut teeth; "he may chance to find he has gone too far an he treat her and me thus."

Then I told of the interview I had had with Mistress Mary, and his face kindled at the recital. As I finished he burst forth,—

"They have made her think she will injure me by her love. I must see her myself, and show her the folly of that belief. Dicon lad, thou art a trusty comrade; thou must do yet one thing more for me. Thou must show me how I may get secretly to the balcony of my lady's room, and so have speech with her, no man but thee knowing it. Once face to face with her, I warrant I will chase away her fears and her doubts. Thou shalt keep thy watch whilst I speak with her; nor will I enter her room, but only stand without as thou hast done. But see her I must, else shipwreck may come of the happiness of two lives. Wilt thou help me in this, good Dicon?"

I think I would have helped him to whatever he asked with such a look and smile; but anything so like a repetition of the romantic story of Romeo and Juliet kindled my ardent enthusiasm and interest. I had very small doubts myself that Mistress Mary would be at her window again to-night, half repenting her of her refusal to send a message, and on the look-out for more news of her lover; therefore as soon as the house was quiet I showed the Viscount how the transit to the balcony might be made, and myself stood in another balcony commanding all the windows, just out of ear-shot, but in full view of the lovers, and ready to give them any assistance by warning or counsel.

It was a bold scheme, but like many such it won its reward. My lord had not waited there above ten minutes before the curtains were drawn back, the casement opened, and then, with a little cry which penetrated even to my ears, Mistress Mary came face to face with her lover.

I was very happy at the success of this experiment; but I confess I had time to grow very cold before the casement closed again and my lord called cautiously to me to join him. I did this without much trouble, and then showed him how he might reach the ground without danger of falling. Soon we stood together in the paved court-yard of the inn, and he grasped my hands in both of his, whilst I could see that his eyes were shining as brilliantly as stars.

"Dicon," he said, "thou art the best and truest of comrades. I will never forget thy good offices this night."

And I felt already abundantly rewarded for what I had done.

It was not my place to ask questions, but surely there was no need in face of my lord's joyous and triumphant bearing. He seemed to tread on air. He passed his arm through mine, and drew me forth into the street with him through the arched gateway, which was not closed at night in quiet times; nor did we pause till we reached the bridge and stood looking down into the flowing dark waters together.

"I could walk all night for very happiness!" cried the Viscount, with that exhilaration of spirit which comes from a deep joy. "Can England itself boast a fairer and more gracious maid than my Mary? Ah, the days will come when my father will rejoice to welcome her as a daughter! None could stand long against such sweetness and beauty."

Then, his energies having been spent in pacing awhile through the frosty night, we turned our steps homewards. I gained ingress by means of a small side door, the key of which I had in my pocket; and my lord slept that night at the Three Cups, and rode forth in the morning; whilst a white hand was waved for a moment from a window above the yard, and then quickly withdrawn.

The next time that I was able, at Will Wiseman's eager instigation, to find my way to Master Simpson's when a meeting had gathered there, I saw Lord Vere enter arm in arm with Mr. Hewling; and Will gave my ribs a triumphant dig with his elbow as he whispered joyfully,—

"See, we are getting nobles to join us at last. Mr. Hewling has prevailed with my lord Vere."

I nodded, keeping my own counsel; but I had a shrewd notion that something else besides the arguments and persuasions of Mr. Hewling had prevailed to make a convert of the Viscount.

CHAPTER VIII.

"*LE ROI EST MORT.*"

"Dicon! Dicon! Come down, lad; come down! The whole town is beside itself, and we want thine eyes and thy tongue here. Get up and come down. Lose not a moment! Heaven help us all if the thing be true!"

I was roused from my sleep on a bright February morning by the hearty tones of my uncle's sonorous voice. I lost not a moment in springing up and hurrying into my clothes, for there was an urgency in his manner which betokened that something unwonted was afoot.

Truth to tell, I was later abed than was my wont, owing to having aided my Lord Vere to another stolen interview with Mistress Mary the previous evening, followed by a second stolen interview at Mr. Hewling's house, where some important letters had been read and discussed, and where Mr. Speke, from Ilminster, had attended, and had given an encouraging report of the state of public feeling in his part of the world.

It was now known all over the country, I suppose, that the King was grievously ill and like to die; albeit there were many who declared that he would be given back in answer to the prayers from the churches. I suppose all men who had any sort of love for their country or interest in public affairs felt grave anxiety just at this time. For there could be small doubt that it would go hard but that bloodshed of some kind there would be, were the Duke of York to succeed to the throne; and yet there seemed no other to take that place, seeing that the Duke of Monmouth was an exile, and that he would have to fight for the crown ere he could hope to wear it. Men who remembered the horrors of civil war a generation back, the disruption of families, and the bloodshed and confusion, shook their heads mournfully, and advised any submission rather than a repetition of such fearsome things; but we of younger and rasher spirit—we who had never tasted of such horrors, but looked only on the glory and honour to be reaped in warfare—felt very differently. I think I, despite my physical deformities, should have been grieved to the heart had any prophet arisen to say that there would be no fighting in our days. The martial spirit had seized upon me. I, in common with others, watched eagerly the marshalling and exercising of the train-bands and militia whenever they assembled under their leaders; and although we knew right well that they were thus mustered and put through their exercises with a view to showing the towns-folk how useless would be any rising of the rabble, when these bands could at once be brought out to crush it, yet knowing the individual men in the ranks, we were certain that half of them at least were hot in the cause of our Duke, and that if the chance for joining him arose, they would come over, arms, ammunition, bright-coloured uniforms, and all.

But I must return to that day when the great news reached Taunton. I rushed downstairs, finishing my toilet as I did so, to find all the lower rooms filled with excited folk who had come in from the streets the moment the news had got wind, and were so crowding round a travel-stained messenger that it was some time before I could approach near enough to hear what he was saying. But I did not need to do that to know what had happened, for the news was in every mouth,—

"The King is dead! the King is dead! God save us all! The Duke of York is proclaimed King in his stead!"

"The King was poisoned by his brother!" whispered a voice in the crowd. I know not whence it came; but the word was taken up in the lowest of tones, and one heard it go surging along accompanied by a sort of shuddering sigh, as though men half feared to utter the fearful words. Other wild whispers soon got afloat. Some vowed it was the Queen who had administered the poison in her intolerant jealousy; others, that it was the notorious Duchess of Portsmouth; but the favourite and most lasting impression of those who believed that foul means had been employed to put the King out of the way, was that his brother the Duke had contrived to poison him, either through his snuff or in his food,—and since he was the man of all others to reap advantage from that death, the opinion flourished and gained ground amongst his enemies apace.

But crowding round the weary messenger, who had galloped to Taunton with the news since noon the previous day, we strove to learn from him every detail of the calamity; and he told his tale again and again.

That the King had been out of health since the fall of the previous year was a thing known to all the country. Some called it gout, and said it was a matter of small moment; others shook their heads over it, and said it showed a break up of the sound constitution which had hitherto marked the monarch. But although there had been much anxious discussion as to the succession, men were not really prepared for this sudden end to the King's life; and when we heard that he had been only four days actually ill, the end did indeed seem to be sudden.

But the terrible thing to us was the story with which the messenger said that all London was ringing—namely, that upon his death-bed the King had been admitted into the Romish Church; that a priest had been found and brought to him by his brother; and that all the courtiers, with the exception of the Earls of Feversham and Bath, had been turned out of the room whilst extreme unction had been administered, and his Majesty confessed and shrived by the priest found with some difficulty for the office.

This was indeed grave news; for if the Duke of York had acted thus, was there any hope but that he would openly profess the Romish faith when he was set upon the throne? At once a vision of Smithfield fires rose before the mind's eye of numbers and numbers of those who heard the story. It seemed to us that with a Papist King, a man notorious for his cruelty and love of inflicting misery and bloodshed, any sort of horror was possible. What wonder that faces grew pale, that we looked at each other in silent amaze, whilst the women wept aloud and gathered their children into their arms as though to protect them from some menacing peril!

"And the King himself, what did he say?" was asked in many quarters. "Did he speak of the Duke—the Duke of Monmouth? Did he say aught of him and his rights?"

The messenger shook his head as this question reached him. The man was one who knew our Duke and thought well of him. He was a West Country fellow himself, and not yet vitiated by the atmosphere of the Court in which he had lived so long.

"His Majesty called for his other children," said he—meaning, of course, children born out of lawful wedlock; for, as all men know, the Queen was

71

childless, to the great grief of the nation—"but of the Duke of Monmouth no word was spoken. The King did not breathe his name—so, at least, it is averred. None dared to speak of him, the Duke of York standing by. Nay, my friends, I fear me there is no hope for England in that quarter. The Duke of York is King in his brother's stead. But what we may lawfully do to stand by the laws and the rights of our nation and our faith, that let every man do to the utmost that is in him. James may wear the crown and be called King, but we will have no tyrant forcing us to a faith against which we have fought and triumphed years ago. He may rule us indeed, but he shall not make of us Papists nor slaves!"

A muffled cheer went round the room as these words were spoken; but many were there standing by who did not endorse the first part of the speech, but cast looks one at another which seemed to say that it would go hard before they would acknowledge a Papist King!

Then a news-letter was produced, and I was called upon to read it loud whilst the weary messenger supped. Of course it stopped short before the death of his Majesty, but it gave an account of the life of the Court up till the time of the King's seizure; and gay and scandalous, indeed, did the history of the last Sunday evening read to us quiet and sober country folks. Women shook their heads as they heard in whose company the King spent his time, and whispered that death had come as a judgment from heaven. Yet few eyes were dry as the letter spoke of the sufferings of the King, and of his fortitude and courage under them.

"After all he was the King, with all his faults and vices," they said; and we all felt how little there was of kingliness in the dark Duke who had succeeded him.

I conjured up before my mental vision the picture of the other Duke as I had seen him a year or two back, his handsome open face, his winning address, his kindly grace of manner, and his care and love for all his poorer subjects (for so did I call them even now in my heart). How could I help trusting in him as the rightful King, when his touch had made me whole, as only the touch of a true King's hand could do?

I found myself telling the story again almost ere I knew it, and the messenger, who was working steadily at the platter of good victuals before him, kept throwing keen glances at me and at the people round, and making odd sounds the while.

I had hardly finished the reading, and the telling of my well-known tale, before a little stir in the crowd announced an arrival; and looking over the heads of the people—for I was set upon a stool to be better heard and seen—I beheld the cadaverous visage and lantern jaws of Mr. Blewer. He came in looking to right and left with his sharp, ferret-like eyes, and his ears seemed to be on the alert to catch any words that might fall from unwary lips. Something in the sinister aspect of the man, and in the loathing with which I had come to regard him, caused the words I was reading to die away upon my lips, and the sudden silence which fell upon me attracted the attention of all present to the entrance of the new-comer.

Mr. Blewer was little beloved in Taunton. It was firmly held by many that he was nothing more nor less than a spy in the interests of the Duke of York, or the King as we must needs learn to call him; unless, indeed—but such things are best not spoken too openly. There were only too many rogues abroad in the world who lived by selling information to one or other of the different parties at Court, and men were strongly of the opinion that the Rev. Nicholas was one of these miscreants. His very appearing so stealthily in our midst at this time of excitement seemed to augur ill, and the murmur of voices died into silence as he made his way into the room.

"Have a care, good people, have a care!" he said, with a leering smile that was uglier than his scowl. "I thought I heard some suspicious word—some phrases that savoured too much of sedition! Have a care how you let your unruly member run away with you! There be birds in the air to carry such words whither ye would not. If God has thought good to take one monarch to Himself, He has given us another of the same name and race to set upon the throne. Let us thank Him from our hearts for this great goodness, and cry aloud in joy and gratitude, 'Long live King James!'"

As he spoke he lifted his hat and waved it above his head, and all who wore theirs instinctively uncovered, and many amongst us, led by the hearty voice of my uncle, strove to raise the shout, "Long live King James the Second!" But the words seemed to stick in the throats of many; and Mr. Blewer looked sharply round upon us, saying, with that evil smile of his,—

"Why, that is but a sorry shout for a new-made King; but perchance your loyal hearts are too full yet of grief for our noble King Charles to give a right royal welcome to his successor!"

"Ay, sir," said my uncle; "that is the case with us. We can scarce yet rejoice in the thought that any other sits in the place of good King Charles, be he never so great and good a prince. Prosperous and peaceful has England been beneath his fatherly sway; and sad are we to learn that he is no more, though I trow that Taunton men will not be lacking in loving loyalty to his successor."

Many asseverations of this kind were made, and the talk grew animated and general. Being no longer required to read the news-letter, which Mr. Blewer had taken into his own hands, I slipped away through the throng, and found myself face to face with Will Wiseman, who caught me by the arm and drew me forth into the street with him.

"It has come then, Dicon!" he whispered, evidently in great excitement: "the King is dead, and another King must sit upon the throne. But whether King James the Second, as in sooth he will be, will be—"

"Hist, Will, be not so rash!" I exclaimed, drawing him into an entry and looking nervously round; for I had caught some caution from the precept and example of my uncle, and I knew that men had paid dear before now for rash words spoken under stress of excitement. "Take heed how thou speakest. If Mr. Blewer were to hear thee, it might go ill with thee in the days to come."

"A pest upon his ugly face and meddlesome, prying ways!" cried Will hotly; for he hated Mr. Blewer even more than I did, and with some reason, since that worthy had done many an ill turn to his master, and had dealt many cuffs and hard words to the lad himself.

Will, as ill-luck would have it, had in his pocket a piece of chalk, and being gifted with the power of drawing lampoons with a wondrous ease and dexterity, he solaced himself by drawing upon the wall, as we stood, two representations of Mr. Blewer, in both of which his hideous face, lantern jaws, and great cavernous mouth were delineated with more truth than flattery. In the first of these pictures the clergyman was represented as preaching from the pulpit, the ungainly action of the man being hit off with wondrous fidelity. In the other he was portrayed as being whipped by the hangman at the cart's tail—a fate we had amused ourselves by prophesying for him sometimes when reckoning upon the good days which Taunton should enjoy when "King Monmouth" should be upon the throne. In both pictures his mouth was equally wide open, and beneath each Will wrote, in rude letters,—

"THE WORSHIPFUL AND REVEREND MR. NICHOLAS BLEWER EXTOLLING THE DIVINE RIGHT OF KINGS."

I doubled myself up with laughter at the clever picture, and a small crowd of laughing men and boys gathered round to admire. We were passing comments far from flattering to Mr. Blewer, and Will was touching up his handiwork so as to make the likeness a little more frightful, when a sudden scattering of the bystanders and a few words of whispered warning made us turn suddenly, to see Mr. Blewer himself regarding us with a baleful light in his eyes, and such a scowl of malevolence upon his brow that I wished Will's talents anywhere else at that moment. I drew him away as fast as I could, but not before we heard the harsh, grating tones of Mr. Blewer's voice following us,—

"Very good, Will Wiseman, very good. It will not be the fault of Nicholas

Blewer if thou dost not taste the discipline of the hangman's whip before he has done with thee."

"O Will, why didst thou do it?" I asked, in an access of fear and trembling. "My uncle ever teaches us to speak with respect of dignitaries, even though they be none of the best. I fear me we were wrong in this, and shall suffer for it. Mr. Blewer is not a man who forgives or forgets."

"Let him remember an he pleases—I care not," answered Will, who had a much higher courage than I, and far more of that reckless daring which I read of with envy and admiration, but never attained to myself. It was one of the things I most admired in him, though it sometimes made me fear that he would get into trouble sooner or later.

We walked back to his home together, talking eagerly of the great news of the day. Personally, we had no especial regrets for his late Majesty, and could not but rejoice in the prospect of the coming strife; for that England would calmly accept James Duke of York as her King was a thing incomprehensible to us, owing to the element of faction in which we had been living. We ourselves so thoroughly believed in the rights of the exiled Monmouth, that we could not credit or understand that these had never been greatly believed in by the mass of the nation, and that the King's brother was likely to obtain all the support of the lovers of established monarchy, as well as of those who, whilst personally regretting the character of the man, would not be a party to a measure of exclusion which should keep the true heir from the throne, or favour a possible usurper.

As days went by the excitement did not lessen. All manner of wild rumours were flying about; but from my lord the Viscount, who came daily into Taunton on one errand or another—in hopes, as I knew, of getting sight or speech of Mistress Mary—I heard the truest tidings.

King James had declared, immediately on succeeding to his new estate, that he would guard the established religion of the country as the choicest treasure of his crown; and a thrill of joy and triumph ran through the country, whilst men swore that the Prince had been sorely maligned, and that whatever his wife might be, he was no Papist at heart.

But then, on the very heels of the first good news, came tidings that the King was going openly to Mass with his wife, that the oratory chapel fitted up for her was to be thrown open for public worship, that the Papists all over the country were rejoicing, and that banished priests and Jesuits were beginning to creep back, certain that good days were in store for them at last.

Then still more ugly whispers (as some thought) got abroad. The King had consented to summon a Parliament, having indeed but small choice in the matter; but it was known in many circles that he had received a large sum of money from the French King in order to make him almost independent of that body, and to bribe and corrupt its members when chosen, that it might be merely an engine for the oppression of the people at the will of a tyrannical monarch.

It was steps like these that so roused the scorn and ire of Lord Vere. Had the new monarch been true and upright in his dealings; had he thrown off the fatal yoke of France, and trusted himself to his loyal people as the House of Tudor (with all their faults) had ever been able to do, I think that even the gentle pleadings of Mistress Mary would scarce have served to turn him back from that loyalty to the crown which was his as by natural inheritance. But this crooked statecraft and treacherous dealing roused all the generous indignation and scorn within him which the young are wont to feel when brought face to face with what is base and false. His father and the elder men might shrug their shoulders, and say that these things had to be; that it was part of the essence of kingcraft; that it was useless to hope for better. But the Viscount could not take this view of the matter. Perhaps he had imbibed more of the opinions and feeling of the towns-folk than he well knew at the time. At any rate, as the days flew by, and we heard more and more of the methods of the new King, a dark frown would often rest upon his brow, and he would say with scornful vehemence, "It is shame that such a man should call himself England's King!"

The dissenters of Taunton—and they were very many—were thrown into great commotion and wrath at the news of the treatment received at the hands of Lord Chief-Justice Jeffreys by that great and good man Richard Baxter, who was brought before him to answer for some rash words spoken in the indignation aroused by the harsh treatment given him for no other offence than declining to use the Book of Common Prayer in public worship. We had just before heard with horror of the inhuman punishment inflicted by the same judge upon Oates and Dangerfield. Not that we felt sympathy with the vile informers who had brought so many innocent persons to the block, but that the ribaldry and cruelty of the judge filled men with horror; and the more so because we knew that this same judge was likely to come again to the West Country for the autumn assizes, and that should any luckless dissenter be brought before him here, he might make up his mind to look for neither justice nor mercy from such a judge. The account of the insults and brutal language to which this aged divine and his friends and advocates were subjected by Lord Jeffreys made the blood boil in the veins of those who read and those who heard. No jury save one chosen by the miserable Sheriffs of

London, mere tools in the hand of the government, would have dared to return a verdict of guilty. And when it was known that Jeffreys would have had the good old man whipped at the cart's tail through London, had it not been that for once he was overborne by his brethren on the bench, a sense of horror and loathing arose in the minds of honest and merciful men, not only against the wicked Judge himself, but against the King who could smile approval on such a debauched servant, and actually associate him with Lord Guildford, the Keeper of the Seals, with the evident intention of promoting him still higher if he continued to go about his work in the same way.

The elections and the coronation all added to the dismay of the Protestant party. It was asserted that the King had so greatly shortened the service that it was most meagre and insufficient, and that this was plainly due to his Popish reluctance to take part in any function of the church he had sworn to uphold and revere. His parsimony was bitterly and scornfully commented upon; for the same spirit of greed which had made him refuse the usual splendid obsequies to the late King (so that men spoke of King Charles as having received "the burial of an ass"), caused him to do away with much of the pageantry of his own coronation, and greatly was this resented by the people, who were by no means too friendly towards him from the beginning.

We of Taunton heard these stories with a species of sombre joy. There was more afoot in the city just now than I knew at the time. My uncle kept me busily employed reading and telling the news. I still continued to take the news-letter into Miss Blake's house and read it to the ladies there. I was often sent errands hither and thither into the country, and kept more busy than I had ever been before; and though I was dimly aware that much was seething below the surface in the hearts of our towns-folk, I was not at all certain whither it was tending.

The elections to which I have alluded took place in May, and the returns were most wonderfully against our wishes, and in favour of the Tory and Court party. The King was said to have got just that sort of packed Parliament which he desired, and would in all probability keep it all through his reign. This was a heavy blow to some amongst us, who had hoped that the leaven working through the land would have acted differently. But at least if disappointed, we knew now what to expect. Such a Parliament as ours would be little better than a tool in the hand of a tyrant monarch. Some small protection it might be against the encroachments of arbitrary power, but so small that it was better to hope nothing from it.

I must not close this chapter (which I fear has been but a dull one; only these things have to be made something clear, or what follows cannot well be understood) without some mention of a piece of work going on within the walls of Miss Blake's establishment, which was destined to bring Taunton almost as much fame as anything that happened within its environs during the stirring days to come.

I had noted that immediately upon the death of the King, whenever I had gone to read to the ladies in the parlour, they were deeply engrossed upon some large pieces of silken embroidery work, something different from anything I had seen in their hands before.

Mistress Mary's was on a large and more gorgeous scale than those of the others, and it was always the same; whilst Miss Blake's and Mrs. Musgrave's varied continually, as they seemed to be putting in the outlines of a pattern which other hands would fill up.

But Mistress Mary's steadily grew and grew, and although always carefully covered up, yet revealed much gold and crimson raised work, and altogether began to have such a wonderfully gorgeous effect that I could not keep my eyes from straying to it again and again as I sat and talked. Busy as she was, I saw that she noted these glances, and one day just before I was about to leave she gave me one of her rare sweet smiles, and said,—

"Come, Dicon, thou needst not eat thine heart out in curiosity. I have good reason to know that thou art to be trusted. I will show thee my work." A flush mantled her face as she unpinned and unfolded it, and she added, with a sudden light in her eyes, "It is a banner for my Lord of Monmouth, when kind Providence sends him hither as our deliverer."

Then she displayed before my eyes the gorgeous golden-worked banner, and I saw that the raised letters surmounted by a crown were none other than these of momentous meaning—J.R.

Nor could I doubt for a moment that their meaning was "Jacobus Rex."

CHAPTER IX.

THE MUTTERING OF THE STORM.

There was a sense of mystery in the air. Life seemed to be flowing in its accustomed channels and with its wonted smoothness; but yet there was an under-current of excitement and unrest which surged through everything and kept every heart beating with expectancy, every ear alert to catch the first breath of rumour, every eye eagerly scanning the faces even of the passer-by in the street, lest haply he might be the bearer of those tidings which some of us longed and some of us feared to hear.

Taunton appeared quiet and peaceable. Mr. Bernard Smith, our Mayor, a man of some force of character, some cruelty of nature, and of known loyalty to the reigning sovereign, kept a close watch upon us, and let it be very clearly understood that upon the smallest indication of disturbance he should call in the train-bands and keep order by strong methods. He was seconded in his good intentions by the influence of the country gentlemen round. Sir William Portman often appeared in the city, and stayed for a few nights in his fine old timbered house, with its many gables, that is still the pride of Taunton amongst those who are learned in the matter of domestic architecture. He frequently appeared in the streets, and when occasion served spoke to the people in such a way as to encourage them to maintain tranquillity and avoid giving cause of offence. Lord Lonsdale and Sir Ralph Bridges followed his example, and were often to be seen in the city, forward to impart to us any items of news from London likely to be acceptable in our ears, and striving to rid our minds of some of the many convictions which recent events had stamped upon them, and especially of that most favourite one—namely, that King Charles had met his death by poison, and that this poison had been administered by the hand of his brother.

But there are some impressions quickly made upon the minds of men which no after labour will efface. We had heard from trusty men of our own party of the black spots which had appeared upon the King's body, of the agonies of pain which had convulsed him, of the sleepless attendance of his dark brother at his bedside, and we thought we knew better than our Mayor or our nobles. So though we listened in respectful silence to their words, our hearts remained unconvinced.

We hated the Duke of York (for there were some who would not speak of him as the King save where prudence compelled) with a deadly hatred, and prayed day and night for deliverance from his malevolent power.

Now as for my own private concerns at this time, I may speak once again of those rides taken in attendance upon the two Mistresses Mary, which began after the inclement winter had passed, and were continued until the great commotion commenced of which I am about to write.

These rides were a source of the greatest pleasure and satisfaction to all concerned; for by means of them the Viscount was able to prosecute his wooing of gentle Mistress Mary, and we were no longer reduced to the more risky if more romantic method of the balcony meetings.

It was easy for me to let my Lord Vere know when and whither we were to ride forth. He was backwards and forwards between Court House and

Taunton many times in the week, like most of the gentry round, and I would make shift to give him the news he wanted. Then upon our next ride, when we were deep in some woodland dell or away across some lonely bit of breezy moorland, the Viscount would ride up, saluting the ladies, and before long the younger Mistress Mary would rein back her steed and join me, leaving the lovers to pace on in front side by side, in the loneliness so dear to all in like case.

Mistress Mary Bridges, albeit but a maid of twelve summers, was wondrous full of life and spirit and imagination. She would talk to me in a fashion which made me marvel at her high courage and dauntless nature; and openly did she lament that she was not a man, so that she might bear a man's part in the struggle which she fully believed was coming.

She came of a family loyal to the Court party and to the reigning sovereign; yet she had heard so much of the other side from her mistresses and comrades in the school, that she might be said scarce to hold either with one party or the other, and in truth this was what she openly averred to be her case.

"If I were but a man," she would cry with kindling eyes, "I would have my own good steed and my own good sword, and I would follow no party, but always fight on the side of right and virtue. I would gather about me a band of followers, as did bold Robin Hood of old, and I would be the champion of truth and liberty and righteousness wherever such were to be found. I hate that false and cruel King James, who will stoop to fondle such vile creatures as Jeffreys and Kirke. Yet I love not your Duke of Monmouth, who can keep a crawling knave like Ferguson in his counsels, and who leaves his virtuous wife and seeks happiness with another fair lady. Were I a man I would follow neither, but be a free lance for the cause of right and liberty!" And the little lady would toss back her ringlets, whilst her face would flush and kindle till I would regard her with admiration akin to awe, and think that a man might well follow such a leader to the death.

But with all her high spirit and courage, she was deeply interested in the courtship of the Viscount and her dear friend the elder Mistress Mary, and confided to me that such a gallant lover was worthy of the prize he had won, though there were few men she had ever seen of whom she would say as much.

"And I trow they had best be quick and wed, even if it be done in secret and in haste," she said one day to me, one bright day in the latter part of May— the last ride (as it turned out, little as we guessed it then) that we were destined to take together; "for I have heard tell that my Lord Lonsdale is anxious to push on his son's marriage with Mistress Edith Portman with all the speed that may be. He thinks that the alliance would be desirable and strengthening for both houses; and the lady is more than willing, since the Viscount is the most gallant youth in these parts. That is why Mr. Nicholas Blewer's suit has been favoured by Lord Lonsdale. He is afraid what the beauty of Mary may effect if Lord Vere ever sees her again. He knows nothing of our rides. He believes his son is forgetting her; but he will not be easy in his mind till one or both are wed. What vile things men are!" cried the little lady, with that flash in her eyes which betokened her headstrong spirit; "they think of naught in the world but their own advancement and their selfish ends! It was told to me, Dicon, by a wise woman, who read my fortune in my hand and in the stars when I was but a tender child, that I should live to slay a man with mine own hands. I trembled when I heard it, and many a time have I lain awake of a night, shivering at the thought; but I shiver not now. Verily I believe I should rejoice to do such a thing were it in a righteous cause. I would it might be the Rev. Nicholas Blewer!" and the maid clinched her right hand and shook it towards Taunton, setting her small white teeth with a ferocity which seemed strange in one so young.

Nor could I greatly marvel at her wrath, for I hated Mr. Blewer as one hates a poisonous and noxious reptile. He was for ever to be seen gliding here and there with his evil smile and stealthy step; and I was certain that he was playing the spy wherever he had the chance. Well did I know that he came to Miss Blake's as much to seek to learn what was passing there as to court Mistress Mary. That the ladies knew or suspected his motive I could not doubt, since in his presence the silken banners were never brought forth, nor was any word spoken of the matters so near and dear to our hearts. He himself would strive to entrap us by seeking to lead us to pass censure on the King or his officers, but we were all resolved not to be thus ensnared; and if cold looks and short answers could have driven the creature away, sure Mr. Blewer would have been long since driven from Miss Blake's parlour. He would have been denied entrance there had the good ladies dared to refuse it; but it was a perilous thing in those days to make an enemy of such a man, and Lord Lonsdale's approval of his courtship made it difficult to exclude him.

As we rode back into Taunton that day—the Viscount leaving us ere ever we reached even the outskirts of the place, since he was very careful never to permit himself to be seen in our company—we were aware of a subdued tumult going on there. Men and women had gathered at their doors or had come out into the streets. Faces were grave and lowering—the faces, that is, of the towns-folk of our fashion of thinking—and one could see that something had occurred greatly to disturb the minds of men.

I dared not pause to ask the reason for it. I feared some disaster had befallen our cause; but my duty to my charges kept me riding close beside them, and, of course, they could not pause to pick up the gossip of the streets, though both must have suspected that something unwonted was afoot. But my curiosity was relieved sooner than I anticipated; for Will Wiseman darted out from a side street at sight of me, and running beside Blackbird at a brisk trot, whispered in my ears the news.

"They have thrown Mr. Vincent into prison!" he said. Now Mr. Vincent, as I have before said, was our minister, and a right godly man, beloved of all his flock; moreover, he was one of those who inculcated maxims of moderation, and patience, and submission to lawful authority—one against whom I am very sure it would be hard to prove either sedition or any other offence. And as I exclaimed in amaze and wrath, Will continued, speaking in the same rapid undertone only just audible through the beat of Blackbird's hoofs, "And they have searched the post-bags here and at Ilminster, and they say that they have found in them enough to hang a score of men in Taunton alone. Dicon, I trow things have gone further than you and I know. The Mayor and Mr. Axe and the gentry have been closeted together this hour and more. Heaven send we be not undone! I would give my right hand to know what they have discovered!"

"I will meet thee anon and hear all I can learn!" I answered in great excitement; "but let me first home with the ladies. I warrant that Mr. Blewer has been at the bottom of Mr. Vincent's arrest. He always hated him with a bitter hatred!"

A fresh shock of surprise awaited us upon our arrival at the Three Cups; for there before the door, looking impatiently up and down the street, stood Sir Ralph Bridges, his horse led up and down by a servant, and several well-stuffed saddle-bags being laid over the shoulder of the man's steed. So soon as he caught sight of the approach of his daughter, he stepped forward and hindered her from alighting, as she was about to do.

"I have come to take thee home, Mary," he said. "Thy place is with thy mother now. Say an adieu to thy companion, and we will get gone. These are no days for thee to be in Taunton."

Mistress Mary looked quickly into her father's rather stern and preoccupied face as though she would fain have asked more. But it was not for a young daughter to question her father's judgment, and all she did was to ask falteringly,—

"Shall I not go to and fro, sir, to continue my studies as heretofore?"

For in other years during the summer months she had often ridden to and fro into the town, as I think I have said, though until to-day she had remained since Christmas beneath the roof of Miss Blake's house.

"No, child," he answered shortly, though not unkindly; "thou wilt remain at home with thy mother. Home is thy place in days such as these."

And in hearing the Knight speak thus, I was more sure, even than when Will Wiseman had been whispering to me, that some unwonted peril was at hand.

I saw that Mistress Mary Mead's eyes had kindled as she heard these words. I read the thought of her heart as well as if it had been spoken in words. The younger Mistress Mary turned and flung her arms about her neck ere she slipped from her palfrey, and I heard her whisper in her friend's ear,—

"It is coming, Mary, it is coming! Heaven send that the cause of right and truth may be victorious! Come what may, nothing shall sever our friendship."

Sir Ralph had already mounted, and after saluting Mistress Mary Mead with courteous good-will, he set spurs to his horse and went clattering down the Fore Street towards North Street with his daughter beside him. I escorted Mistress Mary to her own door and assisted her to alight, and as I did so she said in trembling accents, though it was not fear that made her voice to shake,—

"Go, Dicon, and learn the truth of all this, and bring me word to my balcony to-night. My heart tells me that the deliverer is near. There were fear and anxiety upon the face of Sir Ralph; I am very sure of that. The servants of the tyrant are trembling already. We are thrice armed who know our quarrel just."

With that she turned and went quickly indoors, leaving me with my heart in a flutter of expectation as I led the palfrey to the stable. Will was already there, unable to keep away, and full of the most intense excitement as to what had just transpired.

It seemed that Captain William Speke (the only member of the Speke family who took the contrary side from the master of White Lackington and head of the family) had made a raid on the post-bags at Ilminster—having had notice that suspicious signs had been noted amongst the dissenters of the Western Counties—and had made discoveries which had caused him to send in all haste to the Mayor to counsel him to do likewise. All the Taunton letters, however, had been delivered save eight; but one of these eight, addressed to a certain Mr. Cooke, a good friend of ours, had proved of so incriminating a nature that he was at once summoned before the Mayor and magistrates, and obliged to enter into recognizances for a thousand pounds, and find sureties three in number for five hundred each. Mr. Simpson, Mr. Hucker, and Mr. Herring had willingly come forward for this purpose; and Will told me that they and the Hewlings had gathered in conclave immediately afterwards, and that one of the brothers Hewling had already left the town, though upon what errand he did not know.

"And what was in the letter?" I asked eagerly.

"Marry, that I cannot tell you in full. But this much is in all men's mouths, that it spake of the appearance forthwith in the West of a certain person, and that all the Court party in London are in a most dreadful fear and confusion. It is rumoured, too, that in Scotland the Earl of Argyll is destroying the King's forces right and left. Ah, Dicon, Dicon! With a Monmouth in the south and an Argyll in the north, what may not be done in the cause of liberty and right!"

This was news indeed, and all seemed to confirm it. As Will and I went forth into the streets, we could not but be aware that a great excitement was reigning. The Mayor was hurrying to and fro, and many of his Burgesses with him, seeming scarce to know what he was doing, yet as it were anxious to be everywhere at once to see that the town was quiet. Mr. Axe was likewise walking the streets, but in calmer fashion, and he sought everywhere to persuade the people to remain quiet and orderly. The air was full of whispers and rumours. It was confidently believed that the Duke was nigh at hand. Some said, indeed, that he had already landed, and perhaps might be seen at any moment at the head of a vast army of loving followers marching to the very heart of Taunton.

I knew not what to believe of all we heard; but that more news had reached Taunton than either Will or I knew was more and more evident. We made our way to Mr. Simpson's house, to find Lizzie in a great state of joyful excitement; for she had heard enough to make her quite confident that the Duke was really coming at last. There had been a collection made of money amongst her father's friends—that she was very certain of; and one of the brothers Hewling, she was not sure which, had ridden off with it to the coast, ready to meet the Duke on his landing.

Thomas Dare had had a letter from his father several days ago, in which he had told his son that there had been some trouble in persuading the Duke to take up arms against his uncle. He had been greatly distressed at hearing of his father's death, and had declared at first that, since things were as they were, he should retire into private life, and seek no more to establish what rights he might justly claim. The Prince of Orange had counselled him in this, and the only question under dispute at first was whether the Duke should or should not seek to win distinction in arms by fighting under the Emperor against the Turks, or whether he should retire to Sweden with Lady Henrietta Wentworth, who had followed him into exile, and to whom he considered himself married in the sight of God, and live there in honourable banishment. This course of action had been vehemently opposed by Heywood Dare, who represented to him that all the West Country would rise in his favour if he would but show himself there. Money and men would flow in in streams, so

Dare declared he had affirmed, and he called upon his son in strong and eloquent language to do whatever in him lay to get together men and money and arms, that when their deliverer should appear he might find there had been no idle boasting on the part of the citizen of Taunton. This letter had been read with closed doors amongst a select few some weeks ago, and Thomas Dare had been already absent from the town almost ever since, beating up recruits, and preparing the hearts of friends for what might be expected shortly. All this had been made known to-day to Lizzie by her aunt, and she was as full of the excitement as we were. She told us now fully and freely of the seven-and-twenty banners being worked by the hands of the maidens of the school, and how they hoped to present them in person to the gallant young Duke when he should appear in triumph at Taunton, as it was fully believed he would do, and that right quickly.

How our hearts burned within us as we listened! We could not keep still, nor remain long in one place. We were out in the streets erelong, eagerly picking up every scrap of news, and finding that rumours were flying about as thick as hail in a summer storm.

Public indignation was rising hot against the Court and the King. Not only had the arrest of our Mr. Vincent greatly incensed the towns-folk, but there came citizens from Ilminster to tell of the attempted arrest of Mr. John Trenchard at White Lackington House, and how a tumult had been made, and the Sheriffs forced to run without having secured their prisoner. Again and again were old grievances raked up—the scandalous trial of Richard Baxter, not many weeks old; and the notorious cruelty and tyranny of the King.

"Heaven will fight for us and for Monmouth!" men whispered to each other. And indeed I think that it was our hearts that were glad and triumphant, and those of our enemies that were full of fear as the day waned: for the Mayor looked pale and harassed and full of anxiety, I thought; whilst as for Mr. Blewer, he was so hooted in the streets when he showed his ugly face there, that he hastily retired to his lodgings, and we saw him no more.

"Will," I said, as the sun went down, and we felt so little inclined for sleep that the very idea of bed was a mockery, "what sayest thou to a ride across the moorland to-night by moonshine, and a visit to the witch, to know what she can tell us of what is coming? Methinks I shall stifle within doors; but Blackbird and Lady Jane will carry us rarely, and I can loose them, none knowing it, by a little care. Wilt come with me?"

Will simply jumped at such a proposal. He was as loath to think of bed as I was, and he could ride a horse barebacked right well—saddle and stirrups were abominable to him. In the excitement and stir about the inn, I had no trouble in getting the horses out after nightfall; and making excuse of fatigue to my uncle, I stole away as if to bed, but was soon mounted and scudding through the dim lanes by the side of Will, whilst the moon rose higher and higher in the sky, giving us abundant light. The good steeds, delighting in the freshness of the night air, went willingly and easily; and Blackbird, so soon as we had passed the ridge of the hill and were nearing his old home, became as playful and skittish as a young kitten.

But it was not homewards that our steps were bent. The farm-house at such an hour would be fast sleeping, and I had no desire to wake up the sleepers. It was Mother Whale I desired to find and consult, and unless she were abroad upon her broomstick, she would like enough be awake at her fireside concocting her spells and potions; as, indeed, we found to be the case.

Tethering our horses outside, we lifted the latch and went in, the old woman not even turning her head as we did so, but speaking our names, as though she had eyes in the back of her head, and by some occult magic knew every person who approached.

"Good-even, Dicon Snowe, and thou, lad Will. Have a care, Will, lest thou repent thy rashness in tears of blood ere the year be done. What have you come for, boys? What is your errand here? There be fine doings at Taunton, and will be finer yet. But beware the evil eye that will overlook it—ay, and thee too, Will, ere this chapter close."

I do not make any effort in these pages to try to give the soft speech and drawling vowel sounds of our West Country tongue, not having the skill to spell the same word two ways. I can but follow the model given me by the Bible and those works of the great poets I have named, and let those who know the speech of the West figure it for themselves. It takes a greater skill than I possess to set it down here.

"Mother," I said, "we have come to ask thee to read us that chapter. How will the day turn? Which Duke will be England's King? We know that thou canst read the future in the stars, and the cards, and the crystal. Prithee tell us what will betide, and whether the friends or the foes of liberty and religion will triumph."

It was a bold question; but I had not come empty-handed, and I slipped the golden guinea Lord Lonsdale had given me into the witch's palm. She looked at it with glistening eyes. Money was dear to the heart of the old woman, and I did not doubt for a moment that I should get my guinea's worth out of her; for I verily believed that she read the future as I read the page of an open book.

She bent over the pot, crooning to herself, and seeming to take no heed of us; but I silenced Will's exclamation of impatience by a warning sign, for I knew the old woman and her ways, and that nothing was to be gained by trying to hurry her.

At last the great black cat beside the fire jumped upon her shoulder and seemed to whisper in her ear. I confess that a tremor ran through me, for I verily believed that her familiar was speaking to her, and that we were in the presence of some satanic agency.

A minute or two later she threw her arms above her head, and began to speak in detached sentences, filling up the pauses by a strange crooning chant, wordless and unintelligible.

"Blood will be shed—much blood ... but the glory will come first.... A King will rise and a King will fall.... And blood shall run freely, ay, even as from a slaughter-house. Heads shall be lifted up.... Oh, they shall be raised on high for all the world to see!... A brave show, truly! A brave young King.... And he who now sits upon the throne shall die in exile and disgrace."

That was enough for us. We had heard just the answer we wanted, and the old woman lapsed into a silence which no questions served to break, so we bade her good-even, and went forth again into the night.

"The King will die in exile! Dicon, if she be a true witch, we are to see good days yet," cried Will, dancing in the moonlight like a wild thing. "Blood and glory, and the rise and fall of Kings! Ah, heaven be praised that I live in such goodly days! Dicon, Dicon, let us raise a shout for King Monmouth. Hurrah for the good cause and the King! God save him and us all!"

CHAPTER X.

MY RIDE TO LYME.

I returned to find my uncle not a little disturbed in mind.

The Mayor had summoned the Burgesses to meet him in council upon the morning following my visit to the witch; and my uncle looked harassed and anxious upon his return, and paced moodily up and down the passage—a thing most unusual with him—whilst his jovial face looked more perturbed than I had ever seen it before. My good aunt regarded him with troubled eyes, wondering if evil had befallen him; and Meg anxiously whispered in mine ear, asking if I knew what was amiss. But though I knew that all the town was in a fever of excitement and expectation, and that it was confidently supposed that the landing of the Duke was near, I did not know why my uncle should be more disturbed than other men, nor why his anxiety and fear should be greater.

Towards noon there was a great commotion in the streets, and we heard the tread of marching footsteps and the sound of horse-hoofs on the hard road between the houses. Rushing out in great excitement, willing to believe that the Duke was actually entering the town, I was in time to see several companies of the militia, in their gay uniforms with red and yellow facings, marching towards the Cornhill, followed by one company of horse. But, alas! it was plain to see that they were not only not led by the Duke, our expected deliverer, but that they had been brought in to overawe us and keep order in the town, and prevent us from rising in the cause of the deliverer when he should appear. They were led by gentlemen of known loyalty, and behind the horsemen rode Viscount Vere in all the bravery of a semi-military dress. But I noted that his face wore a clouded expression, and there were stern lines about his mouth that I had not seen there before. He rode between his father and one of the Portman family; but I observed that he spoke to neither, and that he wore an air of aloofness and offence that was rather strange to see.

"Uncle, the train-bands have come into the town!" I cried in great excitement, rushing back into the inn. "Didst thou know they were to be called out?"

"Ay, boy, I knew it," he answered, the cloud still hanging heavy on his brow; and then, we being alone together for the nonce, he spoke with more freedom and openness than he had ever shown to me before. "I tell thee, Dicon, I am in a great strait what to think and how to act. I would fain keep out of this struggle and strife. What am I to judge betwixt prince and prince? When the great and learned of the land are at variance, and know not the truth of the matter, how can a simple man who has never meddled with high things come to a knowledge of the truth? I would have none of it could I help it. But the plague of such times is that men will not let you be. Here is our Mayor on one side reproaching me with being a dissenter, and lukewarm in the cause of the King—a matter like to get me into trouble by-and-by should ill befall this expedition of which all men speak; whilst those of the Duke's side trust me not, and fall into a sudden silence at sight of me. And should he win the day, none will have a good word for me with him, nor say that I was forward in his cause. I am like to get nothing but ill-will from both sides, and all because I would fain manage my own affairs and leave those of the nation alone. It is a hard thing that a man should be so ill thought of simply for attending to his own business, and meddling not with matters too hard for him."

Sooth to say, and put in that fashion, the case did seem hard. But mine uncle was something in the position of the ass in the fable with the two bundles of hay. He had been striving all this while to eat of both, and yet to make choice of neither; and the consequence was that he was now in the position of one not trusted by either party, and not prepared to throw in his lot decidedly with either. By training and choice he was a dissenter, and would gladly have welcomed the Duke of Monmouth as England's King. But he was a long-headed and far-sighted man, and did not think that the power of the reigning sovereign would be as easily overturned as his townsmen fancied, wherefore he was fearful of allying himself with them in their designs. He would fain have rested strictly neutral, and that indeed was his purpose; but it was more difficult each day to avoid making open declaration on one side or the other, and he began to see that if the Duke really landed and marched to the town, it would be increasingly hard to stand aloof from both parties.

"If only I knew which way the day would turn!" he said, pacing restlessly up and down. "I tell thee, boy, I would serve the Duke, and be glad to do so; but I am not ready to be ruined for such as he. My business and my goods are more to me than all these questions of kingship and policy. I love not black King James, and I know we may suffer under his sway; but how do we know that we should do better under another? And civil war is a more terrible ill and calamity than a little tyranny and a few unjust imposts. Let well alone, say I; and nothing very bad has followed King James's accession. I like not the thought of stirring up strife. Yet if strife must come, I would fain be found on the right side—if I could but know which that was!"

And by the right side my uncle meant the victorious one, as I very well knew.

Well, it is not of such stuff that heroes and patriots are made. But then my worthy uncle never professed to be either; and a man who has toiled and laboured to get a good business together, and to stand well with those around him, has many excuses for feeling loath to see all swept away for what may seem to him a fantasy or a dream. I could scarce wonder at his words, though I was all for fighting and dying in a noble cause, and was glad that Heaven had not made of me a man of substance, who feared the loss of goods more than the grinding heel of a tyrant usurper. I could afford to feel pity for my uncle's perplexities. I was sorry for him, and longed to be able to relieve him.

"If I did but know more of the feeling of the country!" he said. "I hear such contrary reports. Our Mayor tells me that it is but just in a few places here and there in the land that men are for the Duke, and that the nation at large will have none of him; whilst others say they have full information that the widespread discontent is ready everywhere to burst into a flame, and if the Duke do but land he may march straight to Whitehall if he will, and by the time he reaches it, will have all the nation and all London at his back. If that indeed were so—"

"Uncle!" I cried, struck by a sudden inspiration, "let me fare forth on

Blackbird, and reap what news I can as I go, and bring thee word again. Let me to the coast, where the Duke, they say, will shortly land, if he be not landed already; and as I go let me ask news of all men—how things are going all over the country, and what men are saying, and what is doing. I am but a lad. I shall not rouse suspicion, and Blackbird knows not how to tire. Let me go, and I will bring thee word again, or ever the Duke appear, how the chances of the day seem like to go. I will talk with men of every degree. Sure I shall gain information worth the having!"

Now this plan, so congenial to my restlessness and excitement, took the fancy of my uncle; and he forthwith slapped me on the shoulder, and said I was a smart lad and a credit to the family, hunchback or no hunchback. And then he took money from his purse and gave it me, and bid me see well to Blackbird, and make a start upon the following morning, the day being now drawing to its close. He was pleased to think of any plan that might relieve him in some sort of his anxieties. He could remain for some days longer without committing himself to either party, and perchance I might reap information for him which should decide him whether or not openly to embrace the cause of the Duke, towards which his private leanings were.

It was reported that several persons had already left Taunton, and it was shrewdly suspected that they were going forth with the prospect of meeting the Duke. When I went to Master Simpson's shop that evening to tell Will Wiseman of my plan, I heard the Master Hucker had gone, and young Dare, and that he believed his own master would not be long in following.

Will did not know whether any place of landing had been yet settled, but he had heard a whisper of Lyme more than once; and it seemed a likely place, being far smaller and less like to be watched than Weymouth, and much nearer to Taunton, which had the glorious reputation of being the city most in earnest in its loyal attachment to the noble Protestant cause.

Lizzie came and joined us, and said she was certain her father meditated a speedy journey; and hearing that I too was bound for the coast, she became greatly excited, bid me strive to be amongst the first to welcome the gracious and noble Duke, and finally took a ribbon from her neck, and fashioned it into a rosette for my hat. Lizzie and I, I must explain, had for many a day made a pretence of being lovers, and I now felt like a knight going forth on his first feat of arms; so it seemed right and fitting that his lady-love should thus adorn him by her token, as Lizzie had decorated me.

With the first light of the morrow Blackbird and I rode out of Taunton, Will Wiseman trotting beside us for the first mile of our journey, and only wishing that he could be my companion all along.

Glad enough would I have been of his company, but I was not altogether sorry that this could not be. Will had a vein of rashness and daring about him that was lacking in me, despite all my brave imaginings; and on the mission upon which I was bent, discretion was needed almost as much as valour.

I resolved to ride leisurely to Ilminster this first day, which was the first day of June 1685. I should learn from my aunt and her friends what was the feeling in that city. And I meant to join company with all of my own degree, or those inferior to me, upon the road, and glean from them all the news that I could.

In particular I was minded to question all those who came from the Devonshire border. For we knew that the Duke of Albemarle, who was the King's deputy-lieutenant of that county, and his very loyal general, was at Exeter with a fine body of train-bands and other troops, and it was of importance to us of Taunton to know whether he proposed to move out from that city in our direction. One traveller whom I encountered at a cross-road, and who lingered awhile to talk with me, declared his belief that if the Duke were to lead his forces against the person of the Duke of Monmouth, and his men were to see that loved face in the opposite ranks, they would all go over as one man to join him; and that the Duke of Albemarle most likely knew something of the temper of his soldiers, and would be very careful how he brought them into action against the Duke of Monmouth. They did very well for keeping the town and district quiet; but he did not believe they would ever take the field against the champion of the Protestant religion, and against one they persisted in looking upon as their late King's lawful son.

This was excellent news, and sent me on my way glad at heart. If this indeed was the temper of the soldiers against whom the Duke might have to fight, his march would speedily become the triumphal progress his friends had foretold.

Shortly after I had parted from this traveller with expressions of mutual good-will, I heard upon the road behind me the beat of approaching horse-hoofs. Plainly the rider was either in some considerable haste, or labouring under the stress of hot emotion, for he was galloping at a great pace. I pulled on one side of the narrow track which we called a road, and which at this time of year was passable enough, and turned in my saddle to look at him, when, lo and behold, as he approached I saw that it was none other than my young lord Viscount Vere.

Great was my surprise to see him riding thus alone and in haste, and with that same clouded look upon his face which I had noted yesterday; and yet more surprised was I to learn, a few minutes later, what had brought him here. On seeing me he drew rein, and a smile broke over his face which was like a ray of sunshine breaking through storm-clouds, and he gave my shoulder a friendly pat, crying out,—

"Ha, Dicon man, well met! And whither art thou away? Are we travelling the same road? If so, let us join forces. I am tired of my own company and my own black thoughts. Tell me whither thou art bound, and what is thine errand."

I told him all, and he listened to the story of my uncle's perplexities with his gay smile of amusement; but when I had finished he gave me a glance of a different sort, and said,—

"Canst guess whither I am bound, good Dicon?"

I shook my head, for I had been wondering all the while whither he could be going at such a time, when the gentry were all gathered about the city to strive to keep the peace.

"Marry, to join company with the Duke of Monmouth when he lands!" cried the Viscount, with a quick flash of the eyes such as bespoke a mind much disturbed. And upon my uttering an exclamation of surprise, he broke forth with much heat of manner,—

"Ay, they have driven me to it! They have driven me to it with their plots and plans and projects! There is but one way of cutting the knot, and cut it I will at all hazard! My Mary's blessing and sweet approval go with me and rest upon me! I have done with the old life. The new may be what it will, but Mary and Mary's weal are bound up in it, and therefore I fare forth fearlessly. When I return I make her my wife, be the issue of this venture what it may. I saw her last night, and had speech of her; and I care for nothing now, so as I win and hold her love. What is the evil black tyrant James to me that I waste in his cause my youth and my strength, and lose the lady of my choice? Rightful monarch he may be, but a vile creature, unworthy the name of King! I will none of him! I will none of them and their machinations! Henceforth I am my own man, and I win Mary, or perish in the attempt!"

It took me some time to learn from this excited outburst the truth of the whole matter, but bit by bit I made it out. Nor could I wonder at the way in which the young man, badgered and beset, had cut the knot of his difficulties and perplexities. It seems that some treacherous spy had reported to Lord Lonsdale that the Viscount had been seen riding with Mistress Mary Mead in lover-like fashion; that this had so alarmed and angered him that he and his friends had forthwith put their heads together; and when Sir William Portman returned from London a few days back, after having been there for the opening of the Parliament, of which mention has been made, he brought back with him the marriage contract, duly drawn up, for an alliance between his daughter and Viscount Vere, and ever since the young man had had no peace because this contract must be signed, and the marriage celebrated with what speed the times would allow.

Now it is not in my young lord's nature to be brutal; and the lady was as willing and eager for so fair a husband as he was reluctant to have her. To his father he had spoken roundly, but had been treated in a high-handed fashion, as though he were but a refractory boy, and must be reduced to obedience. Yet this is not the treatment which can succeed with natures like my lord the Viscount's, and he had been put into a great heat and anger. Last evening there had been a banquet at Sir William's house in Taunton, and he had been one of the guests. At the board open allusion had been made to the approaching nuptials of the Viscount with Mistress Edith, whose bright eyes gave ready and eager response to the good wishes and gratulations of her friends. Nor could the gentle and chivalrous young lord speak open despite to the lady before her kinsfolk, and do insult to her and to his manhood. But his blood had boiled within him at the intolerable position in which he had been placed; for he had believed beforehand that the banquet was for the officers of the train-bands and the gentlemen who had come into the city to help to maintain order, else he never would have gone.

Being thus trapped, and as it were committed to a match to which he never could consent, there seemed to him but one way out of the difficulty, and that was one to which his reckless, defiant mood inclined him, as well as the knowledge that it would be of all others the measure most likely to be approved by his own true lady. He knew that, let him once be accounted as a rebel, the prudent Sir William would none of him for a husband for his daughter; whilst Mary would regard him the more tenderly for all he might lose or suffer in the good cause. Disgusted by the treachery, chicanery, and avarice of the reigning King, eager after the excitements and the glory of warfare, and keenly moved by the expected approach of one who was looked upon in so many quarters as the deliverer of his country, it was small wonder that the Viscount had flung prudence to the winds, and had resolved to fling in his lot with the Duke who was about to come to the help of the perplexed nation. I had no difficulty at all in understanding and sympathizing with the step; my only regret was that he came alone, and not with a gay and gallant following such as beseemed his rank and station.

But he smiled a little grimly as I spoke of this.

"Nay, Dicon lad," he said, "if I be walking into the lion's jaws, I will e'en walk thither alone, and not bring a luckless following of poor knaves after me. Heaven alone knows what the issue of this day's work will be; but all that I have heard on this vexed question tends to the belief that England will not have your Duke for King, like she her present monarch never so little! If that be so, there will be lives lost and heads will fall—it may be mine amongst others. But no other man shall lose his life through fault of mine. I might have brought a score, perhaps a hundred gallant followers into the field, but I would not tempt one to what may be his doom. Let each man choose his own lot in the struggle. I have chosen mine, but I will be answerable for none other besides."

This speech was not a very blithe one, and showed me well that the Viscount had more fears than hopes for the issue of the contest. Yet having once joined with us, I knew he would never turn back; and I thought that a few more such gallant leaders as he might turn the fortunes of any campaign.

We spent that day in company, my lord and I. At the inn where we baited our horses and refreshed ourselves I passed as his servant, and we both, in different capacities, gleaned all we could from those we met. My lord told me afterwards that he saw small indication of any eagerness on the part of the gentry to flock to the welcome of the Duke when he should appear. They were all for maintaining law and order and the tranquillity of the districts in which they lived; but I, on the other hand, heard from the common people of a great joy and gladness in the thought of the coming arrival, and everywhere it was whispered that the soldiers would desert to his standard almost to a man, whilst every rustic or shopkeeper in country or town would raise a shout for King Monmouth, and fight for him through thick and thin.

Wherefore I was more hopeful than my lord of the issue of the contest, and he listened to me with a smile, and said,—

"Ay, ay, good Dicon, believe all thou hearest, and keep up a good heart; there is nothing like it for making brave soldiers at a pinch. Thinking the day won beforehand sometimes proves the best way of winning it at the last."

But I could see that my lord did not think it won yet.

At Ilminster I persuaded him to accept, for one night at least, the humble hospitality of my aunt's roof. He smilingly thanked me and accepted, for he was always of a gentle and affable nature towards his inferiors. Great was the joy of my good aunt, Mrs. Betsy Marwell, when we rode up to her door and I asked her good offices not only for myself, but for my lord the Viscount, whose gallant air, brave raiment, and nodding plumes entirely captivated her from the first moment, and made her eager to put her whole house at his disposal.

However, he had no following, as he explained to her; and for himself, he asked permission to join us at the board. This was not what my aunt would have chosen, since she would have loved to serve him herself almost on bended knee, I think; but he was allowed his own way when he asked it with such graceful courtesy. We were soon seated together at such a supper-table as methinks can only be found in the hospitable West Country; and my lord was paying his attention to our hostess, and making her beam and almost blush for pleasure at being so addressed by a lord, and such a handsome and dashing one to boot; whilst I did ample justice to the noble repast, and felt proud of my kinswoman and of the manner in which she had been able to receive us.

My lord acceded to her desire that he would remain with her as long as business kept him at Ilminster; and he stayed two nights beneath her roof, winning golden opinions from all who saw him, and leaving us quite sorrowful upon his departure.

I did not accompany him for two reasons: one being that he did not ask me, and I feared to force myself upon him against his will; another, that my aunt was resolved to keep me yet a few days longer. And as I was every day suffered to ride far afield and to pick up all sorts of odd but useful bits of information, I was the more willing to do so. It was quite plain that the Duke could not yet have landed, at any rate upon this coast, or we should have known it of a certainty ere now. I was anxious to be there to witness his landing when it did take place; but I could not well refuse my aunt's request, and so I lingered nigh upon a week at her house, pleasantly assured that Ilminster was loyal to the good cause, although perhaps not quite so fervent and warm as the city of Taunton.

My next halt was at Chard, whither my aunt had sent me with a note to a trusty friend of her own, who gave me lodging for two nights, and put me in the way of obtaining all such information as I desired. I could feel the growing excitement of the people, and I hoped that the Duke would not tarry much longer. Men are apt to grow faint-hearted or cold if disappointment and delay fall upon their first ardent longings. It was now nigh upon fourteen days that we had been expecting tidings of the landing of the Duke, and still he came not.

Axminster was my next halting-place, and here I found the temper of the people very hot and eager. There was an Independent chapel there of some importance, and a martial minister, whose name I cannot recall, who was fervent in the cause of the Duke, and who had given out that he himself would lead forth the men of his flock to join the standard of liberty when it should be set up, and that he would fight to the last drop of his blood in the righteous cause. I heard here, too, all the old stories about the poisoning of the King, and the manifold crimes laid to the charge of James now on the throne. The mind of the people was inflamed against the sovereign almost more hotly than I had seen it yet out of Taunton.

One gentleman was known to have store of arms and ammunition in his house, and it was whispered that upon certain news arriving of the landing of the Duke, he would arm his sons and his household forthwith, and any able-bodied men who should desire it, so long as his stores held out; and that he would then march at the head of this band, and tender his and their services to his Grace.

I was fast catching the infection of hot partisan spirit, and feeling more and more certain of the righteousness of our cause and the certainty of ultimate success. There is a strong impression in the minds of all communities that if the mass of the nation are in favour of a cause, that cause will ultimately triumph. I have seen the growth of this conviction during my long life, and I trow that those who come after will see its further development. Whether for good or for ill it is not for me to say, but the people begin to whisper that the power is theirs, and that the voice of the people is the voice of God. It was not put so in the days of which I now speak, but the citizens would lay their heads together and boldly say that they had triumphed over kings before in a righteous cause, and they would triumph again. I listened, and I believed them, and sometimes felt as though the day were well-nigh won.

And in this mood, on one bright evening in June, I found myself riding into the pretty little sea-board town of Lyme.

CHAPTER XI.

OUR DELIVERER.

I had seldom been so near the sea as I was now approaching, and for a moment the boundlessness of the horizon, the sweep of sky and sea, the outline of coast, and the tranquil beauty of the summer's afternoon, filled my senses and drew my thoughts temporarily away from the more personal and exciting matters upon which they had dwelt so long.

But as I sat Blackbird on the brow of the green eminence which overlooked Lyme, and saw the little town nestling as it were beside the blue sea, groups of trees giving beauty and variety to its aspect, and the brooding peace of a cloudless summer's day seeming to rest upon it, I became aware of a small stir behind me, and turning my head saw that a party of some twenty rustics, with flushed faces and damp brows, had come swinging up from below; and as soon as they were within speaking distance the foremost called out to me, asking me, in the broadest and softest of Dorset drawl, whether I could tell him where the Duke was to be found.

"Us have heard that he's coomed," he explained, wiping his brow, and shifting to the other shoulder the great scythe he carried. Five of his companions carried scythes, and three or four sickles, whilst the rest had a miscellaneous assortment of weapons such as bill-hooks and picks. One had an ancient carbine, which looked better able to slay the person who fired it than any other; and a tall lad, with the face of one whose wits were not all under command, brandished with an air of fierce triumph the broken remnant of what had once been a sword.

"They du tell we that he's coom, and us be going tu join him," panted the first speaker as the rest came up. "Happen thee may be able tu put us in the way of finding him. Thee be bound on the same errand, I take it, young master."

"As for that, I have come to seek the Duke," I answered, forgetting all else now in the excitement of the news just imparted; "but I knew not that he had yet landed, nor where. What dost thou know of it, good fellow?"

"Us heerd tell as he'd landed at Lyme. Us have come out to fight for un," was all the answer I could get; and being unable to extract more, and consumed with curiosity to know more of the matter, I wished them a good journey, and set spurs to Blackbird, heading straight down the slope of the down and towards Lyme.

I saw in the bay there two or three white-sailed vessels, and this in itself seemed to give weight to what the men had said. Those white-winged messengers might have brought our deliverer to us; and with ever-increasing excitement and eagerness I drew near to the place, and was more and more certain that rumour had this time not played me false, but that some unwonted commotion was on foot.

I passed numbers of groups of rustics more or less like my first friends, all hastening in one direction; and the question on all lips was not whether the Duke had come, but where he was to be found. That in itself was significant, and seemed to show that something had really happened to awake such certainty in the minds of the people; and very soon this certainty was confirmed by a strange and goodly sight which presently burst upon my eyes.

Just to the east of the town, and hard by the church which raised its square tower heavenwards, was a wide expanse of greensward which went by the name of Church Cliff. Men tell me that since those days a part of this same cliff has slipped into the sea, and that more is like to follow. Be that as it may, when I saw it, many long years ago now, it was a pleasant green plateau, spacious and convenient for the assembly of a multitude of persons; and to-day it presented an aspect which I trow it has never done before, and never will again—particularly if it is like to be engulfed by the hungry waves!

On a small eminence nigh to the church, but not too near for convenience, fluttered in the light summer breeze a banner or standard—for I am not learned in the right names of these things. All I know was that it was planted upon a tall halberd, and floated in the breeze with a gentle swaying motion. Even from a distance I could see that there were letters emblazoned upon it; but only later on, when I was able to come anigh it, was I able to read the device, which ran as follows: "*Pro Religione et Libertate.*" The meaning of that (as I had occasion to explain to many an unlettered hind ere the day closed) was, "for religion and liberty," those two precious gifts to men which the rule of the present monarch so greatly imperilled.

But the standard was not the only thing that took the eye of the spectator. The field was gay with gathering crowds of people of all degrees. Hard by the standard stood a group of gentlemen, as I could see by the colours of their riding coats, and the plumes in their hats. My heart beat as I scanned them. Could the Duke indeed be one of these? It looked like it, for it was towards this group that the crowds were for ever pressing. And plainly there was some order observed in the method of approach; for there was no jostling or crowding in the immediate proximity of this small group, but persons from the crowd seemed to be detached from it and brought up one by one, and then to melt away into the press again, as though their turn had come and gone.

As I advanced ever nearer and nearer, losing my vantage as I drew more close, and finding myself gradually drawn into the throng of eager watchers, I heard men talking one to another, and this was the burden of their talk:—

"The Duke! the Duke! He is enlisting recruits. All the country is flocking to him! Heaven be praised, our deliverer is come! Down with the tyranny of the false usurper! A Monmouth! a Monmouth!"

And this cry was ever and anon taken up by all, and went surging through the crowd like a mighty thunderclap.

"A Monmouth! a Monmouth! God save the noble Duke! God fight for the righteous cause! A Monmouth! a Monmouth!"

I caught the enthusiasm of the people, and forgetting all about mine uncle's errand, the prudence inculcated by him, and the mission on which I had been sent, I flung my cap into the air and shouted aloud for the Duke as lustily as any. Then finding that I could not make shift to get nearer to him on horseback, for the press was very great, I dismounted and turned Blackbird loose on the greensward, knowing well that he would let none but me catch him again, though he would come at my whistle like a dog, and gradually approached to the floating standard, eager above all things else to look once more upon the face of the Duke.

Little by little I made my way into the forefront of the crowd, which had made a ring round the standard and the group near to it, and kept an orderly and respectful bearing, only breaking out from time to time into the joyous shouts of which I have made mention. One of such shouts was being given as I wormed and twisted myself into the foremost ranks, some good-natured spectators making way for me because that I was small of stature, and could not otherwise witness what was passing.

"A Monmouth! a Monmouth!" shouted the crowd, tossing caps and waving kerchiefs. "Down with Popery! Down with tyrants! Down with all usurpers! A Monmouth! a Monmouth!"

And as the people thus shouted, he who stood in the centre of the gay group about the standard lifted his plumed hat with a courtly grace and smiled upon us with a winning kindliness and confidence that made the populace redouble their shouting; and only after several minutes had gone by was comparative silence restored, and proceedings went on as before.

These were simple enough. A man would step forward and ask leave to enlist in the Duke's army. His name would be asked, and duly inscribed in a roll which was being kept by a busy scribe. If he had any arms, he was bidden to one part of the field; if not (as was generally the case), he was sent to another, and was equipped with some sort of weapon from the stores brought over by the Duke or obtained for him by his confederates here.

We believed then that he had arms and ammunition for half England, should so many flock to his standard, and at least for the equipment of as many thousand soldiers as he wanted. It was only later on that we heard that arms had speedily run short, and that scythes stuck upon poles, and other barbarous makeshifts, had to be substituted for the regular weapons of true soldiers.

My friends the rustics came up in due course, and were enrolled in the list; and the Duke had a smile and a pleasant word for each, so that every man believed himself known and remembered by his Grace, and every mouth was filled with his praises.

The difficulty seemed to be in getting the names set down fast enough; and as that fact dawned upon me I plucked up my courage, for being in a state of great excitement and exhilaration, almost like intoxication, by the stress of my feelings, I forgot everything but my desire of winning the approbation of the Duke, and doing somewhat in the good cause. So I stepped up before him, making a low reverence, without waiting to be led or bidden by those who were marshalling up the recruits.

"Well, my good lad, and art thou come to make a soldier in our ranks?" asked the Duke, with that pleasant smile which had beamed upon me once before in my life. "Who art thou, boy, and what is thine errand?"

"May it please your Grace, I am the boy whom your gracious touch did cure of the King's Evil five years agone, and who has never ceased to bless you for that gracious act. Nature has not been pleased to grant me the strength or the stature for a soldier, but I can make shift to wield a pen with any scribe, and would humbly ask that I might help in this matter of writing down the names."

"Well thought, boy," answered the Duke. "Our worthy scribe there will be right glad of thy help. There be so many come to join us that his labours are something severe. Where dost thou hail from, boy, and what news dost thou bring of the temper of the country?"

For my travel-stained garments, and the dust upon my clothing, showed that I had come some distance; and though the Duke's smile was full of light and confidence, methought there was something of anxiety in his eyes.

"All the people be very eager and forward in the good cause, your Grace, and rejoice to think you near," I answered. "I myself come from Taunton, where your friends muster strong. But Axminster and Ilminster are almost as forward to give you welcome, as you will find when you pass through them. But Taunton will give you royal honours, and I pray you tarry not longer than need be ere you set foot in that queen of cities."

The Duke's face lightened at my answer; and truly I spoke only as I felt, and I had no thought to tell more than the truth. Looking round on this crowd of gallant officers and gentlemen, and seeing the hundreds pressing to join the standard, how could I feel that the Duke had aught but a triumphal march before him? He rewarded my confidence by taking me by the hand, and calling me a right brave and honest lad, whom he should remember in days to come; and then, whilst my hand was still tingling with the pressure, and my heart leaping for triumph and joy, I was given a place beside the other scribe, and commenced my duties as writer of names.

I know not how long I had been writing when a hand was laid upon my shoulder, and a familiar voice spoke in my ear,—

"Dicon lad, Dicon Snowe, is this the way in which thou dost follow the behests of thy prudent uncle? Is this how thou dost cater for true news for him? Is this how thou dost prudently wait the issue of events ere thou dost declare for one side or the other?"

Looking up quickly—for the enlisting was well-nigh done for the day, and there were few left to be enrolled—I encountered the gaze of my lord the Viscount's dark-blue eyes fixed full upon me with a glance half of reproach, half of humorous amusement.

Truth to tell, I had indeed forgotten my character of scout, and had flung myself into the very thick of the movement; though the future alone could say whether men would come to call it by the name of victorious revolution or seditious rebellion. I had been carried away by the excitement of the scene and by my personal bias, and I had thrown to the wind alike the prudence inculcated by my uncle and the diplomacy I had promised to exercise on his behalf. Nevertheless I had not betrayed myself, and I had not enlisted as a soldier; for who would enlist a hunchbacked lad like me? Nor had I even told my name, it not having been asked of me; so that I was not exactly committed to aught. Yet I felt a thrill of shame run through me, as though I had in some sort betrayed trust; and I said to my lord with some humbleness,—

"My uncle shall not suffer aught through any act of mine. I will keep my pledge to him, and let him know all I can find ere the Duke enters Taunton; but how may I hold back from him when I see him face to face, and when you, my lord, are serving with him, whom I would fain follow to the world's end or to death?"

The Viscount smiled that smile of his which I never quite understood, but the pressure of his hand upon my shoulder was kindly and friendly.

"It is like enough to be one or the other, wert thou simple enough to throw in thy lot with me," he said in a low voice. "Exile or death is like enough to be the fate of those who meddle in this matter."

His voice was only for my ear, and I heard his words with a start of dismay and incredulity.

"But, good my lord, look on these rolls—look on this list of names! A few hours have brought all these men flocking to the Duke's standard. What will not days do, and when all the country side knows that he is here at last?"

Over the Viscount's face there passed another fleeting smile, and his eye rested upon my scroll with a strange expression.

"A few hundred ill-armed, undisciplined, untrained rustic hinds, who know no more of warfare than I of the plough! Dicon, hast thou read thy history so ill as that thou thinkest England and England's armies can be subdued by such as these?"

"But, good my lord, the train-bands will desert to the Duke as fast as they are brought into the field against him," I answered eagerly. "All men say so; and those I have spoken to have sons or brothers or lovers in the ranks, and they know what they say. O fear not, my lord; be not down-hearted. The will of the nation is with the Duke."

"The will of the nation—the hearts of the people!" repeated the Viscount slowly. "That may be, Dicon, in thy sense, and yet misfortune may not be far off. Dost know, lad, that except my unworthy self, not one bearing the name of gentleman has joined the Duke to-day? Even Mr. Trenchard, who was to have met him with fifteen hundred men, has fled to France out of the way of peril. We will see what the morrow and the morrow's morrow bring forth; but methinks if his Grace be wise he will take to his ships again, and quit the country ere he rouses up the lion to intercept and destroy him!"

"O my lord," I cried in distress, "not that—not that!"

But he made no direct reply, and we could no longer talk together where we were, for a great cry was raised, "The Declaration! the Declaration!" and one whom I may call a herald stood forth before the people with a printed paper in his hand, and forthwith avowed that he would read in the ears of the people the Declaration drawn up by the noble Duke of Monmouth, stating wherefore he had come to England, and what was his object in so doing.

Now all the people were very attentive to hear this, and held a great silence; and I listened with the best of them, striving to retain all in my memory, that I might retail it in Taunton Town when I returned, and have wherewithal to answer the questions which should be put to me.

I cannot set down all here, for it was very long, and would weary both reader and writer; but it was a clear exposition of the wrongs that the people were enduring from an "unlawful and absolute tyranny" foreign to the constitution and rights of the nation. It stated also the perils of Popery and Papist plots, reminding us that the burning of London in the last King's reign was held to have been the work of Papists; that the Duke of York, now calling himself King, had unlawfully instituted all manner of Popish idolatries, had set up the Mass, and was about to persecute with fierce cruelty all those who opposed him or upheld the true religion of the land. Next, we were reminded how he had done to death the late King by poison, and mention was made of others also who had been put from his path by like means; and as these things were read, the wrath and ire of the people grew so great and terrible that they broke at last into yells of rage and execrations against the false usurper on the throne, and some voice raised a shout, which was instantly taken up by hundreds and thousands,—

"King Monmouth! King Monmouth! We will have no King but him!"

Was this cry raised spontaneously at this point, or had it been begun by some person for the sake of effect? At the time I never thought of such a thing, but later on I have wondered whether some agent of the treacherous Ferguson may not have been primed to the part. For the words which followed seemed to fall almost too aptly on our ears, although we none of us felt it at the time. I can repeat this paragraph by heart to-day, having studied it from the Declaration itself, which was once in my hands, though soon it was death and dishonour to have a copy of it in one's keeping:—

"And forasmuch as the said James, Duke of Monmouth, the now Head and General of the Protestant forces of this kingdom, assembled in pursuance of the ends aforesaid, hath been and still is believed to have a legitimate and legal right to the crowns of England, France, Scotland, and Ireland, with the dominions thereunto belonging, of which he doubts not in the least to give the world full satisfaction notwithstanding the means used by the late King, his father, upon Popish motives, and at the instigation of the said James, Duke of York, to weaken and obscure it,—the said James, Duke of Monmouth, from the generousness of his own nature, and the love he bears to these nations (whose welfare and settlement he infinitely prefers to whatsoever may concern himself), doth not at present insist upon his title, but leaves the determination thereof to the wisdom, justice, and authority of a Parliament legally chosen, and acting with freedom; and in the meantime doth profess and declare, by all that is sacred, that he will, in conjunction with the people of England, employ all the abilities bestowed upon him by God and nature for the re-establishment and preservation of the Protestant Reformed Religion in these kingdoms, and for restoring the subjects of the same to a free exercise thereof, in opposition to Popery, and the consequences of it, tyranny and slavery. To the obtaining of which ends he doth hereby promise and oblige himself to the people of England to consent unto and promote the passing into laws all the methods aforesaid, that it may never more be in the power of any single person on the throne to deprive the subjects of their rights, or subvert the fundamental laws of the Government designed for their preservation."

Was it wonderful that such words as these raised our enthusiasm and joy to the greatest height? No more packed Parliaments subservient to the will of the King, instead of breathing forth the will of the nation! No more pandering to France, and receiving bribes from her for the perverting and corrupting of English ministers! No more Mass! No more idolatry! No more absolutism and oppression and tyranny!

Oh, how the people cheered and flung their hats into the air! Was it wonderful that we shouted aloud for "King Monmouth! King Monmouth!"

Who had drawn up that Declaration? I afterwards heard it was the Rev. Robert Ferguson, the man who was ever in the Duke's counsels now, and who was foremost in the cause, and eager to counsel boldness and advance.

Long afterwards I heard it whispered that he was one of those crawling creatures who, to make their own skins safe, play false to their own friends, by giving secret intelligence to the other side, and therefore are bold to urge rash counsel on others. What the truth of this may be I know not. I can only say that Ferguson had the face of a villain, and that I marvelled to see the Duke take so much heed to him.

But I must not omit to mention my other acquaintances and friends whom I saw in the muster about the Duke. Young Mr. William Hewling was there, and Masters Hucker and Herring, both looking very soldier-like in their trappings, and now bearing the commission of captains of the Duke's forces. I quickly distinguished, too, the fine face of Heywood Dare, which I had not seen for some while. He was paymaster of the forces, and seemed much in the confidence of the Duke. His son was ensign to Captain Goodenough, and both gave me a nod and a smile when they saw me.

Besides the Viscount, known to my readers, there was no man of rank in this assembly save Lord Grey, who was in command of the cavalry, and had solicited the assistance of Viscount Vere. Many harsh things have since been spoken of Lord Grey, and methinks he lacked skill and courage in action, as will be seen anon; but he was faithful to the cause of the Duke, and I like not to hear him railed upon.

So soon as I could get away after hearing the Declaration read, I hastened to the town-hall, where the recruits were all taken when enrolled to be provided with arms, and put through certain martial exercises in preparation for what might lie before them. The Mayor of Lyme had fled, we heard, to the Duke of

Albemarle at Exeter, with news of what was passing. Another gentleman, Mr. Dassell, who had striven to induce the authorities to fire upon the vessels of the Duke before he landed, had started off, it was said, for London. We began to understand that we must make the best of our time before the enemy came upon us; but it was needful that the recruits should be trained at least how to carry their arms, and how to obey the word of command, ere they were brought into the field and set in array against trained soldiers.

Thursday evening and Friday were thus spent, my lord the Viscount being one of the most forward and ready to assist in these matters.

In the counsels of the Duke he seemed to take but little part, but he was ready to do his utmost in showing the raw rustics how to shoulder a pike or aim a carbine. And sometimes he would step aside and speak a few words to me (for I could not keep away from the Bowling Green, where these things were going on), and he would say with something of sternness in his aspect,—

"At least the honest rogues shall not be shot down like sheep, or butchered as if in the shambles. They shall learn all that can be taught them in a few days."

But as more and more men kept pouring in, it became evident that arms were giving out, and that all sorts of shifts would have to be resorted to to put them into the field at all. True, we were cheered by the sight of many small companies of armed militiamen deserting to the Duke, and making gay and martial-looking those companies which were forming with all possible speed.

We began to speak of the Blue Regiment, the White Regiment, the Yellow Regiment, according to the prevailing colour of the militia uniform. No enemy appeared against us. No news came of anything but loyal support. It was said by scouts from Devonshire that the Duke of Albemarle was approaching, but that his soldiers were deserting in great numbers—a fact of which we had the best testimony—and that he was more than half afraid to bring the rest against us, lest they should go over in a mass to our Duke.

All faces brightened at this news. We cheered and huzzahed till the welkin rang. Even the Viscount's smile was a little more free and full, and he clapped me on the shoulder and said,—

"Perchance I have been a false prophet after all, lad. At least thou canst bear back good tidings to Taunton and to Mistress Mary. The issue of the day is yet to come, but at least so far the auguries seem happy. Let us live in the present, and leave the future to take care of itself."

CHAPTER XII.

BACK TO TAUNTON.

Had I been free, had I had none else to think of, had I not been bound in honour to my uncle, nothing would have held me back from openly espousing the cause of the Duke, and seeking if I might not at least enrol myself in some capacity amongst his followers. I would have implored the Viscount to let me serve him in the capacity of groom or valet, so that I might be with him, and follow the fortunes of war.

But I knew that until I had fulfilled the task intrusted to me I was not mine own master; and yet I felt the fire burning so hot within me, as I saw the muster of this goodly array and the martial aspect of the town, that I felt my only safety lay in flight, and that I must tear myself away before I took some step which would be disloyal to mine uncle, and a breach of the trust he had reposed in me.

I thought of all this as I lay in a narrow bed in an attic, counting myself lucky to have so much as a straw pallet to rest my weary bones upon—for weary I was with the excitements of the day; and the town was so full of recruits that numbers of these had to camp in the open field or in yards and barns. This was no great hardship whilst the dry warm weather lasted; and all men were so wrought up by the thought of the coming deliverance from Popery and tyranny, that nothing was counted a grievance in the good cause.

On Saturday morning I woke betimes, and after turning over all things in my mind, I resolved that I must not linger longer where I was, but make my way back that day as far as my aunt's house at Ilminster—according to promise— and then on to Taunton on Monday. The Duke, I had heard, would not leave Lyme before Monday, so I should be at home in good time to give notice of his approach.

But I felt that I could not leave without one more look at the Duke; and, moreover, I bethought me that my lord the Viscount might desire to send some letter or message to Mistress Mary: in fine, I had a hundred good reasons for not hastening away, as it might have been wise to do.

I took as good a breakfast as I could get at such a busy time, and putting the saddle on Blackbird, sallied forth in the brave sunshine to find the Viscount, and to pick up as much information as I could as to the plans and route of the Duke.

Now, although I think that this was not very well resolved on my part, I have never regretted it; for it enabled me to witness a most extraordinary and lamentable occurrence, which did much to damp the joy which was in all our hearts, and to send me on my way a sadder and a wiser man. But yet, I ween, there is something in our nature which makes us eager to see all that is to be seen, whether the sight be of sorrow or terror or joy; and therefore, when I approached the place where the Duke's standard had been set up, and saw that some sort of a tumult was going on about and around it, I pressed the more eagerly forward, and soon made my way (thinking less of my manners than of my eagerness and curiosity) into the innermost circle.

I have spoken many times of Old Dare, as he is still called in Taunton Town, where his memory is kept green, and of his forwardness in the cause of liberty and of the Duke; and how that he was always first to be on the spot when there was any fighting and any struggle for freedom. He had spent most of the time since landing in scouring the country for horses for the Duke, and had come in late the previous evening with some forty good beasts—the one he had purchased for himself being a very fine animal.

All this I did not know at the time, but heard it afterwards. What I did see when I approached was that one of the Duke's captains, whose name I had been told was Fletcher (I have not spoken of all the captains, fearing to confuse the reader with so many new names), was seated upon a fine horse, ready equipped, as it appeared, for a journey, and that Old Dare stood beside him with his hand upon the bridle, speaking loud words in a very angry manner.

Now it had been said to me that the Scotchman Fletcher was one of the few men about the Duke who really understood the art of war, and that he was the most valuable man we had on our side; so that I was astonished to hear high words passing between him and Old Dare, and to observe that the altercation was fast growing into a serious quarrel.

But even then I was little enough prepared for what my eyes witnessed. Scarce had I come into full sight and hearing of the disputants, before Dare raised his hand in a threatening manner, as though he would have struck his adversary with the cane in his hand; whereupon Captain Fletcher, roused to a great wrath, drew forth his pistol and shot Old Dare dead as he stood.

I could scarce believe my eyes. A mist seemed to swim before them as I saw the gallant figure totter and sway, and fall helplessly to the ground. Instantly all was commotion and alarm. The Scottish gentleman turned in his saddle and addressed those about him in loud tones,—

"Gentlemen, I call you to witness that the fault is none of mine. No man of honour could suffer himself to be insulted as that fellow was insulting me. I appeal to any gentleman who saw and heard all. Could I have done other than I did?"

A clamour and tumult at once arose of such magnitude that I was glad to back away out of the forefront of the commotion, and trust to chance to pick up later the gist of the matter. But whilst the crowd surged round the body of Old Dare on the ground, and round his slayer, yet mounted upon the fine charger over which the dispute had appeared to arise, Captain Thomas Dare came hurrying up at the head of his levies, and all were crying in loud and angry tones,—

"Vengeance! vengeance! Shall the murderer of Dare go free? Let him be taken before the Duke! Let justice be done upon him! Vengeance—vengeance —vengeance!"

The Duke was already upon the scene, a very troubled and anxious look on his face, as was indeed no wonder, seeing that the day had begun thus badly. There was a great and increasing tumult around him, and I could not tear myself away, although I could hear nothing of what was going on.

After a long time, I saw Captain Fletcher being escorted to the shore by a body of officers and troops, followed by a storm of execrations and hootings. He held his head proudly, and looked indifferent and scornful. I knew not whether he were going to instant death, or what had been decreed by the Duke; but as I pressed forward to look, and strove to learn the truth from those who stood by, I chanced upon my lord the Viscount, who was looking very grave and anxious.

"A bad omen, Dicon," he said as I rode up to him; "a bad beginning when we turn our arms against one another. Nay, I know not where the blame most lay. It was Dare's charger, but Fletcher had taken it in the service of the Duke, the better to perform the duty intrusted to him. It was not matter enough to cause the spilling of blood. And yet it has lost us two of our best men. Dare lies weltering in his blood, and Fletcher has been taken on board the frigate to save him from the fury of the people. He will be carried to foreign shores by the sailing-master, and we have lost the best officer we have amongst us."

I was distressed and grieved at the news, yet full of mine own plans and projects too. I desired (as we do desire such things—I know not why) to carry the news of this disaster to Taunton myself, albeit it would be sorrowful tidings there, for Old Dare was greatly beloved and respected; and my lord encouraged me to leave Lyme and return to my uncle with the news. He sent messages to Mistress Mary, and trusted soon to see her; but all through his discourse I felt that there ran a thread of warning and disquietude. He cautioned me to avoid getting myself too deeply implicated with the cause of the Duke, reminding me that those were safest who stood aloof and took no open share in the quarrel. I could well see that he himself had great doubts about the triumphant march to London of which our mouths and hearts were full. He had been driven himself by several goading motives to take up arms in the Duke's cause, but he was wishful to warn others from following him too blindly.

I rode away from Lyme thoughtfully enough; yet all I saw that day tended to raise my spirits. From all parts men were pouring in to join the Duke. I met them in companies of two or three, up to a dozen or twenty, all bent upon the same errand, and hungry to gain news from one who had seen the Duke and knew what was happening at Lyme. Then there was another sign which gave me food for pleasant speculation: at many cross-roads the authorities had posted constables to turn back the people who should be faring forth in the direction of Lyme. But these worthies were themselves all for the Duke; and though they stopped many travellers and asked whither they were bound, and so forth, yet, so soon as they heard, they wished them good journey, and so let them go, and then laughed between themselves as though it were all an excellent joke.

I made friends with many of these good fellows as I journeyed, and heard from them how all the country was for the Duke; and indeed I could make certain of this myself from the numbers of persons going to join him, many of them being clad in the gay uniform of the militia. My heart grew light as I journeyed, and by the time I had reached Ilminster and my aunt's house there, I had forgotten all my doubts and fears. She received me joyfully, and that evening and the next day I was beset by eager men and women all agog to hear my tale, and ready to dance for joy at hearing that the Duke would pass through their city shortly, on his way to Taunton.

Already they began to hang their windows with bright stuffs, and the town took quite a festive aspect before I left on Monday morning. Children were scouring the fields and woods for green boughs to make arches, and posies to crown staffs. It seemed to me that the Duke had nothing but a triumphal march before him, unless indeed, as some averred, the Duke of Albemarle was on the march eastward from Exeter to try to intercept him before he reached the heart of the Western loyalists.

One thing I must not omit to mention regarding my brief stay at my aunt's house. Of course she had many questions to ask about the Viscount, who had so won upon her a day or two before; and in speaking of him, I could not but say that I feared he was not so hopeful as to the success of the Duke as we were, and that I sometimes fancied he himself looked forward to a death upon the scaffold. At that my aunt looked very grave and troubled; yet both she and I saw that were the Duke to be defeated, it was likely enough examples would be made of the leaders and men of most mark and young Viscount Vere might be one chosen to expiate his rebellious act (as it would then be termed) upon the scaffold.

But such a thought filled us both with great dismay; for I loved the Viscount with a love I cannot hope to express in words. And suddenly my aunt rose and took a lighted taper, and said (it was now dark and late at night, and all her household was abed, we having sat up talking long after all others had gone),
—

"Dicon, come with me. I will show thee a certain thing; and if the day should come when it can serve thee or thy good lord the young Viscount, remember —and I will not fail either him or thee!"

As I followed my aunt, in great curiosity as to what this speech could mean, she led me up and up through the house into a great attic in the roof, whither walking was difficult because of crossed timber beams and chests stored with household goods; and suddenly stooping down in one corner, she made a curious clicking sound—I could not see how—and then, to my astonishment and momentary fear, seemed to sink into the floor, for soon only her head was visible to me.

"Come quietly after me, Dicon," she said; and then I saw that she was pushing herself down through a narrow aperture from which a rickety ladder led somewhere below. Following her through this trap-door—for such it must be, though cunningly hidden, as I saw afterwards—I by-and-by found my hand taken by hers and myself conducted through such strange narrow places as I had never been in before, till we came out at last into a small but not incommodious chamber, where stood a bed and a chair or two and a small table. And then I divined that I was looking upon one of those secret hidden chambers that were ofttimes to be found in ancient houses, contrived as places of safety for hunted priests or monks or Lollards, as the case might be.

My aunt put her lantern on the table, and said in a low voice,—

"I will make provision for an inmate, lest the day go against us; and if thou, Dicon, or the Viscount should come to trouble and be forced to fly, fear not to come hither, and I will shelter you. For myself I have no fears. I am a quiet woman, and take no part in great matters, and all of my towns-folk think well of me. I shall not be disturbed. But I will gladly give shelter to some hunted friend of the Duke's if it be needed. Not a soul in the town knows aught of this chamber. I trow I could keep any man safe for a month here, and none guess at his presence."

I was too much resolved to see nothing but triumph for the Duke to believe that we should ever need such shelter as this; yet I was interested in the chamber, and thankful to my good aunt for her kindness in thus promising me help for myself or my lord should it be needed.

On Monday morning, the fifteenth day of June, I started off with the first of the light to take to Taunton the news of the approach of the Duke. A messenger had come in overnight to say that the Duke would be leaving Lyme that morning, and unless delayed by any encounter with the forces of the Duke of Albemarle, which were said to be advancing towards Axminster, might be looked for at Ilminster perhaps by the evening, or at any rate on Tuesday. So I felt there was no time to be lost in getting to Taunton; and as Blackbird seemed of the same way of thinking, and went his best and fleetest, it was only high noon before we arrived at the outskirts of the town, to see in a moment that the whole place was in a ferment of excitement.

Had I once allowed myself to be stopped and questioned, had it once been known that I came from Lyme with tidings direct, I should never have been suffered to pass on my way, so clamorous were all the people after news. But as I was sure that this would be so, I kept my mouth shut, and put Blackbird to a hand-gallop, never drawing rein till I had him safe within the yard of the Three Cups itself.

At sound of the horse's feet my uncle came hurrying out, and almost fell on my neck in his transport of joy.

"Ah, Dicon lad, how I have watched and longed for thee! Come in, come in! I made sure some ill had befallen thee. Now tell me all—tell me all! The whole place is full of rumours, and never heard I such contrary tales. Our prisons are full of country yokels and farmers, caught in the act of going to Lyme to join the forces of the Duke. They tell us here that he will never reach Taunton; that the Duke of Albemarle will meet and rout him ere the day be done. Tell me, boy, what news dost thou bring? for faith I am half afraid to stir hand or foot, lest I find myself in some horrible trouble."

Well, I told my story as plain as I could, neither making light of such perils as I had heard of, nor yet failing to report how forward were all the country folks in the cause of the Duke. My uncle listened, and his face did not lose its look of perplexity; but after I had told my tale, I was eager to know, on my side, what had happened at Taunton during my absence, and my cousin Meg coming in and exclaiming at sight of me, I quickly got from her the news, whilst my uncle went out to confer with those of his friends who were still left in the town.

Meg told me that the public feeling was rising higher and higher for the Duke, and that soon after I had left Sir Edward Phillips and Colonel Lutterell had come in with several companies of soldiers to keep the town quiet. But on Saturday the latter had marched away with the most part of the troops to join the Duke of Albemarle at Chard or Axminster, and strive to intercept the advance of the Duke, and cut to pieces his army, thus quelling the rebellion at a blow.

Now this had been very grievous news for the people of Taunton, who knew not whether their beloved Duke might not be forced to fly or ever he had come to them as deliverer and saviour. The magistrates now had charge of the town, and were holding the people in check from any sort of rising, both by their authority and through the doubts entertained of the result of the engagement between the forces of the two Dukes.

When I told Meg how many and great were the forces pouring in to the Duke's standard, and how he was surrounded by so gallant a band of officers and gentlemen, and how the militia were deserting to him from every quarter, she took courage and heart again; and others coming in to hear my news, also thought well of it, and ere nightfall a new feeling had spread through the town, whilst whispers were abroad that it would be an easy thing in the absence of the soldiers to make a general rising, surprise the guard, overawe the magistrates, and seize and hold Taunton for the Duke.

But as yet it was only a whisper, and no man dared to speak aloud of such a thing. Order still prevailed, although I felt that the city was like to the hot crust over the crater of a volcano, and that at any moment a tongue of flame might spring forth, and the whole aspect be changed to seething heat and violent eruption.

As I was sitting at table satisfying my hunger after so much talking, and telling those who stood by of the death of Dare—a thing which caused much grief and heart-burning in the minds of his townsmen—my uncle came behind me and said that Lord Lonsdale had come in. After hearing that I had been to Lyme, he had asked to have speech with me; and I rose at once, and found him in the small parlour where guests of the better sort were entertained.

Now although my Lord Lonsdale had not played the part of a good father (in my humble opinion at least) to his son, and though he was known as a determined enemy of the Duke, yet to me he had always shown himself kind and gracious, and I was grieved to see the look of pain and anxiety upon his handsome face.

"Dicon Snowe," he said, as I appeared, "it has been told me that thou hast ridden scout for Taunton, and hast been as far as Lyme, and seen the following of the Duke of Monmouth. Tell me truly, boy, hast thou seen aught of my son? He has vanished no man knows where since the first day of the month, and all that I can hear of him is that he was seen riding south, as though he would make for the coast. I have been consumed with fear lest the foolish boy has run himself into deadly peril. Tell me, Dicon, hast thou seen him? and what was he doing?"

What could I say? I am a bad hand at lying even to my foes, and to lie to one who had ever treated me well would have been a disgrace. I could but tell my lord the truth—that his son the Viscount, goaded by fears of being forced to wed a lady for whom he had no love, had broken the yoke the best way he could, and so he had joined himself to the Duke, his heart not being truly in the cause; and he was now doing all that one man may do to drill the raw recruits, and make soldiers out of men used only to the plough. Having so begun, he would, I was convinced, see this matter through to the end; nor would any misfortune that befell the Duke draw him from the standard, so long as that standard floated over the plains of England.

Whilst I spoke in the finest words I could pick, my lord wrung his hands together and lamented openly the folly of the "boy," as he called him, the hot-headed rashness of youth, and the fearful peril into which he had run himself through his reckless impatience. I was sorry for the distracted father, who plainly feared his son's head would pay the penalty; but my sympathies were all the while with the gallant young Viscount. Nor did I think the cause lost, as the Earl plainly did, although prudence caused me to be silent on that point, and to express no opinion. My journey to Lyme was not thought to be an incriminating thing. Even the Mayor, Mr. Smith, who came to see me and ask questions, rather praised than blamed me for thus faring forth after news. I think I sent that worthy away with a flea in his ear. For I spoke of all the brave sights I had seen, and how joyful the cities were at thought of the approach of the Duke; and I think he wished himself anywhere but in charge of Taunton Town, with the citizens all in a ferment, and the soldiers drawn off elsewhere.

But my day's work was not done until I had seen Mistress Mary and given her her lover's messages; and so soon as I could shake myself free of the crowds that kept coming to hear the news afresh, I stood at the door of Miss Blake's parlour and sued for admittance.

I was welcomed almost with tears when it was known where I had been, and both Mrs. Musgrave and Mistress Mary were summoned to hear my tale, which did not grow less through repetition.

Oh how Mistress Mary's eyes did kindle and glow when I spoke to her of the Viscount, and how he had joined himself to the Duke, and was in command of a fine company of horse-soldiers under Earl Grey! If she had never loved him before, I think she would have loved him then on hearing what he had done, and knowing that for love of herself he had thus thrown all else to the winds and joined the Duke's standard. As it was, loving him heart and soul before, her heart could scarce hold all the joy and gladness that my words aroused; and when I whispered in her ears the messages with which I was charged, her beautiful eyes kindled and flashed, and she clasped her hands together as though hardly knowing how to keep back the words that sprang burning hot to her lips.

In this house there was no fear as to the result.

"God will fight for the right," said Miss Blake solemnly. "He will succour the oppressed in the time of need, and will not suffer His cause to be trampled in the dust."

Then she went out of the room for a brief time, and returned bearing a great burden, which Mistress Mary hastened to help her to undo, and before my dazzled eyes was then displayed the result of those weeks and months of patient toil.

Twenty-seven banners, or colours, as it was the fashion to call them, were spread out before my admiring gaze. The rich materials had been provided by the secret gifts of many wealthy inhabitants of Taunton, but the beautiful needlework had been done by Miss Blake's pupils under her own eyes; and Mistress Mary's banner—the most beautiful and the boldest of all, as I have said elsewhere—was her own work every stitch, and she had purchased with her own money all the materials to boot.

"When the King-Duke comes to his loyal city of Taunton," said Miss Blake with pardonable pride, as she folded the colours once again and laid them by in order, "a right royal welcome shall not be lacking him, shall it, Mary my dear?"

And Mary's eyes kindled and glowed and her cheeks flushed as she lightly passed her hands over the great raised letters J.R. worked upon her banner, and looked up to answer,—

"Nay; and if they call Taunton the 'Queen of the West,' it is but right that the Queen should be ready with royal honours for her King."

Well was it that such words as these were spoken with closed doors! Yet methinks these women had such courage and devotion that they would have spoken them aloud for all the world to hear had there been any cause.

After I had said good-night to these ladies, I found myself so tired out with the labours and excitements of the day, that I must needs find my way to my bed; and in spite of all the stir and tumult which reached me from the street below, I slept well and soundly, unconscious of what was passing, until daybreak on the following morning, when I was awakened by such a noise and commotion as would have aroused even the Seven Sleepers.

But the account of that memorable day and the rise of Taunton I must keep for a fresh chapter.

CHAPTER XIII.

THE REVOLT OF TAUNTON.

I woke with a start from a deep sleep, to find that already a new day had dawned, and to hear in the streets below the sound of trampling feet and the hum of a multitude of voices.

Springing out of bed and commencing to dress myself in a great hurry, I heard steps approaching along the passage, and my uncle came quickly in, looking haggard and dishevelled, as indeed he well might, not having been in bed or asleep for two nights.

"Heaven save us all!" he cried, in a state of genuine alarm. "All the soldiers have been called out. They say the Duke of Albemarle's forces have been overthrown, and that the Duke of Monmouth will be here by noon. Others say that the Duke of Monmouth's army is in full flight, and that the soldiers have been called out to help to cut them to pieces and drive them into the sea, so that not one of them shall remain alive by this time to-morrow. God save us all! What is a man to think or do, with such frightful news pouring in, and none knowing the truth of it!" and my uncle groaned aloud.

Now when I went to bed about ten o'clock the town had been quiet enough, as I have said. The regular soldiers had most of them gone, but several bands of the militia were still there, and these were quite sufficient to overawe the citizens; for they were not at all disposed to desert to the enemy, like those bands in other places of which I have spoken, and the magistrates and the Mayor had taken every precaution that the city should be kept tranquil.

But with the first light of dawn flying scouts kept hurrying in with news that there had been a battle between the two Dukes, and now the whole town was up and astir in the wildest excitement. My uncle could not learn the truth from anybody. The Mayor and magistrates tried hard to persuade the people that the Duke of Albemarle was triumphing, and that he had called upon the militia to finish the good work his soldiers had begun; but the tale told by flying soldiers who made their way into the city from Colonel Lutterell's regiment was very different. They declared that the train-bands under the Duke of Albemarle had given way everywhere before the Duke of Monmouth's troops. The engagement had been more or less in the dark and between hedges. The accounts were so confused that it was hard to tell what was the truth of the matter; but at any rate there were confusion and panic everywhere, and all lovers of order were alarmed, striving hard to quiet the tumultuous citizens and get them to return to their houses instead of running wildly about the streets adding rumour to rumour, till none could tell where the truth might lie.

All through that day this state of wild excitement lasted. Mr. Axe was to be seen in all parts of the town trying to persuade the populace to be orderly and quiet; but when towards evening the news came that the Duke—our Duke, the Duke of Monmouth himself—was in full march for Taunton, there was no keeping down the tumultuous happiness of the people. They cheered, they laughed, they shouted, they sang. When Mr. Nicholas Blewer appeared in the streets (he had been forward in spreading rumours that the Duke was overthrown, and in striving to set the people against him by threats of fearful penalties to be dealt to all traitors), he was so hooted and hustled that he was forced to fly almost for his life; whilst Will Wiseman led a hooting crowd of half-mad apprentice boys after him, and drove him ignominiously into his lodging.

But yet we dared not do more than raise our voices for the Duke when no magistrate was by: for there were still bands of militia in the town, despite the fact that continually companies were marching forth by one route or another; and guards were set everywhere, whilst the constables were busy keeping order, though not quite with that air of authority and certainty that they had shown before; and Mr. Axe and the Mayor worked hand in hand to keep order in the city.

There was no going to bed for me that night. I felt that a crisis was at hand— as indeed proved to be the case; and I sat with Will in a nook in the Cornhill, which was always like to be the centre of any disturbance.

Quiet seemed to have been restored at dark; but that quiet did not last long, for at midnight the roll of the drums began again, and we started to our feet, to become quickly aware that the last of the troops were being marched out of the town. By one or two o'clock in the morning there was not a soldier left, only the guard and the constables; and these, if the truth were known, in a great fright for their own safety.

"The soldiers have gone! the soldiers have gone!" cried Will, in a fever of excitement; and forthwith he went from house to house, knocking cautiously at doors, which flew open without any delay—plainly showing that the inhabitants were not asleep or abed that night; and I followed his example, till from all quarters men began pouring into the street, and the first dawn of the midsummer morning saw all the Cornhill full of people, looking into each other's faces as though asking what should be done next.

I know not who spoke the word first. It is always hard to say when the explosion comes whose hand set light to the gunpowder. For some while it had become known that no militia band was in the town, that the soldiers had gone, that none remained now to impose order upon the citizens. The town was practically in their own hands; they could do what they would.

Then there arose first a low whisper, just a rustle through the moving mass of humanity, but the whisper that became a shout, and the shout that became a yell, and was taken up and passed on, till every throat was vociferating the one word,—

"Arms! arms! arms!"

Now in the tower of St. Mary Magdalene's Church a quantity of arms and ammunition had been stored in case of emergency, and this fact was well known to the crowd. Accordingly a movement was made in the direction of the church, although the doors were known to be very strong; and we still had reverence for sacred buildings, whilst contemning the idolatrous usages of Popery.

But the blood of the citizens was up, and a trifle was not to stay them. Will Wiseman had, as usual, managed to get into the forefront of the crowd, and as they halted beside the church, wondering how to get at the stores, he cried out boldly,—

"Help me up, good people; hoist me on your shoulders. Let me but get footing on yonder ledge, and I'll get the window open and throw you out the arms as fast as you can catch them!"

A shout was the answer, and in another minute I saw the bold Will swarming up to the leads of the church roof, followed by first one and then another active man or lad. To wrench open the windows, to get at the store of arms, to pass them to those below until nothing remained within the tower, was but the work of an hour. By six o'clock every capable citizen of Taunton was armed and equipped. Those who had horses were already talking of going forth to meet the Duke and escort him to the loyal town. Women were hanging their windows with the costliest stuff their stores contained; children were going forth, as from Ilminster a few days before, to get flowers for garlands and green boughs for arches. We laughed aloud in the joy of our hearts. We shouted for the Duke till our throats were sore. Every flying scout who came into the city brought some fresh tale of disaster to the King's forces, and of triumph to the Duke's. Our Mayor had not shown his face since dawn. It was supposed that he and the magistrates, and those of the Burgesses who could not bring themselves to declare for the Duke, were hiding away in fear of the anger of the people, and the possible punishment the new King (as some of us boldly called him) might inflict upon them for their resistance.

Mr. Axe, indeed, came towards us, to try to speak in the name of order and authority; but an excited citizen marched up to him with a musket, and exclaiming, "We will not hear you! the town is ours!" looked so threatening in his aspect that the clergyman quietly retired.

And then the cry broke out,—

"Loose the prisoners! Release Mr. Vincent! Have out the loyal knaves, who will raise a shout for the Duke!"

No sooner said than done. The prison was broken open by the mob. Mr. Vincent appeared before our eyes carried high on the shoulders of the wildly-cheering crowd.

"A Monmouth! a Monmouth! Down with Popery! Down with tyranny! A Protestant King for England! A Monmouth! a Monmouth!"

There was no resisting that sort of shout; we joined in it almost to a man. Even my uncle, who took no open part in these proceedings, remembering perhaps that as Capital Burgess he was expected to be on the side of law and order, could not refrain from adding a cheer as the procession went by. The crowd, despite the efforts of Mr. Vincent to free himself from their well-meant attentions, insisted on carrying him in triumph through all the main thoroughfares, shouting themselves hoarse the while; whilst other inferior prisoners were treated to as much ale and sack as they could drink, and were listened to with admiration and delight as they told the tale of their capture. We were assured by this time that all England would declare for the Duke, and that he would make Taunton his capital in the West, and perhaps even allow himself to be crowned here (so fast did our imaginations and our tongues outrun reason and sense); that his enemies would fly before him, and be scattered as we heard the forces of the Duke of Albemarle had already been. In our great joy we were like men intoxicated, and every sense was strained to catch the first tread of approaching horsemen, which should betoken the coming of the deliverer.

Toward four o'clock that same afternoon a mighty shout was raised: "He comes! he comes! The Duke! the Duke!" And men began rushing wildly towards the road from the south, by which approach to the town from the coast might be expected.

Will Wiseman was at the head of the rushing crowd, and as I tried vainly to keep up with his flying feet, he cried that from the tower of St. Mary's a scout had seen the approach of a band of horsemen; and that was quite enough to rouse the shouts which were echoing down the streets, and to send the whole populace flying forth in one direction.

Although outrun by Will and the foremost of the crowd, I yet reached the limit of the town before the horsemen came up.

Right gallantly did the little cavalcade approach us; yet when they were near enough for us to distinguish faces, we saw that the leader was not the Duke himself, but our good friend and townsman John Hucker, now appearing in all the bravery of his military dress—a Captain in right of the Duke's commission, and bearing himself right gallantly, so that we all looked at him in admiration and amaze.

He drew rein at sight of such a crowd of friends, and his honest face beamed with pleasure.

"Good news, my friends, good news!" he cried. "His Grace the Duke is on his way, and will be here to-morrow with his victorious army, which has put to flight at Axminster all the army of the Duke of Albemarle. We are to march straight to Bristol and secure that for the Duke, and then we look that all the country shall have risen in his favour. London will be the next place. The King and the Court are quaking and shaking. They dare not bring men into the field against us, lest they all desert to the Duke's standard. The stars in their courses are fighting for the righteous cause. Citizens, be ready with a loyal welcome to-morrow for the noble Duke—the future King of England!"

Oh how we did shout and cheer and laugh and weep! This brave message seemed to infuse new life into us. We on our side pressed round Captain Hucker, to tell him how we had risen for the Duke, and gained the mastery of the town in defiance of guard and Mayor and magistrates. We no longer trembled to think of our audacity and the consequences it might lead to. We were full of triumphant gladness; and our townsman promised that the whole story should be told to the Duke, that he might know and appreciate the loving loyalty and devotion of the men of Taunton.

Captain Hucker, however, had private matters to attend to, when he had given us his first good news, and was able to leave his soldiers in our care and ride to his own home.

I think I have said before that Master Hucker—as we had hitherto called him —was a great serge-maker of the town of Taunton. He had his mills in the fair valley of the river Tone hard by the town, and he had a fine house within the city, where he lived with his wife and his daughter Eliza, who was one of the maidens of Miss Blake's school, and had been engaged upon that goodly task of working the colours for the Duke's army.

Captain Hucker now hastened home; and as it chanced that he passed me on the way, he asked news of mine uncle and the rest of our household, and by me sent him a message to ask if he could supply him with any of those notable wines which he was known to keep in his cellar, and which commanded a price higher than men cared to give save on very especial occasions.

"For, Dicon," added Captain Hucker, "thou mayest tell thine uncle that the Duke of Monmouth has graciously promised to be my guest during the days of his stay in Taunton. My poor house is to be honoured as the resting-place of His Grace, and thou wilt see how it beseems me to have the wherewithal for his entertainment. And listen again, Dicon." The Captain leaned from his saddle-bow with a beaming face, though he spoke in a very low and cautious tone. "It behoves us to give a right royal reception to the Duke; for although he enters Taunton but as Duke of Monmouth, yet (if I do not greatly err) it will be as King of all England that he will quit it."

And while I stood open-mouthed in amazement, not seeing how this thing could come so speedily, Captain Hucker laughed and nodded and rode on, only calling back to me not to forget about the wine, and to bring him word in a short space what mine uncle could do for him.

King of all England! The words rang bravely in my ears, but I could scarce credit them myself. To think that fortune's wheel should bring to pass that I had seen and spoken to a King, and had held his hand in mine even for a moment!

I went with my message to my uncle, who forthwith started off to Captain Hucker's house to see and speak with him face to face. Doubtless he wished to learn from him other matters than the amount of wine to be delivered. As for me, I made my way to Master Simpson's; for I had seen his face amongst the horsemen who had ridden into Taunton, and I knew that he would tell us everything that had befallen, and not send me away from sharing the narrative.

He was in the garden behind the house and shop—a right pleasant place, where I had spent many a happy hour with Will and Lizzie. They were with him in the arbour, filling his glass with the mead he loved best, and heaping his plate with such viands as they thought he best relished. He was both thirsty and hungry, as was natural after the day's march, but he was talking all the while nevertheless; and when Lizzie saw me she darted forth and dragged me within the pleasant arbour, exclaiming,—

"Now come and hear all father's tale. Oh, why was I not born a lad, that I might have ridden forth beside him, and joined in the glorious victory!"

But her father fondly stroked her bright hair, and said,—

"Nay, nay, my maid, but thou hast done thy share at home; and the maidens' work shall never be forgotten in Taunton Town.—Well, Dicon, so thou didst find thy way safe home? Thou didst miss the fight at Axminster, and the rout of the King's general there. Ah! it was a goodly sight to see. If all battles end as speedily and as merrily, I care not how many of them we fight."

He told us all the details of that skirmishing fight in the lanes—how so many of their adversaries had deserted to them, and how it was supposed that the Duke of Albemarle had drawn off the rest in fear lest all his army should melt away before his eyes.

"Why did you not pursue them, father," cried Lizzie, "and kill all who would not join you? That is what I should have done. I would not have left alive one soldier or officer who could hurt us afterwards. I would have scattered and slain even as the angel of the Lord we read of in the Bible. Now the Duke of Albemarle will gather his men and bring them up again perchance. I would not have left him even the remnant of an army."

"Well done, little general!" cried the father, looking well pleased at Lizzie's martial ardour; and then growing a little more grave, he added, "I have heard others say that that is what we should have done. Lord Vere was very urgent to pursue and scatter the band; but Lord Grey was against it, and his word prevailed. I am not a soldier born; my duty is to obey my superior. Yet if mine opinion had been asked, I would have said, as my maid here says, that it were better to rout and disperse the band than give it time and opportunity to re-form and harass us as we move."

"I have heard a whisper that my Lord Grey is but a sorry soldier," I ventured to remark in a low tone; for it is not for us citizens to condemn our betters. "Did not men say that at Bridport he fled scarce striking a blow, and left the infantry to be cut to pieces; and no thanks to him that Colonel Wade got them together and brought them safe off? That is a story one man told me. I prithee what be the truth of it, Master Simpson?"

He laughed a little uneasily.

"Oh, as for that little skirmish at Bridport, we take none account of it, being but a small affair," he answered. "We sent to surprise the militia there, and we gained possession of the town right speedily. But there was some blundering and misunderstanding betwixt the officers; Colonel Venner was wounded; and the cavalry under my Lord Grey galloped back to Lyme. But no great harm was done. Colonel Wade brought his men back in good order. They say small skirmishes like that accompany all warfare, but are of small note in the course of the campaign."

"I would the Duke would give my lord the Viscount the command of the horse," I said. "He would not gallop away from the scene of action, and leave the foot-soldiers to their fate."

Master Simpson shook his head at my temerity in thus speaking, yet he could not but say that he thought the Viscount would make the better leader; then we fell to talking of the death of Dare, and the unfortunate loss of two such good men as himself and Fletcher. For it had been found impossible to use Fletcher any more in the West Country, and the sailing-master of the frigate had weighed anchor and taken him off elsewhere. Thus one of the best soldiers was lost to us; and, as we all very well knew, out of those who went in the ranks by the brave names of colonels, captains, and ensigns, scarce more than two or three had been trained in arms or had seen service.

But on a day like this we were not disposed to let grave and despondent thoughts gain the upper hand. The victorious Duke was on his way to the town, and all Taunton was decking itself for the reception on the morrow.

Master Simpson said he must see what he could do to brighten up his house, and went to take counsel with his sister; whilst Will and Lizzie and I went forth together and paraded the streets, watching the erection of triumphal arches, the decking of windows and balconies, and listening to the joyful cries and shouts of the people, as they ever and anon let their spirits get the upper hand, and broke forth into song and cheering.

Lizzie was anxious to see her schoolmistress and take her all the news, so I escorted her thither, and we passed inside together, to find the house all in commotion. The town girls had not gathered for schooling upon such a day of excitement. No study could be thought of at a time like this, yet never had there been a busier day in Miss Blake's establishment.

If every window and balcony in the town was to be decorated, how much was it incumbent upon her to get done before the glorious morrow! All the resident pupils and the two mistresses were working might and main, and at once Lizzie and I were pressed into the service; and as our fingers moved our tongues wagged, and such a clatter as we made amongst us you would scarce believe.

Mistress Mary was there, of course—the most skilful of all, and with her whole heart in the work. Yet she found time to come up to me and ask in a whisper,—

"Has *he* come in to-day?"

"No," I answered; "he comes with the Duke to-morrow. You will see him then, Mistress Mary." And her cheek kindled and glowed; yet there was a sorrowful look in her eyes also, and I noted it the more because upon such a day as this I should have thought nobody could have had aught but thoughts of joy and triumph.

As we were decorating a window together later on, and nobody else chanced to be by, I ventured to ask respectfully,—

"Is aught amiss, fair mistress?"

She looked at me, and suddenly the tears sprang to her eyes. She clasped her hands together, letting her wreath fall to the ground.

"O Dicon," she exclaimed, in a passionate way quite foreign to her usual calm, "how will this end—how will it end? Ah, if I only knew that ill and hurt would not come from it!"

"Why, Mistress Mary," I said in surprise, "you have been ever most forward to prophesy victory, even when things looked dark; and now, when all the world is full of confidence and hope, are you to fear and doubt?"

"Dicon," she said in a low tone, "I had a dream last night—a dream of terror and dread. And yesterday my guardian came to me and said terrible words."

"What did he say?" I ventured to ask.

"He said that I had tempted his son to his own undoing; that I had put a halter round his neck, and had led him to his ruin. He said that none but women and fools could believe that aught could come of this rebellion—that was his word —save a rapid downfall, to be followed, if the King is of the temper he has shown himself ever, by a fearful and exemplary vengeance. He said things which made me shake for very fear, and he spoke with a certainty that rang like a knell in mine ears. And then I had such a frightful dream of dreadful deaths upon the scaffold, the hideous form of the executioner, the crowds of faces, the horror and the agony. And above all, I seemed to see *his* face looking reproach upon me, and his voice saying in my heart, if not in my ears, 'It was for thy sake I did it, Mary. I am dying now by thy act.' Oh, it was terrible, terrible, terrible! I have scarce been able to enjoy this day for the thought of it."

I confess I did not like that dream. I had known before of such that had proved much too terribly true. Also it reminded me unpleasantly of Mother Whale's prediction about much blood and little glory, which had always borne a sinister sound in my ears ever since I had heard it. But then had she not said that the King should die in exile? And if that should indeed be true, why need we fear the rest?

However, to Mistress Mary I strove to make light of the dream, and spoke to her of the prognostications we were hearing on all sides of the triumphal march lying before the Duke; so I think I left her comforted. Nor could any person loving the Duke fail to be glad and happy that night, for we all knew him to be close at hand, and looked to see him bravely welcomed on the

---

CHAPTER XIV.

A GLORIOUS DAY.

I had slept soundly and well upon the night preceding that glorious and memorable eighteenth of June, despite all the excitements of the day; for the previous night I had not troubled my bed, and nature will claim her dues, be the moment never so full of stress and emotion.

But though I slept soundly and well, I awoke betimes; and I was not astir before others, for I heard the sound of songs and glad voices in the streets before I left my room. Below in mine uncle's inn all was life and bustle, for the country folks were pouring in from far and near to witness the arrival of the Duke; and every hostelry was taxed to the limit of its resources to find even sitting room for the merry company, to say nothing of food for man and beast.

I had never seen our stables so crowded with beasts, and we had to tether them in the yard beside heaps of fragrant grass and hay. My uncle's face was wreathed in smiles, and he welcomed every comer with his wonted heartiness. For the time being he was carried away by the stream of popular enthusiasm; and although still carefully refraining from taking any overt part in the day's proceedings, was ready to give welcome to all comers, and was perhaps glad to be tied by the exigencies of business within the doors of his house, so that did he wish it never so much, he could not make shift to leave it, be it the King himself who was coming to the town that day.

We knew that the Duke had slept at Ilminster the past night, and therefore that he could not be here very early, since a march of sixteen miles is not made without considerable loss of time with an army of some thousands of men.

But then there was enough to do, in order to receive that army with hospitality, to keep us all busy, and I would I could describe the appearance presented by Paul's Field and the meadows adjoining, where we guessed the soldiers would encamp; for every citizen, however humble, had some small contribution to make towards the accommodation of the good Duke's army and the hospitable welcome of his followers, and the place looked like a great fair with its tents and roughly-knocked-up sheds, and its supplies of provision for man and beast hastily contributed by the eager towns-folk.

As for the number of horses in the place that day, I never saw the like. Everybody who had a horse, or could by any means obtain one, had it ready to ride forth later on to meet the Duke. I could have sold Blackbird a dozen times over for thrice his value would he but have suffered any other rider to mount him. As it was, several yeomen and gentlemen would not be satisfied without making trial of their prowess; but although one or two contrived by dint of excellent horsemanship to maintain a seat upon his back for a while, yet none after that trial desired to conclude any bargain, and Blackbird remained in mine own keeping, as I was sure from the first he would do.

Towards noon the horsemen began to gather and ride out along the Ilminster road, and I perforce went with them, though I could ill be spared from the inn; but mine uncle saw that my heart was no longer in my task, and good-naturedly bid me go forth to see the show.

Almost needless to say that there in the forefront of the riders—albeit with none but his own feet to carry him—was Will Wiseman; and so soon as he saw me he came to my side, and I gave him hold of my stirrup leather, as we had many times done before when I rode forth, and he ran beside me gallantly, as untired as the horse.

"The witch is not right, Dicon," he cried more than once; "for come what may in the future, is not this glory enow to satisfy the heart of man? Didst ever see town so bedecked as Taunton is this day? And there will be yet more to follow on the morrow!"

For Will and I knew what gay show had been devised for the morrow, and how it would be one that would rouse the enthusiasm of the town to the highest pitch. And Will (who had a wonderful gift for hearing news before anybody else) whispered to me that there would be other brave shows ere the Duke left the Queen city of the West; but when I asked him what he meant, he only laid his finger on his lips and whispered,—

"Hist, Dicon! This be not the time or place to speak of such things. But dost thou think that England will be content to follow a Duke, even though he be the son of a King? We want a King and not a Duke to reign over us. How can men flock to the standard of a Duke, when there is a King upon the throne? We must have a King, too, else all will be confusion and mischance."

This word from Will confirmed what I had heard yesterday about the Duke's leaving the town as King. I confess I was perplexed how such a thing could be, the more so as in the Declaration which I had heard read he had spoken of not insisting upon his title as yet, and only doing so at the request of Parliament. But then I had read enough history to be very well aware that no Prince could always adhere to the resolves laid down at the first. The tide of popular sentiment often carries them beyond the bound originally set; and it might be very true, as Will whispered, that the title of Duke would not be sufficient to content the ardent followers who had flocked to the banner of one whom they hoped to see reigning as England's King.

All this was very exciting, and stirred my pulses not a little. At last my longings were gratified. I was living in times that were truly historic. I was going forth to meet the champion and deliverer of the people. What could heart of man wish more? I should see him and behold his triumphal entry into the city. I should have lived in days which would go down to posterity as the days of a great epoch in our country's story.

Presently the cries and shouts of those in advance of us told us that the Duke and his army had been sighted. The cloud of dust which the horse-hoofs of our advance-guard raised kept us for a time from a view of what they saw; but presently the cloud subsided. All of us drew away right and left upon the turf, leaving the road track clear for the coming vanguard; and in another minute cheers and shouts began to rend the air, and we all tossed up our caps, crying lustily, "God save the Duke! God save the Duke! God be with your Grace! A Monmouth! a Monmouth!"

And one voice was boldly raised to cry, "God save the rightful King!"

The Duke came forward, riding a fine horse with all the grace and manly skill which helped to make him a King amongst men. His face was bright with smiles, he held his head-piece in his hand, and bowed right and left as he passed through the ranks of shouting, cheering citizens and country folk, all come out to do him honour.

Beside him rode a body-guard of some forty or fifty gentlemen, well mounted and equipped; and amongst these I soon singled out my lord the Viscount, whose gallant bearing and golden locks made him conspicuous even amongst so many gay riders. He saw me too, and gave me a smile and a nod. But he kept his place near to the Duke, and we who had come out to welcome him escorted that gallant band at a short distance, the main body of the horse following about a quarter of a mile behind, and the infantry, waggons, and guns (of which there were very few) bringing up the rear half a mile away, and proceeding much more leisurely.

Will had set off running towards the city like a hare so soon as he had really set eyes upon the Duke and had heard from my lips that it was truly he. Therefore on our approach to the city we were surrounded by such a crowd as I surely think no man amongst us had ever seen before. Hundreds of children lined the roadway into the town, flinging posies and garlands before the feet of the Duke's horse. A band of minstrels welcomed him with strains of martial music; and whilst women wept aloud and called aloud upon him as their saviour and deliverer, men shouted his name and made the welkin ring with their cries, till one would have thought the whole place had gone mad with joy.

So thronged were the streets that it was difficult for the Duke to make his way along them, and the many pauses which had to be made rendered it easy for the people to press round him, kiss his hands and shower blessings of every sort upon him. This gave him opportunity to reply to them by smiles and gentle words, such as he was very ready with. And he won all hearts by his gracious demeanour, by the beauty of his person, and by the kingly grace of his deportment.

The procession wound slowly up the High Street towards the Cornhill, and when the open space was reached, the Duke's company moved towards the right in the direction of Fore Street, thus approaching somewhat nearly to the Three Cups Inn, and also to that house where Miss Blake held her school. I think it was by arrangement that the Duke had been thus slowly urged along Fore Street; for as he approached the corner a sudden silence fell upon the crowd, whilst all eyes were turned upon a certain gaily-draped balcony; and immediately there appeared upon it a crowd of white-robed maidens, and to the accompaniment of the band of minstrels their voices were raised in a sweet strain.

They sang several stanzas of some poem, which I afterwards heard had been culled from the writings of Dryden, and which, it was whispered to me, had been obtained with some difficulty and set to music by the organist of St. Mary's Church. Only one verse remains in my memory, and very appropriate did those words sound as they were chanted forth by the white-robed throng: —

> "Thee, saviour, thee, the nation's vows confess,
> And never satisfied with seeing, bless;
> Swift unbespoken pomps thy steps proclaim,
> And stammering babes are taught to lisp thy name."

The Duke listened to the song with bared head, and at its close made a graceful reverence to the young maidens, who retreated from the public gaze so soon as their part had been performed. I saw the Viscount's eyes fixed upon the balcony; and I had well been able to distinguish Mistress Mary's rich voice leading the carol, and giving strength and power to the strain. That she had seen her lover I did not doubt. His face showed that the magic language of love had been exchanged between them as they stood so near to one another.

But there were graver matters on hand than mere songs of praise and shouts of welcome and devotion. A little stir in the crowd betokened the setting up of the standard in the centre of the Cornhill; and then a herald stood forward, and demanded that the city magistrates should instantly be summoned to attend the reading of the Declaration which would forthwith be made.

Eager partisans ran hither and thither to summon these dignitaries, and no doubt they looked upon discretion as the better part of valour, for a certain number of them shortly appeared. Some said that Mr. Bernard Smith, our Mayor, was also present; but of that I cannot be sure, since I did not see him myself, and I can never be certain that what report spoke was the truth.

I have spoken before of that Declaration, and need not more particularly refer to it here, save to remind you how gratefully would those fair promises of toleration and justice fall upon the ears of our citizens who had seen the demolition of their chapel and meeting-places, and had for years been constrained either to go to church against their desire or conviction, or to meet privily to hear the Word preached to them after their own fashion, whilst they were subject to many and grievous penalties for doing even this.

Every clause of the Declaration, then, was received with shouts and cries of joy. The long indictment against the present King fell like music on the ears of those who had regarded him from the first with fear and hatred. Enthusiasm was stirred to its highest pitch by the terms of this long document; and the people crowded so close about the herald, that I was glad to get out of the press, lest I should be trodden underfoot and suffocated.

After the Declaration had been read aloud in the ears of the people, a copy of it was affixed in one or two places about the town, where all who could might read it for themselves; and then a proclamation was read which gave great joy to all the people, showing as it did the gentle temper of the Duke, and his anxiety that justice and mercy should always be done in his name.

This proclamation set forth that whereas, to the great reproach and scandal of the good cause, and contrary to the commands and wishes of the Duke, certain lewd and dissolute persons had, under cover of a pretence of zeal, been guilty of acts of pillage and robbery, and in especial had taken horses from the good and peaceable country folk without payment, it is strictly charged that no such acts be committed any more; and that if any person in the future be robbed of aught he possesses, he is invited straightway to repair to the camp, and to lay complaint before the Duke, when justice shall at once be done.

This proclamation gave great satisfaction to all those who could remember, or who had heard stories of the cruel depredations inflicted formerly by the soldiery in times of war, when redress was practically impossible. I will not go so far as to say that this proclamation had the desired effect of putting a stop to all such depredations; but at least it was evidence of the temper and the wishes of the Duke, and was received with loud acclamations of joy and affection by the people.

By this time the day had fast waned; and although the sun was still high in the sky, being nearly at the summer solstice, yet the Duke and his party were fatigued by their long march in the heat, and by the fervour of their reception. So when Captain Hucker came forward to say that he had all in readiness at his house for the entertainment of the Duke and some of his officers, whilst others were to be received by substantial citizens with whom they would find abundant good cheer, the party was glad enough to betake itself to rest and refreshment; and the good folks from the outlying districts, who had ridden in to see and welcome the Duke, now hastened away to get their horses, and to leave the crowded town.

I heard Captain Hucker invite the Viscount to the hospitality of his house; but his invitation was courteously declined, Lord Vere saying quietly that he had business of his own to see to.

I guessed that that business had somewhat to do with Mistress Mary, nor was I surprised when presently he came and linked his arm in mine (in that friendly fashion he was not ashamed to show even in the eyes of the citizens who knew his rank and my humble birth) and said,—

"Good Dicon, thinkest thou thine uncle can find me a bed to-night? I have not slept in one since leaving Lyme, indeed since reaching Lyme. I would sooner lie in his house than in any other to-night, for I must have speech with Mistress Mary to-day if such a thing be possible; and I trow that I shall gain it best through thy good offices."

I knew my uncle would be glad enough to have Lord Vere as his guest. Lord Lonsdale's son was greatly beloved in Taunton, and to harbour him would not be like to do any man hurt, since Lord Lonsdale was known for a very loyal servant of King James, and most like would use such influence on behalf of his son (supposing that evil days fell upon this expedition, which Heaven forfend) that he would escape the penalty of his rashness. My uncle did not desire to hold too sullenly aloof from all the hospitalities offered to the Duke's followers, neither did he wish too deeply to embroil himself with the rising. So that he was very well pleased when I brought back my lord the Viscount, and at once allotted to him the best bed-chamber, and set before him the best viands left in the house after all the feeding and feasting of the day.

I waited on my lord, and when he had appeased the worst of his hunger, he made me sit down and make a meal myself of the fragments; which I was nothing loath to do, having scarce broken my fast since morning, for the excitement and bustle of the day. As I ate he sat thoughtfully toying with some fruit, and at the last asked suddenly,—

"Dicon, is it true that there be many colours worked by the maidens yonder that will be presented to-morrow to the Duke?"

"I trow so, good my lord," I answered, with secret triumph in my heart. "I have heard and seen somewhat of it."

"And will Mistress Mary Mead be amongst those who will present them?"

"Truly I believe it, my lord. Her banner is the best and most beautiful of all, and every stitch her own. Is it like that upon such a day she would be more backward than others?"

My lord's face was very grave and anxious.

"Dicon, I would have speech with her this night. Canst thou obtain it for me? There may be more peril than she wots of in this thing. I would save her from it if it might be. Can I make shift to see her?"

"Why, yes, my lord; I see no great difficulty about it," I answered. "I am always welcome when I go in with news of the day's doing; and after such a day as this I shall be tenfold more welcome. And if you will condescend to accompany me to the house—any gallant Captain of the Duke's forces will be welcomed with honour by Miss Blake. I doubt not that by this she is in Mistress Mary's secret; and whilst I tell all my news to her, you can get speech with Mistress Mary in another part of the room. I see no trouble about it on such a day as this. All Taunton is on the tip-toe of expectation. None bearing news will be denied entrance at such a time."

"Good," answered my lord, rising to his feet: "I will but arrange my dress and wash away these stains of dust, and present myself to Miss Blake, and gain speech of Mistress Mary if it may be."

How gallant and beautiful my lord the Viscount looked when he came down from his sleeping-chamber a few minutes later my poor pen cannot well say. I felt that such a lover might well win the heart of any maid; and I pretty well knew by this time that Miss Blake was in the secret of Mistress Mary's amours, and that she would do everything in her power to bring about the happy union of two such loyal and loving hearts. Any man serving in the army of the Duke would win her regard and respect; and the personal charm of the Viscount could not fail to make itself felt, whilst the romantic story of his love for Mistress Mary, and the sacrifice into which it had led him, could not but touch the heart of any woman, be she never so hard to please. Wherefore I was very sure that Viscount Vere would receive a warm welcome in the parlour of the ladies.

Nor was I deceived in this. The serving-maid, with a flushed and smiling face, admitted us at once into the familiar room, bright with the last flush of day; and there was Mistress Mary still in her white robes, and the two mistresses flushed and exultant, eager after news and ready with the warmest welcome for me, and with words of deep respect and most sincere good-will for my lord, whose appearance in my wake put them quite into a flutter, and caused Mistress Mary's cheeks to glow as though the sunset sky had been reflected in them.

She remained in the deep window seat, and for a while my lord spoke with the other ladies; but presently he made his way across to where his mistress sat, and we at the other end spoke of many things. I told all I had seen of the meeting of the Duke outside the city, and of his gallant entrance therein.

What the lovers spoke of at first I know not. I heard the low tone of Mistress Mary's voice, but not the words, and I guessed that she might be speaking of those fears and anxieties which she had named to me. However, of this I cannot speak certainly. What I can answer for is that presently the Viscount raised his voice so that we all could hear, and said, rather to Miss Blake than to any other,—

"Ladies, I hear that you are to take a bold step to-morrow. Have you bethought you what the consequences may be should the issue of this revolt be other than the well-wishers of the Duke desire?"

"My lord," answered Miss Blake, with an air of unconscious dignity, "we frail human creatures have naught to do with results; those are in the hands of Him who cannot do amiss. Our part is to do our duty, and show forth our love and service in the cause of right and truth and virtue. This we are resolved to do, and no fear of results will serve to fright us from our appointed task. You men can go forth and fight in the righteous cause. There is little that we poor women can do, yet that little shall not be lacking. You would not, gallant sir, strive to deter us from taking our small share in this noble struggle?"

One of the Viscount's strange smiles hovered over his beautiful face. "Madam," he said, with a bow, "after such words as those, mine sound but poor and mean and faint-hearted. But you know that I love Mistress Mary, and that I would lay down my life to keep her from harm. I know more of the forces at the King's disposal than the country folks here seem to do, and my fears are therefore greater, and my hopes less strong, than those which fill the breasts of the citizens of Taunton. If ill betide this rising, there will be evil days to follow; and those who are most known to have taken a part in it will be subject to most danger. I have no right to counsel you, madam; but I have that claim upon Mary which bids me warn her what she is doing. If she carries forth her banner to-morrow, it may be that some hurt she little thinks of now will fall upon her."

"And if it does, what then?" asked Mistress Mary, raising her head, and looking so beautiful in her generous enthusiasm that I could only hold my breath and gaze at her speechlessly. "Dost think, my lord, that it is only men who are willing to suffer and to die in a noble cause? Nay, in so thinking thou dost greatly err, thou dost greatly wrong us women. I would gladly lay down my life for the cause to which I am pledged, the cause of truth and liberty and righteousness." She turned her eyes full upon him as she spoke, and then suddenly the light in them, which had been proud and even tinged with a noble scorn, suddenly softened, and she laid her hand gently upon his arm, speaking her next words in a different key, and with a tenderness that I can never hope to make you hear. "Reginald," she said softly, and in a moment his hand had sought and covered hers, and I think they both forgot just then that there were any beside to hear what they said, "thinkest thou that I would draw back from any cause to which thou hadst pledged thyself? Thinkest thou that I fear any peril that thou too dost share? Hast thou not taken up arms in the same good cause? and if peril threaten me, it will threaten thee also. Shall I fear to share anything with thee? Thou dost know me wondrous little an thou thinkest that. Together we will live, or together we will die. What matters it so that we be always together?"

As she spoke these last words, he raised the hand he held and pressed it to his lips. She did not strive to withdraw it; and we averted our eyes, that we might not seem to see too much of what is infinitely sacred—that mystery of human love which is the mainspring of all the great actions done in the world. There were tears in Miss Blake's eyes, and Mrs. Musgrave was wiping hers furtively. In a low whisper one of them said to the other,—

"Was ever love so true and beautiful? My Lord Lonsdale may rage as he likes an it reaches his ears, it would be sin and shame to strive to part two such hearts. Heaven has made them for one another. What God has joined together, let not man strive to put asunder."

Just at this moment there was a little stir outside the door. It was opened rather suddenly and hastily, and the serving-maid put in her head and exclaimed in half-angry, half-frightened tones,—

"It is no fault of mine, mistress; he will come in."

And the next minute we saw before us in the gathering twilight the lank figure and evil face of Mr. Nicholas Blewer.

Now Miss Blake had ever hated and distrusted this man, and of late days, gaining courage from the approach of the Duke, she had dared to deny him entrance into her house. But I suppose he had to-day found the maid gossiping in the streets, as maids will do in times of excitement, and so had forced his way in, and now stood looking round upon us all with an evil smile upon his cruel face.

In our part of the room there was not much light; but Mistress Mary and her gallant lover sat together on the window seat where the western light shone in upon them, and her white dress and his festal suit of white and blue caught the last of the evening glow, and seemed to stand out against the window like a picture. I saw the sudden change which came over Mr. Blewer's face as he saw who was with Mistress Mary; and there was something in the tones of his voice that made me long to spring at his throat and throttle him then and there, so full was it of covert malice and bitter hostility.

"I trust I do not intrude. I could not deny myself the pleasure of seeing you all so happy after this strange day's masquerade. Doubtless it has seemed to you like the dawn of a new day. But, dear ladies, it were well to remember that all that glitters is not gold. Be not too sure that your millennium has already come. There be strange chances and changes in the fortunes of war.—My sweet young mistress, I must caution you not to be over-rash in the zeal with which you welcome this new Prince Absalom."

He looked straight at Mistress Mary as he spoke these words, and approached as if he would take her hand; but she suddenly rose and slipped it within my lord's arm, and, looking full at Mr. Blewer with a scorn both in face and voice which I think could not well be surpassed, said simply,—

"With my affairs, sir, you have no concern. I never wish to see your face again, nor to hear the sound of your voice. You have been forbidden this house, and you are here only by a trick. Go! I have nothing to say to you. I distrust and I despise you. There! you have my last word."

"Go, sir!" said Miss Blake, taking up the gauntlet so boldly thrown down; "you have ever been a false friend and a spy in this house. Go! and never darken our door again."

He turned fiercely upon her, his face hideous in its cruel passion. "You threaten me, madam! Have a care, else in the days to come you may bitterly repent the slights you have put upon me. My turn will come all too soon for you; see if it does not!—And as for you, proud minx—" wheeling back towards Mistress Mary with flaming eyes. But that was the last word he spoke in that room. My lord the Viscount sprang forward, and stood before him with such a noble anger and scorn in his face that the coward shrank back in affright, as though he feared a blow. But the Viscount's hand was never raised against him.

"Sir," he said, "you are protected by your sacred calling, little as you are worthy of it, and by the presence of ladies. But utter one more word of threatening, and you will be flung into the streets like the craven cur you are. You with impunity thought to insult and intimidate defenceless women. You have made a mistake, and out of this house you go at the bidding of its mistress without more ado. There is the door, sir. If you do not desire to go forth faster than you came in, go! I shall not speak twice."

Mr. Blewer's eyes seemed to flash baleful fire, but he did not pause or hesitate; he was gone before we had time to draw three breaths. The little maid was heard to slam and bolt the door behind him, but came to say that it was awful to hear him swearing on the other side.

"He will do us grievous hurt if he ever can," said Mrs. Musgrave, looking pale.

"He would have done that in any case," answered Miss Blake calmly; "he was always a wolf in sheep's clothing.—My Lord Vere, I give you great thanks for your action in this matter. It is only a coward who dares to threaten women. You showed him in all his cowardice as it was meet it should be shown him. Methinks he will come here no more, and that Mary will be safe from his persecution. That is a good step gained."

"But he will be an implacable foe to you, Reginald," breathed Mistress Mary, softly and timorously, so quickly do the moods of women change. "Oh, I trust he will never have power to harm you!"

"He will harm us all if he can," answered my lord quietly; "but we will not begin to fear him yet. Perchance he may find his own fate one of these days. It may not be given to him to hurt us. And now, ladies, I must wish you adieu. On the morrow, doubtless, we shall meet. We are embarked together upon a somewhat perilous voyage. God grant that we come at last to a fair haven!"

He took Mary in his arms and kissed her before us all, as though he felt it might be the last time. She clung to him half sobbing, half laughing, from excess of joy and sorrow mingled. The next minute we were once more in the streets, and I found myself saying in my heart, "I would that evil man had not come to mar the harmony of our evening. I would that so untoward a thing had not happened."

CHAPTER XV.

THE MAIDS OF TAUNTON.

I dreamed somewhat uneasy dreams all that night, and woke with a sense of oppression on my spirit; but the bright sunshine streaming in at the windows, the air of bustle and gaiety in the streets, the stir and activity of the house, and above all the feeling that my lord the Viscount was at hand to be waited on and considered, all served to put me into a happier frame of mind. As soon as I had performed some of my rougher duties, and seen to Blackbird and the other horses—for the men were as busy as ever with persons arriving to see the events of the day—I got myself into my holiday doublet as on yesterday, and went down to see if I could help the Viscount at his toilet.

But he was already up and out of his room, and I found him sitting in the parlour at breakfast, and my uncle standing beside him, talking earnestly with him. As I entered I heard these words spoken,—

"Thou hadst best go on as thou hast done hitherto, good Master Inn-Keeper. None can say that thou art slack in serving those who come from the Duke; but there is no need to put thyself forward in this matter. The less a man meddles in these affairs the better it often is for him. Do thy business with diligence, but make no profession, and do nothing to draw attention upon thyself. So thou mayest be safe in troubled days. The keeper of an inn is better placed than many; for none can well lay to his charge the sin of harbouring and entertaining rebels. A man must abide by his calling; and it were unreasonable to expect him to inquire into the business and opinions of all who come and go. Guard a discreet silence on these vexed questions, and walk warily as thou hast done hitherto, and thou mayest safely weather the coming storm. And keep an eye upon that nephew of thine, that he adventure himself not too nearly amongst the rebels. He has more courage than discretion, that lad; and it is sometimes safer to cultivate prudence rather than bravery."

But as I came in at that moment and both saw me, the Viscount stopped speaking, and smiled; whilst my uncle gave me a knowing look and went out, leaving me to finish waiting on the guest.

My lord, however, said nothing to me of what he and my uncle had been discussing, but finished his meal in some haste, saying that he must go to Captain Hucker's house to see the Duke, and learn what the day's duties were to be. I could gather from hints dropped by my lord that he thought the Duke was wrong in not pushing more resolutely forward whilst there was no enemy in his path. In lingering first at one place and then at another he was giving the enemy a better chance of mustering against him before he had made himself master of one important stronghold.

We men of Taunton thought much of our town; but, as the Viscount pointed out to me, it was useless for a garrison, since its walls and fortifications had been demolished. Bristol now would be a valuable place, and it was said that it would open its gates at once to the Duke; but unless he moved thither somewhat quicker, it was like enough that Lord Feversham might bring up his troops and intercept the Duke's on the way.

"If Fletcher had been with us, we should not be lingering thus," quoth my lord, as he girded on his sword and put on a plumed hat to-day instead of any head-piece; "but my lord Grey is all for tarrying and prudence, and methinks that this prudence will end in disaster erelong."

So the Viscount went off down the street on foot, followed by the admiring glances and the reverences of all the people. He replied to these very courteously; but I was grieved that all the brave show at Taunton and the welcome received did not make him more hopeful of the result of the great rising. However, there was but little time to think of these things, for already a mighty muster of towns-folk was assembling about the open space at our corner, and I well knew for what purpose they had thus assembled, and was in no mind not to be in the foremost rank of the spectators.

Will Wiseman came pushing towards me at the last moment, wriggling himself through the crowd like an eel, till he stood flushed and panting by my side.

"I would have come earlier," he said, "only I was called upon by so many to read them the Declarations of the Duke, which can be seen and read by all who know how. I have been at it this past hour. They be never satisfied, these good folks. As fast as one lot goes, another comes up to hear. But I say, Dicon, what has happened to our good friend and preacher Mr. Blewer? He is as yellow as a guinea this morning, as though all the gall in his nature had got into his face. I never saw a more spiteful and evil countenance in all my life. He came down the street, the people hooting him, albeit without offering him any indignity; and I asked him as he passed if it would please him to hear the Duke's Declaration, since I had not seen him at the reading in the Cornhill yesterday. He gave me such a look as would have turned milk sour in the pans, and he told me I should rue the day that I had chosen to insult him. He is an evil hound, and methinks he must be possessed of a devil. When the Duke comes into his own, I hope he will rid the country of such pestilent knaves. I would hang every one such at the cross-roads in chains, to be a warning and example to their fellows."

I whispered to Will the story of last night; to which he listened with infinite relish, and slapped his thigh in ecstasy to think how Mr. Blewer had been ejected from Miss Blake's house by the Viscount.

"Marry, but he will do him an ill turn if he can," he remarked, more gravely, at the end. "Dicon, I almost wish I might make an end of that vile man. I verily believe he will do one of us a hurt else."

But I shook my head. I could not counsel Will to commit a crime, even to save ourselves from possible peril. Perhaps he would meet the due reward of his evil ways without any act of ours.

And now the clocks were striking ten, and all other sounds were merged in the silence of expectancy, as upon the last stroke the door of Miss Blake's house opened slowly, and straightway there marched forth first the two schoolmistresses, clad in such a fashion as was appropriate to their years and calling; and after them more than a score of young maidens, all in white, headed by beauteous Mistress Mary; and each of these damsels bore in her hand one of the colours wrought by their united skill. Now at sight of this goodly procession the people broke into loud cheering, for the thing was one in which almost all had had a share; and though the dainty needlework was the handiwork of the maidens, yet the wherewithal had been found by the towns-folk, and the colours were borne by their own daughters and sisters and kinswomen: so that it was no wonder the whole place had turned out to see, nor that the appearance of the white-robed procession should be hailed with such a shout of welcome.

Miss Blake came first, and she carried no colour, but a small and curiously-bound Bible, and a naked sword with a finely-tempered blade and a hilt set with gems. Mrs. Musgrave waited till all the damsels had filed out, and took up her place in the rear. She carried nothing; and the seven-and-twenty colours were borne by seven-and-twenty young maidens, amongst whom were Lizzie Simpson, who looked blooming and intensely happy, Eliza Hucker, and the Herring sisters, and many others whose names I knew, albeit I will not set them down here, as they have no part in my story.

Mistress Mary was by many years older than these other damsels, most of whom were not aged more than ten or twelve years. She walked alone at the head of the procession, just behind Miss Blake, whilst the others followed in pairs behind her. Mistress Mary's dress was of some soft silken texture, very daintily and dexterously garnished with fair embroidery in silver. She wore a flowing veil over her beautiful hair, and upon her feet were dainty shoes of white embossed leather with silver buckles. Amongst many fair and graceful maidens she was fairest of all in her wondrous grace and dignity, and the golden banner that she held took all eyes; for not only were its size and

137

workmanship more imposing than the rest, but the device of the crown and the letters J.R. drew forth first the wonder and then the rapturous cheers of the spectators, as Will Wiseman shouted out, "J.R.—Jacobus Rex. Long live our new King James!" And although the people were half afraid to take up the cry themselves, yet they shouted might and main as the white-robed throng moved onwards, and following close in their wake, escorted them up to the door of Captain Hucker's house, where it was well seen that their coming was expected.

Gay as were all the houses in Taunton that day, it seemed as though the climax of welcome had been reached here. Flags floated from all the windows. Every window-frame was wreathed with garlands or greenery. The balconies were hung with crimson cloth. There was a great triumphal arch over the door, and to-day there had been laid down in the street before the porch one of those great carpets which were beginning now to be brought by merchants from the East, and which were said to cost fabulous sums of money, and scarce to be seen save in the houses of the nobility.

This carpet, however, made a little island as it were, upon which the crowd did not dare to set foot, but stood respectfully round to witness the proceedings in which such keen interest was taken.

Upon the approach of the ladies, the Duke appeared upon the top of the flight of steps leading up to the door, and with him were assembled a number of his officers and gentlemen, who stood behind him, but in view of the spectators. Miss Blake stepped forward with her book and her sword, and her maidens arranged themselves with simple and unconscious grace in a semicircle round her.

I would that my memory would serve me as well in recording the speech of the lady as it does in presenting before my mind's eye the spectacle of so much youth and beauty and virtue all gathered together to do honour to the champion of a noble cause. But although I know that the speech lacked neither in grace of diction nor in skill of delivery, all that I can remember of it was that Miss Blake besought the Duke's acceptance from his loyal town of Taunton of these colours for his army, telling him that every stitch had been set with a prayer for his success or an aspiration for the cause of liberty. And then when the maidens had waved their banners, and the crowd had raised such a shout as must I think have been heard a mile away, she proceeded to present the sword and the Bible, saying that it was for the sake of the true faith and liberty to read the Word of God and study it each in the way which was most acceptable and comprehensible that they welcomed him here to-day as a messenger from on high. She also added that with the sword he was begged to defend the Bible, so that his loyal subjects and followers might enjoy the blessings of peace, and cease to tremble before the ever-increasing faction of Popery, which had been raising its hydra head menacingly ever since the new King had sat upon the throne.

There was another tremendous outburst of cheering at that, and the Duke appeared transported by enthusiasm and ardour.

Making a step forward, he met the lady half-way up the flight, and taking from her hands (which he proceeded to kiss with courtly reverence) the sword and the book, he held both up before the eyes of the people and proclaimed in a loud voice,—

"Brave men and my very good friends and citizens of Taunton, I stand here amongst you pledged to a noble cause; and these two gifts which have been placed in my hands are fitting emblems of the work which shall be done, God helping the righteous cause. With this sword will I fight for the liberties of all subjects of this realm. I come now into the field with the set purpose to defend the truths contained in this book, and to seal it with my blood should there be occasion for it."

At the sound of these brave words women broke into weeping and blessing, and men into lusty shouts and cheers.

"God save the Duke! God bless and protect our noble Duke! A Monmouth! a Monmouth!" shouted the crowd.

The Duke bowed his thanks, saluted the lady once again, and pressing to his heart the book, gave it reverently into the keeping of one from the house, who carried it indoors. At the same time the Duke's charger was brought up just beyond the ring of white-robed maidens; and still holding the sword in his hand, he sprang gallantly upon its back, whilst at the same time his gentlemen stepped down and presented each his hand to one of the maidens, who remained standing with the colours as before.

Lord Grey was the first, and he gave his hand to Miss Blake, who was, in spite of her years, a personable lady, with much grace of bearing, and with fine eyes and good features. Lord Vere followed next, as his rank warranted, and gave his hand to Mistress Mary, whose face was dyed with a beautiful blush. Other gentlemen and officers followed, and each led by the hand one of the smiling maids, all of whom looked brimming over with joy and pride at the grandeur of their escort, and the brave show that was being made.

The procession having thus re-formed, and being headed by the gallant Duke, who kept his horse at a foot's pace, and paraded slowly onward, so that the crowd might drink its fill of the gay spectacle, proceeded leisurely onwards through the streets in the direction of the meadows where the troops had encamped for the night; and when we arrived there we found them all drawn up in companies, presenting, in spite of all drawbacks in the matter of arms and accoutrements, a right goodly and imposing show.

Colonel Wade had seen to this part of it, and had taken care to have in the foremost rank those men who were possessed of uniforms and proper arms, so that to our unaccustomed eyes the whole rank and file of the great army (for to us it looked mighty indeed) was as grand and as gay as the band of gentlemen surrounding the person of His Grace.

Three thousand men had come with the Duke to Taunton; but I think that five thousand must have already assembled beneath his banner in those meadows. I know that when he marched forth a couple of days later, it was with an army seven thousand strong. Every hour fresh men were pouring in, the militia deserting to him as fast as opportunity permitted. Truly it was an inspiriting and invigorating sight that greeted our eyes as we reached the meadow in the wake of the gallant procession of chivalry and beauty; and when the Duke rode from rank to rank, allotting the colours, and telling his soldiers the story of how they had been made and presented, the shouts and cheers that rang forth will scarce be forgotten by any that heard them; and the maidens received a right gallant thanksgiving from the soldiers, albeit somewhat noisily expressed.

A great concourse had gathered from far and near to behold the spectacle, and as I moved about the field my eyes were attracted by the flutter of a white kerchief. Looking more attentively at the owner of it (for it appeared to me to be waved with a purpose, and that to catch my eye), I saw beneath the closely-drawn hood, which almost hid her features, the bright eyes of Mistress Mary Bridges, albeit she was dressed in so homely a fashion, with a long grey cloak covering her gown, that, seated on a pillion as she was, behind a stout fellow who looked like a countryman, I should never have known her had it not been that I looked at her very closely.

Seeing that she had caught my eye, she waved her kerchief again, and I made my way up to her side as fast as I could.

"Mistress Mary," I whispered, wonderingly, for I knew her father to be a stanch supporter of the King in London, "how come you hither?"

"Hist, Dicon, thou wilt not betray me! I knew not how to keep away when all the world said there was such a brave show to be seen here, and I knew well what it all betided. I felt that I must see somewhat of it. I must see the Duke with mine own eyes, else I should never rest satisfied; and so I sallied forth in my long cloak and hood, and found my good foster-father going to the town. I made him take me up behind, and here I be. Dicon, the Duke is a right gallant gentleman, and I marvel not that the people love him. I would fain raise a shout for him myself. But yet I fear me that ill will come out of this day's gallant show. Dicon, I would whisper something in thine ear."

I came yet nearer still, and Mistress Mary leaned down to speak so that none could hear what was said.

"Dicon," she whispered, "when I hear them talk at home of what is like to follow this rising of the people if the King's troops are victorious, as my father says they will be anon, my heart is heavy with fear for those I have come to love in this town, and above all for my beautiful and beloved Mary Mead. Dicon, thou knowest that her banner is, of all others, like to give offence. It may be that she will be in greater peril than the rest. But be the peril what it may, I will give my right hand sooner than harm shall befall her. Dicon, thou lovest Mary, dost thou not?"

"I would lay down my life to save her!" I answered, with sudden energy. "Twice over would I give my life—once for love of her, and once for the love I bear my lord the Viscount, whose heart is bound up with hers."

Little Mistress Mary eyed me with approval. She too thought of the Viscount almost as I did, and regarded him as a very proper lover for her beloved friend.

"Dicon," she went on in a low tone, speaking in my ear, "thou dost know my home at Bishop's Hull, on the road to Wellington?"

"Yes, Mistress, I know it."

"Dost thou know the lane which leads into a thick wood, and a very marshy tract some two furlongs before you reach the gate to the house?"

"Yes; I have seen it, but never pursued it."

"My foster-parents have a cottage in that copse, so cunningly hidden, and so surrounded by the marshy land, that none save those who know the rights of the way can reach it save with great trouble and difficulty. I lived in that cottage for three years, my parents being absent, and my good foster-mother as good as a mother to me. I know every foot of the ground. My foster-mother will do anything that I ask her; and if peril should ever menace my Mary, take her thither without delay. She will be as safe hidden there as though the earth had opened to swallow her up. I have spoken to her of it, and she is ready and willing. No human foot ever invades the environs of their cottage, and the good folks themselves are retainers of my father, and safe from all chance of harm. Remember that Mary will be safe there, should harm come of this, should hurt menace her. It is in part to tell thee as much, and to give thee this charge, that I have made such shift to come hither to-day."

"Let me come back with you, Mistress Mary, and see the place," I answered her eagerly, for after the look I had seen upon Mr. Blewer's face only yesterday, I did truly think that Mistress Mary might stand in need of an asylum of refuge, even did the political storm pass by without hurting her; and the notion pleased the little lady well. I was on foot, but the distance was not great; and though the worthy countryman had to go into the city on his master's errand (he had not come to see the show, but had seen it, as it were, by an accident), he was glad to put his young mistress in my charge (the Snowes were well known and trusted throughout the countryside), and get her safe out of the throng. So when he had set her down a hundred yards away from the outskirts of the press, he bid us adieu and rode for the town; whilst Mistress Mary and I made our way by by-paths to the thick copse standing in the marsh (now almost dry after the long drought), and I was shown by what way the cottage could be approached even in the wettest season. We were made welcome to a homely dinner by Mistress Mary's foster-mother, who listened eagerly to all my tale of the Duke and the reception he had had, and promised to care for and hide and befriend Mistress Mary Mead, should ever the time come when she needed help.

CHAPTER XVI.

"THE TAUNTON KING."

Now although everything had looked so bright and gay since the arrival of the Duke at Taunton, and though his reception had been so cordial, and we unlettered folk began to think the cause already won, yet there were signs which to better-informed minds were ominous and discouraging; and it was noticed even by ourselves that from time to time a look of sadness would cloud the Duke's face, whilst for a few moments he would be lost in thought, and only rouse himself by an effort to respond to the joyous cheering of the crowd.

And not to be further tedious, I may as well state at once what was the main cause of this anxiety, and why it was that even thus early a presage of coming disaster seemed to fall upon the Duke.

When first it had been put into his mind to invade England in the cause of liberty and justice, he had strenuously refused, saying that he had had enough of the strife of factions, and that since his father had left him no charge, he would henceforth remain as he was, a private gentleman, leading a private life in some foreign city. But he had been persuaded that half England would join his standard if he did but show himself, that it was his duty to assert his rights and stand forth as the champion of the rights of the people; and when the Earl of Argyll had sailed for Scotland to stir up a rebellion there, he had promised to follow to England in a few days, and gather round him there all who would join the cause of liberty and Protestantism.

Nevertheless he had passed his word to the Earl that he came not as King, but as the supporter of the Commonwealth, and that it was some such form of government that he should establish were he to be successful. It will be remembered that in the Declaration made first at Lyme, and afterwards read in other places, it was fully stated that he did not insist upon his title as yet, but left that matter to be decided by a Parliament fairly chosen from the people; although he declared that he was a legitimate son of the late King, and could prove as much should need arise.

Directly upon his landing, as I have been told, there were those about him who desired that he should cause himself to be proclaimed King; but he refused, saying that it was contrary to his pledges and to his Declaration—which no man could deny.

But many days had now passed, and instead of the whole of the West Country flocking to him in a body, only the humbler amongst the people had come forward. Not one single gentleman with a following of servants and retainers had placed himself under his standard. The Viscount was the only man of rank who had joined him since his landing, and he came alone and unattended, in defiance of his father's wishes and conviction, and more from personal desire to be quit of the perplexities of his position than from sympathy for the cause. Rustics and yokels came flocking in, as has been shown, and the militiamen likewise by hundreds. But it was too significant a fact that the gentry stood absolutely aloof; and even Mr. Trenchard, who had made brave promises beforehand, and who was known to be forward in the cause of liberty, had betaken himself suddenly to France—a thing which had caused the Duke not a little discomfort and sorrow.

Soon after his landing, two messengers had come in hot haste from London with the news that things were ripe for a revolt there, and that Colonel Danvers was only waiting for the signal of the insurrection in the West to raise the whole city in the Duke's favour. This, together with the expectation, everywhere rife, that Cheshire was on the point of breaking into open rebellion, had cheered his spirits greatly, as had also the brave reception he had met on his route to Taunton. But nothing more had been heard of the rising in London. Many of his followers, who best knew the character of the man, told him plainly that Colonel Danvers was a time-server and hypocrite, and that no reliance could be placed upon him; whilst as day after day went by and still no men of any mark came forward, every person about him began to feel that matters were growing serious.

I have to explain all this at some length in order to make it to be understood why, after his declaration to the contrary, the Duke at last permitted himself to be proclaimed King, to the great joy of the citizens of Taunton, who had desired it from the very first.

It was urged upon him vehemently now that the reason why the gentlemen stood aloof from his cause, even whilst heartily hating and distrusting the reigning King, was partly because they hated the name of Commonwealth even more, and would not take up arms in any cause that did not promise the continuance of the monarchical system; partly because, as things were now, there was too much peril for his followers, and that in case of disaster they were all dead men.

Now at first sight it may seem strange that such should be the case. One might naturally suppose that the peril would be greater to those who followed him (in the case of defeat) if he had proclaimed himself King; but men who understood the law said that this was not so. And they further explained their words to the unlettered by telling us that there was a statute made in the reign of King Henry the Seventh (who, it will be remembered, obtained his crown by force of arms) sheltering all those persons who should obey a king who was king *de facto*, as it was termed, even though he should not be a king *de juro*. And I understand by this that a king *de facto* is one who, like the Duke, comes with a great following, and for the time being proclaiming himself king, and being obeyed as one, does exercise royal prerogative, although in law he may be no monarch, and may never live to wear a crown. If therefore those who obey such a king could shelter themselves behind this statute, it would naturally give men courage to join the standard. For instead of being considered mere rebels following an obscure insurrection, they would be following one who was for the time being their king.

This is what was argued upon one side, whilst others said that if the Duke once took such a step he would make the breach between himself and his uncle irreconcilable, and seal his own doom in case misfortune attended him. But the Duke answered to such words that for himself he cared nothing, that his desire in all things was to do what was right and best for his followers, and that he would abide by the counsel of the majority of his advisers.

There were other matters to discuss also to-day in the council of war which was held after the grand spectacle of the giving of the colours which I have described. It was now known that the Duke of Albemarle was following hard after the rebel army, and that he was either at Wellington or not far away. Scouts had even come in to say he was marching upon Taunton, but that had proved untrue. The question arose as to whether the Duke's army should march back and give battle to him as early as possible, or march on towards Bristol, which, if once captured, would be a weighty prize in the hands of the party; for it would give him a basis of operations which he never could have so long as no garrison town was in his hands.

Whether what was decided was wise or the reverse, I cannot say, having no knowledge of such matters; but I was told by the Viscount that evening, when he returned to his quarters from the council, that it had been decided to march in a northerly direction, and that probably the move would be made on Sunday. It was now Friday night, and when I asked why not to-morrow, since time seemed of much importance in these matters, one of his curious smiles passed over the Viscount's face, and he replied significantly.

"To-morrow is needed for another matter. To-morrow will give to us a new King James."

Then, with a thrill of intense excitement, I realized what was about to happen, and I quickly ran out into the streets to spread the news. It was known already in many quarters, and the town was alive with citizens all crowding together and talking of the coming event. Nothing but approval reigned in Taunton. We were proud to think that our town would be honoured by being the one in which the new King should be first proclaimed. Mistress Mary Mead's banner, although her own workmanship and design, did but reflect in its legend the feelings and opinions of the citizens.

All night long the good folks were up, renewing the wreaths in their windows, and adding to the festive appearance of their city. And when soon after break of day the heralds went about giving notice that all loyal subjects were invited to attend at the Market Cross in the Cornhill to the proclamation to be made, the press of people gathering there was almost greater than even upon the day previous; whilst the windows which gave upon the place were crowded to suffocation, and the city seemed again to have gone mad with joy.

Several magistrates were there as on Thursday, wearing their gowns, and striving to conduct themselves in such a fashion as should give no cause of offence to either side. I believe they were forced out of fear to be present, lest they should be torn to pieces by the populace; but it was against the grain with many to appear, and as soon as they were able they withdrew, and hid themselves in their houses so long as the new King remained in the city.

The Duke was mounted upon his charger, and surrounded by his small band of gentlemen, as usual. His face was pale, I thought, and although he returned the vociferous salutations of the crowd with his usual courtly grace, I thought there was an air of anxiety and restlessness about him, and in my heart I doubted if he himself desired this honour which was thrust upon him.

Places of honour near to the Duke and his *cortége* had been reserved for Miss Blake and her white-robed maidens, who appeared once more before the eyes of Taunton. I noted that Viscount Vere shifted his position a little so that he stood very close to Mistress Mary Mead, and I think that they had some minutes of conversation together from time to time. At any rate their eyes must often have met, and I suppose that the language of the eyes is often full of eloquence, and says as much as the tongue can do.

After a great blowing of trumpets and the usual preliminaries, the proclamation was read in loud tones by Mr. Tyley, who stood upon the steps of the Market Cross to do so; and whilst he read a deep silence fell upon the listening crowd, who drank in every word with eager avidity:—

"Whereas, upon the decease of our Sovereign Lord Charles the Second, the right of succession to the Crown of England, Scotland, France, and Ireland, with the dominions and territories thereunto belonging, did legally descend and devolve upon the most illustrious and high-born Prince James Duke of Monmouth, son and heir apparent to the said King Charles; but James Duke of York (taking advantage of the absence of the said James Duke of Monmouth beyond the seas) did first cause the said late King to be poisoned, and immediately thereupon did usurp and invade the Crown, and doth continue so to do: We therefore, the noblemen, gentlemen, and commons at present assembled, in the names of ourselves and of all the loyal and Protestant noblemen, gentlemen, and commons of England, in pursuance of our duty and allegiance, and for the delivering of the Kingdom from Popery, tyranny, and oppression, do recognize, publish, and proclaim the said high and mighty Prince James Duke of Monmouth our lawful and rightful Sovereign and King, by the name of James the Second, by the Grace of God King of England, Scotland, France, and Ireland, Defender of the Faith.

GOD SAVE THE KING.

Proclaimed at Taunton, the twentieth day of June 1685."

What cheers and shouts went up from the people as the last words were read!

"God save the King!"—"God save the King!" Men shouted themselves hoarse, women fell a-weeping, and thanked God aloud amid their tears for sending them such a deliverer. Children, held aloft in their fathers' arms, flung posies and wreaths at the feet of the newly-made King; whilst Miss Blake, at the head of her pupils, stepped forward to claim the privilege of being first to kiss the hand of royalty.

All the maidens followed in turn, and the King, after permitting each to kiss his hand, saluted them upon the cheek, as was the custom of the day, though from royalty a marvellous condescension. Then after the white-robed procession of virgins had retired within their own doors, followed by the cheers and good wishes of the people, the Duke was beset by a loving crowd of men and women, all desiring to kiss his hand and do homage to him; whilst from the church towers the bells pealed forth, and that very day in the evening service he was prayed for as King. Mothers with children afflicted by the King's Evil brought them to him to be touched, and I heard that many were thus cured in a few days, though I speak from hearsay and not of mine own knowledge, having more to think of than the matter of the children.

Our hearts were made glad to-day likewise by the arrival of Colonel Basset, one of Cromwell's captains, who came in with a company that he himself had raised. This looked indeed as though good were to come out of this step; yet men said that the Colonel looked ill pleased when he heard of the proclamation just made, being far more in favour himself of the setting up of a Commonwealth.

Thus it may well be seen how hard it is to please all men; and every step gives offence in some quarters, however it may be desired in others.

Another man of some note who joined the Duke here was one Colonel Perrot, from Southwark near London. Men whispered of him that he had been concerned in that extraordinary attempt of Blood's upon the crown and regalia; but as I know not the details of that story, and as it has no concern with the present narrative, I will say no more of it. Colonel Perrot was warmly welcomed, and thought to be an addition to our staff of officers; of which, indeed, we stood in need, so many thousands of common people having flocked to the standard at Taunton.

And now the Duke, being proclaimed King, and so acknowledged throughout the town, sent forth almost at once other proclamations which were eagerly read by the people. The first set a sum of money upon the head of the usurping James of York; the second declared the present Parliament a seditious assembly; a third commanded all men to refrain from paying any taxes levied by the Duke of York; and a fourth declared the Duke of Albemarle and many others rebels, and authorized all loyal subjects to wage war upon them till they were destroyed.

Each proclamation was received with enthusiasm and joy by the people, and Will Wiseman was kept busy until his voice gave out in reading them to all who desired to hear. Such bold words seemed to augur success; and as we said one to another, the Duke would not make such sounding phrases, nor breathe forth such threatenings and slaughter, did he not know himself prepared to carry on the war to a successful issue.

It was soon known also that our King had sent letters both to the Duke of Albemarle and to Lord Churchill commanding them to lay down their arms; and we did not doubt that this would greatly perturb and alarm those generals, who must be by this time finding out the temper of the people, and how little they could depend upon their soldiers to fight against their new King.

But the day was not to be one of entire joy and triumph, for as evening drew on there began to be some fresh commotion in the streets; and running forth to see what it might mean, I found people looking scared and grave, whilst women began to cry out,—

"The Duke of Albemarle is coming! We shall be destroyed! Our town will be demolished! There will be a terrible and bloody battle ere nightfall. God have mercy on us all!"

And amongst these cries I heard several whisper, as though half ashamed of their own words, as well indeed they might be,—

"Would to Heaven he had not come! We had at least peace before. Now no man can say what will become of us!"

In a state of some alarm and more indignation—for it seemed to me a coward trick thus to speak because the hour of danger might be near; but then women have no stomach for fighting, and perhaps mean not the half of what they say —I ran towards the field where the army was encamped, thinking I should get the news soonest there. As I did so I met my lord the Viscount coming towards the town, looking grave and thoughtful, but with no haste or urgency in his manner; and when his eye fell on me he paused and smiled.

"Is there to be a battle, my lord?" I cried, panting in my haste. "In the town they say the Duke's army is upon us. The people seem in a sudden fright. Hath aught of hurt befallen?"

"Nothing of grave moment," answered the Viscount. "A few men of ours have been killed not far from Chard, whither they had gone to reconnoitre. They were fallen upon by a body of the enemy's horse, and some were killed, whilst the rest rode back thither post-haste. But the Duke and Lord Churchill are generals of no mean valour, and their close proximity to the town has decided the Duke—nay, I must now say the King" (and a smile passed over his face that was beyond my power to read)—"to leave Taunton on the morrow, and seek to reach Bristol as soon as possible. If we can find entrance there and make it our own, all may go well for the time; but if we fail in that, it were better to face our enemies now at once, than go forward with them hanging on our rear, and Lord Feversham and Colonel Kirke in front."

"But, my lord, how can we fail, with all the country flocking to the King's standard?"

"My good Dicon," answered the Viscount, "dost thou not know that already we have exhausted our supply of arms, and the recruits who would fain join our muster have perforce to be sent back, because we have nothing wherewith to equip them? Hast not heard yet that one of our frigates sailed away with Colonel Fletcher, after the mischance at Lyme, and that the other two have been seized upon by our enemies, and such arms as they contained have all been lost to us? If gentlemen with armed retainers will now join us, they will be gladly welcomed; but for unarmed country yokels—why, we have enough and to spare of such. We are now forced to send them back to their own homes; nor do I think the cause loses much by so doing. It is not with such forces as these that the kingdoms of the world are won."

"But others will join now that the Duke is made King!" I cried eagerly, having heard some of the reasons for that step.

"We shall see," answered the Viscount, with his peculiar smile. "At present it seemeth to me that we have succeeded in disgusting the advocates of Commonwealth and republican opinion without winning those whom we have sought."

"But, my lord, it is but a few hours."

"Right, Dicon. I speak not from what has happened——or not happened—in these few hours, but from my own knowledge of the world I come from. A King proclaimed in Taunton forsooth—at the head of five thousand scythe-armed rustics! A wondrous thing indeed! A right royal personage! Dicon, Dicon, methinks the Duke of Monmouth might have won some following, for men are deeply discontented with the rule of the tyrant James; but they will not raise a finger for a puppet-king—the King of a rabble of low-born knaves and varlets! I speak not these words of scorn of mine own self; I do but rehearse what will be the words in the mouths of those gentlemen from whom such brave things are expected. Ferguson, Wade, Hucker—they know no better; but my Lord Grey should have lifted his voice against it. It is a blunder we can never repair now; but methinks it will be the death-blow to the cause."

"My lord, my lord, say not so! All Taunton is rejoicing. All Taunton will stand by His Majesty to the death!"

"Is that so, Dicon? thou wilt see erelong. I think it would not take much misfortune to turn Taunton back to her grudging loyalty to the present King."

"O my lord, Taunton has ever been true to the cause of liberty!"

"Ay, but not to the cause of monarchy. There is the rub. The King is now pledged to rule as a monarch; and methinks Taunton has been dreaming all this while of a Commonwealth."

"But, my lord, think how they greeted the King to-day!"

"True, carried away by love for him, and the excitement of the hour. Well, Dicon, thou mayest know thy towns-folk better than I do. Yet I misdoubt me if Taunton will long lift her voice for her new-made King; and I would that there had been less of pageant within her boundaries, and that it had been some other place which had given him such royal honours. I would that those colours had never been worked and presented in Taunton, and that my Mary had had no hand in the matter."

"Dost think harm will come to her, my lord?" I asked anxiously.

"If this rebellion, or revolution, or what you good folks choose to call it, come to naught, I verily believe that a signal vengeance will be taken by the outraged monarch; and if so, the town of Taunton, thou mayest be sure, will be one to win for herself the first place in the royal disfavour. Dicon, hast thou ever seen the Lord Chief-Justice Jeffreys? He came on circuit not so long since in the West. Didst thou see him then?"

"No, my lord," I answered, slightly shivering at the name of one who was held in terror and execration by all dissenters in the West of England. "It so chanced that when he came I was on a visit to my father's farm. I heard of him when he had gone."

"Dicon," said the Viscount gravely, "if thou hadst seen that man, thou wouldst have felt that thou hadst seen the devil incarnate. If ever the spirit of a devil looked out of human eyes, it does so from the eyes of that man. And, Dicon, he stands high in the King's favour. If a cruel and bloody piece of work has to be done, it will be my Lord Chief-Justice Jeffreys who will be sent to do it. When I think that my peerless Mary may in the days to come be brought face to face with that monster, my blood freezes in my veins with horror. Dicon, I am too deeply implicated now to be of use to her, and she may need a protector in the days to come." He broke off suddenly, biting his lips, as though to subdue an inward agitation, and then he suddenly began again, "Boy, I think that thou dost love me?"

"My lord, I would die for you if I might save you from peril!" And in truth I meant what I said, for it is easy to think and speak of death when the peril is far off. It is another matter when it seems to be looking you in the face; but then I did not know that, and spoke in all sincerity.

My lord smiled, and put his hand for a moment on my shoulder—a thing which sent the blood tingling through my veins.

"I ask none such sacrifice as that, good Dicon," he said. "My life is of none such great value; yet I believe in thy good-will, boy, and I thank thee for it. Thou lovest me, I know well, and methinks that thou dost love my gentle lady too?"

"My lord, I would die for her too," I answered, not able to think of any other way of expressing the devotion I felt.

"Good," he answered; "to die in such sweet service would not, methinks, be hard. Yet I would not have thee die, good Dicon, but live to serve and perchance to save her. Boy, I lay this charge upon thee; and if thou lovest me thou wilt perform it faithfully, in so far as it may be possible. When the issue of this insurrection is known, and if that issue be disaster to this new King's cause, and that peril threaten Taunton and Mary, and I am unable to help or succour her, then do thou watch over her with all such care and diligence as is possible to thee. Guard her from harm if such a thing may be; and strive at all risk to save her from the evil power of Mr. Blewer, if he should seek (as is like enough) to advantage himself by the winning of her hand and her fortune when there be none to defend her from him. It may not be possible, Dicon, that thou canst do this; yet thou hast a shrewd wit, and thou livest so nigh at hand that thou mayest be able to contrive what another could not do. Wilt thou at least take this charge from me, and seek to fulfil it by every means in thy power?"

And with a heart swelling with pride and devotion I answered, "I will, my lord."

CHAPTER XVII.

ON THE WAR-PATH.

"Uncle, I cannot help it! I will do nothing to injure any who bear my name! I will change that name if needs be—but I must go! I cannot stay behind, knowing nothing of what is happening save what the voice of rumour whispers. I must see and know for myself. None shall be hurt through me. But prithee let me go. It may be that I will be able to send thee word of things that thou wouldst fain know. Hinder me not, good uncle, for needs must that I fare forth with the King!"

My uncle regarded me reflectively and gravely, as I poured forth these words early upon the Sunday morning that had so little of Sabbath stillness in the air. I had been up and about already, although the day was yet young. I had heard that the camp was to be broken up forthwith, and a march made towards Bridgewater. The thought of seeing the King and all his soldiers march away, and of remaining behind in the city a prey to all sorts of fancied terrors, and in suspense as to what might be happening elsewhere, seemed intolerable to me. The fever of war had got into my blood, and though I knew I could never be a soldier, I felt that I must needs see war, or I should die of disappointment.

Perhaps my uncle felt sympathy with me; more possibly he thought that such a hot partisan of the new-made King was more of a peril to him in his house than following upon the path of the soldiers in that mob which always waits upon the steps of an army. There few would know or take note of me. Here I was known by pretty well every one in the city. If I was resolved upon throwing in my lot with the army, I might be in less peril myself and cause less danger to others there than in the town of Taunton. So after steadily regarding me for a while, and revolving the matter slowly in his mind, after his fashion, he answered,—

"Well, well, well, a wilful lad will go his own way. Thou must e'en choose thine own path, Dicon. I will not keep thee here against thy will, but I counsel thee not to run into greater danger than needs must be. We may all be in peril of our lives for all I know ere this matter be settled; and where the greater danger lies Heaven knows and not I. Wherefore take thine own way, but use all prudence and caution. Thou hast a good head of thine own, and quick wits when thou dost use them aright. See that thou walkest as warily as may be in the perilous days that be like to fall upon us."

"I will be careful, I will be wary," I answered eagerly. And in great excitement and joy at having so easily won my uncle's good-will, I ran to tell Meg and Will Wiseman, and then to groom and feed Blackbird, and decide what to take with me in my saddle-bags; for I knew little as to what might lie before me, but desired to be at charges with no man, and to pay for everything that I might need.

Meg, whose heart was almost as much in the cause as mine, gave me some crown pieces out of her store for my needs, and my aunt did the like. I had money of mine own too, and some of this I took; yet I would not dip too deeply into my hoard, because I had a feeling that I must keep it for other needs than mine own. Should evil days fall upon us, and should I have cause to keep the pledge I had made to my lord the Viscount, I might need the golden guineas I had earned bit by bit by my letter-writing, and so forth, and had stored away so carefully these two past years in a secret receptacle of mine own. The silver coins I took with me, but the golden guineas I left where they were. A few groats would go far to keep me; to say nothing of shillings and crowns, of which I had many. But gold might prove a peril, and I would none of it.

Out into the streets I went next, to find the citizens in hot discussion together, and not all of them well pleased at what was doing. There were many amongst them who had confidently hoped that before the Duke left he would have raised up fortifications around the city, have built up the ancient walls, and left there a garrison to keep and defend the place for him.

Colonel Hucker was the centre of this group, and he was speaking warmly in favour of this thing.

"What use to the cause is a city without walls?" he was asking. "Why, if we march out to-day, the Duke of Albemarle can march in to-morrow, and none can let or hinder him!" [And in very truth that was just what did happen, for the new King's army left on Sunday afternoon, and the Duke of Albemarle was in the city on Tuesday, albeit he made no long stay, but continued his pursuit of our army towards the north.] "What we want is to leave behind us garrisoned cities holding for his Majesty. If one King can pull down fortifications, surely another can build them up! Taunton has held her own gallantly in times of war, and has stood notable sieges in a good cause; nor has the temper of her citizens changed. Give her but walls and towers and a few good soldiers to lead and direct her citizens, and she would hold out as gallantly as ever. What do you say, fellow-townsmen? Shall not Taunton be restored to her former glories? Can she not do even as she did before?"

"Ay, ay; that she can."—"Give us walls and soldiers, and we will show the usurping tyrant what Taunton can do."—"Where is the King? Let him but give the word, and every man among us will become for the nonce a stonemason, that we may begin to build our walls afresh!"

Such were the cries of the citizens, and such their enthusiasm in the cause. There is nothing so catching as the martial fever, except it be the panic which sometimes sets in afterwards. But though the zeal of the city was great, the young King could not be brought to see the matter as Colonel Hucker sought to show it him. He said there was no time to build walls—which was true enough—and that he could not spare men to garrison it if it were fortified even in a most hasty and rapid way.

Colonel Hucker, who had looked to be made captain of the garrison and Keeper of the City, was not a little disappointed, and all Taunton with him; but there was too much right on the King's side for us to urge the matter beyond a certain point; and as the Viscount said to me, as we rode out at last towards Bridgewater,—

"If we can once secure Bristol, there we shall have a fortified city at our command forthwith. That is the task we should set ourselves to do without delay. Would that we were already before its walls! These delays will be the undoing of us, I fear. Already has the King in London had ten days in which to muster and send forces out west. Had we been quicker, we might have had a fortress of our own already. Heaven send there be no more such tardiness!"

My Lord Vere was one of those men who seem to be soldiers born. He had not had the training and experience of some of the others, including our new King himself, yet it seemed to me that if his counsels had but been followed from the first we should have been marching to victory now, and making the usurper shake upon his tottering throne. As we rode along I could not but tell my lord of the witch we had visited, and of what she had told us. I hoped that it might give him more heart (for I knew by many signs that he thought the enterprise well-nigh desperate), but he only gave me one of his curious smiles.

"A wise woman truly, Dicon, to foresee more blood than glory in this undertaking."

"Nay, but, good my lord, she said that the usurper would die in exile. How may that be, if our gracious King be not victorious?"

"It may be that thou wilt live to see such a thing one day, Dicon," answered my lord, "and yet not see King Monmouth on the throne. Knowest thou not that there be men who have already fixed their eyes upon the Prince of Orange, husband to the King's daughter, as a possible saviour and deliverer? The witch knows more of such things, I trow, than thou dost, boy, in spite of all thy learning."

"The witch hath a familiar who tells her what the future will bring forth," I answered quickly, for I liked not to hear my learning compared with that of an ignorant old woman, who would be nothing without her familiar. And at that my lord smiled again, but said nothing; and indeed I forgot the whole matter next moment, for we saw approaching us from behind, in hot haste, Lord Lonsdale himself, whose face wore a look of such anxiety and pain that I was quite sorry for him.

Now it so chanced that the Viscount was not with his company at this time. He had been detained by some duty which the King had set him to do, and had not been able to leave the camp so soon as the soldiers. This was the reason why, when he came riding after us a little later, he had drawn rein upon seeing me on the outskirts of the crowd of followers, and had paused to ask what I did there, and to gently chide me for my folly in leaving a safe shelter for the uncertainties of war.

It was whilst we were riding together thus in the rear, having by this time left behind the crowd who pressed after us on foot—Will Wiseman amongst them, to see the last of us—that we heard the sound of these hasty pursuing horse-hoofs, and turning round beheld Lord Lonsdale riding apace after us. I thought the Viscount's face changed and hardened slightly as he saw his father; but he drew rein and waited till he came up.

"My son, my son," began Lord Lonsdale, in whose face and voice anger and anxious fear seemed to be struggling together, "what madness, what folly is this? A son of mine to be in arms with a rebel Duke, daring to lay claim to the crown of England! Vere, Vere, you are not like these ignorant rustics whom any one can delude by a specious tale. You know that England will never submit to see a base-born King sitting upon the throne. Be the present King never so much the tyrant, he rules by his hereditary right; and you know that this young Duke has no more chance of being England's King than thou hast thyself. Boy, thou canst not look me in the face and tell me that thy heart is in the cause! I know thee too well for that!"

Lord Vere made no attempt to meet this challenge, although he looked his father unflinchingly in the face for all that.

"Sir," he said, in a low, resolute voice, "your remonstrances come too late. I have unsheathed my sword in the cause, be it a good or an evil one; and honour forbids me to sheathe it again until that cause is either lost or won. You know well who and what drove me forth to break a bondage that had become unendurable. If I give you pain now, it is only because you have driven me to it!"

"Boy, boy, what folly is this! Why didst thou not tell me how thine heart was bound up in that maid?"

"I told you many times, sir, that my heart was so bound up with Mary Mead's that death itself would be preferable to life without her. I said all that a man could say, and my reward was that I was made by strategy to appear in public as the plighted husband of Mistress Edith Portman. It was your hand that severed the bond of mutual confidence which once existed between us. I have no more to say. I follow in the steps of one to whom I have done homage as King."

"Vere, Vere, Vere!" cried the agitated father, almost in tears, as it seemed to me, his face pale with agitation, "only come back with me, only give up this mad folly, and thou shalt wed the girl when thou willest. I will say no word against it. Anything is better than that thou shouldst put a halter round thine own neck. Come but back with me, and all shall be as thou desirest!"

There was sadness now in the Viscount's face—sadness and even a little bitterness—but no sign of wavering.

"Sir, it is too late," he answered. "Hadst thou spoken those words but ten short days ago, I would gladly have followed thee home, and given to thee a sweeter daughter than son has ever given to father yet. But it is too late now. Mine honour is pledged, and not even for the sake of my duty towards you nor my love towards the lady can I lay aside that honour and break my plighted word. Nay, were I to do so my lady would be the first to cry shame upon me. She is a soldier's daughter, and holds honour in more esteem than life itself. A deserter from the cause so near her heart would find no favour with her. She might have let love win the day had I not taken up arms for this young King—"

"King!" breathed Lord Lonsdale, in a tone only just audible, but full of bitter scorn; "knowest thou what he is called—he and his army—by all loyal and honest folk? 'King Scott and his vagabonds' is the name he goes by. My son, my son, to think thou shouldst be following such an one as he!"

The Viscount's face wore a look half sad and half bitter—like his voice when he spoke.

"Yes, it seemeth strange sometimes even to me; but there be strange shifts in a man's life, and a Viscount may sometimes come to be ranked amongst vagabonds. Father," and here his tone changed and became softer, "believe me, I am not ungrateful for your care and thought for me, and it pains me to give you pain. But I cannot go back now. I would things had been different with me; but since they are not—since I have been driven to this step—I cannot and I will not draw back. If you lose your only son by a traitor's death, it will be a grievous sorrow to you, I wot well. But even if things go ill with us, there will be many that may hope to escape with life. Perchance I will be one of these. For my Mary's sake as well as yours I shall make a battle for my life."

Lord Lonsdale would have stayed to reason longer, but his son shook his head as though to say that argument was useless, as indeed it was when both father and son thought really alike upon the question, and only a sense of honour bound Lord Vere to the cause he never professed to believe in with his heart or soul.

"Farewell, father," he said softly, and put out his hand; but the Earl drew back with a look of such pain as I shall not soon forget.

"I may not touch the hand of a rebel," he said; and so father and son parted with more bitterness and sorrow than I like to think of even now.

My lord was very grave and silent for a long time after this, as indeed he well might be, but presently rode on ahead of me to join the army.

As for me, I could please myself what I did and what pace I travelled at. The infantry had gone on in advance that morning, and had covered the distance well. I thought that they would reach Bridgewater easily by nightfall, and I decided that for my part I would stop for the night at my own home and tell all the news there.

I was a little depressed by what I had heard between Lord Lonsdale and his son, and perhaps it had slightly damped my enthusiasm in the cause. I began to see that war could be a very hideous and evil thing, and I almost found it in my heart to wish that the Viscount had consented to return with his father, and marry Mistress Mary Mead forthwith, thus saving both (as I trusted it would) from all future perils. I knew that I loved and honoured him for his words, and for ranking honour above life and happiness, and I well knew that could Mistress Mary have been there she would have upheld him with all the earnestness and enthusiasm of her nature. I was resolved that she should one day hear the story, and know what a noble heart she had won; but just for the moment I was sorrowful and sad, and I thought that the welcomes of my family would prove a pleasant diversion for my grief.

Nor was I mistaken. I found all the house in a great stir, my mother more hot and bustling and excited than I had ever seen her; for it seemed that the Duke (I find it hard to say King as I should; wherefore I think in the future I will still call him the Duke, although for many days we all of us gave him the royal title, and were proud and glad to do so) and his company had paused at the farmstead, and had asked refreshment there. His handsome face and courteous ways had won all hearts. My mother and sisters could talk of nothing but his beauty and grace. They had refused all payment for what they had set before him, and he had kissed my mother ere leaving, and set her all in a flutter of excitement. To have been kissed by a King was an honour which none of her friends or relations had ever received. She felt lifted into a region beyond that of her daily life.

I was pounced upon for news, and made to talk the whole of the day and far into the night—a thing very foreign to our home ways—so that when at last I gained my couch I slept as soundly as a dormouse, and was ashamed to find the sun high in the sky when I awoke.

Although my parents and brothers and sisters intermeddled not with such troublous matters as the rightful succession of Kings, and so forth, their hearts were all for the gallant young Duke, and I received a handsome addition to my small stock of money from my father, who bid me good-speed on my journey and a safe and prosperous return. All the country side in these parts believed that the cause of the Duke would be crowned with glory and success; and it was amusing to hear their stories as to how they had evaded giving any help, and put hindrances in the way of those who were on the royal side, but how they did everything to speed the cause of the Duke.

Blackbird was somewhat heavily laden as we started forth to Bridgewater, for my mother was in sore fear lest I should not find enough to eat on the road, and she would fain have hung all manner of things around my saddle, had I not declared that I should be the laughing-stock of all the army.

Then with many adieus I rode off, and was not long in finding my way to Bridgewater, where, as I have before stated, I had another uncle with whom I was familiarly acquainted.

It really seemed to me as I rode into the town that Bridgewater had striven to outdo Taunton in the welcome she gave the Duke. I heard that already he had been proclaimed King there; that the proclamation had been read in great state, the magistrates in their gowns standing by, and, as I also heard, not unwillingly either. Flags were flying, and windows and balconies were decked as in our town, whilst the faces of the people looked as gay and happy as though no such thing as doubt or fear existed.

I made my way with all speed to my uncle's house, which I found as busy as was like to be on such a day. My kinsfolk had scarce time to give me a welcome; but I set about making myself of use to them, and in so doing picked up many a piece of news of a welcome nature.

It seemed that although the recruits were still of the lower class of the people, much money had been collected for the cause in this place, and that the Duke and his officers were in better spirits on that account, and also because of the warmth with which they had been welcomed.

The citizens and common people were beginning to think scorn of those above them, who showed themselves so backward in the good cause, and to whisper amongst themselves upon the subject.

"We wonder the gentlemen come not in," they began to say. "But we will show them that we can do the work without them; and then when we are the masters we will have their estates!"

That evening, as I wandered through the streets of Bridgewater, I suddenly met Lord Vere walking rapidly and hurriedly, with a preoccupied look upon his face. Seeing him thus thoughtful, I was drawing aside—for I feared to presume upon that kindness which he had ever shown me—when he suddenly saw me and paused.

"Ha, Dicon!" he said, "I was just wondering where thou wert to be found. I want speech with thee, boy."

I was at his side in a moment, eager and flattered by his words.

"The matter is this, Dicon," continued my lord, speaking rapidly and in a low voice:—"Thou knowest enough of matters in the camp to understand that it is of the greatest moment for us to win Bristol. If we fail there, I see naught for it but to be destroyed between the two armies which are marching upon us— the Duke of Albemarle in our rear, and Lord Feversham and perchance Lord Churchill (for there are contrary reports brought in daily and hourly) in front, or marching from the eastward. We hear that the people of Bristol are anxiously awaiting us; but even of this there seems no certainty, for they say, too, that the Duke of Beaufort with a large body of troops has recently come into the city to hold it for the King—the King in London, Dicon—and that we shall find it a tough nut to crack. All agree in saying that if once we can get possession of it we shall find arms and money and provision in abundance, and shall have achieved the first step towards a lasting success. But the question is whether we may find entrance there, and if so what will be the wisest plan of attack; and there be few men here who know the city and have friends therein who may be trusted."

"They say Colonel Wade is from Bristol," I remarked; and the Viscount nodded assent.

"He is; but he cannot be spared from the counsels of the Duke. In fine, Dicon, what I have offered to do is to ride alone, or with but one trusty servant at most, into Bristol myself, to see certain men of the city with whom I have some acquaintance, and to learn how matters be there. I am then to return and advise the Duke what he should do; for never was man so beset before with counsellors all advocating different views, and sure never had general such a strange company of captains under him, scarce a man of them trained to war, and some scarce knowing how to handle arms!"

"You are going to Bristol then, my lord?"

"Yes: I shall start with the first light of dawn to-morrow, which will be shortly after three o'clock; and I have sought thee, Dicon, to know if thou wilt be mine esquire for the nonce and ride with me. That black pony of thine will carry thee bravely and well, as I know; and there be few of the steeds our men have of which I could say the same. Thou hast no air of martial valour to raise suspicion. I shall but appear like a traveller upon the road with my servant behind me. I think we shall not be in danger's way till our errand is done, and —"

"My lord, I would follow you to the world's end, be the dangers never so great!" I cried, my heart swelling with pride that he had made choice of me out of all the company in that great army. "I have been longing this many a day to do some service either for you or for our gracious young King. Let me go with you. I will serve you as no servant would, and lay down my life for you if need be."

He smiled at my protestation, and answered kindly,—

"I trust that may not be needful, good Dicon; but if thou wilt thou shalt serve me in this thing. Canst meet me then here in this spot by three of the clock to-morrow morning? Good! I shall look for thee. See to thy steed to-night, for we must travel with all speed. I shall strive to reach Bristol to-morrow, and as early in the day as the distance will permit."

"I will not fail you, my lord," I answered proudly, my heart beating high within me. "And shall we return to the army when you have fulfilled your errand? Shall we see the fight when the foe is before us?"

"Truly I think we shall, Dicon," answered my lord with a smile. "The enemy seems in small haste to attack us; but whether that be a good or an evil sign I wot not. Yes, boy, I mean to be in the thick of that fight whenever it does take place;" and his eyes shone for a moment from beneath their bent brows with the battle light which the thought of action brings into the faces of all true soldiers. "I too would bear my share in that fight, as I see thou wouldst too. But I doubt not we shall be in time for that. It is not fighting, it is this delay, these pageants and proclamations, which sicken me. Would we were intrenched before Bristol now, doing and daring all, instead of trusting that some great thing will come to us. Well, boy, thou and I will see what is like to be our fate in that city. To-morrow before sunrising; and Heaven give us a good journey!"

CHAPTER XVIII.

IN PERIL IN A STRANGE CITY.

Of our long day's ride from Bridgewater to Bristol I do not purpose to speak in detail, being anxious to get on to more stirring scenes; and yet it was upon this day that I began to understand somewhat more clearly the nature of the enterprise on which we were embarked, and to see that the progress of the Duke was not much longer to be a march of unmixed triumph.

As we pursued our journey, sometimes along the roads, sometimes across open tracts of country, where Blackbird's cleverness and sagacity gave us great help in picking our way, we encountered bands of stern-faced men riding along with an air of purpose—men clad in such armour as was worn by regular soldiers, and showing in their air and bearing a martial bravery which was greatly lacking in the ranks I had lately seen.

These men looked at us with sharp glances as they passed; but our appearance was so harmless that nothing was said to us of a disquieting character. Sometimes we were asked if we had seen aught of "King Scott's army;" and though the gibe in the voice of the questioner made my cheek flame, my lord would answer quietly enough that he believed it to be encamped somewhere near to Bridgewater.

Once we journeyed some little distance with a party of these men. The commanding officer rode with the Viscount in front, and a couple of the troopers, who were greatly taken by Blackbird, and would fain know his history, came and rode beside me. I learned from them that they were on the way to Bristol to join the garrison there. They had been sent by the Duke of Albemarle, who was advancing upon Taunton, but had had to make a wide circuit to avoid the army of "King Scott" at Bridgewater, and were glad to fall in with travellers upon the waste of moorland, being but little acquainted with the country.

I asked them why they spoke of the Duke of Monmouth as "King Scott;" and they laughed, and said that he had forfeited his right to the title of Duke by his act of high treason. They told me that since his marriage, when quite a lad, he had taken the name of his noble wife, wanting one of his own, and that that name was Scott. They jeered and gibed at him and his feeble insurrection in a fashion that made my heart beat fast with mingled wrath and fear, and kept me in constant dread of betraying myself by some unguarded word. But for my lord's sake I strove for patience and discretion; and being accounted but a boy, and a hunchback to boot, I misdoubt if any words of mine would have been taken seriously by the troopers who rode for a time with us.

Still I was glad when they left us; and though my lord's face was the graver after they had gone, he did not tell me aught that had passed betwixt him and the captain. Indeed a heavy rain began falling soon, which, though sorely needed by the country after the long drought, was not a pleasant thing for travellers, and made us wrap ourselves in our mantles and draw our hats over our brows, and so pick our way with care and pains.

It had long been dark, and the rain was pouring down steadily and pitilessly, and our good horses were growing weary and jaded before the lights of Bristol flashed through the night, cheering us into a better pace than we had been able to get out of the horses for the past hour. The road too became better, and our hearts revived within us; but still I can remember little of our arrival at that great city, I was so dazed and wearied and confused by the long journey and the strangeness of everything about me.

There were a halt and a parley at the gate ere we got in, but my lord seemed to have no great trouble in obtaining entrance; and soon we found ourselves at a snug little hostelry, where there was good accommodation to be had for both man and beast, and where we were soon seated at a table set before a grand fire, the damp rising in clouds from our wet garments as we buckled to over our trenchers and ate as only men do who have fasted many hours, and travelled far to boot.

Our host waited himself upon us, many of his people having already gone to bed, and he was full of the rebellion, and the excitement prevailing in the city. He was very cautious for a while in telling us what was the feeling within the walls; but my lord had a way with him which quickly won the confidence of those with whom he spoke, and by-and-by I woke up from the doze into which I had fallen to find our host whispering many things to my lord with an air of eager secrecy. He said that the people were very discontented with the present King and with the Parliament, with the way in which justice was administered, and, above all, with the spirit of persecution which was springing up.

"If the Duke had but landed here or marched here straight," continued the man, in a husky whisper, "the town would have been his almost without the striking of a blow. But now His Grace of Beaufort has come in with the regulars, and they say the Earl of Feversham is close at hand, and may be looked for to-morrow or the next day. What can the citizens do when the iron hand of the army is at their throat? If only he had come sooner!"

Interesting as all this was to me, I was too weary to listen to more, and in fact was taken with such a fit of shivering that my teeth chattered in my head, and it was with much difficulty that I dragged myself up the stairs to bed, pulled off my wet clothes, and crept in there. My lord came himself to see me, and brought me a hot spiced posset, which, as soon as I had drunk it, sent me off into a sounder sleep than I think I ever slept before; for when I awoke again I found that the next day had slipped quite away, and that it was evening of Tuesday, and I had lain abed like a log when I had meant to be up and about after any business my lord might give me to do.

I arose in a great shame, and finding my clothes dried and brushed by my bedside, I dressed with what speed I might, and went below.

The room was filled with people of the lower sort, all talking together in excitement and heat. I sat in a corner and ate a piece of bread whilst I listened to all that was being said, and strove to gain knowledge of what had happened during the day.

One thing I heard which troubled me much. Lord Feversham had entered the city with a large body of troops—two hundred and fifty horse-guards, as I learned later. But there was more than this; for I heard, too, that the bridge over the great river Severn had been broken down by the Earl's men at Keynsham, so that it should be impossible for the Duke of Monmouth's army to approach the city.

This was very bad news for me, and, as it seemed, for the people also. In this place, at least, there was no hesitation as to which rule was preferred—that of the Popish King on the throne, or that of the champion of liberty and Protestantism come to wage war upon him. If men spoke with bated breath of the coming deliverer, it was not because they were half-hearted in the cause; and here and there a voice would be raised to ask why, if all the citizens were agreed, the soldiers could not be outnumbered and overawed? why the will of the people should not prevail over some few thousands of hired mercenaries, who at heart most like did not love the King better than the towns-folk?

These high sounding-words were taken up and passed from mouth to mouth; but yet I could see that none knew how concerted action amongst the citizens could be begun now that the town was guarded by soldiers and a close watch set about the walls and even in the streets. Yet as the night drew on other men kept dropping in, and it was whispered that the Duke of Monmouth was after all approaching; that some of the horse had already reached Pensford; that another day might bring them beneath the walls of Bristol; and that then would be the moment for all the city to rise.

I listened with beating heart and straining ears to all this, wondering what the truth of it might be, and if indeed the city would open its gate to our new-made King. Presently I ventured to enter into conversation with some of those nearest to me, and told how I had been in Taunton when Monmouth had been proclaimed King. This excited great interest in the minds of those about, and I was made to tell the story out aloud, whilst the people listened with mouths agape, and I could see by their eager faces how they longed to see him proclaimed here in Bristol.

Presently, however, some soldiers came marching in and ordered wine. They looked about upon the people with an air of suspicion and severity which quickly changed the aspect of the assembly. First one group and then another broke up and went out, and in a short time there were scarce half-a-dozen persons left.

"Your good customers seem mightily afraid of a buff jerkin and a musket, landlord," remarked one of the soldiers as he drained his goblet. "Have a care that you harbour not seditious malcontents in your house, or it may chance to go ill with you one of these days."

And then the soldiers clattered out, having probably done what they came to do; whilst the landlord's face, which had been pale and submissive in presence of the troopers, grew dark with fear and hatred.

"Those cursed soldiers!" he hissed beneath his breath. "A man goes in fear of his life and his property when the city is beset with them."

"Heaven send us a speedy deliverer!" breathed another, with clinched hand and frowning brows. "All the city would rise to greet him, I verily believe—soldiers or no soldiers!"

Late at night the Viscount came in, and told me something of how his day had been spent. It was quite true that the citizens were as much in favour of the Duke here as in the other places where we had seen the welcome they gave him. But the presence of a strong garrison and a determined Commander put a very different face upon the matter in this fortified town. The garrison had possession of the walls and citadel, and could turn their arms upon the towns-people as well as upon the foe if there were any tumult or rising. Some were in favour of stirring up a revolt within the walls so soon as the Duke should be without, engaging the soldiers in defence of their gates and ramparts; but men who knew as much of war as the Viscount were doubtful whether such a rising would be attended with success. There was something in the presence of regular troops which acted as an effectual check to burgher risings. A panic quickly set in at the sight of cold steel and the remorseless action of trained soldiery. Forty years of peace had weakened the warlike traditions of the past generation who remembered the civil war.

"Citizens talk, and speak great swelling words, but too often they run like sheep at the first sight of pike and musket," said my lord; and when I remembered how the crowd in this very room had dispersed like a mist before the handful of troopers who had come into their midst, just after having spoken such great things of defying the army, I could not but think that he was in the right.

Next day I too wandered about the streets of the great city, full of curiosity and amaze at what I saw. I had never been within a fortified town, and the frowning walls and gateways struck me with awe and amaze, as did also the great quays and wharfs where vessels larger than any I had ever seen lay at anchor. And nothing would content me but that I must go aboard of one, which I did through the kindness of a sailing-master with whom I got into talk; and I spent two wonderful hours amongst the shipping, both hearing tell of the wonders of the deep, and learning something of the desire amongst seafaring men for a better King upon the throne, and the hope that the Duke of Monmouth would "come into his own."

I asked whether, if there were to be fighting around Bristol, there were any ships that would help the cause of the Duke by firing upon, or in any way injuring, the soldiers; but he did not seem to think that there were any vessels in the harbour that could be trusted to do any good that way. There had been a close watch kept on all vessels coming into the river, and some had been sent to the right-about, and not suffered to make the harbour.

Towards sundown I retraced my way towards the hostelry where we were lodging, when I was suddenly brought up short by a most unwelcome sight. I was aware that a pair of dark sinister eyes were steadily regarding me; and looking to see whose they might be, I encountered the malevolent gaze of the Rev. Mr. Blewer, whom I believed to be far away in Taunton.

I can scarce say why it was that this gaze troubled me so, but I felt a sensation as though some person had walked over my grave (as the saying is); and I was not made any more comfortable by seeing that Mr. Blewer immediately beckoned to a sentry who was standing near and pointed me out to him, though what words he spoke I could not hear.

I found myself trembling all over as I walked onwards, and I railed at myself for proving nothing but a coward. I was relieved when I got in to find the Viscount there before me, to whom I told what I had seen.

But he only smiled, and said,—

"I am well pleased that that pestilent fellow is far away from Taunton and from Mary. I doubt if he would gain speech of her now were he never so near; but I would sooner he were anywhere else than there."

"But can he do hurt to me or to you, my lord?" I asked, rather anxiously; and was answered by a smile of amusement.

"It is like enough he might if he set himself to it; but we shall not be here much longer. I have found out all I came to discover; and if it be true, as men say, that the Duke will be at Pensford to-night with his whole army, we will join him early and give him the intelligence he seeks. Thou hadst best go to thy bed early, Dicon, for this may be the last night for many that thou wilt have a bed to sleep in. Are our horses in fettle for the road to-morrow? We must be astir right early, and leave the city with the dawn."

"The horses are as well as ever they were, my lord; they have been shod afresh, and well fared and cared for. They will carry us another fifty miles to-morrow if needs be."

"Nay, it will be but a short way we need take them; but perchance they, like ourselves, will fare only badly for a while. Time will show—time will show. Get thee to bed now, Dicon, and be ready for the start to-morrow."

I went to bed, little dreaming of any further adventure that night; and I suppose I had slept for some hours, when I was awakened by such a tumult in the street below as made me spring up in a sudden fright, and I heard men shouting out in every key and tone,—

"The Duke! the Duke! He has come! he has come! God be praised! Our deliverer is here!"

Although there was no moon in the sky, in which the rain-clouds still hung heavily, albeit it was not raining that night, my room was almost as light as day with a red glare that spoke of fire. I was up and into my clothes faster than I can write all this down, and I dashed across to my lord's room, to find it already empty—he having been still up and dressed when the first shout was raised, so that he was in the streets before me.

Down I rushed, all the household being awake and alarmed, and the door standing open like half the doors in the town, as I hurried along not knowing whither I went, but only agog for news.

The people were all running and shouting, and the great palpitating glare in the sky lighted the whole city, and gave a weird brilliance to the strange scene. All the time the streets were echoing to the cry,—

"The Duke! the Duke! To arms, citizens, to arms! The Duke has come! Down with tyranny and Popery! Down with the usurper! A Monmouth! a Monmouth for the people!"

"Where is he? What has happened? Where is the Duke?" I asked, first of one and then of another. At first none heeded me, but others taking up the question, we began to get answers bit by bit.

"He is here! He is coming! That is the beacon light to bring him! Perchance he is beneath the walls! He may be entering the city even now! Hark! is not that the sound of arms? He is coming! he is coming! Heaven be praised, our deliverer is at hand!"

The people seemed to have gone well-nigh mad. I never saw such a sight in my life as the streets of this city with all the men and women swarming out, shouting, weeping, crying, praying, and the great red cloud swaying over us in the black sky, and at last the steady tramp of mailed troopers swinging along down the wide thoroughfare.

"The soldiers! the soldiers! Pray Heaven it be the Duke's men!" shrieked the women. But the next moment the cry went up, "The King's troops! the King's troops! Have a care, citizens! Hist! hist!"

They came swinging along with their great pikes menacingly pointed at the crowds, which dispersed and fled before them; whilst at intervals a halt was called, and a voice from their midst rang out in a threatening word of warning,—

"To your beds, citizens; to your homes and your beds. The Duke of Beaufort makes it known through all the city, that if there be any rising this night for the rebel Duke of Monmouth, he will fire the town about your ears in a hundred places at once. Take your choice, men of Bristol, take your choice. Either disperse in quiet to your homes, or see yourselves, your houses, and your children burned before your eyes!"

A horrified silence fell upon the people as these words were heard; and only one woman dared to raise her voice to ask, "But where is the Duke of Monmouth?"

"Ten miles away if a step, woman, and with a swollen river without bridge 'twixt him and Bristol.—To your homes and your beds, good people, if you wish to save yourselves and your city to-night."

Away swung the soldiers, to give their dread message in other places; and away to their homes scuttled the cowed citizens, led by their trembling wives; whilst news came that there were twenty companies of foot drawn up in Redcliffe Mead, ready at a moment's notice to march through the streets and fire the rebellious city if it should prove troublesome. Another report said that the fire was in the river; that a ship there had caught light either by accident or by design; and that had it not been high tide, with plenty of water in the harbour, so that other vessels could sheer off, there might have been a fearful destruction amongst the craft lying there.

"Some miscreant of the Monmouth faction did the damage," said one party of soldiers parading the streets to keep and enforce order. "Spies from the rebel camp have been seen prowling about the streets to-day, and along the wharfs. Let us but catch them, and their heads will adorn the city gate by the time the day dawns."

At these words I shrank into the shadow of a doorway, with my heart thumping against my ribs as though it would burst out of them. I did not doubt for a moment that I was reckoned as one of these spies, and perhaps my lord for another. If Mr. Blewer had seen him he would not forget it, and would take advantage of any incident to raise a tumult against him. I realized the fact that we stood in no small jeopardy so long as we remained in Bristol; and my first thought was to seek the shelter of the hostelry, to get ready our horses, and then strive by what method we could best escape from those environing walls. It was a terrible thing to think of having to pass the sentries if we were under suspicion. But I trusted that my lord, who knew the city and had friends there, would have some plan for escape; and to go home and await him there seemed the best and wisest course to pursue.

I wished the streets had been a little more full now—that the citizens had not been so easily cowed and scared back to their homes; then I should have had a better chance of slipping through the crowd and making my way unseen. Still, as it was, one of the sides of the street was in deep shadow, and I was flitting warily along in it, when suddenly I heard a sound in front like that of shouting and pursuit. The next moment round the corner, as if with wings to his feet, came my lord the Viscount, hatless, and with his doublet half torn off his back, his breath coming in deep gasps, his hair streaming in the wind, looking like a golden cloud where the red firelight touched it.

The moment I saw that sight, before the pursuers had rounded the corner, I sprang out upon him, as one who joined the hue and cry. I felt as though every muscle in my body had suddenly turned to steel. I seized him by the hand, and darted with him down a narrow entry that I had noted that day in coming up from the river.

"My lord, my lord! this way, this way!" I gasped in his ear, not knowing whither we were speeding, but perceiving that we were in a labyrinth of small back streets which might baffle pursuit for a time. We fled onwards, although I was certain that I had heard a hoarse cry raised from behind,—

"There goes the other of them! Now we shall have them both! After them! they cannot escape! After them, men! ten pounds to the man that brings them, dead or alive!"

I do not think my lord heard, his breath was coming in such deep and laboured gasps. He let me turn and double whither I would; and I think that I had the greater skill to baffle pursuit, having a more lively fear in my heart, perhaps, and knowing something of the ways of wild things when running for their lives.

But still I could hear cries and shouts following us, and that word of evil omen, "The spies! the spies!" and I wondered whether we should be able to escape them after all, when we suddenly dived down a dark entry, and were brought up short by a house that stood at the end, blocking all egress, and as it were enclosing us in a trap.

"Heaven help us, we are lost!" I cried in despair, realizing that to return the way we had come would probably throw us into the very arms of our pursuers, who had scattered hither and thither, and could be heard coming nearer and nearer. My lord spoke no word, being indeed past speech, but I saw his hand go to the hilt of his sword, which he still wore, and I knew that he at least would sell his life dearly. But then all of a sudden a door behind us opened cautiously, and a woman looked out.

"Come in, come in quick!" she said. "This way! along this passage—mind the holes in the floor—and up yon stair. Go up and up and up to the top, and out upon the leads. There's an open trap; but ye can shut and bolt it, and give yourselves a few moments' grace. There's a mile of leads up there, and spouts and gutters leading from place to place. I'll keep them here in parley as long as I can. Hide yourselves somewhere in the holes or behind the chimney-stacks. Men have hidden away there before now and escaped. If ye be from Monmouth's army, ye shall not die in Bristol town if Jenny can save you."

"Heaven reward you!" I cried, as I darted along the passage and up the stairs, my lord after me; but he paused to ask the woman if she ran no risk herself ere he would go (which shows the difference there is between gentle blood and blood like mine; for I thought only of my own skin, whilst he had thought to spare for her), and I heard her words come clear and mocking,—

"They shan't hurt me—nay, not a bit of it! I'm too well known for that. Not a man of them would lay a hand on old Jenny; and I'll say I was knocked down by a pair of insolent, swaggering fellows, who have made their way out of yon window at the back. Some will go up to the leads for all that, but some will stay below and search the courts behind. I know the ways of them; and if there be but two or three to follow you, slay them one by one as they slip and scramble over the roofs. Oh, it is rare sport, it is rare sport! I have seen the likes of it before."

The woman's uncouth speech and mocking laugh baffle description. I almost shuddered at her words whilst hurrying up the rotten stairs and pushing open the trap-door at the top. The next minute we were both out in the free air upon the leads, with the fading glow of the fire very near at hand; and we bolted down the trap and made it as firm as we could before we spoke a word.

"At least we have a chance of our lives now, Dicon," said my lord; "and if we have to lay them down, we will at least sell them as dearly as may be."

He drew his sword half out of its sheath, and his eyes glittered in the glow of the fire. I felt a curious thrill run through me as I heard and saw him, and I felt that to-night I was to receive my baptism of blood.

CHAPTER XIX.

A BAPTISM OF BLOOD.

For the moment we were safe, but only for the moment. From what the old woman had said, we knew that our pursuers would soon be after us; and there was another peril of which I had not thought till my lord's voice spoke in my ear,—

"If the woman has played us false, we may be in a trap from which there is no escape. But at least it was certain death to remain there."

I felt a cold shudder run through me as I said,—

"I do not think she was tricking us, my lord."

And he answered in the same low voice,—

"Neither do I; but such things have been before. We must be on our guard. Walk warily, Dicon. These leaden roofs are treacherous. Yet what a labyrinth they form. Methinks we can baffle pursuit yet! See, lad! we are not far from the river. It may be we shall make shift to find our way out from the city by water. Canst swim, Dicon?"

"Ay, verily; better than I can run."

"Good; yet thou didst run manfully just now with those hell-hounds after us. Dicon, thou knowest that our enemy Mr. Blewer is in the town?"

"Ay, my lord."

"It was he who set them on at me for a spy. He thought to have rid himself thus easily of a rival and a foe. It may be he will do so even yet; but if I die to-night, I sell my life dear!"

He spoke through his shut teeth, and I felt the strange quiver, that was half like fear and half like exultation, run down my spine again. All this while we were rapidly picking our way along the leads and roofs, lighted by the glow of the burning ship upon the river, which I had no time to stay and look at, as I fain would have done; for the question of life and death was paramount with us, and it was no moment for pausing to admire the blood-red river like a flaming mirror, nor the strange fantastic shadows cast by the leaping flames. We were glad of the light for making our own way amongst the leads and chimney-stacks and along narrow parapets, where a false step would have been destruction; but all the while our ears were strained for the sound of hammering and pursuing footsteps, and we knew that as soon as we heard them we must crouch down in some of the many deep niches and hiding-places of that strange region, else would the brilliant light lead to our instant discovery.

All the while we moved my lord kept casting his eyes hither and thither, and at last I heard him exclaim,—

"Hist, Dicon! they are after us. And here is the very place for us. In with thee, boy! There is room for thee, I trow. I will follow and guard the entrance. He shall pay dear who seeks to hale us thence."

My lord spoke through his shut teeth, and I was quaking all over as I looked about, yet could see nothing like a hiding-place. But the Viscount's eyes had been sharper than mine, and the next moment he pushed me gently but firmly into a narrow, narrow niche between two great chimney-stacks—a long black crevice filled with masonry at the farther end, looking like a mere slit in the wall, and in which, unless I had tried, I would not have believed that I or any other man could stand. But the crevice widened a little after I had pushed myself into it; and it was in the deepest of deep shadow, for the dark chimney-stacks rose high above our heads, and the narrow, narrow aperture by which we had squeezed ourselves in faced away from the river, so that not a single shaft of light crept into our retreat.

I drew a gasping breath of relief as I found myself at the far end of the niche, with ample room to turn round and move my arms; and I said to my lord, "Surely we are safe now." And he made answer, "Unless they know the place, perchance we are; but even so it will go hard to oust us. Methinks I could hold the entrance against a score of enemies, and run every one of them through as he approached."

And in truth only one man could approach the place at a time, as I saw very well; and it made me think of the story I had read in Roman history of the passage of the bridge that was kept by Horatius and his two supporters. The Viscount was to me as great a hero as any in the pages of history or romance, and well could I picture him holding this place against the onslaught of a hundred foes.

But the next minute all thoughts save those of a personal nature were lost in the overwhelming trembling fear which assailed me as I heard the sound of hurried tramping all along the leads, voices calling one to the other, and brutal threats shouted out to the accompaniment of brutal laughter.

Although the heavy masonry in which I was enclosed hindered me from catching every word, yet I could well follow the drift of what was said, and well did I understand that a long rope and a short shrift was the best we could hope for were we caught. Once I heard a soldier in passing say to his comrade,—

"The clergyman promised a liberal reward to whatever man would show him the head of the dainty gentleman. We'll have him and get the reward. I'll run him through with my own sword—I've no pity on a spy."

All the place seemed alive with searching soldiers, shouting one to another— sometimes bawling out that they were here or there, sometimes cursing loudly at having been deceived by a shadow. Some declared they saw them getting down by a spout, and a rush would be made to this side or that. Others vowed they had got away from this block altogether, and would be found elsewhere; and they would fall to cursing this region of house-roofs and chimneys, which it seemed had favoured the escape of fugitives before now, as indeed the old woman had implied.

I cowered against the wall, quaking in every limb. I must needs tell the truth, even if I am dubbed coward for it. Sometimes the voices were so near that it seemed as though we must be discovered; then again they would move further off, and I began to breathe once more, till some fresh footstep again brought my heart into my mouth. I felt then as if anything would be better than to be trapped like this without hope of escape; but when the footstep had passed by again, I felt thankful for the protection of the friendly niche, which plainly was not known to the soldiers.

Gradually the sounds of pursuit died away. Voices angry and disappointed called one to another that we must have taken to the lower roofs, or that old Jenny had been right in saying we had got out by a window, and had not taken to the leads at all. Cursing and swearing, the men appeared to draw off, and I was just about to approach nearer to my lord, who had remained all this while close to the entrance of our retreat, his drawn sword in his hand, when I was deterred by the sound of a new footfall coming steadily onwards. This footfall did not pass by our niche, and against the lightness of the sky beyond I saw outlined a tall martial figure, and knew that this last soldier had noticed this chink in the masonry, and was speculating about it as he passed by.

"A likely place," I heard him mutter, "but an ugly one to enter alone. Where are the rest? Have all gone? A pretty search they have made. I will call them back."

Thump, thump, thump went my heart against my ribs. In spite of its clangour I heard a sound which I knew was just the beginning of a shout that would have the effect of bringing the scattered searchers all rushing back to this place. But one slight hoarse note was all that was uttered. With a quick rush my lord had sprung out, sword in hand. There followed for two or three seconds the sound of clashing blades, another effort at a call, and then the thud of a heavy fall, and a gurgling noise, which I shall never forget to my dying day. In the dead silence which followed I heard my lord speaking in a low voice.

"You can come out, Dicon; I think all is safe now."

I came out trembling and giddy. There upon the leads, run through the heart by a swift sword-thrust from my lord, lay the man who had been a second or two before full of strength and life. His glazing eyes were upturned to the sky; his tall form lay so still that I could not bear to look at it. I had never seen a man killed before, and the horror of the thing was stronger upon me at that moment than the relief of our escape. My lord was binding with his scarf a gash upon his wrist. That sight brought me out of my stupor, and I asked leave to help him, though my hands trembled, and I was clumsy at fastening the knot. I saw my lord look at me with something of a smile upon his pale, resolute face.

"Warfare is a grim thing, Dicon. Thou hast scarce the stomach for it yet. But, boy, thou wilt see grimmer things yet, I take it, if thou dost hold to thy purpose of following the Duke's army. Such things as these are scarce the beginning of horrors. Come now, we must not linger here. I reckon we shall be safer to seek old Jenny in the house now than to linger longer on these leads, where soldiers may be posted watching and spying. Go cautiously, Dicon, and keep in the shadow. Belike the woman will not be far off."

This surmise proved a true one, and before we had retraced our steps we saw the creeping form of old Jenny coming towards us.

"Hist!" she whispered; "ye have done well to hide and outwit them. Ye are safer here now than anywhere. How many did ye slay? Only one? I would it had been a score! Better luck to ye next time! Now, follow me, and I'll take ye safe to the water-side, and put ye in a boat that'll land ye further up the river, where ye may find your way to the Duke. Tell him that all loyal folks in the city will rise for him if he will but bring his army to the walls. Who cares if the soldiers do fire the city? Fire means plunder! Who cares for danger where plunder is to be had? We'll fling the cursed soldiers into the flames they have kindled, to roast there as they deserve; and for us there will be plunder—plunder—plunder!" and the old hag waved her arms wildly over her head, and looked the very embodiment of some fury breathing out curses and threatenings of coming doom.

"The Duke shall hear all that I have learned," answered my lord, "and he shall know that we owe our lives to you, my good woman. But set not your heart too much upon seeing him here; for Bristol with its present garrison will be a hard nut to crack, and the Duke has few guns, and fewer men who know how to handle them."

The woman had wrapped us each in a heavy cloak, which disguised the cut of our garments, and bidding us follow her, she glided through the house once more and out into the street, where it was now very dark. She passed us, I scarce know how, through a little postern door giving upon the river, where, at the sound of a whistle, a boat quickly appeared out of the darkness, and she held a parley with the man who held the oars.

"He will take ye as far as a mile beyond the walls," she said, "and ye will give him a gold piece for his pains. They say the Duke is at Keynsham, building up the bridge. Ye'll find him there right enow."

"But our horses, our horses!" I said anxiously, being loath indeed to part from Blackbird. And when old Jenny learned where the nags and our belongings were to be found, she nodded her head many times, and said at last,—

"If they be at honest Job Candy's, I'll get them thence directly it is dawn, and bring them to ye by the wood ye'll see on your right when ye leave the boat. Never fear, sirs; old Jenny never fails to keep her word. Farewell to you, and a good voyage. I'll see ye again before many hours have passed."

She slipped away into the darkness, ignoring the outstretched hand of my lord, which would have pressed a golden guinea upon her.

"Don't linger, sir," said the gruff voice of the boatman; and the next moment we were speeding up stream with the last of the flood-tide, the man being anxious to land us at the appointed spot before the strong ebb should make his task a hard one.

I had never been on so wondrous wide a river, and looked about me with awe as the boat flitted along in the shadows. The burning ship farther down towards the mouth of the great tidal stream had drawn all traffic away from the upper reaches. Ships had weighed anchor and sheered away into the wider reaches, to make sure of escape should the fire spread; whilst small craft had gone to help the burning vessel, and left this part of the river quiet and lonely. The fire was still burning, but not fiercely. The ship looked like a phantom one of glowing flame, reflected double in the sullen water, and illumining the other vessels in the river with a sombre brilliance. I had never seen such a sight in my life before, and could not take my eyes off it. When at last we rounded a bend in the river which hid the fire from view, I saw the first faint tinge of red stealing into the eastern sky, and knew that another day had dawned, and that we were alive to welcome it, as once I had scarce believed we should be.

The walls of the city seemed to be slowly sinking behind us. The tide grew slack, and began to turn. Our boatman looked over his shoulder and pointed towards a wooded hill not far from the left bank of the river, which was on our right hand as we sat facing him in the stern; and we gathered from his uncouth words that he was about to land us there, and that we were to wait in the wood for Jenny and our horses.

Ten minutes later we stepped ashore, and the Viscount gave the man his appointed dole, together with words of thanks and courtesy, which seemed almost thrown away on such a fellow. It was beginning then to get light, and I saw that my lord's face was ashy pale, and that the bandage we had made for his arm was soaked through with blood.

It seemed that our rough boatman had noted as much as that, for he gave me a look, and then jerked his thumb in a certain direction; and following the direction of his glance, I saw a little wreath of smoke curling up through the trees, and gathered that we should find some sort of a dwelling-place there.

Nor was I disappointed, for when my lord had dragged his faltering steps a few furlongs, we came in sight of a thatched cabin belonging to a woman; and when I knocked at the door and asked admittance, saying that we had been forced to fly from Bristol by the King's soldiers, and were on our way to the Duke's army, we were welcomed with open arms.

The wood fire on the hearth was made bright and cheery with faggots from the store; and albeit there was nothing in the house but rye bread and milk, and a little hard cheese, yet the milk, made hot, brought the colour back to my lord's wan cheek; and we soon stanched his wound, which was not deep, and bound it up afresh, so that it hindered him but little in the use of his arm.

We were both somewhat spent by our night's peril and fatigue, and I quickly fell asleep by the fire, and slept for several hours without once waking. When I did open my eyes, it was to find the rain pouring down, the fire in the cabin burning cheerily, and my lord sitting at the table with his head resting on his hand, lost in serious reflection.

As I started up he smiled at me kindly. His face was still pale, but he was not otherwise changed.

"Awake, boy," he said, "and ready for a march? Old Jenny has not failed us; and our horses are in the shed hard by, refreshed by their rest in the city. The good folks here declare the army to be no further than Keynsham; and say that the bridge was mended yesterday, and that the Duke will be passing over to the Gloucester side of the river to-day. We had better join him as soon as may be, if indeed thou wouldest not rather go home than see more of the perils of war."

I felt that I had not distinguished myself in my first adventure, and my face burned with shame, although I knew my lord had no thought of mocking me. I stood up and said resolutely,—

"If you are going back, my lord, I go with you."

"I have no choice," he answered gravely; "I am pledged to the cause. I have my company to lead into action. But the case is different with thee, Dicon; bethink thee well."

"I have thought of everything, my lord," I answered. "I go not back unless it be with you."

"Thou art an obstinate lad, Dicon," said my lord, with a smile; "yet I like thee the better for thy stubbornness. Then if thy mind is made up, let us forth without loss of time. If we wait for the skies to smile again, we may have long to tarry."

We had soon thanked and rewarded and said farewell to our hosts, and were in the saddle once more. Travelling was becoming bad by reason of the persistent rain, albeit the land sorely needed it. I wondered how it had fared with our soldiers, and whether the cold and the wet had damped at all their martial ardour.

It was but some seven miles, I take it, from where we started to the bridge at Keynsham, or Cansham as some write it; and long before we reached the spot we knew that the army was nigh at hand, because all the people of the scattered villages were going forth to see, and we saw horsemen scouring the country in search of provisions wherewith to feed the men. Sheep and oxen were being driven towards the camp, and though in the main payment was made for what was taken, yet there were some amongst the farmers and peasants whose faces were dark and lowering, and who muttered that a bad King was better than an army on the march.

The bridge over the river at Keynsham, which the enemy had broken down, had been repaired by Captain Tyler with skill and despatch; already the Duke and his gentlemen had passed over it, and the rest of the army was following when we got up. Pressing on after the Duke's party, we were not long in coming up with it. Then I fell into the rear, and mingled with the men: whilst my lord went straight to His Grace, and was welcomed very graciously, as I heard.

The news which I brought from the city, despite the favourable feeling of the common people, did not seem to the soldiers to be very encouraging. They shook their heads when they heard of the Duke of Beaufort's threat, and more than one veteran who had seen something of war in Holland, from which country they had come over with the Duke, said that in a walled and garrisoned city the towns-folk were helpless as sheep if the soldiers kept true to their leaders; and so far as we had heard, there had been no disaffection amongst the regular troops. It was only the militiamen that deserted to the Duke.

Later on word came that the Duke had been very sad on hearing the news brought by my lord the Viscount, and had been heard to exclaim,—

"God forbid that I should be accessory to the ruin of my friends, or that for any consideration I should subject so great a city to the double calamity of sword and fire!" And although many amongst us loved him the better for his gracious care of his people, yet the veterans shook their heads, and whispered together that thoughts like these would be the ruin of any cause, and that by no such arguments had the victories of the world been won.

Still there was talk of an attack upon Bristol that very night; and since now they were so near to that city, it was suggested that the troops should fall back upon Keynsham, rather as though they were retreating, but still encamping upon this side the river, should wait for nightfall and then march rapidly upon the city and seek to surprise it. Now this was right good news to the more warlike portion of the army, who had longed all the while to make a bold stroke. I, too, was rejoiced to hear it, for methought that if the townsmen did but arise as one man and attack the garrison in the rear, whilst we engaged them in front, surely the place must yield; and if our Duke were but master of Bristol, arms and treasure and stores of all kinds he would have in abundance, as well as a walled city, and a seaport to boot, whence supplies could be brought from his friends in Holland, who we were assured were working for him there.

Having no post or occupation of mine own, I wandered here and there as I would, watching the men take up their quarters as if for the night, and always ready to do any errand for my lord, if he should desire it. His company of horse was posted in the rear, to guard it from attack; and as the evening began to fall wet and murky and cheerless, I chanced to be standing beside him, both of us being mounted, when a scout came rushing breathlessly out of the town, crying lustily,—

"To horse! to horse! the enemy is upon us!"

In a moment all was confusion and dismay—all save the demeanour of my lord himself, which was perfectly calm and intrepid.

"Steady, men, steady!" he kept crying, as his troopers gathered round him; and as they fell into line, inspired and controlled by the calmness of their leader, he asked a few questions of the scout, and was told that two companies of the enemy had come charging into the town, and would be upon us almost at once.

And, indeed, whilst we were speaking, there came to our ears the sound of on-coming horse-hoofs, and the next minute the Viscount had shouted,—

"Stand to your arms, men! Be ready! Charge!"

In a moment his horse sprang forward, and Blackbird after him. I had no manner of business in the action, not being armed with anything but a poniard in my belt, and knowing nothing of warfare; but where the Viscount's horse went Blackbird must needs follow, nor had I then the will to check him. Behind us thundered the men, following their gallant young captain as almost all Englishmen will follow their leader if he be brave and resolute. They were but country yokels for the most part, who had seen nothing of fighting, and who knew nothing of the tactics of war; but they set their teeth and lowered their weapons, and followed the dashing charge of their leader.

What happened next I know not. It seemed as though, with some frightful shock, I was hurled against a solid rock. Sparks danced before my eyes. There was a sound of singing in my ears; and then another sound—that of the rattle of musketry. And at that sound I felt Blackbird rear up on his hind legs as though he would fall over backwards; but he righted himself, and then, with a swiftness and skill with which I could scarce have credited him, he dashed off through the heaving mass of combatants. How he did it I know not to this day; but with the sound of musket shots and the clash of swords in our ears, he galloped off as though for dear life as hard as hoofs could take him.

So bewildered and breathless was I that it was long ere I could check him. I felt all the while like one in a dream, and knew not whether the thing were true or no, nor, if it were, whether I had received some grievous hurt in that first fierce onslaught. But gradually as I succeeded in pulling up my foaming horse, I came to the conclusion that I was sound and whole, and was grievously ashamed at having been thus carried out of the battle by my terrified and refractory steed. But Blackbird had never been in such a terrible scene, nor had he ever heard fire-arms save at a distance, and then it was hard to hold him. I could not wonder that he had served me so; yet I was grievously ashamed that I had seen none of the fighting, and had left my lord the Viscount in such a fashion.

But as I urged the reluctant Blackbird back whence he had come, I saw that he was not the only horse who had been seized with a like panic at the rattle of musketry. Horses—some with riders and some without—were careering wildly about in extremity of terror, and quite unmanageable; whilst, to my display and terror, I speedily singled out from amongst these the fine charger ridden by my lord, who so soon as he saw his friend and comrade of the past days, came and ranged himself beside Blackbird, as though ready for another charge.

My heart was full of fear and woe as I saw this, for I knew that Bucephalus had no fear of fire, that he had been trained to such scenes, and that to see him thus riderless betokened some hurt to my lord.

Already it seemed as though the brief tide of battle was turned back. I saw a compact body of horsemen, looking like the enemy, riding fast away. Later I discovered that they had taken us for friends at first, and had been riding to join us, when they suddenly found out their mistake, and had been compelled to meet and repel our charge before they could re-form and retreat. Had our horses and soldiers been trained, we should have made prisoners of the whole company; as it was, only a few prisoners were made. The rest galloped off in safety; but they left lying on the ground as one dead the gallant young captain who had led the charge against them; and with a cry of fear and horror, I saw my lord stretched out upon the miry earth, looking as still and rigid as the soldier on the leads at dawn that day, who had been struck dead by a blow from my lord's sword.

CHAPTER XX.

IN SUSPENSE.

With a lamentable cry I flung myself from Blackbird's back, and knelt beside my lord's prostrate figure; and almost at once there was a crowd about us, and presently I heard a voice speaking in tones of authority, "Make way, men, make way! Here is the surgeon!"

The next moment somebody else was kneeling beside me, and I saw the grave, clever face of Mr. Oliver, one of the Duke's surgeons.

"Is he dead? is he dead?" I moaned; for I felt all the courage and life taken out of me at sight of that white still face.

"Killed! not a bit of it, boy. It is but a swoon from loss of blood. Here, let me get to him to stanch the bleeding, else he may bleed to death!" and the surgeon's busy hands moved to and fro, whilst the flow of life-blood was quickly checked. But over and above the deep gash in the shoulder from which the crimson stream flowed, the bone of the sword-arm had been shattered by a musket-ball; and Mr. Oliver, as he drew forth the bullet and proceeded to swathe up the injured limb, shook his head with the remark,—

"This will be the last of your fighting for some time to come, my good sir. The cause will be lost or won without your aid before you can cross saddle or wield weapon again."

The Viscount heard not a word, being still sunk in deep unconsciousness; but a voice above us said in sorrowful accents,—

"And so I lose another of those very few who know the art of war. Soon I shall have not a soldier left!"

Raising my eyes, I saw our Duke looking down upon my lord's white face with eyes full of compassion and regret.

"To lose such a soldier in so small an affray! and he one of the very few who had the art to command his men!" said the Duke again. And I loved him the more for his words and his look, seeing that he, too, loved my lord right well.

"It is greatly to be regretted, sire," answered the surgeon, who was now adjusting the torn doublet, and looking about as though to know what next was to be done with the patient. "Lord Vere is a heavy loss to us; but he must be well tended and have care and nursing, or it may go hard with him after such a hurt. He has not that iron frame which a soldier needs. He is an instrument something too finely tempered for such rough and ready warfare.
—Boy," he said, looking straight at me, "art thou his servant? I have seen thee ofttimes beside him. Where can we carry him, so that he shall be well tended whilst he lies helpless and sick?"

"His father's house would surely be his best asylum," said the Duke; but I shook my head doubtfully.

"I misdoubt me if my lord would go there. His father has cast him off for joining your Majesty. But if I could get him taken back as far as Bridgewater, I could there get him all he needs, and he would be well cared for and tended."

"He will need that," said the surgeon, with his hand upon the wrist of my lord. "He will probably fall into a fever from his wounds. But, boy, let not any leech take more blood from him on that account. He has lost more already than he can spare. See that further loss is spared him, if thou be with him. A little more, and they would drain the life from him altogether—as has been done before now!"

"I will see to it," I answered eagerly, vowing in my heart that nobody should do a thing for my lord that I could do myself. He seemed all at once to have become my charge. My heart swelled with happiness in feeling this, and yet sank at the thought of the many perils and difficulties which lay before me. How was I to get him all those long miles back to Bridgewater? and if I could not get him there, how could I tend him and care for him in a strange place, from which all stores had been taken to feed the army, and amidst strangers who would pay little heed to my prayers, and to whom my lord's life would be of no moment?

"I pray you, sir, stay with him but a brief time, and I will see where I can take him," I petitioned of the doctor; and he nodded, being in fact still busy over his patient, striving to restore him to consciousness after his long swoon. We had carried him beneath a group of fir trees, where the ground was soft and dry; and his cloak had been rolled up for a pillow beneath his head.

Leaving him there in good hands, I made my way to the rear of the army, where the baggage-waggons and guns were, and where I was sure I had seen a familiar face not long since—the face of a farmer from the neighbourhood of Bridgewater with whom I was acquainted, and who was, as I well knew, a kindly man, and a person of substance and importance. I had seen him in Bridgewater, too, and he had told me there that he was bringing six of his men to join the Duke, as well as two loads of provisions for the army. He had shown me one of his waggons—and waggons were not then so common as they are becoming now—and he was mighty proud of it. It was laden with provender for man and beast, and was to follow the army till the corn was all gone. It came into my head that if that waggon were to be returning empty now, I might get my lord conveyed as far as Bridgewater therein; and once at Bridgewater I should be amongst his friends and mine, and could get him tendance and comfort without fear of rebuff.

And not to make too long a story of it, I found the farmer, and the empty waggon too; and not only did he enter into my plans for my lord, but he said he would come back himself with us, which was a mighty comfort to me. He had seen enough of fighting—for there had been skirmishes all along the road these past days—to see that he was not made for a soldier. He had been somewhat scurvily treated by some of the officers, and though still loyal to the cause, he was weary of the long wet marches. He wanted to be at home again, to see how matters were going there. His ardour for a personal share in the campaign had considerably dwindled, and the whisper which was going round that it would not be long before the King's army was upon them four thousand strong, in which case a real engagement would become inevitable, added very much to his desire to find himself amongst more peaceable surroundings.

So he threw himself with great zeal into my plans for the Viscount. Together we collected moss in great quantities, and made a deep bed of it on the floor of the waggon; nor were we content till we had piled it up two feet high, so that it made the softest of beds for a wounded man. It was rather damp, to be sure; but the farmer's sacks were spread in great numbers upon the top, and we were both proud of our handiwork before it was done. There was some trouble in getting the two strong horses which had drawn the waggon; for horses were greatly needed by the army, and it was easier to bring them in than to take them away again. But by using the Duke's name, and by my making over my lord's charger, which I knew he would not want for many a week to come, and which was of real use in battle, we succeeded at last in getting our horses and yoking them to the waggon. The farmer had kept victuals enough for the journey, and we were resolved to start at once, and take a little-trodden route, so as to avoid the bands of soldiers hanging about the rear of the Duke's army, and perhaps by the morning to be clear of them.

Whilst thus bustling about in the camp, I heard news that I thought augured ill for the success of the Duke's arms. Since the capture of a few troopers of the enemy, with whom we had engaged not long since, in the engagement which had cost the Viscount so dear, it had been decided not to march on Bristol to-night. The Duke had heard that there was an army of four thousand men close at hand, and he was afraid that he should be attacked before and behind if he pursued his intention, and be discomfited altogether. He spoke now of turning aside to Bath, and trying to obtain possession of that place. For my part, I grieved to think that he should not seize upon the more important city, and one which was so well disposed towards him and so full of stores and all things that he needed. But I was no soldier, and moreover I had other matters to think of; and by the time we had reached the Viscount once more with our waggon, I had almost ceased to think of the Duke or the army, or indeed of anything in the world except my lord.

His eyes were half open now, and he gave me a feeble smile as I approached; but his voice was so weak that I was frightened, and had much ado to keep back my tears. I began to wonder whether we should ever get him to Bridgewater alive; but both the surgeon and the farmer were inclined to laugh at my fears, and to tell me I should make but a sorry soldier if I were so disconcerted at the sight of a little blood.

They both approved the plan of carrying him to Bridgewater, out of the immediate tide of battle. As for himself, he was so spent with pain and loss of blood that he could scarce take note of our words, and let us do with him what we would. He had lost much blood in the morning before this second wound laid him low; and I never saw living man look more like death than he did when at last he lay upon the couch we had made for him, wrapped up in his cloak and mine against the sharpness of the night air.

The surgeon looked at him thoughtfully.

"Take him gently, take him gently, and give him frequently to drink of this cordial. Get him away out of this harassed country, where nothing can be had save the bare necessaries of life. Get him to some quiet place where he can be tended and watched. He should do well then; but he lacks the toughness of fibre which a soldier needs. He is all fire and force, but the body is not seasoned. He has the soul of a soldier, but the frame of a girl."

I was rather indignant at the last words, albeit there was some truth in them; for my lord looked almost like some fair young maiden with his white face and golden hair, as he lay with closed eyes upon his couch. It was too much like the marble face of some sculptured monument not to awaken a sense of pain within me; but I fiercely held back my fears, and declared that I would save him yet—for Mistress Mary.

As we journeyed slowly through the summer night—and the night was fair and starlight, though the ground was heavy with the recent rain—I mused much of Mistress Mary, wondering how matters were going with her, and whether I should be able to see and speak with her when I was as near as Bridgewater, and whether perchance I might so contrive that she should have sight and speech of my lord.

I rode Blackbird close behind the waggon for the most part, and when we halted I strove to give the cordial to my lord, and to get him to take food; but this he could not be persuaded to do, and sometimes seemed so sunk in mists of weakness as to know neither me nor what was happening to him.

That long journey, which we accomplished safely in two days and three nights, seems always like a dream to me. We met with no mishap. We saw no soldiers or foes. The country people were kind, and brought us milk for my lord whenever we passed a village or farmstead, and listened with wondering eyes to our tale. I was just absorbed in striving to keep my lord alive till we could get him proper help and tendance. He lay almost like one dead, save when the pain of his wound would rouse him, if the road were more rough and bad than usual. Then he would strive to raise himself and ease his pain, and would sometimes speak my name in a tone of gentle fondness when I sought to do aught for his comfort. But the fever was ofttimes upon him too, and he would lie back with his lips moving and his eyes seeing things invisible to us; and at such times he would seem to be in converse with Mistress Mary or with the Duke, or commanding his men in some sudden attack of the enemy. It was often hard to keep him from rising and hurting himself; and night and day I had to watch him, afraid to close my eyes lest he should be wanting something or doing himself a mischief.

Right glad was I when at last, upon the evening of the second day, the sight of the familiar walls and chimneys of Bridgewater rose up before my weary eyes. My lord was lying like one dead in the cart, sunk in a deep unconsciousness, and I verily began to fear that he would die ere ever we could reach the town.

I took him straight to my uncle Robert's house—the Cross Keys Inn, as it was called—and there we met such a welcome as cheered my heart and took a load of anxiety from my mind.

All Bridgewater was agog for news of the army, and any follower of the Duke's was welcomed with the greatest love and kindliness. There was something in the beauty of my lord that appealed to all hearts at first sight of him; moreover, in Bridgewater he was well known and well loved for his own sake, and the people were ready to make an idol of him forthwith when they understood that he had given up everything to join the Duke, and that he had met his grievous wound in the good cause.

He was carried forthwith to the best bed-chamber in my uncle's house, and before long all the leeches in the town had gathered round him, and I was in the greatest fear lest they should want to use their lancets upon him—for such was the custom for almost every malady—and I had to repeat the words of Mr. Oliver many times over; but having done so, I saw that they would prevail.

The doctors looked at each other and nodded and shook their heads: one said that there might be something in the argument, whilst another said that an army surgeon ought to know what he was talking of. A third, the eldest, remarked that perhaps a sound sleep would be the best thing for the patient, and that he had a potion which would probably induce a long and sweet sleep, and he said he would at least try that before resorting to any other methods. All having agreed to this, the potion was given, and soon the furrows of pain smoothed themselves from my lord's brow, and he sank into a sleep very different from the trance-like condition in which he had lain often for half a day together in the waggon, and which seemed to me like a harbinger of coming life.

As soon as this was so I stretched myself on a couch at the foot of the bed and slept also; and I think never was sleep so sound or sweet as mine that Saturday night.

During the week which I spent in Bridgewater many things happened, and I scarce know in what order to tell them, nor which will seem of most moment to the reader. Perhaps that which at that time seemed of most moment to me— namely, that I succeeded in getting Mistress Mary Mead to ride out with me one day from Taunton, and spend a few hours beside my lord. Such a thing might not have been so easy to compass but for the excitement and stir prevailing at this time in both towns. It was a period of intense suspense. We knew not from day to day what news would be brought in. We heard all manner of rumours of which no man knew the origin. Sometimes we heard that the Duke's army had been cut to pieces and was in full flight; at others, that he had obtained a mighty victory over the King's forces, and was in full march for London, which was ready to receive him with open arms. One flying scout declared that there had been a fight at Philip's Norton, that at the first experience of real warfare the Duke's army had begun to melt, and that thousands had departed to their own homes. Another report said that Mr. Adlam from Wiltshire, with a great body of horse, was on his way to effect a junction with the Duke; whilst the club-men, ten thousand strong, had gathered somewhere upon Pedwell Plain, and had sent a message to the Duke promising to join him.

Perhaps some may not know what manner of men these club-men were; and indeed their proffer of assistance came to almost nothing in the end. I have heard that the club-men had their origin in the days of the civil war, when the people, finding themselves robbed and plundered by two rival armies without hope of redress or compensation, resolved to defend themselves from such attacks, and refuse to allow their property to be taken from them by either party. The men thus banded together were armed with clubs, and went by the name of club-men. Whether they were ever much of a power I know not, but from my boyhood I had heard them spoken of in the country; and now it was said that they were up and in arms, and ready to join the Duke in considerable numbers.

Another and a very disquieting rumour also reached us during this week, which was that the King had issued a manifesto to those engaged in the service of the Duke, to say that if within certain dates they should quit the Duke's army and join that of the King, they should be pardoned their rebellion, and be safe from all punishment. This promise, it was said, had had the effect of inducing many to quit the Duke's army; and so disheartened had our young uncrowned monarch become (so the voice of rumour said) with these desertions, and the failure of the Bristol project, and the slackness of the gentry to join him, that he had seriously spoken of flying with his officers to some neighbouring seaport and taking ship for Holland, leaving his army to avail themselves of the King's promise of clemency, and be safe from further harm.

You may guess what a ferment was stirred up in men's minds by all these contrary and disquieting rumours. Bridgewater and Taunton were all in a tumult from morning till night, waiting for fresh news, discussing what had last been brought, and sending messengers to and fro to seek tidings and ask their neighbours what they had heard. It was thus easier than it would have been at any other time to ride unnoticed from place to place. By the time Thursday came my lord began to show real traces of amendment. He was as weak as a sick child, and could scarce lift his head from the pillow, and at present he asked nothing of the news of the day, seeming too weak to wish to be disturbed. But the fever had left him, and the good soup and possets which my aunt made for him were bringing back his strength little by little; and so I felt that I might safely leave him for a day, and go to Taunton to seek tidings of my relations there, and, if possible, to gain speech of Mistress Mary and tell her of her lover.

All Taunton was in a fever of excitement when I arrived; and I heard that news had been brought thither that the Duke's army was actually in retreat, that no help had come from Wiltshire, that Argyll had been defeated in Scotland, that the army was deserting fast on all sides, and that the Duke, in great depression of spirits, was falling back upon those cities which had welcomed him at first. Also a messenger had come in with the notice of the King's promise to deserters from the cause, and a great tumult had been thereby stirred up, none knowing what effect such a manifesto might have upon the soldiers.

But what I chiefly noted was the change in the feelings of the Taunton citizens. They who had been so forward to welcome him at first were now talking together at street corners, and the words that I heard were such as these:—

"Let him not come back hither! Let him not return to Taunton! We gave him all we had last time. We plundered ourselves to furnish him. We have no more to offer. We shall be undone by a second visitation! Let him not come hither again. Let us send word whilst there is yet time that we want no second visit!"

What a change from the Taunton of a fortnight ago! I could scarce believe my ears. Well indeed has it been written that there is no confidence to be placed in any child of man! When I reached my uncle's house, I found the tone of his talk quite altered. Without openly asserting enmity to the Duke, he spoke in a way which made me certain that his heart had turned against him in the hour of adversity. Since no capture of Bristol had been made, and no rising amongst the gentry had followed the proclamation of the Duke's title to the throne, doubt and despondency had fallen upon Taunton; and my uncle, ever prone to sail with the wind, was amongst the first to listen with respect to Mr. Axe's persuasions and the arguments of the Mayor and magistrates, and avow himself on the side of law and order. He was sincerely relieved to find that I had been so little with the army, and that I was now at Bridgewater in quite a humble capacity as body servant to my lord. He advised me to dissuade my lord from mixing himself up any more in what he now termed a rebellion; and I was able to answer that I thought this would be an impossibility in the future, for my lord was like to be a long while healing of his wounds; whilst, if things did not take a turn, the Duke would scarce be here in arms more than a short time longer.

But I was very sad to find Taunton so changed: for I loved the Duke, and still cherished bright dreams of what England would be like living under the righteous sway of such a King. I thought I would go to Miss Blake's without delay, and give my account of my lord to her and Mistress Mary. I had scarce put into form my hope that she would come back with me and see him, and yet such was the case; for scarce had she fully comprehended that he lay in Bridgewater sick and wounded—wounded in the righteous cause—than she went up to Miss Blake, who was listening with tears of sympathy in her eyes, and said,—

"Prithee, dear madam, take me to him! I must see him, my gallant love, who has gotten this hurt in the good cause which, for love of me, he embraced. Ah! dear lady, the days be long and the way is short! Dicon will find us horses to take us. Prithee, take me there, dear madam, and I will bless thee to the last hour of my life!"

I know not what heart could have resisted Mistress Mary's sweet pleading; certainly not that of Miss Blake, who was as full of romance and enthusiasm as any girl, and whose loyalty towards the Duke had never failed nor faltered through good report or evil report. That is the way, I think, with women. Love is with them an instinct, and it is far more faithful and lasting than with men, who reason and think and weigh matters again and again in the balance. It mattered not to them that the cause was beginning to look gloomy, that some even went so far as to say it was lost. They loved and trusted just the same, and believed that right would be done at last; and since the Viscount had got his grievous wound in the righteous cause, and Mistress Mary must needs see him, her good friend rode forth willingly with her that day, and we reached Bridgewater before the sun had begun to get low in the sky.

As I have said, there was too much astir just then, too much coming and going, and talking and discussing, for the doings of quiet people to excite much comment. We rode forth without meeting any questions, and at Bridgewater, where the ladies were not known, no one paid any heed to us. The town was full of excitement because it was said that both the army of the Duke and the army of the King were drawing near, and some thought there would be a battle nigh against the town; whilst others averred that only the Duke was coming, and that he had already routed his foes. Any way, there was so much stir in the streets that none paused to look at us; and soon we alighted at my uncle's inn, whilst my aunt came forth to welcome the strangers, and listened in smiling amaze as I whispered my story in her ear.

"Nay, but thou hast brought him the best medicine of all, Dicon!" she exclaimed at the close; and when she had taken the visitors to the parlour, and had seen Mistress Mary without her riding-hood, her heart was more than won, and nothing was good enough for her. She bustled about to get the table set, whilst I went to my lord's room, and found him lately wakened from a sweet sleep, and looking more like himself than he had done since he was first laid low.

I did not tell him that Mistress Mary had come; I only told him that I had been to Taunton, and that I had seen and spoken with her. Even that word brought a flush of colour to the wan cheek—the first I had seen; and as he lay looking at me whilst I told of her, and tried to remember some of her words, the door behind us opened softly, and a light footstep crossed the floor.

The next moment I saw such a light leap into my lord's face that I knew in a moment who had come in.

"Mary—my Mary!" he cried, and would have lifted himself but that she came swiftly forward and laid her hand upon him to restrain him.

"Reginald," she said softly, "you have gotten your wound for my sake. I must needs come to help to heal it."

"It is healed already at sight of thee, sweetheart!" he said; and then I rose and stole forth from the chamber, for I felt that it was no longer any place for me.

CHAPTER XXI.

BACK AT BRIDGEWATER.

"The Duke back in the town—here!" cried my lord, and he half rose from his pillows in his excitement; whilst Miss Blake and Mistress Mary, who were sitting together near to the pleasant oriel window, started up, and Mistress Mary exclaimed,—

"Sure I thought that I heard the sound of a distant tumult but now. Dicon, Dicon! art sure of it? What has brought him hither again? not misfortune? Say it is not misfortune!"

"Mistress, I know not the rights of it yet," I answered, breathless with the haste with which I had rushed back with the news. "All I can say is that he is here, and his army is fast following; that all the town is gone out to meet him, and that the streets are full of people all talking and welcoming him. There is no cloud on their faces. They are as glad and as loving as when he entered last. I stayed to ask nothing, but fled back with the news. I saw him riding bravely amidst his officers, and I missed no familiar face. If some of his soldiers have deserted him, I think his captains are stanch."

"Back at Bridgewater!" repeated my lord, who had sunk again upon his pillows, being indeed too feeble to sit up. "That is strange! Is it a retreat, or but a piece of strategy? Dicon, go forth and ask more, and come and tell us again. Where are the Wiltshire horse of which we have heard? Ask that, good Dicon. And how about the march upon London? Has that, too, been abandoned? Does the Duke think his work is done when but a few ungarrisoned towns in the West stand for his cause?"

"Dear love, be not dismayed," said Mistress Mary, rising and coming towards him with that light in her eyes which I knew so well. "What does it matter to God whether deliverance is wrought by many or by few? He is the God of battles. He fights ever upon the rightful side. Why need our hearts quake or feel fear? All will be well. The Lord will arise, and His enemies will be scattered!"

I saw a strange smile cross the Viscount's face as Mistress Mary spoke these words in that full, sweet voice of hers that was like music in his ears. He did not answer, but put out his uninjured hand, and she came and laid hers upon it. Then they looked into each other's eyes, and I think that all thoughts of the Duke or of coming warfare passed out of the minds of both. I have lived to see something of the power of love in human lives, but I think I never saw such beautiful and perfect love as that which existed between my lord and fair Mistress Mary. From the time, only a day and a half now, since she had first appeared beside him, he had made a wonderful advance on the road to recovery; and Miss Blake had, of her own accord, offered to stay for a few days at the inn, that Mistress Mary might help to nurse her lover back to health and strength. Just now the whole country was so disturbed that the movements of private individuals were not like to attract notice. Lord Lonsdale had gone to London, Mr. Blewer was away none knew whither. There was nobody to note the absence of Mistress Mary from her accustomed home; and if any asked for her, he would be content on knowing that she was away with Miss Blake upon a visit. Her guardian, the only person who could interfere, was at a safe distance, and there was no schooling going on at such a time of excitement. Many parents had removed their daughters in affright at the turn affairs were taking, and at the prominent way in which Miss Blake and her pupils had come forward on the occasion of the proclamation of the kingship of the Duke. So it was easy for both to be absent just now; and it was the best of medicines for my lord to see the sweet face of Mistress Mary beside him, and to be ministered to by her gentle hands. I was never afraid to leave him now, and just at this exciting time was glad of my liberty.

I rushed forthwith into the streets again, and soon found my way to the soldiers' quarters, where they were being bountifully done to by the loyal towns-folk. There was nothing of dismay or fear in their aspect, and they told us of a gallant victory they had won at Philip's Norton over the enemy. I never had a very clear idea of what that battle was like, for some said one thing and some another; but it was plain our army had discomfited that of the false King, and that after some sharp fighting, and a good deal of cannonading which had made great noise but done little hurt, the rival army had drawn off in retreat, leaving our bold fellows masters of the field.

Why they had not then marched forward instead of retreating backward is a matter I have never fully understood. I think the men themselves did not know. Some said that they had not enough horse to cross Salisbury Plain, since Mr. Adlam had not brought his promised troop; and others, that the Duke was still thinking of a retrograde move upon Bristol. But however that may have been, the men were very bold of aspect and full of martial ardour. They admitted that there had been a good many desertions after the fight at Philip's Norton. Numbers of poor yokels, who had never seen war before, and had been scared by the guns and disheartened by the hardships of the wet marches and lack of food, had deserted to their homes upon finding themselves so near. But the stouter-hearted fellows who remained laughed at the poor spirit of these comrades, and vowed themselves better off without them. Mistress Mary, when she heard, looked at her lover with one of her radiant glances, and said,—

"Is it not like that sifting of Gideon's little band? All who were faint-hearted were to go to their own homes. In a holy cause we want none but those whose hearts are set upon the noble end, and who know not a thought of faltering and fear. Oh, I am glad there has been such a sifting! I think that God will never work with unworthy instruments. Dear love, how I would that thou couldst go forth with them again! Yet I will not even repine at that, since thy hurt was gotten in a righteous cause, and I have the sweet task of ministering to thee."

Such sweet words and looks went far to reconcile my lord to the fret and weariness of sickness. I think he scarce felt the pain of his wounds when Mistress Mary was by; and if his nights were sometimes restless and full of feverish visions of disquiet (for my lord always felt that ill would come of this thing), by day his lady's presence would chase these visions away, and give him that rest of body and mind which his state so greatly needed.

The next day, Saturday, completed the week which we had spent at Bridgewater, and certainly a great change for the better had taken place in my lord's condition. He was so much stronger that I sometimes thought he would ask speech of some of his brothers in arms, now in the town once more; but he never did. And it may be that this thing was the saving of him in the days which quickly followed, for I do not think his presence in the town was ever really known. Men had so much to think of in those days that faces and names slipped out of their minds, and there was such coming and going that none could rightly say who was here and who was not. We had not thought to keep my lord's presence a secret, yet I verily believe the thing remained hidden from knowledge. He lay in a large chamber well out of the way of the noise of the inn, and Mistress Mary took the charge of him, with Miss Blake to help her, and in all the excitement and stir in the place that quiet upper chamber and its occupant were well-nigh forgotten.

Saturday was a day of rejoicing to the town. It was said that help was at hand, though none knew exactly from whence it was coming. A report that eight thousand troops from France had been landed to quell the insurrection in the West was proved to be untrue. Messengers had been sent out from the Duke in various directions, and the people believed that great things would come of it. The march upon London was still eagerly spoken of, and it was in all men's mouths that news was daily looked for of a rising there; whilst lower whispers declared that there was a plot on foot to stab the usurping King in Whitehall, and that Colonel Danvers had declared he believed it would soon be done, the people being so incensed against him, and that then the Duke would only have to march boldly forward to find himself King of all the realm.

The temper of the soldiers was so loyal and fervent that all the Taunton men were permitted to go home to see their wives that day, on the promise of returning on the morrow; and that promise they faithfully fulfilled. And I trust that Taunton felt something ashamed of its panic of a few days since when tidings reached it of the bravery of the Duke's army, and the successes it had gained.

My lord heard all this with great quietness, and it was Mistress Mary's eyes that kindled and glowed and flashed as I came in and out with news. Not that any plot for assassination found favour in her pure eyes; but she said with grave severity of mien,—

"A man does but reap that which he sows. If ever monarch has sowed evil and cruelty and injustice, it is he who now sits upon England's throne. God is in heaven, judging right; and if He send him a quick retribution in this life, it may be that he will find pardon in the world to come."

Sunday dawned fair and clear, and we had no thoughts of what a day it would be for us. I had heard that the Rev. Robert Ferguson, of whom mention has been made, who was one of the Duke's chiefest advisers and the chaplain to the army, was to preach to the soldiers upon the Castle Green that morning; and I was very anxious to hear him, albeit I had taken a great dislike to the man from some words dropped anent him by my lord, who made no secret of his distrust of the fellow. He had been hoping to preach at Taunton in St. Mary Magdalene's Church two Sundays before, had it not been decided to move from that city upon that day. He had even made a raid on Mr. Harte's house in Taunton, where he seldom was to be found, since he lived at his Cathedral residence, and left Mr. Axe in charge there, and had robbed him of a gown in which to enter the pulpit. But the sermon had after all never been preached, and now we were to hear it in Bridgewater.

I remember little of the discourse save the text, which was received with a murmur of approbation when it was spoken, though afterwards I remember that I thought of it with a certain thrill of dismay,—"The Lord God of gods, the Lord God of gods, he knoweth, and Israel he shall know; if it be In Rebellion, or if in transgression against the Lord (save us not this day)."

Mistress Mary was with me, and listened to every word, and went back to her lover with a new light in her eyes and colour on her cheek. I fear I looked more at the people than at the preacher, and that his eloquence was lost upon me. But men said that he had preached a fine sermon; and when I heard Mistress Mary quote pieces of it to my lord, I thought it sounded finer and better and purer than it had come from his lips. I think my lord felt the same, for he presently said with a smile,—

"I think that thou couldst convert me to anything, sweet Mary; but I fear the reverend gentleman's remarks would have found but little echo in mine heart. A man must be true to himself and his cause ere he can look for others to trust him; and if treachery was ever written upon any face, it is written on the face of that man."

"But he will not betray the cause?" asked Mistress Mary, breathlessly.

"May be not. He has more to hope from the Duke than from any other man or any other cause. Self-interest may keep him stanch; but such a man as that would sell himself anywhere to the highest bidder. I misdoubt me now that he is not half a spy."

Leaving Mistress Mary and my lord to talk these things over together, I strolled into the sunny street, for to-day was bright and fine; and hardly had I gone a few furlongs before I was met by a fellow whose face and name were known to me—one Richard Godfrey, servant to a gentleman of the neighbouring village of Chedzoy. He was hot with the haste with which he had come, and on seeing me he cried out,—

"Hi, Dicon lad! dost know where the Duke of Monmouth—the King—is to be seen?"

At first I thought him jesting, and answered with a jest; but he quickly made me understand that he really meant what he said.

"My master has sent me," he said, "to tell the Duke that the King's army has encamped not six miles away on the plain of Sedgemoor. We saw them from the church tower this morn, and he sent me to spy out their numbers, and to bring speedy news thereof to the Duke here. There be several thousand lying there, close to the village of Weston Zoyland on Penzoy Pound—thou knowest the place, Dicon. But they be drinking and revelling, and have no thought, as it seems, of attack. Bring me to the Duke, and let me tell him all. So is my master's will."

After hearing this, I lost not a moment in conducting the messenger to the Duke's quarters; and, as good fortune would have it, we met him coming forth with several of his officers, all of whom were speaking of a move that day, though whether upon London, or whether into Gloucestershire, we humble folks did not know.

Upon hearing Godfrey's message great excitement prevailed, and a rapid move was made towards the church tower, from whence, by the aid of spy-glasses, we could descry the position of the enemy, and see that our messenger had brought us true tidings.

Now instantly there came into the minds of the Duke's counsellors the desire to make a sudden attack by night upon the careless and unsuspecting foe. We could not see whether they had intrenched themselves or no, but Godfrey said he would go again and bring us word, and then guide us over the plain of Sedgemoor by night; for there were various rhines—as we call the deep water-drains which intersect it—to be crossed, and only those familiar with the district knew the places where these were fordable.

Meantime the waggons were loaded up, the soldiers were drawn up and fed, and preparations made for a march out so soon as the evening should be come. The soldiers returning from Taunton, whither they had gone to see their wives or friends, found that they were to be led into battle that very night, to cut to pieces (as we fondly hoped) the whole army of the Earl of Feversham!

The greatest joy and enthusiasm prevailed. The men who had seen the King's troops draw off from Philip's Norton, and who had never met any serious check, despite the fact that they had not been led to the walls of Bristol, or been called upon for any very great achievement, felt confident of winning a great victory over a sleeping and careless army. When Godfrey returned with the news that the enemy was not intrenched, that the greatest carelessness prevailed, that officers and men were drinking themselves drunk, and that Lord Feversham was at Chedzoy with one of his bodies of horse, the men huzzahed aloud, and tossed their caps into the air. Visions of easy victory, a routed army, and abundance of plunder rose up before their eyes, and they only clamoured to be led against the foe as fast as they could travel.

Godfrey was our leader. He advised the Duke not to take the direct route to Weston Zoyland, because the Earl had placed bodies of horse to guard that road; and we must also make a circuit to avoid Chedzoy, where more dragoons had been posted. Our way lay along the Eastern Causeway, as the lane is called, as far as Peasy Farm, and then bearing round to the south, we should march straight down upon them, leaving Chedzoy on our right.

How shall I describe the brave show that our army made marching forth in the bright sunshine of that July evening?—the horsemen with my Lord Grey (the Duke would not divide the cavalry, as some wished him to do, though, had my lord the Viscount been there, methinks he would have put one half under his charge); then the foot-soldiers, the Blue, the White, the Red, the Green, the Yellow regiments, as well as the independent company from Lyme; and behind these the waggons of artillery and the four field-pieces. Never had I seen a more gallant sight; and I could no more keep away from following than a bee can tear himself from a flower. Blackbird was as eager as I, and as much excited; and I rode ahead beside Godfrey, and let him ease himself by resting a hand on Blackbird's neck as we went.

At first we did not hasten, for we wanted the darkness to fall before we emerged from the shelter of the lanes upon the open moor. And as we wended our way through the gathering dusk, we talked of the great things that would follow this coming victory, and how, when once the King's army had dispersed before us, we should march unimpeded to London to set the crown upon the royal victor's head.

The march of a great host is a more tedious matter than one would believe who has not seen it, and darkness had fallen before we reached the moor. This was what we wanted; but the darkness was bewildering too, and the crossing of the two great rhines which lay in our path became more difficult than had been supposed. Indeed Godfrey lost his way altogether for a time, so that some have said he betrayed us and the cause, and have spoken much ill of him. But I am well assured that such was not so, for I was hard by him all that strange journey, and I am very sure that he did his best to lead us by the right road.

The troops, as you may guess, were thrown somewhat into disorder by the passing of these fords; and now believing that the rival army lay before us without intrenchment or defence of any kind, and being hot and eager for the struggle, the men marched very fast, and so increased the disorder in their ranks.

After passing the second rhine, we were (according to Godfrey) not more than a mile from the enemy; and here the Duke halted, and I heard that the cavalry were ordered to advance, followed by the guns, and that the foot were to get into rank and follow to support the horse so soon as the first charge had been made.

And how shall I describe that battle, fought in the darkness of a summer night, about which so many stories are told that one's brain reels with the effort of trying to understand and piece together all that is spoken concerning it? Perhaps I had better content myself with telling as far as I can remember what I myself saw and heard, though my recollections are indistinct, and so mixed with the tales afterwards heard that sometimes I scarce know what it was I saw in person, and what it was that was afterwards told me.

But at least I know that when the horse had started I followed behind them on Blackbird, too eager to feel fear, and resolved, should a splendid and victorious charge be made, to be the first to carry back the news of it to the Duke, who remained with the infantry.

Up till now we believed that our approach had been unknown to the carelessly-guarded army; but we knew that it could not remain unknown much longer. The horse were charging straight upon the camp, when suddenly there came a halt, some angry and dismayed exclamations, and the sudden accidental discharge of a pistol. Who fired the shot has never been known; it was believed to have been an accident, caused by the dismay which seized the horse on finding that a deep rhine—the Old Bussex Rhine—of which Godfrey seemed to know nothing lay between them and the camp on Penzoy Pound.

Immediately confusion reigned, but the word was given to skirt along and find a ford. In the darkness and disorder I knew little of what passed; but the whole place was astir—sentries were calling, the rattle of arms was heard, when suddenly I heard a shout which told me that our men were across the rhine. Next moment the darkness was lit up by a flash of fire, whilst the terrible roll of musketry rang through the night air. These volleys were repeated again and again; yet it seemed but a few minutes before I was almost carried off my feet by the return of our horsemen, who came galloping back in confusion and dismay.

"What has happened?" I cried breathlessly, as Blackbird was carried along by the backward rush of the snorting horses, terrified at the flash and smell and noise of fire-arms, so that their riders could not control them even had they desired to lead them again against the foe.

Then one said one thing and one another; but all agreed that we were betrayed, that the cause was lost, that the enemy was securely intrenched behind a deep fosse, and that those of the horse who had crossed it would never come back alive.

At that methinks some spirit not mine own possessed me, for I fell into a kind of fury, and called out to those about me,—

"Men, if you be men and not cowards, follow me for the sake of England's honour, and strike one blow for freedom and the Duke, if we die for it!"

Then pulling up Blackbird, and making him wheel round sorely against his will, I seized an axe from the belt of one of the men near to me, and galloped furiously back toward the camp, where the battle was raging hotly.

I know not how many came with me; some twenty or thirty, I think. I trow I must surely have been mad at that moment; but I cared not what befell me, so that I struck but one blow for the cause I loved. And I think that the fury of my spirit entered into Blackbird, for he no longer feared to face the flash of fire nor the rattle of the muskets, and even the boom of the great field-pieces only made him gallop the more willingly. I think it was his instinct that led us to the place where the rhine could be crossed, or else he leaped clean over it. For the next minute I and some score of followers were charging through the enemy's camp, scattering right and left all who opposed us, and for the moment spreading confusion in our train.

"King Monmouth! King Monmouth!" I shouted at the top of my voice, as I waved my axe about my head, feeling that I could slay the veriest giant as though he had been a child; and indeed I did cut down more than one adversary who aimed a blow at me as I swept past.

"Down with all usurpers! Death to all traitors and Papists! King Monmouth! King Monmouth for England!"

Shouting these words, and charging through the camp like furies, I and my few followers dashed on madly, whilst behind us we heard the tide of battle raging, and knew not how the day would turn. Suddenly we were brought to a halt by a shock the like of which I had never felt before. We had flung ourselves in the darkness upon a compact mass of horsemen, drawn up in Weston Zoyland by the Earl of Feversham himself (as I heard later), and about to start forth to the relief of those in front.

"Down with the traitors! No quarter!" I heard shouted, as the awful shock brought Blackbird to a standstill, flinging him back on his haunches, and nearly knocking the breath out of my body.

I remember setting my teeth and trying to pray; for I was assured that my last hour had now come, and was surprised that I felt no fear, being yet full of the overmastering fury which had first possessed me when I saw the flight of

Lord Grey's horse. But quicker than lightning Blackbird had recovered himself; and wheeling round with that dexterous agility of which he was such a master, he was off through the darkness like a flash, whither I knew not. I heard a rattle behind me; there was a whizzing and singing in my ears. The right arm, with which I was still holding my axe, dropped numb to my side, although I felt no pain. A sort of mist came round me. The sound of the battle reached my ears like a continuous hum. I found myself thinking that I was in church, and that the organ was playing; then I remember nothing more for what seemed to me an immense time, and woke to find myself lying in a ditch with Blackbird above me, and the clear light of a summer's morning breaking slowly in the east.

Where was I? what had happened? and what meant all that noise of crying and shouting, groaning and shrieking, which assailed my ears?

CHAPTER XXII.

FATAL SEDGEMOOR.

Was I alive or dead, sleeping or waking? Was all this tumult part of a horrid dream? or was I in the midst of unknown and undreamed of horrors? With a sense of strange suffocation I strove to rise, but was unable to do so. I was lying in a dry ditch, and Blackbird was on the top of me, not crushing me by his weight, but so placed that I could not do more than lift my head and look about me.

Day had broken, the long low shafts of light fell across the plain, and I saw, as in a dream, the figures of men in hot pursuit one of another. I saw men smitten down by their fellows, falling sometimes without a groan, sometimes with shrieks of agony. I saw worse things than that too; for even as I lay and watched, scarce knowing who I was nor where I had got, nor what this fearful sight could mean, I saw fierce-faced men with bloody swords striding amongst ghastly heaps of writhing human forms, and dealing awful blows here and there with remorseless fury, sometimes even laughing at the suppliant cries and groans of the wounded wretches, but only driving home more fiercely their gory blades, with a brutal oath or the exclamation, "There goes another traitor!"

As I watched with that awful fascination which a scene of horror always inspires, shivering and shuddering lest my own turn should come next, sense and memory returned to me. I remembered the events of the previous night—

the strange dark march to Sedgemoor, the attack in the dead of night, the rout, the fierce irresponsible onset that I had made, and the roar of battle which had been in my ears when I was smitten down, I knew not when nor how.

But now the battle was over. Now there was nothing but an awful carnage that was not warfare but a shambles. And I lay and watched it, and tried to pray to God to spare me, or to give me courage to die; and I kept asking in my heart how the battle had gone, though I knew all too well by the sights I saw.

For they were not our men who were marching to and fro upon the bloody field, slaying without pity all whom they could find. They wore the dress of the regular army; they had the mien and air of practised soldiers. They challenged one another in the name of the King, and they shouted, "Down with all rebels! down with Scott's vagabonds!" as they sent poor half-armed, wounded rustics to their last account.

I verily believed that Blackbird saved my life that day; I will say how anon. As I lay in the ditch, wondering whether he too were dead, and whether I should ever be able to rise and stand on my feet again, or whether I should be despatched by the sword-thrust of one of these bloody men, a groan close at hand told me that I was not alone, and I spoke low, asking who was there.

"A wounded soldier," was the answer. "I thought that all were dead here in this ditch save me. Art thou from Monmouth's following?"

"I came to see the battle. I am no soldier, but only a lad untrained to arms. Who art thou? And how came the battle to be lost? Surely we outnumbered the foe; and we took them unawares in the darkness."

"It was those accursed horsemen," groaned my unseen companion, who lay behind me in the ditch. "We always said that my Lord Grey would ruin any cause. Had the horse but stood their ground even without striking a blow, we would have won the battle without them. Curse upon those cowards who taught them to flee! A plague upon Lord Grey and his poltroons!"

"What did he do? what did he do?" I asked, in great excitement and indignation.

"Do? why, fled like a coward after the first charge; and though we of the infantry came up rank after rank and fired for hours, and would have stood firm and won the battle for the Duke yet if we had had ammunition, those cursed horsemen charged back into the rear and cried that all was lost; so the waggons made off, and the rear ranks took fright, and all fled helter-skelter as they could. As for us, we stood firm, and fired all our ammunition; and when all was done, and no waggons came up, and we kept calling, 'Ammunition, ammunition! for the Lord's sake ammunition!' and none was brought us, we had to lay aside our muskets and take our pikes. And when at last the enemy's horse formed and charged, we were broken to pieces, and fled; and they came and cut us down like sheep. A curse upon those horsemen who lost us the battle!"

The poor fellow did not speak all this in one breath as I have written it down, but in gasps and disjointed fragments; and I found he had heard a part from other fugitives, who had fled with him, but had become confused, as he was himself in the darkness, and had lost themselves upon the moor, wounded and faint, and had been struck down by the weapons of the pursuing soldiers.

"Where is the Duke?" I asked; and the answer came with another groan,—

"Fled—fled with my Lord Grey, long before we had ceased firing, and when we would have won him the battle yet if the horse had returned and the waggons come up. Ah me! ah me! it is not hard to die in a good cause; but it is hard to be deserted by those who should be our leaders and commanders when the battle is still being fought."

It was very terrible to lie there and hear all this, and picture that gallant stand of the untrained foot on the edge of the rhine; and to know that whilst they were firing, firing, firing, and throwing death and confusion into the enemy's ranks, they had been deserted by the Duke, and left to their fate by the cavalry and the rest of the army. I could well understand that it might not be all the fault of my Lord Grey, that the untrained horses might soon become unmanageable in the darkness and the tumult, and that a rout was due more to that than to the cowardice of their riders; but still they need not have communicated panic to the rear of the army. They should have encouraged and not discouraged the fellows behind. But what boots it to muse or to speak thus? The battle was lost; the Duke was fled; and now what lay before those who had embraced his cause?

I was soon to see something of that all too near. Steps were heard approaching, and a brutal laugh sounded so close above my head that I shut my eyes and set my teeth, believing verily that my last hour had come.

"Here is another of them," cried a voice. "A militiaman too—a deserter to the rebels! Let us take him to the Earl to be hanged, as an example to all loyal folks."

"Get up, you hound!" cried another voice; and I heard the sound of a blow or kick, followed by a groan from the voice of the man who had talked to me.

"I cannot," he said faintly; "I am sore wounded. Have mercy, sirs."

"Mercy for a rebel cur! You and your fellows will soon see what the mercy of the gracious King is like. Get up, you hound!"

Another blow, another groan, and then the first voice said,—

"Never mind him; he's not worth the trouble. Kill him, and come away."

The next moment a sickening sound reached my ears, as a sword was buried in the unhappy man's body, and he expired with a gurgling groan.

A cold sweat broke out over me. My head fell back, and my eyes closed. I felt the horse above move slightly, and his head seemed to come down upon mine. For a moment I thought I should be suffocated, and almost cried aloud; but fear held me mute, and almost at once the steps passed on. Then I felt another movement of Blackbird's, and presently his whole body moved, there was a struggle and a quiver, and he rose and stood upon his feet, looking down at me, and touching my face with his velvet nose, caressing me in his silent fashion, as though he would ask how I fared.

I had thought him dead all this while. But he was only exhausted, and I verily believe some instinct of self-preservation and the preservation of his master had kept him perfectly still and quiet all this while; for it was not till the field at this part was deserted of soldiers that he rose to his feet. And when I struggled upon mine I was alone with the dead, and nothing but the reddened earth and heaps of slain to say how the conflict had sped.

I felt all my limbs, but found none of them broken. I had a wound on both sides of my arm, where a ball had passed through it; and the effusion of blood must have made me faint, and then have stopped. I bound the wound with a kerchief and slipped it under my sleeve, that I might not look like a wounded man. I washed my face and hands in a ditch, and rearranged my disordered habiliments. My plain leather doublet and gaiters did not tell tales, and Blackbird's glossy coat was soon restored to order by a little careful grooming. I had lost my cap; but there were many lying about the field, and I found a plain one suited to my appearance, and put it on, with a shudder as I thought that its owner was probably lying cold in the sleep of death.

Having done all this, I mounted Blackbird, and began to pick my way across the plain in the direction that I saw by the sun must lead me back to Bridgewater. I knew that I was liable to be caught and slain at any moment if I met a party of soldiers who suspected me; but I was too dazed with horrors to feel anything but a sort of numb desire to save myself if possible. If I did perish, I did perish. There was certainly nothing else to be done than to try to get back home.

As I picked my way across the plain, Blackbird snorting and turning aside again and again from heaps of corpses, I suddenly became aware of a strange sight. Across the plain in front of me there came at lightning speed a wild young horse galloping madly. A rope was round his neck, and the other end of the rope was tied round the neck of a fine-looking young man, who was stripped of almost all his clothing. And fast as the horse ran, the man kept pace with him step for step; till just as they reached one of the great rhines of which I have spoken, the horse tripped, and fell exhausted, and the man upon him.

Behind came a number of horsemen, galloping as hard as they could, with much shouting and laughing. Curiosity got the better of prudence, and I rode up and asked what was going on.

"Marry, it is the Earl's sport," cried the fellow I had addressed. "Yon man was to purchase his life by running with the horse. It was told my lord that he could run with any steed, and he was promised his life if he proved it true. Verily it was a brave run. The horse fell before the man. He has earned his ransom well. Why are they bringing him back?"

For the runner had been taken by two troopers, and, panting and exhausted, was being led back in the direction in which all were now moving.

"Where take they him now?" I asked, looking with curiosity and awe into the face of a gallant-looking soldier, whose arms and accoutrements and mien pronounced him to be a leader and general.

"To the camp at Weston, I suppose," answered my informant. "We are about to hang a batch of rebels. Thou hadst better come and see the fun, boy. There will be rare times for the country now! First they will have military vengeance from my lord the Earl of Feversham, him yonder with the stern brow and eagle eyes, and from Colonel Kirke and his Lambs, of whom doubtless thou hast heard; and when these have done their part, the Lord Chief-Justice Jeffreys will come down and do his office. And a rare time you good rebel folks will have when he comes. Ho! ho! ho!"

The laugh which followed made my blood run cold; but I dared not refuse to follow the band, lest I should draw suspicion upon myself. It did not appear that anybody so far had troubled to waste a thought upon me. My youth and my hunched back preserved me from suspicion.

The camp at Weston Zoyland presented a strange and animated appearance. Already the news of the defeat and flight of the Duke had reached far and wide, and farmers and gentlemen anxious to propitiate the victors had come crowding out with hogsheads of beer and wine and provisions of all sorts for the soldiers, together with loyal expressions of good-will, and every appearance of delight at the termination of the ill-starred rebellion. Mirth, revelry, and cruelty were reigning rampant; and there were nigh upon a score of trembling prisoners only waiting the word of the Earl to be hanged upon the great oak tree, still known as the Bussex Oak, and called by the peasants

"Hangman's Oak."

"String him up with the rest!" cried Lord Feversham, pointing to the man who had won his race, and whose life had been promised to him as the reward; and in spite of his pleading and remonstrance he was dragged off to the tree with the rest. A great fellow with a horrid-looking knife came forward from the group of soldiers, and I knew that his office was to dismember the miserable wretches, probably before they were quite dead, that their heads and quarters might be nailed up in high places, a terror and a warning to others.

But I could not stay to see it done. A sickening horror possessed me. I turned Blackbird's head, and dug my heels into his sides; and unnoticed in the crowd and in the midst of so much revelry and excitement, I galloped off along the near road into Bridgewater, which I reached faint and exhausted some time not long after noon on Tuesday morning.

What a changed place it was from the one I had quitted on the Sunday evening! Then all had been hope and brightness and enthusiasm; now a look of blank terror was seen stamped upon all faces. The people went about as if afraid each man to look at his neighbour; and in many houses the shutters were shut and the windows all shrouded, because the families had fled from the expected vengeance, and were striving to put the sea between themselves and their remorseless enemies.

In the market-place there were still drawn up some bodies of troops, which had fled there with the horsemen on hearing that the Duke had taken flight and deserted his army. Colonel Hucker was there with his troop, and I sometimes think that even then if the Duke had but remained, something might yet have been done to retrieve the fortunes of the day.

It has been reported of Colonel Hucker that he betrayed the cause of the Duke on Sedgemoor, first by firing the pistol which gave the alarm to the foe, and then by flying with his men before defeat had become a fact; but those who thus speak do him an injustice, for he never sought to save himself. It is true that had Taunton been fortified he would have been made governor, and he was anxious that this should be done; but his disappointment on that score never made him disloyal to the cause, as was proved by the fact that he sealed it with his blood, when he had ample opportunity to make good his escape had he been so minded.

The news which I brought of the hangings and massacres on Sedgemoor added to the terror and despair of the people. The bands of soldiers melted away, the poor wretches fearing for their lives, as well they might; and Bridgewater was left defenceless to the fury of the avenger.

All that day, men were at work all along the road betwixt Weston and the city, erecting a row of ghastly gibbets; and before two days had passed, every one of these gibbets bore a horrid burden of human forms—some hung in chains, to remain there for months and years, the last being not removed until the landing of William of Orange.

I think that when I brought the evil tidings to Mistress Mary and my lord, I gave her a blow from which she found it hard to recover. I well remember the white face and wild eyes she turned towards me, and the way in which she wrung her slim white hands together, looking first at me and then at my lord, as she cried out,—

"I brought him into this—and the cause is lost! God has not been on our side. And perhaps he will even have to die for it. And the fault is mine! the fault is mine!"

Then she put her hands before her face, and we saw the tears forcing themselves through her fingers; and my lord rose up on his elbow and said,—

"Mary, sweetheart, come hither to me!"

She came weeping, and kneeling down beside his bed she prayed,—

"Reginald, canst thou forgive me?"

"Nay, I have nothing to forgive, sweetheart. And, dearest, if the cause be good, it is none the less so for being unfortunate. If I have taken up arms for liberty and right, and God sees not fit to crown those efforts of ours with victory, it is not that the cause is not rightful, nor that He will desert the right, but that His time is not yet, or that He has other means in store by which to work. Be not faint-hearted, be not cast down. All this has drawn us but close and closer to one another. I would not have it otherwise; and thou dost know well, sweetheart, that I was never very sure of present victory. I did not enter the cause with blinded eyes; and if I have to lay down my life, as many will, I shall die happy in knowing that thy love has been mine, and that thou wilt be loving me and praying for me to the last."

"Ah, Reginald, talk not so! I cannot bear it, I cannot bear it! Thou shalt not die—thou must not die! it will break my heart!"

"Mistress Mary," I cried suddenly, "methinks indeed that my lord shall not die. Let him but rest here in secret, none knowing where he is, till he be able to take horse again, and I will convey him to a safe asylum, where he may lie hid until the hue and cry be past." And then I told them of the secret chamber in my aunt's house, and how she had promised to hide my lord there if ever he should need a safe hiding-place from his foes.

Mistress Mary's face lightened and brightened as she listened, and my lord smiled too, and gave me a look which reminded me of the charge he had given me to care for Mistress Mary likewise should peril threaten her.

None knew in the days that must follow who would escape and who would suffer. I might be in no small peril myself, for I had been with the Duke's army again and again; and though I think that none knew how I had borne arms in that last battle and had charged so madly into the enemy's ranks, yet I knew not that I might not be accused of other crimes, and have to suffer for my love and loyalty in the cause of the Duke. My youth and hunched back had many times saved me from suspicion, but it might well cause me to be known and noticed where others would escape. As I thought of these things I trembled for myself; but in times of common danger it is strange how quickly one forgets the pressure of fear and personal peril. One grows used to it and ceases to think of it; and indeed we had too much to think of in the days which followed, too much of present horror to see, to have thought to spare for possible horrors to come.

"Colonel Kirke is coming! Colonel Kirke is coming! He and his Lambs are on their way!" cried the terrified towns-people on that well-remembered Tuesday afternoon, and they all fled to their houses, as though afraid to look upon the face of the conqueror, although they could not but crowd to the windows to see him and his soldiers bringing in waggon-loads of prisoners and miserable wounded wretches, who were to be hanged and quartered at leisure.

And I must not here omit to mention the noble and godly labours of our good Bishop Ken, the Bishop of Bath and Wells, who came amongst us at this time, and himself went amongst the prisoners, the sick, and the wounded, striving to prepare them for their fate, and doing all that man can do both to ease their condition in their prisons, and to win from the stern military tyrant grace and pardon for numbers who would otherwise have perished. Nor were his labours in vain, for he gained pardon and freedom for many; and many others were brought to peace and repentance before they met their end, so that they were able to lay down their lives cheerfully and with a good courage.

But to return to my story and Mistress Mary, of whom I must now write. I stood with her at an upper window of the inn to see the soldiers enter, and as evil fate would have it, there amongst them, riding not far behind Colonel Kirke, was the Rev. Nicholas Blewer; and it so chanced that his evil eyes, roving restlessly about as they were wont to do, glanced upward in passing at our window, and fixed themselves upon the face of Mistress Mary.

She did not see him, and resisted when I would have pulled her back, so that he saw her plainly; and I saw an evil light flash into his eyes, and knew that some plan had instantly formed itself in his cunning brain against my sweet mistress.

Making a hurried excuse to leave the room, I went straight to my lord and Miss Blake, who were together in his sick-chamber, the elder lady having altogether refused to see the sight of the enemy's entrance into the town. To them I told what I had seen, and at once both declared that Mary must at once leave Bridgewater and return to her home in Taunton.

Amidst her own towns-people, where the name of her guardian, Lord Lonsdale, was known and respected, she would be as safe as any person could be at such a time; but here in Bridgewater, with an army fresh from plunder and slaughter close at hand, in a public-house where entrance could be denied to none, and where nobody knew or had any care for her, she was not safe for a day. She must therefore depart instantly, before Mr. Blewer would believe it possible to accomplish the flight, and never rest till she was safe beneath the roof of Miss Blake's house, which the citizens of Taunton would not permit to be invaded without due and sufficient reason. Mr. Blewer had no friends in that city. He would not be able to effect there (where he was known and distrusted) what he might be able to in this place.

"And, Dicon," said my lord, when Miss Blake had gone to make instant preparation for departure, "come not back to Bridgewater; but remain at Taunton, watching over Mistress Mary—"

"But, my lord, you need my care and tendance."

"I can do without it if needs be, good Dicon. I have been thinking I would rather thou wert otherwise occupied than with me since the defeat on Sedgemoor has put my head in peril." Then as I was about to protest, he silenced me with one of those movements of his hand which I knew so well, and continued, speaking quietly: "Go to Taunton, and remain there. I am for the present safe; and more than that none can say for himself. I can pay for the tendance thou hast hitherto given me. And thou must be beside Mistress Mary, to see if any peril threaten her, and convey her away if it do to that cottage where her friend and companion will hide her till the storm be past. Wert thou here I should fret myself into a fever thinking her being carried off by yon miscreant; but if thou art close at hand and on the watch, I shall feel that she has a protector."

I could say no more. Indeed I so loved both my lord and Mistress Mary that I knew not which stood first in my heart, albeit it was to the service of my lord that I was pledged. But if he dismissed me on any mission, it was but for me to obey; and forthwith I went down to the stables to prepare the horses, and before half an hour had passed we were riding forth together, Miss Blake and Mistress Mary wearing their riding-hoods drawn deeply over their faces, and I riding just behind them, as though I were their servant—as indeed I was.

All the town had gathered to see the entry of the soldiers—all the people, that is, who dared to leave their houses; people of the poorer sort, to whom a show was a show, be the cause never so evil.

The streets were almost deserted as we rode through them, and Mistress Mary's head was bent low. She was weeping to herself, as I well knew, thinking, doubtless, of her joyful entry into the town a few days before, full of hope for the cause, and happy in thinking of seeing my lord again, even though he lay sorely wounded.

Now she had bidden him adieu. She was parted from him, and in such a time as this none dared to say when and how they would meet again. He was in sore peril, and she in something of danger herself, though I know not if she guessed it. He might well be arraigned for treason, being found in arms against his sovereign. She was the object of vengeful love of a bad man, who would seek to win her by foul means, and having possession of her and her fortune, proceed to break her heart by his cruelty. In sooth, I scarce knew whose peril was the greater; and right glad was I to reach the shelter of Taunton Town with my fair charge, having seen and heard nothing of pursuit, and having plainly given the slip to the cunning Nicholas left behind in Bridgewater.

CHAPTER XXIII.

TERRIBLE DAYS.

How is it possible for me to make any understand the unspeakable horror of the days that followed? Were I even gifted like the great Shakespeare himself, methinks I should scarce succeed in drawing a picture of those days and nights of fear, which were prolonged till men became almost dead to a sense of the peril in which they stood, until some fresh panic and new report set all hearts quivering with fresh affright.

Soldiers were scouring the country. Miserable fugitives from the army taken in barns and ditches and cabins were either hung up then and there by the soldiers, or brought before the officers to be judged and condemned by them. And these fared even worse than those butchered by the troopers, for they received the horrible sentence of traitors, and had their hearts torn out before their faces or ever the breath had quite left them, and their members and heads dispersed throughout the country to be exposed to public view.

How well do I remember seeing the first consignment of these ghastly trophies passing along the road, and the inn-keepers and such like being forced to nail them up before their doors as a warning and terror to the village. Sometimes the air was rendered foul and pestilential for miles by the hanging corpses and horrid trophies. Women kept within their doors for weeks together, being so filled with horror at the sight; and the whole country was filled with stories of marvellous hairbreadth escapes, or of captures of innocent persons, who were treated with the same cruelty as those who had been in arms—the soldiers scarce taking the trouble to listen to their protests, and brutally telling them that since so many deserving death had escaped, they must needs die in their stead.

What fearful days to fall upon England, who had called herself a free country, and whose people had always believed that the innocent were protected from violence by the strong arm of the law! Alas! we were soon to find that the most fearful things of all were enacted by those who came in the name of Justice and Law.

I forget exactly what day it was that news reached us that the Duke had been captured, and was now on his way to London, where, as all men said, nothing could save him from the wrath of the King. Some said that had he not proclaimed himself King he might have had a chance for his life, but that having done this he had nothing to hope, and would end his life upon the scaffold.

Yet there were numbers of people who declared that he had got off safe to Holland in disguise, and that he who was on his way to London was not the Duke himself, but some follower whose outward aspect was very like, and who had changed clothes with the Duke and allowed himself to be taken, that his lord might safely escape and live in retirement for a while, and then appear again in his kingdom and fight more successfully for his crown. This belief was held by hundreds and thousands of people in our western counties for years and years, and I remember how long it was before the expectation of again seeing the Duke died out. Some maintained to the end of their lives that he still lived, and that he would have come again to save England had not the tyrant monarch been forced to fly, whilst the just William of Orange ruled (with and in right of his wife) in his stead.

But we in Taunton had other things more near and personal to think of than whether or not it was the Duke who was taken. The bloody victors were at our very gates, and none in the town knew who would escape when once inquisition for blood was about to be made. Was it not in Taunton that the Duke had been proclaimed King? Was it not in Taunton that he had received such royal honours, and such help in money and men? Were not many of his leading officers Taunton men? And if such signal vengeance had been taken already on the innocent rabble, who had acted ignorantly, how should the citizens of Taunton hope to escape?

Well do I remember that Thursday morning when we heard the people in the streets shouting out,—

"Colonel Kirke is coming! Colonel Kirke is coming! God have mercy upon us! Kirke and his Lambs are on their way!"

I rushed out into the streets to hear the news, and even as I did so I met a horseman riding into the yard of the inn, as though he came from the army. But I stayed not to ask news of him, for the people were crying out that twenty men were to be hanged in the city that day, and that Master John Mason was of that number.

All the town was in a terror and tumult, for Master John Mason was a man of most excellent repute, and though he had taken arms in the Duke's cause, he had only fought at Sedgemoor; and that he of all men should be a victim was a thing not to be borne.

At our inn, so near to the open Cornhill, all was hurry and confusion; for Colonel Kirke and his officers were to lodge there, and a banquet was to be prepared for them at the very hour at which the victims were to be slain. The town stood aghast at the horror of the thing, and awful stories were whispered of Kirke during his governorship of Tangiers. Some believed that he had caused miserable Jews to be burned alive there; but others said that he had not burned them himself, but had sent them to the Inquisition in Spain to be burned there—which seemed not much better. His soldiers were called Lambs, but whether in derision because of their fierceness, or (as some said) because when in Tangiers their banner bore the sign of a lamb, I cannot tell. But at least at the thought of their coming all men's hearts shook with fear, whilst the ladies of the town resolved that they would so petition for the life of Master Mason that even Colonel Kirke would not have the heart to slay him.

There was one, Mistress Elizabeth Rowe, a beautiful and godly matron, blending the graces of youth with the dignity and softness of maturity, and well known to every resident in Taunton. There was also a legend in that city, that a "white woman or woman in white" could always obtain pardon for a condemned criminal; and good Mistress Elizabeth declared that she would be that woman, and that she would intercede for the life of Master Mason. On hearing that there was great joy, for it seemed to all as though not even the bloody Colonel Kirke could resist so much goodness and beauty; and as we toiled at our preparations for the ghastly feast, we spoke in whispers of the appeal to be made, and wondered whether it would succeed.

What a terrible day that was! The memory of it is yet as clear before my mind as when it was but a week old.

It was afternoon when we heard the sound of martial music, fifes and drums, and the marching of many feet. All Taunton rushed to window and balcony to look out, and beheld the dark-faced Colonel riding along at the head of his troops. What a difference from the last triumphal entry into Taunton, when all the town was decked with boughs and garlands, and every face beamed with joy! Now almost all faces were grey with fear and grief. Hardly a citizen but trembled for his liberty or life, or for that of some near and dear one. The few voices raised in acclamation as the Colonel rode through the streets sounded hollow and faint. The drums and fifes and martial strains of their own men kept the silence from being too ominous.

At the Three Cups all was hurry and confusion. A great banquet was being prepared in the long upper chamber with the balcony which looked up the Fore Street and towards the Cornhill. But we scarce dared look out of the window ourselves, for just outside, a little to the right, where the space was wide and free, soldiers were hastily setting up a scaffold and gibbet. Close beside this gibbet had halted a cart filled with groaning and wounded prisoners, amongst whom was good Master Mason; and a whisper had already run through the crowd that they were to be hanged and dismembered that very day as an accompaniment to the Colonel's banquet.

I am proud to say that no Somersetshire man could be found to do the hideous work of executioner here. The Colonel had had to send for the executioner from Exeter to do his horrid work. This functionary, whose gigantic frame and scowling face were enough to inspire terror in the hearts of all beholders, was already preparing for his bloody task. He had a great axe and two or three sharp long butcher's knives laid out before him, and he was calling to the people to bring faggots and billets for the making of a great fire.

We knew not for what the fire was intended, but we were to know all too soon.

Sounds of revelry and mirth soon arose from the upper chamber where the Colonel and his officers were feasting. Little recked those fierce men of the horror and terror and agony that reigned in Taunton. They had come to punish rebellion, and to strike terror into the hearts of all who had been concerned in this thing; and Taunton above all places had been most deeply implicated.

How shall I speak of the horrors of that day? When the carouse was at its height, the Colonel, inflamed with wine, appeared upon the balcony, and his half-drunk officers with him, and gave the signal to the executioner to commence his task. Already a row of twenty gibbets had been erected, and the twenty white and wounded prisoners upon the carts had been set in order beside them. Master John Mason, whom all Taunton knew and loved, was kneeling devoutly, praying for himself and his fellow-sufferers, and heeding nothing of what was passing. Some of those near to him followed his words with tears and ejaculations, and most of these were calm and resigned; though some, seeing their dear ones weeping in the crowd, could not keep back their own tears, though all striving to face death bravely.

Then before our eyes in that upper balcony appeared a white-robed figure, and those of us—there were not many—who were in the secret of the petition held our breath to listen, whilst good Mistress Elizabeth upon her knees pleaded for the life of the righteous citizen. Now I was very near to the balcony, being, in fact, just under it, and the parley lasted so long that I feared respite, even if granted, would come too late; for the halters were about the necks of all the prisoners, and the cart was about to be pushed away from under their feet.

Suddenly I heard a harsh voice above me saying, "It is granted, madam;" and then in another tone the same voice said, "Go you, Bushe, and see to it. Tell the executioner to cut the fellow down."

The next moment one of the younger officers came swaggering half drunk from the inn door, and went up to the executioner and spoke to him. There was a brief parley, and he cut one of the halters through. A man leaped from the cart and dashed away in the crowd, and immediately the rest were swung into the air, and remained hanging betwixt heaven and earth.

"Give them music to their dancing!" cried the voice of the Colonel, as the legs of the dying men twitched and moved in their last agony; and the drums and pipes struck up a jubilant strain, which was continued all through the final scenes of that horrid spectacle.

Why did I wait and watch? In truth, I was paralyzed by the awful horror of it. One by one the dead or half-dead wretches were cut down, the fierce executioner cleft the senseless trunks asunder by a blow of his axe, and seizing the heart of the victim, tore it from his body and flung it into the fire, exclaiming as he did so, "There goes the heart of a traitor;" and at each repetition of the words the martial music struck up again, as though some jubilant and joyful thing were being done.

Yet after all good Master Mason perished with the rest. The Lieutenant Bushe sent by his Colonel to save the prisoner had not the least idea of which one the lady had spoken, and on reaching the gallows had said to the executioner, "Cut down that fellow." "Which fellow?" had been the question, since twenty were there, and Bushe had no idea which it was. Master Mason, absorbed in his prayers, took no heed of what had been passing in the balcony; but another man had seen the whole, and when the executioner and lieutenant paused in doubt what to do, he looked up and said that he was the man for whom the lady in white had pleaded. So the executioner cut the rope, and he sprang away and vanished in the crowd, as we saw; and in the confusion it was not known till afterwards that good Master Mason had perished, although his life had been granted to him at the instance of Mrs. Elizabeth Rowe.

Such things are too often done in the bloody days of war.

Twenty victims (save one) perished that day, and thirty upon the day following, each time the Colonel holding a great feast, and turning off on the second occasion ten victims with each of his three great toasts—one for the King, one for the Queen, and one for "the great Lord Chief-Justice Jeffreys, who is shortly coming to finish the work that I have just begun."

As those words were heard, a shudder and a shiver passed through all who heard them, and a groan went up that was not altogether a groan of compassion for the last of the batch of victims who were being butchered in cold blood almost in sight of the revellers. We all knew what terrible days would follow the appearance of the Lord Chief-Justice amongst us. We had heard enough of his ferocity and brutality before now; what would it be like when we were forced to drink to the dregs the cup of his wrath?

Acts of singular ferocity and brutality were daily perpetrated under our very eyes. One man was hanged whilst in a dying state, unable to move hand or foot, scarce living when he was swung into space. Another was hanged three times, and three times cut down to ask if he repented of his crime; but he boldly answered that were he to have his life given him to live again, he would do just the same. He was at last hanged in chains, and left upon the gallows, like several more, till the coming of William of Orange.

But amongst all these tales of brutality and horror, I must not omit to mention one incident which reflects credit if not honour upon the cruel and bloodthirsty Colonel Kirke; and this thing I was witness of with mine own eyes, so I can testify the truth of it right well.

In spite of all the horrors of that time, business went on at mine uncle's house as before; and it so chanced that whilst the Colonel was in the town, and his soldiers more or less ravaging the whole country side, an order arrived from Bishop's Hull (the home of Mistress Mary Bridges) to send thither a hogshead of beer without loss of time.

Now with the Colonel and his officers quartered in our house, we were not a little pressed in those days; and my uncle not knowing how to get this hogshead sent, I asked if I might not take the cart and drive it over. I had two reasons for this. One was that I desired if possible to get speech with young Mistress Mary about Mistress Mary Mead; another was that I sometimes felt as though I should go mad with the fear and horror of the sights of Taunton Town. For day by day and all day long the black-browed executioner, and an assistant whom the townsmen called "Tom Boilman," were engaged in boiling in pitch the quarters of the victims of the rebellion; and the whole place reeked of the awful brew, and turned me sick with horror every time I passed that way. I felt I must get out into the green fields, if only for a few hours. I had been too busy to be spared all this while; but this errand was in my uncle's service, and I went gladly.

It was not a long journey to Bishop's Hull; but the cart travelled at a slow pace, and I did not hurry the horse. It was a relief to leave the streets of the city and the careworn faces of the inhabitants behind, and to see the smiling meadows and innocent, careless life of bird and beast, unshadowed by the horrors that had fallen upon the land.

But one could not forget even here that a reign of terror ruled. Bands of soldiers still scoured the country, seeking after fugitives; and in almost every principal house in the country round men were quartered, to keep watch both upon the inhabitants and upon any flying to them for succour.

I knew that there had been soldiers living at free quarters at Bishop's Hull, and doubtless it was for these that the ale was needed. I drove my cart into the great yard of the house, and delivered its contents to the servants there. But being anxious to obtain speech of Mistress Mary, I did not immediately go away, but tied up the horse to a ring, and entered into talk with the men of the place.

Sir Ralph was away, I heard. He had been summoned to meet the Duke of Albemarle, it was thought, or Lord Churchill, and before he left he had arranged for the removal of the soldiers who had lived for some time in his house. But to-day some of these had come back and demanded their old quarters, and some perplexity reigned in the place as to what was to be done with them. There was confusion in the house, and one of the servants to whom I spoke, asking news of Mistress Mary, answered,—

"Methinks she is somewhere in the great hall. Go in, lad, and fear not. There be too many coming and going to-day for thy appearance to be noted. Go seek her for thyself; I have no time to go with thee."

And in truth every servant about the place seemed flying hither and thither. I followed the command given me, and made my way towards the hall of the house, coming upon a scene as strange as any it has been my lot to witness.

Seated in a high-backed chair beside the great empty hearth, that was in this summer season decked with green boughs and great spikes of foxglove— Mistress Mary's hand in every inch of it—was the stately lady of the house, surrounded by some frightened-looking maidens, who were gathered together behind her chair, and seemed to be shrinking in terror from something or somebody. As I advanced a few steps further into the hall, I saw that it was half filled by swaggering and tipsy soldiers, who appeared to be clamouring for something which the lady of the house was not willing to grant, and whose scowling and angry looks were the cause of the fright in the faces of the maids.

A few paces away from her mother, standing at the other side of the hearth, her slight, strong figure drawn to its full height, her face in a quiver of anger and scorn, was little Mistress Mary, such a light in her eyes as I had never seen there before, her hands locked together, and her whole figure instinct with suppressed passion. What had passed before I know not. I think the men had been demanding free quarters again, and that the lady had been telling them that they had been withdrawn by their officer, and that they had no right to come again in such a fashion, or to take that tone with her in absence of her husband, the master of the house and a loyal servant to the King. However that may have been, I can answer at least for what happened next; for as I appeared upon the scene, one great tipsy fellow, who seemed to be the foremost of the band, came lurching forward, and offered so great and gross an insult to the stately lady sitting there, that my pen refuses to put it on paper. But mark what followed. Almost ere the words had passed the fellow's lips, with a bound like that of a young tiger Mistress Mary had sprung forward; and ere any man of us knew or guessed what she was about to do, she had seized the fellow's sword from its sheath, and had run it through his heart as he stood, so that he fell dead at her feet without a groan. A deep silence fell upon us all as we saw this deed; and Mistress Mary, her face as white as death, but with her eyes still flaming fire, faced round upon the rest of the soldiers and said, pointing first to the corpse and then to the door,—

"Take him, and go!"

Mechanically the men obeyed her; but some half-dozen, more sober than the rest, lingered behind and said, firmly but respectfully,—

"Mistress, you must answer for this deed before the Colonel. You must come with us at once."

"I am ready," answered Mistress Mary, with heroic firmness. "The sooner the better; I fear none of you!"

And indeed she spoke no more than the truth. And never have I seen a more dauntless mien than was carried by that brave child as she rode beside her mother into Taunton that day, guarded by a band of soldiers, and followed by me in my cart; for I felt I must see the end of this thing, and bear my testimony, if I might be heard, when the tale was told to the fierce Colonel.

He was, as was usual at that hour of the day, in his room at the Three Cups; and upon hearing that a prisoner had been brought to be tried by court-martial, he at once summoned his officers to the long banqueting-room and ordered the prisoner before him.

When his eyes fell upon the tender maiden, not more than twelve years old, with the dauntless mien and steady eyes, his face changed and even softened as I had never thought that face could do; and he sternly asked his men why they had brought a woman before him, and she scarce more than a child.

When he heard that it was a military offence with which she stood charged, he bent upon her a searching look, and commanded that all should be told him. Then the men who had brought her told the tale, not indeed extenuating the offence of their dead fellow, but putting the case fairly enough. There was no need for me to speak; there was no need for Mistress Mary to defend herself. When the Colonel heard the words which had been addressed to the dignified matron standing just behind her brave young daughter, and recognized in her the wife of one of the King's loyal supporters, and the mistress of a house where much kindness and hospitality had been shown to His Majesty's soldiers, his face took an expression of mingled sternness and approval which it is hard to describe; and he said, looking round upon the men who stood by, —

"Where is the sword with which the deed was done?"

One of the men had chanced to bring it, and it was handed to the Colonel. The stain of blood was yet upon it, although it had been wiped clean from blood-drops. The Colonel took it and rose up in his seat. He made a low bow to Mistress Mary, and handed the sword to her.

"Mistress Mary Bridges," he said, "you are acquitted of the crime laid to your charge. The action you performed was not only pardonable; it was legitimate and noble, and does you every honour. Would that there were more such women in this land to become the mothers of a soldier race! Take this sword, fair maiden, take it and keep it; and let it pass down in times to come to other Mary Bridges of your name and race. May your house never want such a Mary as you have shown yourself, to act with such courage and resolution in the hour of need.—Madam, farewell!" (this to Lady Bridges). "A brave mother makes a braver daughter. Guard well your child, and honour her as she deserves to be honoured. A maid who will risk her life for her mother's protection is one to grow up the pride and glory of her house.—Mistress Mary, I salute you. Farewell; I could almost wish that you had been born a boy, that I might have numbered you among my own picked soldiers!"

And stooping his dark head the Colonel saluted Mistress Mary on the cheek, and bending low before her, as did also all his officers, saw her pass from the room, holding the sword in her hands.

A burst of cheering greeted her as she appeared in the streets clasping the trophy of victory. Her face was flushed now, and her eyes sparkling betwixt excitement, triumph, and tears. Her mother's face was quivering now that the peril was past as it had never quivered whilst her daughter stood arraigned before the fierce Colonel.

"Dicon, Dicon, I cannot face all these people with my sword!" cried Mistress Mary, a girlish shrinking suddenly possessing her, showing that she was still a maid, though she could act with the courage of a man when need was. "Take me to Miss Blake's! Take me to Mistress Mary; I must see her ere I go back!"

Lady Bridges was willing enough to get out of the cheering crowd, and quickly we found ourselves beneath the shelter of the next roof. Mistress Mary, hearing the tumult, came down the stairs to see what it meant; and the younger Mary, rushing into her arms, and dropping the sword upon the floor, cried out, betwixt laughter and tears,—

"Mary, Mary, I have done it! I have slain, with mine own hands, one of your Duke's foes!"

CHAPTER XXIV.

THE PRISONER OF THE CASTLE.

I scarce know how many days had passed after these things before there happened that which was to me more terrible than all.

The military executions in Taunton were over. Many soldiers remained, but the people ceased to go in terror of their lives—for the moment. An awful sense of coming judgment hung over us. None knew who would be arrested for complicity in the plot, and haled before the terrible judge who was coming shortly. But for the moment there was a slight lull, and the wheels of life revolved just a little more in their accustomed grooves.

Sorrow and mourning and fear prevailed in too many homes, however. Master Hucker was a prisoner awaiting his trial. Master Simpson had fled none knew whither, and his sister feared him dead. Both the gentle brothers Hewling had been taken, and were in London for the time being, though it was said that they would be sent down to Taunton to be tried. More homes than I can mention here were desolated by the events which I have been striving to record, and I felt almost heart-broken now when I went to my friends the Simpsons; for Lizzie's face was pale and tearful, and even gay Will Wiseman, ever of a joyous courage in olden days, looked gloomy and troubled. He had loved his master well, and was faithfully serving him now in his absence, and acting almost like a son to good Mistress Simpson, the sister. But they lived in daily fear of hearing of his arrest; and sometimes Lizzie, weeping with my arm about her—for we were like brother and sister in love—would say,—

"Sometimes I think I would almost rejoice to hear that he were dead! It is such a fearful thing to think that he may even now be brought before that terrible judge who is coming, and have to suffer the awful death of traitor. Oh, if we only knew him safe—even if it were in the safety of a soldier's death!"

For the prisons were filling fast with fugitives and suspected persons, and none knew who might be the next to be haled off, there to linger until the Special Commission headed by Judge Jeffreys sat to judge and condemn those who had been concerned in this matter. Many judged those happy who had met a soldier's death, or had been hanged by the soldiers in the first onset. To linger in suspense in a dismal dungeon, often laden with irons, and subjected to cruel privations, only to be brought at last before that merciless man in whose hands the issues of life and death were to rest, seemed harder than a short shrift and a long rope at the hands of Kirke and his men. I know I often thought (shivering lest I might be recognized and sent to prison) that if that were so with me, I should live to wish I had perished on the fatal field of Sedgemoor. But my uncle stood high in favour. No word had been breathed against him. Colonel Kirke had called him an honest knave, and a credit to his trade; and the Snowes had always held a good repute in the town for loyalty and order, wherefore I was let alone.

But to return to the point from which I started, how may I tell the grief and terror I was thrown into by a sight I saw during the days of that lull which came betwixt the departure of Colonel Kirke and the arrival of Lord Chief-Justice Jeffreys?

I was coming through the streets toward my home, when I perceived a small knot of soldiers, who seemed to be bringing in a prisoner in their midst. Now this had become so common a sight that I might not greatly have heeded it, had it not been that I saw Mr. Blewer riding with the soldiers, his face wearing its most evil smile of malevolent triumph.

At that sight I looked again at the party, and as I did so my heart stood still within me. There in the midst of the soldiers, partly held and partly tied upon his horse—for he was almost fainting from sickness and his wounds—was none other than my lord the Viscount; and the party were heading straight for the Castle, into which they presently disappeared with their captive.

I had followed, speechless and like one in a dream; but when the portal closed behind them and I was left standing without, I heard a voice in my ear saying in accents of mock sorrow,—

"Alas, good Dicon, that one so young and fair and highly born should be a rebel! The best grace the young lord can hope to win from the great Lord Justice is the axe instead of the halter. His would be a pretty head to set up over the gateway here! Alack! what will Mistress Mary say? Methinks she had a maid's passing fancy for the fair face of our young warrior."

The speaker was Mr. Blewer. With a sense of sickening loathing I turned away from the man and rushed homewards, putting the saddle upon Blackbird as quickly as I could, and scarce drawing rein till I stood before the house of my uncle Robert in Bridgewater.

I found my aunt in tears, and I had no need to put a question before she burst out with the tale.

"Dicon, we could not help it. We breathed no word of his being here; and when the soldiers had done their hanging and had gone—at least some of them, and the rest were more for carousing and feasting than anything else— we felt able to breathe once more. But there was an evil-faced man for ever prying about, habited like a clergyman, but with little of the nature that befits that office. He asked so many questions from one or another about a maiden he had seen here, that we could not hide from him that Mistress Mary Mead had been a guest here for a while; but not a word did we breathe of the young lord upstairs—I give you my word we did not!"

"I am sure of it, good aunt; I know you had learned to love him right well. None could fail to do so who came into his presence."

"Indeed thou speakest sooth, Dicon," she answered. "I waited on and tended him myself; and never have I seen a gentler and more perfect gentleman, so patient, so grateful, so anxious to avoid giving any trouble—as though we grudged what we did for him—and he paying for all like a prince! I loved him as a son, if I may say it. And yet that evil man, by hook or by crook, and by dint of ceaseless spying and prying, got scent of his being here; and to-day there came a troop of soldiers with an order to search the house for a rebel who was known to be sheltering here in disguise. Dicon, when that befell us, what could we do? To have resisted would not have saved the poor young gentleman, but would have brought all the rest of us to the gallows."

Her tears broke forth afresh, and I could almost have joined with her in weeping, had it not been that my heart so burned within me in hot indignation against the miscreant who had spied and betrayed us. As it was, the tears would not come to my relief, and all I said was,—

"Did he come with them?"

"Ay, he did! They knew not the face of the young lord; and even when the monster had found him, they would scarce have taken him, so weak and ill as he yet was, as white as a lily, and not able to rise. But yon brutal minister— whom I would I could see beneath the hangman's hands!—he swore at them that they were traitors and rebels themselves an they took him not. So he was forced to rise and dress, and was set upon a horse, though no more fit than a new-born babe; and whether they get him to Taunton alive the Lord only knows! Oh may He take a speedy and a bloody vengeance for all the deeds of blood and horror that have been committed in this city in these last days!"

But I could not linger to listen even to sentiments so congenial. I had learned what I had come to learn, and now possessing myself of all my lord's property, and of a considerable sum of money which my good aunt was keeping for him—he had contrived to get supplies sent him before I left—I took horse again, Blackbird having been well fed and as willing as ever, and was in Taunton once again ere set of sun.

What to do next I knew not. At home I was resolved I would not breathe a word of this matter. Mine uncle was striving to forget all other feelings in the one of loyalty to the powers that be. From him I should get nothing but a warning to have nothing to do with rebels and prisoners. From his own point of view he might be right, but I could not rest so long as my lord lay in durance vile, and with nothing before him but the mercy of a judge who was pledged to show no mercy.

Yet I was so distracted by sorrow and fear that I could think of nothing alone; and after tossing upon my bed that night in a restless misery, I suddenly came to a resolve.

"Mistress Mary will counsel me!" I cried, sitting up and pressing my hands to my hot brow; and even as I took the resolution to see her so soon as the day should have come, I grew calmer and more hopeful, and was able to snatch a few hours of much-needed sleep before I had to rise to my day's work.

Miss Blake's maidens had some of them come back to her, but there was little of regularity in the hours kept, and many pupils had been altogether removed by cautious parents. I was a welcome guest now whenever I appeared within those doors, and my request to-day to see Mistress Mary at once soon brought her down to me into the little parlour, her eyes full of anxious questioning.

I fear me I broke the evil tidings to her but clumsily, for she went so white that I feared she would swoon away; but recovering herself with all speed, she clasped her hands together and cried,—

"Dicon, we must save him, we must save him! It was I who led him into this peril and strait. Thou and I together, good Dicon, must win his release. Dicon, he must be got out of yon Castle! He must not stand before that relentless judge! We must save him! we must save him!"

"Mistress, I will die to save him if I can," I answered; but she gave me one of her own beautiful smiles as she answered,—

"Nay, good lad, thou must live to save him. Dicon, there is no time to be lost. We must think what can be done!"

It was this that I had come for, and greatly was I surprised by the ready wit and shrewdness displayed by Mistress Mary when we sat down to talk. Methinks she must have spent many hours thinking and pondering upon such chances as these, for she seemed to have a plan already in her head, and she quickly set it before me.

"Dicon, by what thou sayest, I think that they will not dare to cast my dear lord into a dungeon, sick as he is. He is known in Taunton, and the soldiers and keepers there are not monsters like Colonel Kirke's Lambs. Our towns-folk are humane men, and a soldier is but a man after all though he follow a bloody trade. And then money, Dicon, will unlock many a door, and it has pleased Providence to make me rich."

"I have money, too, laid aside." I answered eagerly, "and every penny of it shall go towards freeing my lord!"

Again she smiled sweetly, but checked me by her gesture,—

"Nay, faithful Dicon, thy money will not be wanted for this; but thy shrewdness, thy cleverness, thy good-will, shall serve us instead. Thou art under no suspicion, therefore go boldly to the Castle and ask leave to bring to my lord such things as he needs. Prisoners, as thou knowest, live at their own charges, and thou canst represent thyself as sent by his friends with the things needful for him. Then by bribes thou canst win leave to take these things to him thyself. This carnage and slaughter has sickened men's souls within them, and they are readier now to listen to the promptings of mercy than they were awhile back. Make friends with him who has charge of my lord; make him see that it will serve his purpose best to let thee come and go at will. Doubtless with one weak and ill as my lord, there will be more of mercy and less of strict watch kept than where the prisoner is hale and strong. Be it thine, Dicon, to do all this; and having thus done, come yet again to me and bring me word, and we will talk of what shall be the next step."

I left the house with many a golden guinea of Mistress Mary's in my pouch, for she would have none even of my lord's money for this; she would do it all herself. And forthwith did I set myself to the task I had before me, rejoicing that I was able to find so good an excuse for my first visit to the Castle. For it came into my head (my wits being sharpened by all this) to ask my aunt if she could not spare a pair of good fat capons for the Governor there. And this being thought a happy notion by mine uncle, who was, as I knew, all in a fever to keep in the good graces of the authorities, I was quickly laden with a basket containing various good things, and amongst them a bottle of rare good wine, which, however, never found its way to the Governor's table.

For before I got to the Castle I took and hid this bottle about my person; and when I had delivered my message and my load, I began talking first to the porter and then to one and another of the guards who came and went, and who were willing enough to stop and chat about what was going on in the town, and how soon the trials were likely to begin; until at last I came across the man who had the keeping of my lord the Viscount, and him I asked to speak aside for a moment.

He had a little slip of a place at the end of a long corridor, where he kept watch; and when I produced my bottle of wine, his eyes sparkled, and we were friends at once. He told me of the prisoners he had in his charge, and of Lord Vere, who had been brought in wounded and sick but the day before. He asked me if I thought His father would send him those things that he needed, as it would go ill with him if he had not some care; and when I (concealing my exultation under a mask of indifference) said I would ask, and also asked if I might see Lord Vere and learn from him what he chiefly needed, the man made no objection at all, but led me along the passage to a certain door which he opened. I went in with my finger upon my lips, which sign my lord instantly perceived, and spoke not as though he had any special knowledge of me, though most people in the place knew my name by this time.

He answered my questions, and told me what he most needed. I asked if his wound were severe, and he answered that it was mending, though the ride yesterday had inflamed it and brought back some of the fever. But he looked less feeble than I had feared; and I took great heart at seeing that he was not in a dungeon, but in a small and fairly commodious chamber. The warder told me that the dungeons were full; and I told him I was sure I could get him money from my lord's friends if he could make shift to keep him there. The man winked at that, and said that so long as he was sick he would not be moved; and I winked back and said he had better keep him sick, and he would get money.

Next day I was there again with such things as my lord had asked for. I did not seek to go into the room that time, feigning no especial interest in him, but stayed chatting with the warder, and I gave him a broad crown piece as an earnest of more to follow if the prisoner were well looked after. Next day I brought some things I professed to have forgotten, and another bottle of wine for the man; and this time he bid me go in to see how well he had cared for the patient, that I might tell the same to his friends. And as he was anxious to finish the wine before his fellow came to relieve guard, he locked me for a short while into the room with my lord; and I spent every moment in eager talk, and in examining the place, that I might know whether there was any hope of getting him safe away out of it when he was strong enough for flight.

I soon saw that this little chamber was in the south side of the building, a little to the left of the gateway as you stand facing it, and situated about half-way betwixt that and the round tower at the corner. From the window, which was heavily barred, there was a drop of perhaps forty feet into the enclosure behind the wall which lay all round the Castle. But this wall was neither very high nor very closely guarded; and I had a wild hope that it might not prove an insurmountable difficulty if once we were free of the Castle itself. A dark night would have to be chosen, and many things would have to be thought of first; but I did not despair either of bribing the jailer to secrecy, or of making him an accomplice in the flight. Then let us but once get quit of the Castle, and I knew of a safe place of retreat for my lord till all hue and cry should be over.

Days and even weeks flew by all too fast for us; for my lord recovered but slowly, and until he was sound once more it would be hopeless to think of such a thing as escape. A long ride of twelve miles into Ilminster was the first use he must make of his liberty; and if he had not strength to accomplish that, what use to get him out of prison? July had merged itself into August, and August was waning towards September, and men spoke with shuddering dread of the coming Great Assize, when the fate of all prisoners would be settled, and yet only by very, very slow degrees had my lord struggled back to health; and even now, for lack of air and his wonted exercise, he was wan and white and thin, albeit now able to leave his bed, and walk to and fro for an hour together in his chamber.

Meantime with the jailer I had become great friends, and he was quite fond of my lord likewise; moreover, he whispered to me that the Governor was greatly interested in the young man, that he was very friendly with Lord Lonsdale (who had been in London all this while, and had not sent a message to his son), and that he was very sure he would be glad, and indulgent to those concerned, if the young nobleman should make good his escape before the bloody work of Jeffreys should commence. The warder told me this with bated breath, and a look in his eyes which gave me my cue; so I told him that I knew I could get him twenty guineas forthwith from one who loved the Viscount, and twenty more if the thing should succeed, to help me to get him safe out of the Castle before the Judge should come.

At this the man's eyes glistened, and he said that I might count upon him. He would have done it for less, seeing that the young lord was so gentle and kind to all, but for that sum he would take care that nothing miscarried; and I went to Mistress Mary triumphantly with my news.

But I found her less exultant than I was myself when she knew all; and she said with anxious eyes,—

"To get him safe out of the Castle is much, good Dicon, but it is not all. The city is full of soldiers, and these be not kindly men such as they in the Castle. Some are Colonel Kirke's Lambs, and others the fierce soldiers of Lord Feversham. They watch with terrible sharpness those who come and go, and they keep watch by night as well as by day. Two riders faring forth at any hour of the night will scarce get clear of Taunton streets; and to be caught and taken back to prison will be worse than to wait there for what may betide."

I listened aghast to Mistress Mary, recognizing at once the truth of her words, and feeling my heart sink into my very shoes. All this while I had never thought of aught but getting my lord safe out of the Castle; and now, when this seemed to be a thing possible at last, I was confronted by another and perhaps a worse danger.

"Could he not be hidden away?" I asked.

"Mr. Blewer would find out he was escaped, and raise all Taunton after him," answered Mistress Mary, "and such places as thou or I know, Dicon, would first be searched."

She was silent then a great while, and I had no heart to speak; but suddenly she raised her head and looked me full in the face with shining eyes.

"Dicon," she said, "I see how it must be done!"

"Oh how, fair Mistress?"

"It must be done, not in the dead of night, but at break of day. He must ride forth with thee when the town is beginning to stir."

"Mistress Mary," I cried aghast, "all the town will know him!"

She smiled, and touched my hand with her slim white fingers.

"Foolish boy!" she said softly; and then after a pause for thought she added, "Dicon, wilt do as I say?"

"To the death, Mistress!"

"Then at sunrising to-morrow morning be at this door with Blackbird and Lady Jane, and we will forth into the fresh morning air together. Then will I tell thee more."

"I will not fail you, Mistress," I said; and I went home in a great perplexity.

With the first grey light of dawn I was before the house with the horses, and Mistress Mary came forth clad in a long grey riding-dress and a grey cloak and hood. This hood she wore drawn well over her face, as indeed it was the fashion of maidens to go in the streets, with so many bold soldiers swaggering about.

We rode quietly down the roads, the soldiers looking at us, and sometimes challenging us; but there being naught about us to excite remark or suspicion, we were suffered to go on our way.

We rode some miles almost in silence, and as we were returning Mistress Mary said, "Dost understand, Dicon?"

"No, Mistress, not yet."

"Come every day at dawn for me so. We ride forth thus day by day till every sentry in Taunton knows us. Then some morning there shall another rider sally forth with thee in this grey habit and cloak, and this hood well drawn over his brows. He shall ride this steed and on this saddle—though his own good horse shall be waiting at some appointed place. And who will seek to stop you then, or even give a passing glance? Say, good Dicon, dost thou see light now?"

CHAPTER XXV.

JUST IN TIME.

Days fled by apace. Mistress Mary and I continued our daily morning ride till every sentry and guard within the place must have seen us. Often we were stopped and questioned at first, or looked at with suspicion; but by degrees less and less notice was taken of us, and at last we came and went unmolested, and we knew our object was gained.

Meantime my lord steadily regained his strength, but not so fast as our impatience wished. We were ever in fear lest something should go wrong, lest something should happen to remove our friendly warder from the charge of my lord; and every day as it passed was crowded with anxieties and terrors.

These terrors were not lessened by what was happening all around us.

Every day arrests were made of persons suddenly accused of favouring the rebellion of the Duke. The Bridewell by Tone Bridge was crowded to suffocation with helpless, hapless prisoners awaiting the coming of the merciless Judge; and one day, to my horror and amaze, I heard from the weeping Lizzie Simpson that Will Wiseman had been haled off to prison that very day, she was certain at the instance of that wicked man the Rev. Nicholas Blewer!

I might well tremble with fear on hearing that news; for if Will's youth did not protect him from the malice of his enemy or the penalty of the law, neither would mine protect me; and the rancour of Mr. Blewer against me might be, for all I knew, as great as it had always been against Will since that unlucky drawing of his. I shook in my shoes as I heard the news, and I said to myself in breathless gasps,—

"Suppose they came and took me—before my lord was safe!"

Already the implacable Judge Jeffreys had reached Winchester, and with shuddering horror and many deep-toned execrations we heard of his vile and inhuman treatment of the noble and innocent old Lady Lisle. If an aged and honoured matron of high birth and spotless character could be ruthlessly condemned to a fiery death, and a reluctant jury bullied and coerced into passing a verdict against her, what could we of Taunton hope? A thrill of terror and horror ran through the whole place, and every face one saw was white and stern and set.

I went that very day to take my lord some provisions and other things, and to see if the flight might not be made that very night; and when I had crossed the moat and made my way into the Castle, where I was well known by this time, the friendly jailer beckoned me aside into his little narrow room, and whispered some news in my ear.

"Some prisoners are to be removed to-night from the Castle to the other prison," he said. "They must have more space here now that the Assize is coming so near, and there be so many to be lodged here. I have orders to remove my lord elsewhere—not to Bridewell, but to some underground place here, whence we might never be able to get him out. But I will make shift to bring him forth with the rest of the prisoners who are to be taken away; and then, boy, thou must be ready to hide him somewhere for the night, and get him forth from the town at daybreak. He will not be missed from the Castle till I give the alarm on the morrow—and I will take care to do that none too soon—and at the Bridewell he is not expected, so there will be no question as to him there. Thou must lie in waiting beside the deep recess nigh to the bridge; and when we pass towards the prison, I will see that in the darkness my lord is pushed out of the line and into thy keeping. Have the maid's hood and habit to throw over him forthwith; and then get him safe away to some friendly place of shelter till you can ride forth without fear from the town in the early morning light."

I listened with all my ears, my heart beating joyfully, for the detail of my lord's flight from the Castle had always been full of difficulty even with this man's ready help. My lord was weak, and unable for great efforts, and there were the outer wall and the moat to be crossed; and save by swimming one scarce knew how that last transit was to be made at such an hour of the night as we must choose. We had waited and hoped for some favourable conjunction of circumstances; but none had as yet arisen, and the guards were often changed at the gates, so that overtures of friendship commenced and carried on for a time became so much labour lost when the next change was made.

Now, however, came this happy chance, only just a short while before the dreaded day of the Judge's entrance.

How my heart beat as I posted myself in the appointed place that evening after dark! The night favoured us, for it closed in very gloomy and wet, the rain falling softly and steadily from low-hanging clouds that quite obscured any faint light from moon or stars. In my hiding-place it was as dark as pitch; and I crouched against the wall for shelter, straining my ears as the minutes passed by for the sound of approaching tramp of feet, my heart often growing sick within me as I waited and watched, in fear lest some fresh fiat had gone forth and the change of the prisoners' habitation had been given up.

In my anxiety to be in time I was much too soon, and the time of waiting seemed well-nigh interminable. I had almost resolved to come forth and wend my way to the Castle for news, when I heard in the distance a measured tramp of feet, and drew back once more with a sense of sickening expectation for the procession to pass.

Nearer and nearer came the tread of many feet. I heard the voices of the guard as they uttered maledictions on the weather and on the dirty and uneven state of parts of the road. I crouched in my hiding-place and held my breath. They were close beside me; they were already passing! Oh, had this plan failed? where was my lord?

"Hist, Dicon, be ready!" It seemed as though the whisper was in the air. A second body of men passed me. I could hear, but could see nothing. In a moment I felt a figure slip beside me in the embrasure, and with a great throb of heart I whispered,—

"My lord! my lord!"

"It is I, Dicon," answered the well-known voice, though the tone was very low, and methought sorrowful. But I said no word, only hasted to get the grey habit and cloak and hood arranged in the darkness; and by the time that was done every sound had died into silence, and nothing but the murmur of the river and the plash of the rain fell upon our listening ears.

"Come, my lord," I said, and took his hand, and together we glided out of our hiding-place and began retracing our way through the streets. It was late, and the towns-folk were in bed. The prisoners had been moved only after the hour for the city to be asleep. Perhaps the Governor feared some attempt at rescue, perhaps some moving and heart-rending scene on the part of friends or relatives. At any rate, his orders had been given for a night move; and to this, and to the clever management of our friendly jailer, we owed my lord's escape from those grim walls.

He let me lead him whither I would; and I had his place of hiding all arranged. My low knock at a side door was instantly answered; and the next moment the door closed upon us, a ray of light streamed out upon the little group gathered in that place, and my lord passing his hand across his eyes, spoke for the first time in the exclamation,—

"Mary! Mary!"

For it was Mistress Mary who was standing before him, and Miss Blake who held the lantern and gazed with eager joy upon the rescued captive. It was to the house of this brave and generous lady that I had brought my lord, and that by her own desire.

"It will be safer so," she had said when I told her of the plan. "Come to the little side door. None will hear or see you; and then when the morrow comes, and my lord fares forth disguised as Mistress Mary going for her morning ride, it will be best that he should sally forth from this door. Bring him hither then, Dicon. Let the children see each other once again; for in these perilous times there is no telling, when we once are sundered, when we may meet again."

This was almost the first knowledge I had that Miss Blake looked upon her own position as one of peril. But I read in her eyes then that she did; and yet she was willing to harbour a fugitive beneath her roof, knowing that for such an offence Lady Lisle had but just been condemned to be burnt alive!

I think that weak women are often braver than men. All honour to the lady who opened her doors to us that night!

I could not, however, linger. I wished not to arouse suspicion by my movements, and I slipped away and into the inn and up to my room without meeting a soul. My uncle did not trouble much about my comings and goings, and I knew how to go in and out at will, even when the doors were closed. But there was little sleep for me that night. I tossed and turned upon my bed, thinking of every sort of mishap that might occur to hinder my lord's flight; and with the very earliest of the dawn, when there was scarce light to dress myself by, I arose, and was soon in the stable feeding the horses and wondering how I should feel when next I performed that office here, and whether I should ever return to Taunton save as a prisoner, to await my trial with the rest.

I dare not go much before my usual time to fetch my charge from Miss Blake's house, else might our unwonted promptitude excite remark. It was a clear, bright September morning, and the sun was beginning to rise in the east when at last I stood before the door and knocked, feeling all the while as though my own heart were knocking at my ribs loud enough to be heard by all the town.

The door opened, a veiled and muffled figure came out, and but for the extra height—and Mistress Mary was taller for a woman than my lord for a man, so that the discrepancy was not so very great—I should never have guessed but that it was my lady herself. In another minute we had commenced our ride through the yet quiet streets, few persons being about save the sentries, who scarce cast a glance upon us as we moved leisurely along; and indeed, now that he was sitting the horse woman fashion, it would take a clever pair of eyes to detect any difference from my companion of every day. And with each turning passed my heart leaped up within me, for safety seemed to be already gained, and once free of Taunton—

But there my meditations came to a sudden end, my heart seemed to stop beating till my head felt like to burst, and a mist swam before my eyes; for there half a street ahead of us, but standing still as if for us to come up, was Mr. Blewer, mounted on a horse, and looking at us with such an ugly leer in his eyes that I felt as though he already knew all, and that we were undone.

There was shadow still in the street, and my lord wore the hood drawn right over his face, as Mistress Mary was wont to wear it. Nothing could be seen of his face at such an hour; but what if the cunning foe had divined our plan, and insisted on looking beneath?

"My lord, my lord, have a care," I whispered, "or we are undone! Mr. Blewer is about to address us."

That was all I had time to say. Already we were approaching the waiting horseman; and he, making a sweeping bow with his hat, and giving one of his most hideous smiles, reined alongside my lord's horse and said,—

"Fair Mistress Mary, I have seen thee pass up and down these streets these many days with thy faithful servant. Methought thou wouldst not disdain another escort, and the temptation to join thee was too strong for flesh and blood to resist. Say, sweet mistress, hast thou no kind word for me? Knowest thou not yet how deep is the devotion of thy poor servant and humble suitor?"

There was no answer from the veiled figure, only the head was drawn up with a haughty gesture, so like that of Mistress Mary when angered that I could have smiled had I dared. I breathed a little more freely. I saw that no suspicion had entered yet the evil mind of this man. He believed that he was addressing Mistress Mary; and I racked my brains to think of any means whereby this delusion could be kept up, and our most unwelcome attendant dismissed without his suspicions being aroused.

Giving him a look and a wink, as though I had something to say to him, I drew his attention off for a moment from the one he supposed to be Mistress Mary. Having done so, I dropped behind; and he, after speaking once more to the silent figure beside him, and receiving no answer, looked back at me, and on receiving a nod, fell behind too; whilst the grey-clad figure rode on ahead, as though glad to be rid of us both.

May Heaven pardon me for my falsehood that day! I have learned, since I have come to think seriously upon such matters, that it is wrong to seek to meet evil by evil, and that to be false in order to outwit the cunning of others, or to stoop to evil practices to secure good ends, is a thing abominable in the eyes of God, albeit there is too much of it mixed up in the things of this world. But I was then only a lad. I felt that I would risk all I possessed in this world and the next for the safety of my lord; and I had not been taught to look with abhorrence upon all crooked ways. Wherefore I had rapidly turned over in my mind how best I could deceive the miscreant who rode beside me, and I spoke to him false words without a qualm of conscience.

"Sir," I said, in a whisper that bespoke good fellowship, "if you really would wed with Mistress Mary, you would do well to wait three more days till my Lord Lonsdale be come back to his house. I have heard that he will then summon Mistress Mary home to him there, thinking Taunton no safe place for her when once the inquisition of blood begins. Then let her once be there, safe in his care, and I am sure he will welcome any godly man who comes to woo and wed her. Mistress Mary has said as much herself. I sometimes think her heart is failing her, and that she will soon be willing to save herself from peril by doing her guardian's will, and wedding with the husband he has chosen."

Mr. Blewer's eyes sparkled greedily. Sometimes I wonder that he believed me, knowing, as he must certainly have done, of the way in which I had been mixed up with the cause of the Duke and with my lord. But then, again, mine uncle had given it out all through the place (although I knew it not at the time) that I had gone forth as a spy, and that my mission was to send him news of the movements of the rebels—and there was enough truth in this to bear out his words; and since he himself had gained a character for trimming his sails to the prevailing winds, it was not altogether unlikely that I, his kinsman, should have caught the trick from him. Also a man is always prone to believe that which accords with his desires.

Wherefore Mr. Blewer looked eagerly at me, and asked in a yet lower whisper, and with an air of confidence and good-will,—

"Then thou thinkest, good Dicon, that her heart is already inclining towards me?"

"I think it will incline more and more if you, good sir, will hold aloof for a while, and let her feel her loneliness. My lord the Viscount, for whom she had a maid's fancy, is in prison, and like to die, as all men say, if not of his wounds, yet by the hand of the executioner; and all those whom she most loves are in prison or in peril. Doubtless she will soon feel the need of some strong man's arm to lean upon. Only try her not too soon. Let her first feel her guardian's displeasure. Let him first set before her the peril in which she stands for her handiwork, and meddling in the matter of those banners and colours. Afterwards she may incline the more to one who seeks her in her hour of trouble and desertion. But seem to come to her then as a deliverer. Trouble her not now, whilst her heart is still proud, and she is still buoyed up with false hopes. Let her hear a little more of the work of the Judge, which has but now commenced. Methinks that will bring her to her senses."

"Boy, thou dost talk like a philosopher and a student of women. Whence dost thou get such wisdom at thy years?"

"Nay, good sir, it is not wisdom; it is but knowing something of the whimsies of maids from having sisters at home who are as contrary as the winds of heaven. And now, an it please you, sir, I must join my lady; but if you will wait for another day, I think your suit will be the better forwarded."

Mr. Blewer looked first at me and then at the figure in front as though in deliberation; but at last, to my infinite relief, he reined in his horse and said,—

"So be it, Dicon; thou mayest be right. And I will make my lady answer for this pride and haughtiness in days to come."

So then he turned and rode back whence he had come, whilst I joined my lord; and we soon left Taunton behind, and knew that for the present our perils were over.

Three miles away, at a little obscure farm-house, I had a horse ready for my lord. All that had been settled days ago, none knowing what sudden change might cause us to make our attempt without much warning. I intended, however, to take Lady Jane the whole way, and to let my lord ride woman fashion into Ilminster in the dusk, cloaked and hooded as before; for there were soldiers on the watch in every town, and we should be far less like to draw notice upon ourselves thus than if my lord rode openly into the city, where his face might like enough be known.

So we had a very gentle and easy day, stopping long at the lonely farm to rest; and I wondered at his silence and sadness, since our journey had so far been crowned with success. But he smiled when I asked him, and made answer,—

"My sadness is not for myself, good lad; thanks to thy courage and quickness and my Mary's devotion, all has gone well with me. But I cannot forget those poor, simple fellow-prisoners of mine, who went with me from the Castle but yesterday, and who may so soon be called upon to die a terrible death. They have been so much less guilty than I. They followed like sheep where they were led. In their simple souls was no thought but of victory and an easy triumph for a rightful King. And they must die like sheep; whilst I, who knew better the two sides of the picture, and who rebelled against the reigning sovereign with open eyes—I am to escape all consequences, whilst others suffer the full penalty of the law. I cannot but be sad. I could weep tears of blood. Were it not for my Mary's sake, methinks I would even now give myself up, and die with the rest."

I loved him for his gentle words, but I sought to comfort him too.

"It would not help them for you to die, my lord."

"No, else would I die for them," he said.

The day passed in short journeys and frequent halts, chiefly at places where I knew the people and was sure of a welcome. The last halt we made was but three miles from Ilminster; and there we abode till the dusk fell and we could ride into the town under cover of the evening shadows, yet not so late as to attract notice or remark.

My lord donned the grey habit once again, and leaving his own horse at the farm till I should fetch it thence, took Lady Jane and the side saddle, and so rode through the gathering twilight into Ilminster. There I was hailed by one or two friends, all anxious for news of relatives and friends in Taunton. I showed no haste nor anxiety in holding parley with them; and when one asked me who was my companion, I answered at once that it was a maid on her way to her friends at Lyme, and that I had promised her a bed at my aunt's house, whither her friends would fetch her on the morrow.

And thus talking and explaining we rode through the streets, till we alighted at my aunt's door.

Right gladly did she receive me, and right kindly did she greet my companion, whom she took at the first to be a maid, until I whispered a word in her ear, and got a squeeze of the hand in reply. But so long as her servants were about the place, she made as though my lord were in truth a maid, and only when we were alone together in the guest-chamber did she permit herself to welcome him as his own self.

The secret chamber was ready, and with some pride and pleasure she took us up, and showed us all the arrangements made for the comfort of the fugitive.

"If it be but changing one prison for another, my lord," she said as he would have thanked her, only that she put his words aside, "I will answer for it that you shall lack nothing here; and that so soon as this cruel and wicked Judge has gone, and peace settles down once more upon this unhappy land, its doors will open for you, and you will go forth to your friends, whilst I shall have known the honour and pleasure of saving the life of Lord Lonsdale's son."

"Madam," said my lord, "words are all too poor as a medium of thanks. But tell me, are you sure that no hurt can fall upon you for this good deed? If peril were to threaten you for this act of charity to me, I would sooner go forth into the street now, and give myself into the hands of the guard to do with me as they would."

"Hoots, my lord, talk not so wildly!" answered my aunt, giving him a motherly pat on the shoulder. "There is not a soul in this house that knows of this chamber here. Not a soul in the town wishes me ill, or would speak a word to trouble me. We will soon contrive, Dicon and I, that the household believes the maid who entered my doors leaves again on the morrow. Go to bed, laddie, go to bed—that is the only place you are fit for—and leave Dicon and me to settle all the rest. He shall bring you a supper before long that will be better than prison fare; and then to rest and get sound and strong is all you will have to think of this many a day."

I waited on my lord, and soon saw him betwixt the fine woven sheets of my good aunt's spinning, on a bed so soft that he said it was enough to send him to sleep of itself. Indeed after he had partaken of the good cheer prepared for him, he quickly sank to sleep, feeling that at least no prison walls enclosed him, and that if he were not yet a free man, he was on the way to freedom. The terrible days that were threatening Taunton would not touch him.

My aunt and I sat far up in the night talking in low tones of the fearful things that were everywhere happening. Every fresh person one saw in those days had some new story of horror to unfold. Ilminster had its tale of citizens languishing in different jails till the Judge should pass sentence upon them; and every house had its cause of fear, or at best was saddened by the shadow which had fallen upon others.

With the first light of day I was up, and had brought round Lady Jane, saddled for the maid; and out to me came my aunt, robed in the grey hood and habit— for her figure being tall and spare, none who saw her would know any difference; and the neighbours beginning to open their windows nodded to me and wished me a good journey, whilst they spoke kindly to my companion, whom they took to be a girl in a humble walk in life, and who gave them a low-toned answer of thanks.

Then we started, I leading the horse by the bridle; and only when clear of the town did my aunt dismount from her unaccustomed perch, take from the bundle she carried her own head-gear and cloak, and, leaving me to dispose of Lady Jane as I would, made her way back by another route to the town, and was seen in the market as usual making her daily purchases.

As for me, I took Lady Jane to the farm where Lord Vere's horse was stabled, and then made my way back to Ilminster. I remained one more night with my aunt, saw that my lord had all he needed for comfort, and was well pleased with his surroundings; and then taking Blackbird on the following morning I rode him back to Taunton, leaving the other horses with the farmer till I could reclaim them with safety.

I got back to Taunton to give the other twenty guineas to the kindly jailer, and to be in time for the terrible pageant which was to take place now within its environs.

CHAPTER XXVI.

THE TERRIBLE JUDGE.

"Dicon, my father says he has heard that that terrible man will have up Miss Blake and the Taunton maids who made and presented the colours. Heaven alone knows what fearful thing will happen to them then! Dicon, let me have speech with Mary! She must be got away; she must be hidden till the storm be overpast! I have an hour to spare, whilst my father has business with Sir William. Dicon, dost thou know that Lord Jeffreys abides with him in his house here in the town? But he has sent all his women folk to Orchard Portman. He will not let them meet yon wicked and terrible man. Methinks a King who can use such instruments is little fit for his place! Dicon," lowering her voice to a whisper, her eyes flashing with a noble indignation as she spoke, "dost thou know what is said?—that if only this monster in human shape slays enough men here in the West to satisfy that bloody tyrant his master, he is to be rewarded with the great seal of the Chancellor! Truly the people had right on their side when they rebelled against such a tyrant; only they needed one to lead them whose title was above reproach, and who came not under false pretences. Surely the day will come when such a champion will arise, and England will free herself from the hateful yoke of an unjust, an illegal, and a cruel tyranny."

The speaker was Mistress Mary Bridges, and since her heroic act, of which I have already spoken, she had become an idol of the people of Taunton and a companion to her father such as she had never been before. She had ridden in with him that day, and now was all eagerness to see Mistress Mary Mead; but when she returned to the inn-yard after her visit was paid, it was with a grave face and anxious mien.

"Dicon, I have argued and entreated in vain. She will not fly! She will not leave Miss Blake to meet the storm alone. Her pupils are nearly all of them fled. Some few remain in Taunton, but many are conveyed away I know not whither. Mary says that she had as much to do with those banners as Miss Blake, and she will not flee and leave her. She says were all to be done again she would do as she has done. She has no fear. She is not afraid even of the wicked Jeffreys. She will stay and confront him, and will not let herself be hidden. But, O Dicon, though I love her the more for her courage, I fear that ill will come of it!"

"What can they do to her?" I asked with a shudder. "They will not kill her?"

"Oh no, no!" answered Mary. "I asked my father just now, and he said that the penalty for such an offence was not like to be more than a heavy fine. Even that monster would not dare to condemn a maid to worse than that. But it is the being brought before him, being subjected to his brutal words and looks, his hideous jibes and his inhuman threats. O Dicon, the stories of yon man in other places make my blood run cold! To think of Mary exposed to his baleful glance. But she knows no fear; she will not let Miss Blake bear it alone."

"It is like her!" I answered, with warm admiration. "And, Mistress Mary, I will watch over her all I can; and if there be need later, will take her to the cottage in the marsh, where she will be safe."

"Ay, she will be safe there; and truly after these rains it is few who could find the way thither. Dicon, let not Lord Lonsdale take her to his house. They say he will not return till after the trials. He is in a great fear for his son, but has been told that the Viscount is not numbered amongst the prisoners. There has been some error or mistake. He was taken, as many aver; but he has either died of his wounds or else has escaped in the confusion—no man clearly knows which. Lord Lonsdale went to Court to seek to win his pardon from the King should he be brought up for trial and condemned; and he remains there till the Judge has gone, having a special messenger here to bring him instant word if his son should be arraigned. But he himself stays where he is till all peril is past. Then he will come back, and if I mistake me not, his first act will be to wed Mistress Mary Mead to some man of known loyalty, both as a protection to herself and as a means of keeping her away from his son, should the Viscount ever return. Dicon, guard her from that an thou canst. I trow that my lord will return one day to claim her, and she must be free to wed him."

I promised young Mistress Mary to use all heed and diligence; and then I watched her ride away with her father, who came to find her, and thought that two such noble Marys did not live in all the world as the two who honoured me with their confidence.

But all Taunton was in a tremble, and within the town there was that state of things best described by the words of the prophet—"lamentation, and mourning, and woe."

The great Assize Hall in the Castle was being prepared for the coming tribunal, and I must needs go to see. It is a very fine hall, as all men of Taunton know, a hundred and twenty feet long and thirty wide; and when Taunton was under the Bishop of Winchester's ecclesiastical jurisdiction, his court used also to be held here. So that still over the porch were the two keys and the sword, the arms of the Bishop of Winchester, together with the three bugle horns which were the private coat of Bishop Horn, who no doubt was a great personage when the place was built or repaired. Four cherubs occupy the corners, and within the surrounding garter are the two mottoes, "Honi soit qui mal y pense," and "Crux et Vanitas."

Over the two strong arches of the inner gateway stood the grand-jury room, soon to be occupied by the trembling jury, who, badgered by the wicked Judge, feared to return any verdict save that of Guilty, however insufficient the evidence against the unhappy prisoner. We had heard already how the monster had raved and foamed with fury at any other verdict, and had driven the unhappy men away again and again, until he had terrified them into submission. To begin with, the juries were selected by the Sheriffs; and since the Sheriffs were all loyal King's men, they had chosen men all in favour of the King's policy. But even so, they could not altogether throw to the winds all sense of justice and right; and yet if they dared to give any verdict save that which the merciless Judge indicated, they went almost in terror of their own lives. To such a pass had things come under this Special Commission, instituted by James the Second and conducted according to his own heart by his chosen tools!

The great Assize Hall was being hung with crimson cloth in honour of the important occasion. Methought the colour something ominous of what was coming; but it was said that Lord Jeffreys always looked to be received with due honour. I had a great and lively curiosity to see this wicked man, and as I was known to one or more of the custodians of the place, I was promised entrance that afternoon, when his charge to the jury was to be given; though after that, when the trials themselves came on, I must take my chance with the rest of the people. The place would be thronged to suffocation, and if I wished for entrance I must seek it at the doors with the others.

I did very much wish to be present, but knew not whether I should achieve my desire. But at least I was there in a fairly good place that afternoon, when I knew that the great and wicked Judge had arrived, and that he was to address the jury at once, so that the business of the day could commence upon the morrow.

How my heart beat when at last he came, with his brothers of the bench in attendance, who seemed of no account beside that great burly figure with those extraordinary eyes, and that bloated face seamed and lined by passion and drink till it was more like the face of a devil than of a man. Although I had heard much of Judge Jeffreys, never had I pictured such a monster in human shape as I beheld that day, as the western light, level and clear, illumined the great hall and made plain all the persons assembled there. It was as if the devil himself looked out from those eyes; and in the loud rasping tones of the voice, full of fierce invective coupled with brutal taunts and threats, it was impossible to conceive that there spoke the voice of a monarch's servant. Oaths of the most blasphemous description fell from his lips, mingled with such ribald jests as made one's blood run cold. What was the nature of the charge I cannot tell, for I seemed to hear nothing but taunts and threats and profane jests all jumbled together in one hideous medley. No wonder the jurymen stood huddled together, as if only longing to be out of reach of those basilisk eyes. No wonder that amongst the crowd assembled to hear those who had relations or friends amongst the prisoners felt their hearts sink within them. That all the men declared the Judge to be drunk seemed small consolation. We had heard before this that it was his habit to be more or less drunk whilst performing his duties. Possibly in the morning he might be something more sober; but there were those who averred that he was even more to be dreaded sober than drunk. In either case he was a devil incarnate. About that there were no two opinions. And it was passed quickly through the town that the only chance a prisoner had was to plead guilty, and so save the court the trouble of trying him. Those who did this were condemned to death in a mass; but many were respited. It was said that the Judge had openly declared he would hang every man who dared to plead "not guilty," and that these would be at once hung up, whilst those who pleaded "guilty" would be respited for a time, and possibly escape the final penalty of the law. This was the Judge's artifice for shortening his bloody work, and it invariably put him in a tempest of passion when prisoners dared to plead "not guilty."

Do as I would, I could not get into court upon the first day of the trials; and I ran down to Master Simpson's house to see how things were going there, and if aught had been heard of Master Simpson himself. Here I found Miss Hannah Hewling mingling her tears with those of Lizzie and her aunt; for her brother Benjamin was awaiting his trial now at Taunton, and the gentle William, only nineteen years old and so full of sweetness and piety, had already been done to death at Lyme, in spite of all the favour brought to bear on his behalf.

Amid her tears Miss Hannah read to us a letter he had penned to her just before he suffered. "I am going to launch into eternity," he wrote, "and, I hope and trust, into the arms of my blessed Redeemer, to whom I commit you and all my dear relations." And as he was going to the place of execution, he repeated to one of his comrades some of the beautiful words contained in the fourteenth chapter of St. John's Gospel; and then he added, "Here is a sweet promise for us, 'I will not leave you comfortless: I will come to you.' Christ will be with us to the last." And to another who bid him farewell he said,

"Farewell till we meet in heaven. Presently I shall be with Christ. Oh, I would not change conditions with any in this world! I would not stay behind for ten thousand worlds." And to a friend who came to comfort him at the end—not one of the condemned—the friend who had given all these particulars to Miss Hannah, he said, "Pray remember my dear love to my brother and sister, and tell them I desire they would comfort themselves that I am gone to Christ; and we shall quickly meet in the glorious Mount Zion above."

And so greatly were the officers who carried out the mandate of the Court touched by his piety and sweetness and gentleness that some wept, and others declared that had the Chief-Justice himself been there he could not have let him die. So though no mandate had been given to that effect, yet the body of the pious youth was given to the people of Lyme for Christian burial, and was laid in the grave by a number of young maidens of that place, who had heard the story of his faith and resignation, and took this Christian office upon themselves.

It could not but comfort the sister's heart to hear all this, though her tears fell fast as she told the tale. Her heart was sore troubled too for the brother yet living; but her parents in London had sent her large sums of money, and it was hoped that the Judge might be bribed into showing mercy, even though he had condemned the prisoner in court.

Upon the day when Master Benjamin Hewling was to be tried, I was resolved that I would be there, and would find room too for Miss Hannah and for Lizzie as well. Money would always do much, and of this there was no lack; and I went beforehand to the keepers of the doors, and got a promise that if I would come very early, and keep very quiet when admitted, they would see that we got smuggled in before the crowd came thronging and surging in. And this in fact was done; and though afterwards we were well-nigh suffocated by the press, still we were placed where we could see and hear. I was the more glad of this because I heard a whisper that this would be the last day, and that the case of the Maids of Taunton would come before the Judge at the close of the more bloody proceedings, and also that of Will Wiseman, the accusation against whom was only the reading of the Declarations of the Duke to the populace; his other daring acts seeming not to have become known to Mr. Blewer, who, we felt certain, was his accuser.

How my heart quaked when I saw the Judge's terrible countenance beneath its wig of office! The red robes were scarcely more red than the inflamed visage, and the eyes rolled from side to side with a sullen fury that was almost more terrible than the ferocity of their gleam when first I had seen them.

The scenes I saw that day will never be effaced from my memory. I would that I had the skill to tell the tale as it should be told, but I can but state a few bald facts. Let the reader fill up the outline as he will.

Let me speak of the trial of Mr. Simon Hamling—or Hamlyn, as men indifferently call him. He was a worthy citizen of Taunton, who had borne a good repute there for long; but had for the last three years of his life lived some three miles out of the town, and come to and fro on business. When he heard that the Duke had come, he went to the town to speak to his son, to advise him to have nothing to do with this matter of the rising; as he expressed it in his defence, "That as he expected his blessing and countenance, he should not at all concern himself in the matter, but submit himself to the will of God in all things;" and having so delivered himself he went home, and was never in the town again whilst the Duke was there, save that he came to buy some provision for his house, as was his custom, on the Saturday. But he was a dissenter, and the Mayor owed him a grudge. When nothing could be proved against him as having been concerned in the rebellion, the Judge fell into such a rage as I have never seen in my life before, so that all the court quaked and trembled, and he bawled out, "The rascal is a dissenter! I can smell 'em forty miles!" and forthwith foaming at the mouth he bid the jury find him guilty, which to their shame they did; and sentence of death was accordingly passed upon him. Hearing which the Mayor, being smitten with shame and remorse, strove to get the sentence reversed; but the Lord Jeffreys turned upon him with one of his awful oaths, and cried, "You have brought him on; if he be innocent, his blood be upon you!" and immediately called for the next prisoner, which was Mr. Benjamin Hewling.

In such a mood as the Judge was now in all saw that the poor young gentleman had no chance. Many stood forward to try to bear witness to his blameless character, but were yelled down by the Judge, who would hear nothing. The prisoner had been in arms in the rebellion, and should die the traitor's death. Then enraged by the dauntless and dignified bearing of the young man, his judge stormed and cursed and raged at him, and made the horrid words of the sentence tenfold more horrid by the way he flung it at him, till half the women in the place fell weeping, and Miss Hannah drooped her head and for a minute quite swooned away.

But the spirit of her brothers possessed her too, and she recovered herself, and was able to make her way out of the court holding Lizzie's hand. I must needs stay to see how Will Wiseman fared, and to hear what befell with regard to the Maids of Taunton, as they were beginning to be called by the world. Several cases came between, all of which were treated in the same brutal fashion by the Lord Jeffreys; and when one thought of the pious and blameless lives many of these men had lived, their godliness and honesty of purpose, and their piety and sweetness of disposition, it seemed a strange thing to see them arraigned before this drunken and blasphemous judge, and feel that he had the power, in despite of the clearest evidence, to doom them to a frightful and hideous death.

But my heart beat with a more personal interest when I saw the familiar face of Will Wiseman in the prisoner's place. He had grown thin and white during his captivity; for the prisons were crowded and unwholesome, and the prisoners were but poorly fed. I had done what I could for him; but I had not succeeded in seeing him, nor could I be sure that the things I took him from the Simpsons' house ever reached him aright.

Jeffreys glared at poor Will as though he would have done him to death on the very spot; but Will looked at him back without any sign of fear—though, unless he were double and treble as brave as I, he must surely have been in a sad affright. And then the witnesses suborned by wicked Mr. Blewer, who had by this time edged himself very near to the judges, and was looking on with cruel malice in his eyes, came forward and bore testimony to the fact that Will had read the different Declarations of the Duke to the people who wished to hear them; and thankful indeed was I that none came to tell how he had led the assault upon the arms in the church tower, for I was not sure that that would not have been a hanging matter. I thought they could not do much to poor Will for such a small thing as this; but Jeffreys was licking his cruel lips, and his face had that smile upon it which was almost worse than his scowl, and he cried out in his husky, rasping tones,—

"A young rogue, but a veritable villain! He must be taught to curb that mischievous tongue of his! Pity the good old plan of boring it through with a hot iron is out of fashion now! Never mind; we will find a cure nevertheless. What does the wise man say? 'Spare the rod and spoil the child.' Well, we will not do that. The rod shall not be spared. I give sentence that the prisoner, William Wiseman, be whipped through every market town in Somerset.— Executioner, warm him well. The weather is growing sharp. See that he take not cold in the open air. He will needs be shorn of his clothing. Warm his back for him! warm it well!" And doubling himself up in brutal laughter at his jest, the Judge signed for the prisoner to be removed.

My heart went out in pity and rage; but to myself I kept repeating, "My hoard of guineas—my golden hoard is still almost untouched. Sure it can win for poor Will an abatement of his punishment. The executioner at least will not be as brutal as the Judge."

When I came to myself, after having been wrapped in thought for I know not how long, I felt a curious thrill going through the court; and there I saw Miss Blake and Mary Mead standing side by side before the wicked Judge, who was regarding them with a face of curiosity and malevolent interest.

"And where be the other fair maidens?" he asked, looking at a paper before him.

The usher of the court replied that only Miss Blake had been summoned; that the pupils could be found when necessary, but that they were taken by their parents, and were scattered here and there, save Mistress Mary Mead, who had claimed to accompany Miss Blake.

The names of twenty or more maids were read out as having been concerned in the making and the presenting of the colours; and much ribald jesting was indulged in on the part of the Judge, who, however, seemed in not so evil a humour as heretofore. Whilst the proceedings were going on, I observed with uneasiness that Mr. Blewer edged himself up to Lord Jeffreys; and my uneasiness did not decrease when I saw them laughing together as if on very friendly terms, and keep throwing glances in the direction of Mistress Mary, who stood white and calm and collected beside her more agitated mistress. I think perhaps she had never looked so beautiful as she did then in her devotion and courage; and I hated to see the eyes of those two bad men scanning her at their evil pleasure.

After a while the Judge took up the word again, and said that for the high misdemeanour of Miss Blake and all the persons named upon the list which had been read, a fine would be laid upon them by the court; but that this fine should be the Christmas Box of the Maids of Honour of her Majesty the Queen, and that they should levy it upon the Taunton Maids at their will and pleasure. How the sentence was worded I cannot remember, but that was the substance of it. The Taunton Maids were to remain at large, but to be given (as it were) to the Maids of Honour for a Christmas Box; and they were to have liberty to exact as much money as could be wrung from the parents and guardians of the maids. But after having so disposed of the irresponsible culprits, the Judge turned with a heavy frown upon Miss Blake, and thundered out that as she had been the planner and contriver of all this, and knew what she was doing, which the young maids did not, she was condemned to be imprisoned in Dorchester jail at the King's pleasure, where doubtless she would come to repent her of her evil ways.

Then whilst poor Miss Blake turned pale and seemed about to swoon, and the women in the court who had known her for long fell a-weeping, the Judge turned his evil eyes upon Mistress Mary and said,—

"As for you, young Mistress, who are old enough to know better, yet have been led into evil practices by those about you, I will pass over your misdemeanour in this matter but lightly. You shall pay your share of the fine imposed; but for the rest, your imprisonment shall not be in any jail—that were something too hard for youth and beauty. Yet inasmuch as you have proved stubborn and rebellious, and are not fit to be custodian of your own fortune nor of your own person, we give you here in troth-plight to good Mr. Nicholas Blewer, a godly and a loyal subject; and he will guide and teach and admonish you, and train you to be a submissive wife and a good subject. To-morrow we will see you wed ere we leave the town,—And so, ladies, farewell!"

I listened aghast. My eyes turned helplessly from the evil face of the Judge to the triumphant one of Master Blewer, wreathed in smiles that turned me sick; and then to the cold, calm visage of Mistress Mary, who seemed scarce to take in the meaning of these terrible words. After standing for a minute, gazing as if horror-struck at the Judge, she suddenly pulled her hood over her face, and went out walking unsteadily, so that many thought her weeping.

But I knew better: Mistress Mary's spirit was one that rose under stress of peril when that of another would have sunk. I was near to a door, and I pushed my way out and fought my way through all sorts of places where I had no business, till I found myself at her side. Her face was as white as death; but she grasped me by the hand when she saw me, and said, in a low, strained voice,—

"Take me somewhere, Dicon, before *he* can get out!"

"Come with me!" I said, rapidly reviewing the situation, and striving to know what to do; and as we passed out together, I heard people saying one to another, "She is ill! she is stricken to death!" "The evil visage of that man has killed her!"

"Yes," I cried, seizing my opportunity, "she is ill—she is very ill. She is stricken with a fever. I must take her to those who can tend her.—Lean on me, Mistress Mary; I will take care of you."

She obeyed me mechanically. I do not think she either heard or saw. There was a stunned look upon her face, as though somehow the soul had gone out of it. I knew that her mind was working inwardly all the more keenly and intensely; but to others it looked indeed as though she had been stricken for death, so ashen grey was her face, so fixed and irresponsive her eyes.

She put her hand upon my arm, and by many by-ways and alleys I led her away, none following, as all interest was still centred in the doings of the court. Still I was resolved to baffle all pursuit; and since poor Miss Blake was committed to prison, there was no safety for Mistress Mary beneath the accustomed roof.

So I took her straight to the Simpsons' house, where Lizzie welcomed her with open arms; and after I had whispered long in her ear, a look of keen intelligence beamed over her face, and she whispered back in eager accents,
—

"Trust us, good Dicon. We would do more than that for sweet Mistress Mary to save her from such a fate!"

CHAPTER XXVII.

THE JUDGE'S SENTENCES.

And what then was our plan? If, reader, you will trouble yourself so far as to read the annals of Taunton for this time, and especially the part of it which refers to the Taunton Maids, you will find it set down that there was one maid who appeared in court besides Miss Blake; and that the terrible looks of the bloody Judge struck such terror into her heart, that she pulled her hood over her face and fell a-weeping, and so left the court; and that so great was her fright that she went home and sank down in a swoon, and was dead of sheer terror before the sun had set. And if you will seek amongst the graves in the churchyard here, you will find one that bears the name of Mary Mead; and you will be told by the sexton that it is the grave of the fairest of the Taunton Maids, who worked the most beautiful of all the banners that were given to the Duke of Monmouth by Taunton Town, and who fell sick upon the very day on which she had borne herself so bravely in court before the wicked Judge Jeffreys, and died and was buried, though she was to have been wed on the very day of her funeral.

The story says that it was to a handsome young Viscount that she was to have given her hand, and claims sympathy for the maid on that account; but those who remember the real scene know better than that, although there are but few who know that Mary Mead does not lie in that grave, but that therein lies only a coffin filled with books and stones; whilst she—but I must not get on too fast with my story.

In the confusion and excitement of the town at this time, and the universal fear and indignation inspired by these trials, it was so easy to arrange the thing. A coffin was brought to the Simpsons' house that very night, for a maid stricken with a fever; and after it was filled with heavy substances, the lid was screwed down, and an order for burial was easy to obtain. For all had heard the story of Mary Mead in court, and how she had been stricken as it were for death upon receiving her sentence from the Judge, so that none were surprised to hear how sudden the end had been; and since Mr. Blewer had drunk himself drunk with Lord Jeffreys that night, as a fitting preparation for his nuptials with a pure and virtuous maiden on the morrow, even he did not trouble us with any inquiry. Then as all men had a wholesome horror of fever, the coffin was promptly screwed down, and all made ready for the burying before the dawn of the day.

God forgive us if we did amiss; but those were hard and cruel days, and poor persecuted folks were driven sometimes to sore straits if they were to escape worse than death. I, at least, felt no qualm at that time, whatever falsehood I told to stand betwixt Mistress Mary and the peril of being wedded to that wicked man, who would make of her fair young life a veritable hell upon earth. For her sweet sake, let alone for my lord's, I would have done more than I did. As I say again, God forgive us our sin; for sin we did, albeit I scarce know now how I should act were such a thing to come into my life once more.

So whilst all Taunton slept after the excitement of that day, and in prospect of the near excitements of the coming executions, Mistress Mary and I slipped from the town on foot, and by unfrequented routes; and before the first streak of coming day appeared in the east, I had piloted her through the marshy tract of ground nigh to Bishop's Hull, and had left her, exhausted but in peace, with the kindly cottage folks, who had had their instructions from their well-loved foster-child, and who received this other Mistress Mary with open arms.

Indeed the story of the scene in the Assize Hall roused within them feelings of the keenest indignation. They would have done much more than was asked of them to save a victim of wicked Judge Jeffreys from the fate he had assigned her. They lived near enough to Taunton to know somewhat of Mr. Blewer and his evil report; and when I sallied forth again at break of day, it was to feel that no surer place of refuge could have been found for Mistress Mary, and no more loving guardians.

But there was plenty of work awaiting me still. I knew not the day nor the hour when Will's punishment would commence; and it was needful that I should see and bribe the hangman, that he laid the stripes but lightly on my poor comrade's back, despite the charge of the Judge. The execution of the prisoners condemned to death was fixed for the thirtieth of the month—only a few days distant; but Will might be whipped at any time, and if I knew Mr. Blewer aright, he would seek the pleasure of seeing it done right speedily. Well did I know that it was his spite alone which had caused Will to be arrested. And the only marvel was that I had escaped his rancour, the more so that I had deceived him about Mistress Mary and Lord Lonsdale's speedy coming. But perhaps he had thought that I spoke in good faith, and was myself deceived. At least he doubtless saw his way to a more speedy and triumphant accomplishment of his wishes by gaining the ear of the wicked Judge, and therefore laid his plans accordingly, caring nothing for the guardian's consent, now that he had the mandate of the Chief-Justice.

I reached the town again before daylight, and found Master Simpson's house straitly shut up. For already it had been whispered abroad that Mistress Mary had died of the plague—the report having been set afoot by the gossip of the excited maid-servant, who had seen the grey and rigid face of the maiden as she was brought in, and hearing almost at once that she had died, ran forth in a great fright to her own relations, and declared that she had seen a dark spot on the brow of the lady; and in a short while it was being whispered about that the plague had suddenly stricken her and carried her off—which was thought only too possible in those days.

Nothing could have turned out better for our purpose, albeit we had not ourselves set the rumour afloat, nor did we hear anything of it till that morning, when a mandate reached the household from the Mayor, ordering instant burial for the body, and that none should come forth from that house till leave was given from him.

Luckily for me I was away when that mandate came, so I escaped the imprisonment which Lizzie and her aunt suffered for fourteen days, very willingly. And this saved them from any questioning or trouble from Mr. Blewer, who did not dare to came anigh the house; and though they say he raved and raged horribly at the ill turn fate had done him, he did not suspect for a moment that any trick had been played upon him. He, like all Taunton, believed in the death of the maid; and only when no more signs of the plague appeared in the house or the place did men say it was most like to have been a virulent fever, caught perhaps in court from some prisoner from the fetid jail, or engendered by the fright of being brought face to face with the Judge.

As for me, being unable to obtain entrance to the Simpsons' house, I went straight home and took from my store several golden guineas; and then I made my way to the Bridewell, to seek speech with the hangman, and see if I could bribe him to treat Will but lightly and mercifully.

Whilst I was passing through the streets I saw a great crowd gathered. Coming hastily to the edge of it, I asked what was going on, and was told that Mistress Hannah Hewling had been waiting outside a certain house where Lord Jeffreys was known to be, to petition him on coming out for a respite of her brother's sentence; for she verily believed that such interest would be made by their parents and friends in London town, that if he could but be respited a few days his pardon would be assured.

I heard a woman's voice in the midst of the crowd raised in imploring tones, and I heard the brutal laugh of the wicked Judge—that malicious laugh I had heard so often of late, and which seemed the most evil thing about that most evil man. Then suddenly the crowd parted with cries of, "Have a care! have a care!" and I saw that the Judge had stepped into his coach, and that the prancing horses were just starting.

But even then Mistress Hannah would not cease her pleading. She hung upon the coach, still rending the air with her cries, and offering—I think it was a thousand pounds for just two days' respite. But Jeffreys looked forth from the window, his eyes scintillating with passion, and he cried out to his coachman,
—

"Whip her off! whip her off! Cut her hands to pieces! I will not be badgered thus!"

And the man, who seemed to be a worthy fellow of such a master, took his heavy whip and lashed at the poor lady's white hands as they still clung to the coach; and the people started forward and caught her as she fell away, half fainting with pain and anguish. And methinks if the Judge could but have heard the curses with which he was followed as he drove away, he would scarce have felt comfortable for the rest of the day.

Now it so chanced that Mother Whale was in Taunton that day, and she was standing in the crowd when this thing happened; and suddenly tossing her withered arms into the air, she burst into a torrent of execration that sounded almost like words of prophecy. The people stood agape with a stern joy as she hurled her maledictions upon him, and screamed after him that his turn would one day come—that he should himself be a fugitive from mankind, and should sue for the mercy which should be refused him, and should perish miserably at last like the wretched brute beast that he was!

Then all the people cried, "Amen! Amen!" and Mother Whale was taken into many houses that day and treated sumptuously; but she would add nothing to the words she had spoken, nor say how and when they would be fulfilled. All Taunton, however, was whispering that a frightful fate would follow this monster, and a stern satisfaction was upon the faces of those who heard and those who told the news.

So many interruptions on the way hindered my errand, and I was but just in time. Poor Will was to be whipped through the streets of the town this very day; but the fellow who had charge of the whipping was known to me, and had small relish for the office, seeing that Will was a favourite with all who knew him, and had won golden opinions in the prison by his wit and cheerfulness, and the way he had served and entertained his fellow-prisoners, keeping up their courage and making light of hardships.

It needed little of my gold to win the promised leniency.

"I would not lay a finger on the lad if I could help it!" said the man; "but were I to put the office on another, the poor fellow might fare worse. He is a right brave and good lad. I would it were yon black-coated knave of a parson that I had under my lash! I would not spare him. I would warm his shoulders well, and give them a red jacket to boot that he should carry for long enough!"

Mr. Blewer was not beloved in Taunton, and his spite towards Will had long been known.

Will came out looking pale, as he had done in court yesterday, but resolute and fearless for all that. His eyes lighted at sight of me, and he gave the hand I held out to him a hearty squeeze.

"It's all for the good cause, Dicon," he said. "Art not thou ashamed to speak with one who is to be tied to the cart's tail yonder?"

"Ashamed of thee, Will? I would I were half the man that thou art!" And then coming a little nearer, I whispered in his ear,—

"He will make thy punishment as light as he can, Will; and after the Judge be safely gone back out of the West, men say that prisoners will have little to fear. The Mayors and people of the towns will have none of his brutal sentences carried out. Thou wilt not be sent from town to town as he said."

Will gave a nod, but could say no more; for the executioner had come to tie him to the cart, and Mr. Blewer came hurrying up that he might witness the pain and shame of the boy he hated. But this was too much for the crowd. Whether or not this man was a friend of the dreaded Judge who had not yet left the town, the crowd was not to be quelled. A storm of groans and hisses arose at sight of him; women shook their fists in his face, and children took up stones, and would have cast them at him but for the restraining hands of their mothers. One great brawny blacksmith came forward with his hammer in his hand and stood right in front of the white-faced poltroon, who was looking this way and that, as though he knew not whether to fly or to hurl threats and defiance at the mob.

"Look you here, sir," said the man, speaking loud enough for everybody to hear. "You'd better watch this thing from somewhere else than the public streets, if you don't want the coat, which you're a disgrace to, to be torn off your back! I tell you, sir, that it would not take more than a few words from some amongst us to get you stripped and set where that poor lad is now; and there's not a man amongst us but would be glad to lay lashes on your back— ay, and we would too, if once our blood was up. So if you value a sound skin, go while there is yet time! Taunton Town is not trodden so much in the dust yet that she cannot rise in revolt against a monster like you!"

Yells, hisses, and groans filled the air, and Mr. Blewer's face turned from white to purple, and again faded to an ashen grey. If ever man looked cowed and beaten, he did then. But he took the hint, and made off as fast as his legs would carry him; and I verily believe had it been any other time—had the sense of fear inspired by recent events not been still strong upon the people— that he would have been pounced upon then and there, and whipped at the cart's tail through the streets of Taunton by the infuriated populace.

As it was, it was poor Will who was whipped, though the lashes were but lightly laid on; and I think the boy scarce felt the pain in the sense of triumph at the discomfiture of his foe, and in the encouragement and sympathy of his townsmen. I walked beside him all the way, and he looked at me every now and then with a smile. All sense of shame—which to some natures is the bitterest part of such a punishment—was saved him; for he was regarded by the people as a sufferer in a noble cause, and as a youthful martyr might have been in days of old. Women wept and blessed him; men called out brave words of praise and encouragement. He held his head up to the very last; and though he sometimes winced and shrank, he did not utter a cry the whole way through the town and back.

But alas, alas! we had only raised in the breast of his implacable foe a spirit of hostility which would not be satisfied without a speedy vengeance. As we entered the yard of the prison again, there was Mr. Blewer waiting for us; and as he cast a scrutinizing glance upon poor Will's back lined with blue wales, he uttered a snort of contempt and anger, and turned upon the executioner with an air of stern displeasure.

Will was led away by the jailer, who treated him kindly enough; but the hangman was detained by Mr. Blewer, who said severely,—

"Why, fellow, what do you mean by carrying out my lord's sentences in such a fashion? He straitly charged you not to spare the rod; and you have not only spared it, but have scarce let him feel it! I tell you, fellow, the Judge's mandates are not thus to be set aside. I will report the matter to him, and see what he says!"

And at that the fellow broke out in a great passion, as well indeed he might.

"Sir," he cried, "men talk with horror of the cruelties of the Popish Priests; but commend me to a Church of England Priest for downright cruelty! You are like the country Justices who will not believe that a man is burnt in the hand unless they can see a hole through it! Shame upon you, sir. You would not dare to speak thus were the citizens of Taunton here to listen!"

Mr. Blewer's face expressed all sorts of evil emotions. He raised the cane he held in his hand and slightly threatened the man with it.

"Have a care, fellow! have a care how you speak, or you may chance to get a taste of your own rope's end one of these days!"

"I would I could give you a taste of it!" muttered the man as he walked off in a rage; and as I followed him to get speech if it were possible of Will, he broke out again and cried, "I verily believe the whole place has gone mad. Men seem to be drunk with blood. Surely this is like the great whore of the Scriptures who is drunk with the blood of saints and martyrs! The King and his ministers will have a deal to answer for when the books come to be opened at the Day of Judgment!"

My heart swells even now with indignation when I think of the rest of this story. What passed betwixt Mr. Blewer and that wicked Judge I know not, nor can any man tell, but (although I knew it not till after the evil deed had been done—whereby I was saved some suffering) a mandate was sent down that very day to the keeper of the prison, saying that the boy Wiseman was to be whipped again upon the morrow; and that another man was to be chosen for the office, that the sentence of the Judge might be adequately carried out! And this thing was done in the prison-yard—for methinks the keeper of the prison was afraid to do it in the open streets—and the poor lad was so cruelly whipped that they say the bones of his back were laid bare. And it was in almost a dying state that he was carried back to the prison, where he fell into high fever, and might well have died had not news come of it to our ears, and had we not procured for him a separate room, where he could have ease and quiet, and such good nourishment and tendance as his state demanded.

But when I saw him first he knew me not; and though I came day after day, he lay in a death-like stupor, muttering to himself, but speaking no word that any might understand, and only moaning a little when his wounds were dressed by the godly woman whose services we had bespoken for him.

"Never weep for him, Dicon," said the good woman to me, as my tears fell fast at his sad state. "Methinks the Lord will yet raise him up. And this fever is a merciful thing for him, for it dulls his pains, and he knows naught of his sufferings: it would be far worse were he himself. We will get his wounds partly healed before he comes to feel them. He takes his broth and milk, and he gets a sort of rest by day, though he is wakeful and feverish at night. Yet I can see that he makes progress day by day. He is a bold lad and full of spirit. He will be a sound and whole man yet, please God."

So I received comfort, though my heart was still full of rage and grief; and methinks Mr. Blewer would have been well-nigh torn in pieces in Taunton streets had he dared to show himself there, but he took himself off to Wells when the Judge moved thither, and for a short time we saw him no more.

There was one more terrible day for Taunton upon the last of this month of September, when the bloody sentences of death were executed upon the prisoners condemned to die there—nineteen in number.

Great numbers of other prisoners, who were condemned on pleading guilty in a body, did not suffer death, but were sold by the Judge to various persons, who either extorted from their friends a ransom for them, or in the case of meaner persons, whose friends had no money, shipped them off to the plantations to be sold there, where it was said that they fetched about ten pounds a head. Great numbers of these unfortunate men perished on the outward voyage; but some reached there alive, and of these some very few returned in after years to their country and their friends. I have myself spoken with more than one such, who has told me moving stories of the sufferings they underwent first in the vessels which conveyed them to these torrid zones, and afterwards at the hands of cruel task-masters. But of this I cannot more particularly speak now. It belongs not to my story, save to account for the fact that whilst so many, many hundreds, and even thousands, were condemned to death, the greater number of these were not executed, but were treated in this manner.

I will not describe further the horrid side of the execution of our friends and fellow-citizens of Taunton; but I will speak of their bravery, their resignation, and the words and bearing of them, which made even their enemies say afterwards, "If you want to learn how to die, go to the young men of Taunton to learn."

No respite of his sentence had come for Mr. Benjamin Hewling, and he was one of the most courageous and steadfast of them all. Of those to die with him whom I have named in these pages were Master (or Captain) John Hucker and Mr. William Jenkyns. The only favour that their friends could obtain for some amongst these was the right to bury them in the churchyard after death. To save his corpse from dismemberment, Miss Hannah Hewling had to pay the thousand pounds she had offered for the life of her brother; and there were a few others who gained this privilege also, though upon what terms I have never heard. Surely this Western Assize must have been a fortune in itself for Lord Jeffreys. It was told us afterwards that he bought a fine property on the proceeds of the bribes received and the sale of prisoners living or dead. Methinks that such a house as that must surely have been haunted by the shades of many an innocent sufferer!

When the prisoners were brought forth from the Castle by the Sheriffs, and the sledge brought which was to convey them to the place of execution—the

Cornhill, where already a large fire had been lighted, so that those who were to be dismembered and their hearts burned might see the flames beforehand—they came forth looking calm and glad, and speaking brave words of comfort both to one another and to their friends, Mr. Benjamin Hewling being (like his younger brother) most sweet and tender in his fashion of speaking, so that tears ran down all faces. But the Sheriffs hurried them upon the sledge, grudging to them even the last words and embraces of their friends; and then the procession started. But a very strange thing then happened: the horses kept stopping short and refusing to draw the sledge, and they snorted and shrank back, and broke out in a sweat, as horses will do when greatly frightened. And all men marvelled at it, and whispered one to another that sure the Angel of the Lord stood with a drawn sword in his hand to keep back His servants from their bloody doom. I believe indeed that this was so; for I, who was mounted on Blackbird, that I might see above the heads of the crowd, felt him shake and grow rigid beneath me, as though he too saw some strange sight. At last the Mayor and Sheriffs had themselves to come forward and actually pull and force the horses onwards, although to the very last they resisted, and showed every sign of terror and reluctance.

Upon the scaffold the prisoners embraced each other and joined in prayer; but they were rudely interrupted by the Sheriff, who doubtless feared some breaking forth on the part of the people.

"May we not pray a while ere we are brought before our Maker?" asked one; whereupon the Sheriff answered by a rough question,—

"Will you pray for the King?"

"I pray for all men," was the answer; and having thus prayed, he further asked if they might sing a Psalm.

"It must be with the ropes about your necks then," answered the Sheriff brutally; but with a smile they consented joyfully to this.

Sure never was Psalm so sweetly or strangely sung as the twenty-third of David that day by our brothers just with their last breath. So touched were all by the scene, that it seemed as though all the town had come forth to bear to their graves those for whom this favour had been purchased; and as we stood to see the earth thrown upon them, we broke ourselves into the words of the same Psalm, and felt indeed that the valley of death had had no terrors for those who walked with the staff of the Lord in their hands, and were comforted by His presence even there.

CHAPTER XXVIII.

PEACE AFTER STORM.

The Judge was gone; the prisons were emptying fast; men began to breathe again after their long terror; those who had fled their homes, and had been living in hiding in terror of their lives, came out once more, and appeared to gladden the hearts of their friends. It was said that a general pardon would now be issued to all those who had not suffered, and that the terrible time was over at last. The King, we heard, had been excellently well pleased by what his Lord Chief-Justice had done in the West, and soon rewarded him with the Chancellorship, as had always been believed. I think perhaps it was the knowledge of these things which went far to stir the hearts of the people against their sovereign, and to pave the way three years later for the bloodless revolution which set a Protestant and a Constitutional ruler upon the throne in place of the Papist tyrant. I sometimes think that had we of the West Country had more patience, and had we waited till the time was ripe, we might have been called patriots and saviours of our country instead of rebels and traitors, to be massacred and hanged by the hundred. But then, again, I have learned to doubt whether the Duke of Monmouth would ever have been received by the nation, or have made a wise ruler had he been so received. Men who best understand him and the matter say that he could never have made good his title to the throne, that he was not born in wedlock, and that the people would never have suffered a sovereign with a stain upon his birth. Queen Mary with her good husband proved a kind and a wise ruler, and beneath her gentle sway peace, order, liberty, and prosperity were quickly restored; and yet there be men who even now talk as though the Duke or his son might yet come back to put forward a claim, and many declare that he never died upon the scaffold, but that he was personated to the very last by a devoted follower.

All this is looking ahead. In the days of which I speak we had no knowledge of the good times to come. We breathed indeed, feeling that the iron hand of military and judicial vengeance was relaxed from our throat; but it seemed to us then as if the bloody James were seated all the more firmly upon his throne.

And now what shall I tell next of all the events that followed in such quick succession? Perhaps whilst my mind is upon the subject I will speak of Mr. Blewer and the vengeance which fell upon him for his cruelty to a Taunton boy.

I have mentioned before good Bishop Ken, who did so much to ease the condition of prisoners, and who was beloved throughout all his diocese. He came to visit Taunton not long after these things had happened; and going into the prison, he found poor Will in a sad state still, although greatly better than he had been.

It chanced, as luck would have it, that I was with him when the Bishop came; for Will's case had excited much comment in the town, and he was permitted to see his friends and enjoy many small privileges, which indeed his state demanded. And after the kindly Bishop had spoken to the boy, and had prayed beside him a beautiful prayer, he asked me how he came into so sad a state. Then I told him everything I knew, striving to hold my wrath in check, as was due to my superior, but scarce able to keep it from breaking out when I spoke of Mr. Blewer.

I thought that the Lord Bishop's face grew stern as he listened, and I hoped that some punishment might fall upon the man who was a disgrace to the sacred calling he had embraced; and in truth I was not mistaken in this, as I will proceed to tell.

I think it was the next day that the Bishop and Mr. Axe were walking together through the town, and talking of many things—Mr. Axe, as I have many times said, being a reverend and godly man, well thought of by all, a loyal servant to the King, and a lover of order, but always on the side of mercy and justice.

Well, as these walked and talked there came towards them Mr. Blewer, mincing and bowing, and plainly resolved to gain the notice of the Lord Bishop; for he had an eye to promotion to some office in the Church, and trusted that he might gain the good-will of this good man, and so be appointed to some living. As he approached, the Bishop looked at him, asking his companion who the person was who evidently desired to attract his notice. Mr. Axe replied with some brevity and coldness that his name was Mr. Blewer, and that he had been living for some time in Taunton, appointed by Mr. Harte to assist in the services of St. Mary's Church.

At the sound of that name the Bishop's fine face became very stern; and as Mr. Blewer came up with mincing steps and hat in hand, believing that the Bishop had paused to permit his approach, he fixed his eyes upon him, and spoke in a tone that all the bystanders could hear.

"Mr. Blewer," he said, "I have heard of you before. Indeed I have had it in my thoughts to summon you to my presence."

"My lord, you do me too much honour!" was the delighted answer, as the creature stood bowing and mincing before the Bishop, his evil face wearing its expression of submissive adulation, such as had been seen upon it in presence of the Lord Chief-Justice. "It is very true that I have done all in my poor power in the cause of law and righteousness during these troubled days, but I had scarce hoped that my poor services would have reached the ears of my gracious lord."

"Sir," answered the good Bishop, with gathering sternness, "the less you speak of righteousness the better, for there has been little of it in your conduct during these troubled days. Sir, think you that at a time when every man calling himself the servant of God should have been straining every nerve in the cause of mercy and tenderness, it is for the clergy to disgrace themselves by acts of selfishness, rapacity, and barbarity which make all honest men shudder and breathe forth curses? Nay, sir, answer me not. It is for me to speak and for you to listen. I have heard of you, Mr. Blewer. I have heard how you persecuted an innocent maiden, and how you cajoled and bribed a certain high personage to grant you her hand in marriage, not for any love you bore her—for you had openly boasted that you would rid yourself of her in a year's time—but because she had money, which you desired to possess; and how she was only saved from your malice by the merciful hand of death. Sir, you are as guilty of that sweet and tender maiden's death as though you had slain her with your own hands. Small wonder that the very thought of being placed for life in such cruel hands caused that deadly fever of which she quickly died. I blush with shame to think that one who has dared to take upon himself the sacred calling and the holy office of the priesthood could ever thus disgrace both himself and his calling!"

"My lord, my lord, you have been misinformed. Some enemy has been wickedly slandering me. Alas! in this evil town a godly man has but too many foes. I swear that I loved the maid—that I would have made her the best of husbands. My lord, I have been cruelly maligned. There is no man in Taunton with a tenderer heart than mine. God be my witness that I speak the truth!"

The Bishop raised his hand in stern displeasure. "Sir," he said, "take not that Holy Name to profane it by falsehood. Can a man who will drink himself drunk with the Lord Jeffreys and his boon companions, and join with him in profane swearing and ribald jesting—can he be a fit spouse for a godly and a pure maid, to whom evil is but a name? Mr. Blewer, think not to deceive me by false swearing; I know too much of you and of your practices. And as though it was not enough to seek to wreck the life of this maiden, you must seek also to do to death in a most cruel and barbarous manner a lad whose only fault has been a boyish lack of discretion. Sir, my blood tingles in my veins at the thought of this thing. Were our prisons not crowded enough with men taken in the very act of rebellion, that you must needs lay an accusation against a young lad of excellent character for a mere indiscretion, and get him also incarcerated in those filthy dens, to languish there for weeks? And having done this, and having borne witness which gained for the poor child a whipping far in excess of his fault, what fiend possessed you to carry a tale to the Judge in his cups, and gain for the boy such handling that his life has barely been saved by the exertions of his friends and the leniency of the prison authorities, themselves ashamed of such a deed? Man, man, I almost forget myself in anger as I think of this thing. You calling yourself a priest and servant of the Most High God, a minister of His children, a messenger of peace and righteousness—you to show yourself such a monster of cruelty that the blood curdles at the tale of your deeds! Go, sir; let me never see you again. And do not dare ever to pollute a pulpit, or perform any holy office in the diocese over which I reign, lest I take upon myself to excommunicate you, as in the good old days of ecclesiastical discipline would have been done for a far less offence than yours!"

And the good Bishop walked on with a stern face, leaving the miscreant he had so worthily lashed with his tongue cowering and shivering with rage and fear, his face livid with passion and disappointment, and his hands nervously clutching at the cane he carried, as though in an instinctive longing to lay it about the shoulders of some innocent victim.

Not daring to follow, or to say another word to the good Bishop, who was known to be a most tender-hearted man, and whose scathing rebuke was therefore far more telling than it would have been in the lips of the military Bishop Mew, who had actually taken the field in person, the wretched creature lingered staring after the retreating figures until they had turned the next corner, and then, gnashing his teeth in impotent shame and rage, he turned towards his own lodgings, and made as though he would have retired thither.

But he was not destined to attain this shelter so speedily as he had thought. A crowd had gathered in the street to hear the Bishop's reprimand, and murmurs of applause and approval had greeted every scathing rebuke. The very fact that the Bishop had not scrupled to speak thus in public to a clergyman showed how greatly his indignation had been aroused; and as the evil creature turned to leave the scene of his humiliation, he found himself suddenly confronted by the brawny blacksmith who had given him a taste of his tongue on another occasion.

"Ho, ho, Sir Priest! so the good Lord Bishop is not a friend to drunkenness and debauchery and savage cruelty! And so the discipline of the Church is relaxed, is it, and its evil servants cannot be touched? Sure that must be a sore matter of regret to so righteous a man as good Mr. Blewer.—Friends," and here he turned his face with a not too pleasant grin upon it towards the crowd now pressing closely round, "since the good gentleman here is debarred from the discipline of the Church, suppose we good citizens give him a taste of such discipline as our town cudgels can bestow."

A yell of delight answered this suggestion, and a hundred staffs were immediately waved in the air. Mr. Blewer's face turned a livid green tint, and he looked at his tormentor with a sickly smile, fumbling in his pocket the while.

"Very good, very good, my merry friend. Thou art quite a wag in thy way,"he gasped in his coward terror at the ring of fierce faces around him. "An excellent jest in truth, and one which I will myself tell to the good Bishop when I go to clear myself in his sight of the slanders he has heard against me. All friends of the people have enemies who malign them, and so it has been with me. Here, my good fellow, take that, and bid your friends disperse. I am a man of peace; let us have no unseemly disturbance here in the streets."

He would have pressed a golden guinea into the blacksmith's hand, but that honest rogue turned away with an expression of scorn and disgust.

"Thy money perish with thee!" he cried, in a great access of wrath; and bringing down his heavy staff upon the shoulders of the luckless Mr. Blewer, he shouted out, "Take that, thou coward and craven monster of cruelty! take that and that, and think of Will Wiseman! Would I could break every bone in that wretched body of thine!"

With a yell of pain and terror, and an agonized cry for the watch—which, however, never came—the wretched man sprang away and hurled himself through the crowd, every man of which, who was armed with a stick, hit him a blow as he passed, and every woman snatched at his coat or scratched his face, till his clothing was half torn off his back, and his face was running down with blood; and every one who struck him called out in savage accents, "Remember Will Wiseman!" or, "Take that for Will's sake!" or some phrase like that, till the wretched man must have wished from the very ground of his heart that he had let Will Wiseman alone. And when I heard the story, and how Mr. Blewer had been beaten almost into a jelly ere he reached the shelter of his house, I felt indeed that Will had been avenged, and that God had wrought vengeance even by the hands of the lawless and violent men.

Nor was any notice taken of this outrage by the authorities. I think both the Mayor and the magistrates felt that Mr. Blewer had only met his due. The rebuke of the Bishop was known to them, and there was no desire to take up the cudgels for a creature of such evil notoriety. All the town was sick of bloodshed and confusion, and was breathing once more in the hope of quieter days to come. To raise an inquiry and to punish the ringleaders of the mob would only stir the city into anger and even rebellion once again. So Mr. Blewer made his plaint in vain, and got no redress; and it was said of him that he went to Bristol as soon as he was able to travel, and drunk himself to death there before the year was ended; but of this I know nothing certain. I never saw the miserable creature again, and I can only think it very like him to come to such an end after the disappointments and the violent usage he had received.

The news of this discomfiture of his enemy, and of the vengeance taken upon him by the citizens, did much to hearten up poor Will after his long illness. I told him the story myself as he lay on his pallet bed upon his face—for his poor back was still all raw, and it would be long before his wounds would be healed. But the old spirit was coming back into my comrade, and I saw his eyes glow and flash just in the old way.

"O good Jem Truslove, good Jem Truslove! methinks I can see and hear him! O Dicon, it were a thousand pities I was not there to see it with mine own eyes! Had it been somebody else, how I would have thrashed him mine own self! So they made him remember Will Wiseman, did they? Ah, it was good of them! it was indeed a kindly act! Dicon, methinks after all he may have done me a good turn yet, for all that he meant to have killed me: for the Governor was here yesterday after thou hadst gone, and he told me that so soon as I could be moved I was free to go back to my friends; that my sentence had terminated, and that he was sorry I had been so roughly handled. Now that that monster of a Judge is gone, men are ashamed to think what he made them do. They are sick to death of bloodshed and cruelty, and would fain save all his victims from the fate he desired for them."

This indeed was very true. The Bloody Assizes, as men began to call them, had produced an indelible impression all over this West Country. The gentry, who had been all along against the rising for the Duke, and had joined hands with the party of order, on seeing the horrible and bloody vengeance taken upon the wretched inhabitants of their towns and villages, experienced a revulsion of feeling, and a great hatred of the King who could rejoice in and applaud such wholesale slaughter. They had believed that the ringleaders would of necessity suffer death—that was a necessary consequence of such an act of rebellion; but after the Duke had been beheaded, and after the rising had been so completely quelled, it was said by all moderate and merciful men that but a slight punishment should be inflicted upon the mass of lesser prisoners, who had been led away by ignorance and enthusiasm misplaced, and were like sheep following one another they knew not whither.

The sending down of the bloodiest and most iniquitous Judge upon the bench with authority to massacre wholesale, and the unbridled ferocity with which he had carried out his bloody task, had thoroughly displeased and disgusted all moderate and merciful men; and the honours heaped upon the bloody wretch by his admiring sovereign on his return had added to the universal execration in which he was held. All mercy that was possible was therefore fearlessly shown now to those who had escaped the peril of the law, or lay under some sentence like that of Will Wiseman. Other men—ay, and women too—had been condemned to be whipped through various places at intervals; but the magistrates took it upon themselves to release them after a very small part of the punishment had been inflicted. A sense of peace and security settled down upon a region so long rent by faction and fear. The citizens felt that the gentry were at heart with them in their indignation against the King, and in their desire after purer government; and although at the moment there was no thought of any fresh rising, the people began to whisper that a deliverer would come some day, and that the oppressed nation would turn as one man, and hurl the bloody tyrant from his throne.

So although there was mourning and woe in too many homes in Taunton, yet there was rejoicing in others; and amongst these latter was the house of Master Simpson, which was gladdened by the return of the master, on the very day when poor Will Wiseman had been got back, after having been so long away and suffered so much.

I had brought him back myself in a coach which my uncle had sent from our inn; and I had made him comfortable upon a couch, and Lizzie and her aunt were hanging over him and asking him all manner of questions, and making as much of him as though he had indeed been their brother and nephew, when we were startled by a heavy footfall up the flagged garden walk (for the impulse of fear was still strong within us, and we were easily alarmed at any unexpected sound), and Lizzie suddenly uttered a little scream of ecstasy, and the next moment had sprung right into her father's arms.

Oh, what a clatter of tongues and clamour of voices there was, everybody speaking at once, and nobody able to listen till the first joyful excitement had passed!

Master Simpson—he would never let himself be called Captain again—had a long story to tell us of his narrow escapes from the bands of soldiers after the fatal field of Sedgemoor. He had been amongst those who had made such a gallant stand upon the edge of the rhine, and had fired volley after volley into the surprised and disordered ranks of the enemy long after the Duke had fled at the instance of Lord Grey, and in fact until every round of ammunition had been used. He confirmed the story told me by the poor soldier in the ditch, that if the ammunition-waggons had but come up, and the cavalry had but re-formed even at a distance and shown something of a front, the day might easily have been ours. He spoke bitterly of Lord Grey, and declared that if Lord Vere had been there things would have gone very differently. But I have often thought since that Lord Grey was scarce as much to blame as our people always said. I doubt whether the untrained horses would have stood the sound of firing had their riders been never so stout of heart. It is a long time before the mettlesome creatures can be made to understand that they must face the flash of fire-arms and the terrible noise and smell. Sometimes it takes two years before a horse is seasoned; and these animals had been but a few weeks at most with the army, and had only smelt powder once or twice before.

Yet if the horses would not stand, their riders should have sent on the ammunition as fast as possible, instead of spreading dismay through the rear of the army and keeping back both the waggons and the rest of the foot. There was nothing to excuse the confusion which their rout created in the rear of the army. But what boots it to talk of these matters now? The day was lost, and Master Simpson, slightly wounded and greatly exhausted, had crawled into a ditch to hide himself, and was passed over by the soldiers in their first search. Afterwards he got up and slunk away in an opposite direction from Bridgewater, and received much kindness at a woodman's hut, where the people took care of him for several days, and where he healed him of his wound. Then fearing to remain so near to the scene of Colonel Kirke's activity, he fled towards Philip's Norton, knowing the country from having traversed it before but recently; and many narrow escapes did he have of falling into the hands of the soldiers. But fortune favoured him, and he escaped each time, though once he was up hiding in the rafters of an old barn, whilst the soldiers were eating and sleeping on the ground beneath him; and he almost gave himself up for lost once, when the beam creaked beneath his weight, and somebody called out, "Is anybody up there? Speak, man, or I fire!"

He did not, however, speak, nor did the soldier fire. The men laughed, and the officer swore at them for waking him up; and so they settled to their slumbers again.

That was the nearest shave he had, but many were his perils; and Lizzie sat holding his hand, and looking into his face with eyes full of terror and ecstasy; whilst the aunt bustled about to get the best supper the town could produce upon a sudden, and Master Simpson turned to Will and made him tell all his history.

He shook his head, and his face looked stern as he heard of the cruel Judge; but it brightened as he heard how Mr. Blewer had been served, and said, rubbing his hands together,—

"Good lads of Taunton, good brother citizens, would I had been there to add a sounding blow to theirs! Would that we could serve the Judge the same! Would that he might be at the mercy of the West Country lads some day!"

"Somehow," said Will slowly, as he lay white and thin upon his couch, a strange light coming slowly into his eyes as he spoke—"somehow I seem to think that I shall have my turn some day even with Judge Jeffreys! I think that I shall avenge upon him the wrongs of our people before he lays down his wicked life!"

CHAPTER XXIX.

MY LORD AND MY LADY.

I have spoken of other matters first; but it must not be thought that the affairs of Mistress Mary and my lord had been forgotten all this time.

Both, however, were in safe hiding; and until the wicked Judge had left for London, and till peace and tranquillity had settled down upon our distracted country, it was better that they should remain there. No one knew exactly what turn might be taken by affairs from day to day; and especially until Mr. Blewer had left Taunton, I was in continual anxiety as to Mistress Mary's safety, being haunted by a fear that he would get wind somehow of the trick played upon him, and discover the maid in her hiding-place.

Not that I thought now he could do aught to molest her, for all the place was hot against him; but the Judge's words were that he had liberty to wed the maid, and who could tell what steps he might not take in order to obtain possession of her once more?

So Mistress Mary lay in hiding, whilst her towns-folk talked of her as dead; and so the days slipped by. I heard also good news of my lord at Ilminster, when I rode Blackbird across to ask for him. I had but a short while to stay; but I saw him for a few minutes, and told him that Mistress Mary was safe, albeit I gave him not the whole history of her peril, fearing that he would incontinently come forth from his hiding-place to defend her, and perhaps put both their lives in peril thereby.

For the pardon, although talked of, had not yet reached us; and it was scarce safe for one of my lord's rank to show himself openly, though others might venture to do so, as Master Simpson had done.

I think it was two days after this visit that Mistress Mary Bridges sent for me on some excuse about her pony—for I had chosen one for her not long since, and had helped to break it in. When I arrived she took me into the paddock, dismissing all others; and whilst we stood there seeming to be talking of the pony, who came and stood beside us, she began, in her quick, eager fashion, —

"Dicon, what are we to do next?"

I knew what she meant, and I had asked myself the question many a time before, but I had never found the answer. Mistress Mary continued, in her quick, imperious fashion,—

"Mary cannot stay where she is much longer. It is no fit place for her when the winter days come. Only those born in the marshes can live there, and they ofttimes suffer from ague and marsh fever. Mary cannot stand it much longer. But where can she go? Mary Mead is dead. I know not whether she would suffer some penalty—or her friends—if she came to life again; and Lord Lonsdale hath her money, for he is her heir. And how can we get it back for her without telling all? And I fear Lord Lonsdale. He is not like my father; and he is a King's man every inch. What are we to do for her next, Dicon? Methinks that thou and I have this secret to ourselves. Sometimes I half fear at what we have done, and then again I say that were it to do over again I would do just the same. But Mary cannot always lie hidden; and how is she to appear again? That is what is perplexing me. Dicon, what shall we do?"

"Marry her to my lord!" I cried suddenly, struck by an unexpected inspiration. "So she will be my Lady Vere, and Mistress Mary Mead no longer. If she has lost one name, let her have another bestowed upon her. Let her be married to my lord!"

Mistress Mary's eyes brightened like stars.

"Ah, Dicon, a good thought!" she cried, clasping her hands over the pony's neck; "but how may that be accomplished?"

I was not quite so ready with an answer; but after a pause I said,—

"Mistress Mary, suppose you tell your lady mother all, and ask for her advice; and I will think over a notion which has but just now entered my head. Let us meet again upon the third day from this, and speak of what we have done. If you could get Mistress Mary safely to Ilminster in a secret fashion, perchance the rest might be managed; but until the pardon be issued, my lord cannot openly show himself, for he does not know that his own father might not give him up to justice, so grieved and wroth was he at seeing his son in arms against the King."

"Ah no; he is not so bad as that!" answered Mistress Mary. "And men talk very differently of the King from what they did a few weeks back. He has lost many of his friends, and will likely lose more."

"Then things will be all the better for us and our plans, Mistress," I said; and after some more conversation of no especial moment, I left her and returned to Taunton full of my own plan, which was indeed one of much boldness, seeing how humble mine own birth was, and that it was something bold of me to think of speaking with the great ones of the earth.

Yet my idea was nothing less than to strive to win the good Bishop Ken to stand our friend; and as he had always given me a friendly smile and nod since the day when he had seen me in the prison, I thought I might even presume to seek speech of him, since all men said how gentle and courteous he was to all who approached him, and how he was striving to bring back peace and prosperity to his distracted diocese.

Moreover, he was still in Taunton at this time; and I had heard it said that he was shortly going to visit Mr. Speke of White Lackington House, near to Ilminster, of which mention has been made before. Mr. Speke had lost a son in the rebellion, executed at Ilminster, and he himself lay under charges to pay a very heavy fine for his supposed or real share in the rebellion. The Bishop's visit was one of condolence and friendship, and was likely to last a week or more. If I could but get speech of him before he started, I felt hopeful of bringing this matter of my lord's to a happy conclusion.

Fortune favoured me; for I met the Bishop the very next morning, walking and meditating quite alone in some of the meadows beside the stream. I had heard that he had been seen to leave the town, but I scarce hoped to light upon him thus easily. He gave me a smile and a nod as usual, and then paused to ask how Will Wiseman fared, and was pleased to hear that he had been released and taken back to his master's house, where he was treated now as a son. And when we had spoken a few minutes of him, and the Bishop would have passed on, I plucked up my courage and said,—

"My lord, may I speak a word to you concerning something that lies heavy upon my heart?"

He gave me a quick, keen look, and then motioned me to walk beside him; and although he was so high and great a man, before whom all men bowed as he went along the streets, yet I am very sure that he told me as he walked that he was my servant, and that I need not fear to speak openly of what was burdening me. And I have thought, both then and since, that the holier and greater men are, the humbler and gentler they show themselves. Sure no man could have listened with so much kindliness to my story had not his heart been as full of the love of God as our good Bishop's was.

And I told him everything from first to last—all that I have been laboriously striving to set forth in these pages—all of it, at least, that in any way concerned my lord and Mistress Mary; and how that she was living all the while, though held dead by her towns-folk and acquaintance; and how my lord was in hiding with mine aunt, and that I believed it was commonly reported that he had died of his wounds in the prison, though of that I could not speak certainly. But I spoke of the love those twain had ever borne one another, and how that death would be more welcome to either than to be sundered through this life; and at last, with tears starting to my eyes (for I had worked myself up to a state of great excitement), I stopped short and threw myself at the Bishop's feet, and cried through my sobs,—

"And, O my lord, if you would but be their friend and marry them, so that none could sunder them more, they would bless you for ever, and I trow you never would repent it; and methinks even Lord Lonsdale would rejoice to have his son given back to him—with so fair and sweet a bride at his side. He loves Mistress Mary—he always loved her; and sure to have them both brought back as if from the grave would gladden any father's heart! O my lord, think of it—think of it, I pray you on my bended knees!"

"Nay, nay, lad," answered the Bishop, laying a kindly hand upon my head; "it is to God alone that prayers must be addressed upon our bended knee. I am thy brother and fellow-servant; no such prayers should thy lips frame or my ears listen to. Get upon thy feet, lad, and calm thyself. I can make thee no promise as to what I will or will not do in this strange case that thou hast laid before me, but I will at least relieve thy young shoulders from the burden they bear, see Lord Vere myself, and that right soon, and hear what he has to say of all this. I knew him as a fair child, and I have some knowledge of his father. I am deeply interested in thy tale. I say not that all has been well done; but I will not condemn thee, because thou hast been sorely tempted, and in these dark days of fear the best and strongest are ofttimes led to swerve from the straight path of virtue. There, boy, go home with thee. I would think more of this. And if thou knowest what becomes of Mistress Mary, let me hear it ere I leave for Ilminster three days hence."

I raced homewards with a heart wonderfully lightened of the load which had begun to press sorely upon it. And it was still more lightened when I next saw Mistress Mary Bridges, who told me that she had whispered her story of Mary's escape into her mother's ear; and that although the mother was rather disturbed and uneasy at the daring scheme, she had not chidden her daughter overmuch, and was helping now to get the other Mary conveyed away to Ilminster, where her face was not known, and where she might remain in safe obscurity until something had been decided. Lady Bridges had a sister living in that town, and was about to send her daughter to her on a visit, the elder Mary accompanying her as her maid. It was no longer safe for her to remain amid the unwholesome marshes, and as soon as Sir Ralph should return from town the matter was to be laid before him, and he would advise the next step.

My heart bounded with joy when I heard that Ilminster was to be the place of Mistress Mary's residence; for was not my lord there? and if he were there and the good Bishop too, what might not happen to bring all things to a happy conclusion? I did not tell Mistress Mary of my talk with the Bishop, fearing lest I should stir up hopes which might not be fulfilled later; but I hugged the knowledge in my heart, and I thought of little else during the days which followed. My heart was in Ilminster, but I was kept at Taunton by my work in my uncle's house. Life was beginning to move in its accustomed grooves again, and I had my set duties to attend to, and could not rove about almost at will, as I had done during the months of distraction and excitement during which life seemed to have entirely changed its conditions. I could run to and fro in the town, and visit friends there at leisure moments; read or tell the news to poor Will; and make a little boyish love to Lizzie, who grew dearer and dearer to me every week. But I could not get off to Ilminster for some while, and no letter reached me from thence. Mistress Mary Bridges, as I heard, was still with her aunt; and that was all I knew.

The house next door stood blank and empty. Poor Miss Blake had died in prison of jail fever or small-pox (as was severally reported) very soon after her admission there. Mrs. Musgrave, who had always kept much more in the background, had now retired, and the school which had obtained such a sudden notoriety ceased to exist.

The general pardon, so anxiously waited for by the still half-fearful people, came at last; and we were glad when it did so that Miss Blake was no longer in this world, for her name had been excepted from it, and figured upon the list of those whom the King refused to pardon. The Maids who had presented the colours (or rather their parents and friends) were still being harried by the Maids of Honour for the fine-money, and the negotiation was long of settlement. The rapacious Court ladies demanded seven thousand pounds; but after long wrangling I believe they were forced to content themselves with less than half. From time to time I used to hear from the indignant Lizzie that the matter was still under negotiation; but how it was finally adjusted I cannot now remember, nor is it of any moment to these pages.

The arrival of the general pardon was the signal for a public holiday. Bonfires blazed, bells rang joyfully from the church steeples, and I asked and obtained leave to take myself off and ride to Ilminster to see how my kinswoman there fared.

All the town was astir and in holiday guise, as Taunton had been when Blackbird and I rode forth in the morning. Although the wind was sharp and keen, the sun shone merrily, and all faces looked beaming and happy. At my aunt's house I saw an appearance of stir and festivity by no means usual there; and when I stopped at the door and asked for her, I was told that she was at the church, and that I had best follow her there. This I was ready to do, for I took it to be some special thanksgiving service that was going on, and I was willing enough to add my voice to that of a glad and happy people, relieved from a long oppression and fear. But when I neared the church, I saw few persons going in or coming out, and concluded that my aunt must have gone to repeat her private thanksgivings there.

Nevertheless having come so far, I was not to be turned back, and I entered the building with bent head and hushed footfall, hearing a voice at the upper end reciting some office, though the seats about the lower end of the church were all empty.

Treading cautiously so as not to be heard, I advanced towards the choir, when I was suddenly arrested by a sight that sent the blood surging into my head till I felt that I must grasp something solid or I should surely fall. For the service going on was a wedding. The bride and the bridegroom were even now joining hands, and speaking the irrevocable word which made them man and wife. I did not need to look to recognize the clear tones of my lord's voice, nor the soft sweetness of Mistress Mary's, nor yet the beautiful mellowness of the good Bishop's. Yet when the mist had cleared from my eyes, I gazed and gazed as though I could never satisfy myself. Yes, there was my lord, looking more beautiful than ever with his golden hair, his deep-blue eyes, his face still pale from sickness and confinement, but with a look of restored health, that made my heart bound. And there beside him, in a long trailing gown of white that gave to her the air and dignity of an empress, was Mistress Mary Mead— though that name had but now passed from her keeping for ever—a veil just

265

shading her fair face, but unable to hide the beautiful features and the glories of the dark unfathomable eyes.

Close beside her, as being the one who had given her in marriage, was Sir Ralph Bridges, tall, upright, and soldier-like; whilst clinging to her mother's hand, sparkling, kindling, brimming over with joyful excitement, was the younger Mistress Mary, who can henceforth claim exclusive right to that title; and behind them, some paces distant, my aunt, looking proud and happy beyond all words; and some score or more of persons who had heard the romantic story, and were anxious to be present at the nuptials.

The marriage over, the Bishop gave a fatherly blessing; and soon the little procession moved down the long aisle to the door, to which I had now retreated.

As they came out, my lord's eyes suddenly fell upon me, and at once kindled with such a look as sent the hot blood surging into my face.

"Dicon—it is good Dicon!" he cried, and held out his hand; whilst over Mistress—I mean the Viscountess Vere's face there flashed such a sweet, tender smile, that I cherish the memory of it to this very day. "Good Dicon, my only sorrow to-day was that thou wert not here to see it," said my lord. "What fairy messenger brought thee here in time after all?"

I could not reply categorically to the question. My lord in his white-and-silver suit, his golden locks flowing over his shoulders, the sunlight streaming upon him, his face full of light and unspeakable happiness, was a vision so bright and so beautiful that my eyes were dazzled, and my heart too full for speech. I think they understood, for the lady smiled at me and then at her husband, and she said in a gentle tone,—

"We will see him again anon, Reginald.—For the present, good Dicon, farewell. Come to us again another time."

Bowing low before them as they moved towards the coach that awaited them, I could only exclaim in a gasping voice,—

"My dear lord! my gracious lady!"

CHAPTER XXX.

A CHRISTMAS SCENE.

The great dining-hall of Bishop's Hull was wreathed in greenery and all ablaze with lights. In the gallery overhead a band of musicians discoursed sweet music, whilst below were assembled a party of gay and merry guests, gathered round Sir Ralph Bridges' hospitable table; and the only sorrowful face to be seen at that board was the grave, anxious countenance of Lord Lonsdale.

I was there, clad in the livery of the house, and waiting at table with the practised skill which I had learned in my uncle's inn. My heart was beating fast as I came and went, and caught here and there a word of the talk passing between the merry guests. Now one gentleman would relate an anecdote or give us a reminiscence of his youth, or another would speak to his neighbour, perhaps with bated breath, of some of the recent events which had made this year so memorable in our part of the country.

Although it was the eve of Christmas, and the prevailing wish was to drop care and keep in the background all sorrowful topics, yet it was impossible altogether to forget or keep in abeyance thoughts so easily suggested by the passing mention of persons or places.

Moreover, the sight of the sword hanging upon the wall in a conspicuous position—Mistress Mary's sword—called forth towards the close of the repast an account of that incident, which had become known far and wide by this time; and when Sir Ralph told the tale, with pardonable pride in his bright-faced young daughter, whose rosy countenance glowed half with pleasure and half with modest shame at all the notice bestowed upon her, every glass was raised to be drained to her health, and a cheer went up from many throats in honour of the maid who had not feared to strike so goodly a blow in defence of her mother.

It was just when this buzz of acclamation was going round that I heard Lord Lonsdale say mournfully to his host, next to whom he was seated: "Ah, if my poor boy were living yet, how happy it would have made me to seek for him the hand of that brave daughter of yours in marriage. Methinks the maid could soon have learned to love him. I never knew any whom he had not the power to win by his handsome face and winning ways."

"He was a very goodly youth," answered Sir Ralph, quietly and gravely. "Have you given up all hopes of seeing him again? Are you assured of his death?"

"I have ceased to hope now," replied the father, with steady gravity. "It seems probable that he died of his wounds in the Castle, albeit the Governor was not informed of the fact, and in the general confusion of those days was unable to trace whether he had died or been removed by mistake to the pestilential Bridewell, where he was like to perish quickly, enfeebled as he was, or whether he made good his escape. For long I hoped that this last had been the case; and from the day on which the pardon appeared I have been eagerly looking for tidings of or from him. His name was not upon the list of exceptions. There was no fear for him once that was out. If in the land of the living, why does he give no sign? Alas, alas! I fear there can be no doubt but that he is dead. And I must bear about with me the life-long remorse of having driven him to his death."

"Nay, my good friend, how could that be so?"

"I thwarted the lad in the dearest wish of his heart," answered Lord Lonsdale sadly. "Ah, how often have I mourned that step and its dire consequences! Thou knowest my ward, Mary Mead, one of the sweetest maidens that ever walked this earth? Ah, why did I not see things then as I do now? I loved her as a daughter, and yet I had never thought of her as a wife for my son, being anxious to ally myself through him with the Portman family, as you know. And when, as little more than children, the pair plighted their troth and sought my blessing, I denied it harshly, and sought to separate them by sending her away to that place where she learned those lessons which have been her undoing and that of my poor boy also."

"Ah, I see! Had she remained with you and been wedded early to Lord Vere, she would have been saved from the influences which worked so strongly upon her—"

"Ay, and were the cause at last of her death, as well as the cause of my son's joining the rebels. His heart was not with the Duke of Monmouth, albeit his soul doubtless swelled within him at the tales of coward cruelty and tyranny which he heard of his Majesty. After all, good Sir Ralph, if you and I can foresee a day when perhaps some such struggle must again be fought, though with another and a more righteous and legitimate champion, ere this land can be freed from the curse of tyranny, can we blame so harshly the younger and more ardent souls who saw in this young Duke a champion of liberty and religion? Had all England known something more of the temper of the King and the nature of the tools he employed, and purposes yet more fully to employ, I sometimes wonder whether more of our class might not have joined issue with the Duke of Monmouth, in despair of ever serving such a monarch as the treacherous and unkingly James."

Sir Ralph Bridges bent his head with a look of sternness upon his face; and I hearing these words, marvelled at the change already creeping over the minds of the gentry, who but a short time back, in the hour of his peril, had rallied so gallantly round their monarch, even though for his own person they held but small love.

Surely the coward cruelty of the King and his officers had done much to estrange the hearts of his subjects from him.

Then, after a brief pause, Sir Ralph took up the thread of the discourse.

"And so you did truly love the poor maiden, who was said to drop down dead, or nigh to dead, at sight of Jeffreys' evil face? You would not have forbidden her union with your son had things turned out differently with both?"

"Had my son but been restored to me, he should have chosen his wife when and as he would. I would have never said him nay, never striven again to force my will upon his. But indeed I sometimes think that had he returned to find her dead, he would have never recovered the blow. His heart has been set on her ever since their childhood. I can see it now. Would to God I had never thwarted them! The load I have to bear about with me is well-nigh too heavy for me. The death of both lies at my door! I shall never see grandchildren sporting at my knees, and the fair mansion in Devonshire prepared for Vere and his bride will remain desolate and empty till it passes into the hands of aliens." And Lord Lonsdale's voice quivered as he spoke, and I thought that there was even a glint of tear-drops in his eyes.

At this moment Sir Ralph gave me a signal—the signal for which I had been anxiously waiting all through that long banquet.

Without a moment's delay I crossed the floor, then opened a pair of folding doors which shut off a smaller apartment within; and immediately there stepped forth, in all the bravery and beauty of their wedding garments, my lord the Viscount and his fair young wife, the latter so changed and transfigured by the few weeks of wedded happiness that I was startled by the wonderful radiancy of her beauty.

At the same moment the band struck up a measure so full of joy and triumph that no heart could fail to beat in unison with the glad strain; and to the accompaniment of this soul-stirring music the Viscount led forward his bride, and kneeling with her at his father's feet, said in accents which could reach only the few who stood nearest,—

"Father, I have come to ask your forgiveness for everything in which I have failed in filial duty towards you, and also to beg your love and fatherly blessing for me and for my wife."

Well, they call Lord Lonsdale a proud man, and one whose feelings lie deep hidden, and perhaps they do in the main. But there are moments in a man's lifetime when he cannot but show of what his heart is made—when love will not be hidden, but will force itself through the crust of pride and reserve and show itself to all the world, no matter who may be there to see.

The next minute Lord Lonsdale was weeping upon the necks of his long-lost son and his fair young bride, whilst the guests sprang to their feet, filled their glasses, and shouted as with one voice, "Long life and happiness to Lord Vere and his bride! Welcome and happiness and honour to the bridal pair!"

Yet whilst others shouted and laughed and made the hall ring with their acclamations and glad congratulations and wondering questions, I turned aside and wept for joy. For until this happy hour I had not known with certainty that all would be well; and now that I knew the best, my heart so swelled with happiness and triumphant gladness that there was nothing for it but to weep, although never in all my life had I known such a moment of unalloyed happiness.

But one surprise was yet in store for me, and an honour that I little deserved; for you who have read these pages will know that I am no hero, albeit it has been my lot to witness some stirring scenes, and to find myself sometimes in perilous places. Whilst I wept in my corner I felt a touch upon my arm, and there was my lord standing before me all shining in his white and silver; and he took me by the hand and led me forward and presented me to his father and the company as the person who had saved his life more than once (though how he made that out I know not, my head was in such a whirl), and my lady put her hand upon my shoulder and told how I had served her—but that was not me, but Mistress Mary Bridges. Then the guests shouted again, and drained a bumper to my good health; and when I left the hall, it was carrying in my hands a small but weighty packet, which was placed there by my lady, but which I was too dazed even to look at then. And only when I got to my own room in the hall did I find that it was a purse containing five hundred golden guineas, and that I, Dicon Snowe, at the age of fifteen and a half years, was made a rich man for life.

EPILOGUE.

My story is done, in so far as I set myself the task of telling the tale of the ill-fated rising of the Duke of Monmouth. Yet methinks it will be more complete if I add but a few more words, and tell of how Will Wiseman revenged himself upon that wicked Judge whose cruelty and injustice wrought such misery and havoc in the prosperous and happy homes of the West.

Whilst the King was rousing hatred and anger throughout his realm, which ended in his being forced to fly the kingdom but four short years after the events I have related, I was living happily at Master Simpson's, having elected to join with him in his business (though later in life I became possessed of the Three Cups Inn, and left the shop to my eldest son, as being a place of less temptation for a youth than a house of entertainment), and being at the age of eighteen betrothed to pretty Lizzie, who loved me in spite of my crooked back, and has made me the best and most loving of wives.

Will Wiseman remained with us, rising from apprentice to shopman in due time; and when the kingdom was all in a turmoil of excitement at the reports flying about as to the flight of the wicked King, and the landing of his son-in-law, William of Orange, nothing would serve Will but that he must go up to London to see and hear the news. And since he had had no holiday for many years, we gladly encouraged him to do so; and thus it came about that he became, through God's Providence, an instrument for the punishment of that most wicked of wicked men, Lord Jeffreys.

Will stayed in the house of a poor scrivener at Wapping, and this man had the most terrible fear of the great Judge, having been once brought before him, and having never forgotten the gleam of those rolling eyes nor the frightful aspect of those bloated features.

All London was in a ferment. The King had fled, so it was said; and rumour said also that the wicked Chancellor, in awful terror of what might now befall him, had fled likewise, and that he was about to leave the kingdom in disguise, hidden away in some coaling-boat.

No one was perhaps more excited than Will by this intelligence; and when further information was brought by the mate of a coaling-vessel lying in the river to the effect that the Chancellor (if indeed he could be so termed seeing that the King had taken over the Great Seal into his own possession to destroy it) had come on board in disguise, and was actually lying hidden there till sailing-time next morning, Will was one of the excited and furious crowd who rushed off to the Justices of the Peace in that neighbourhood to obtain a warrant for his arrest.

But the Justices complained that since no specific charge was brought against Jeffreys, they could not grant this; and perhaps they were, in truth, still afraid of the man before whom so many of them had trembled in the days of his power. The people might have been baffled by this rebuff had it not been for the firmness of Will, who suggested that they should demand a warrant from the Lords of the Council; and from these dignitaries, who were still sitting, they obtained a warrant to arrest him on the charge of high treason, those ministers thinking it injurious to the welfare of the kingdom that he should be allowed to leave.

Armed with the warrant, they went on board the coaling-boat, and searched it through and through, but found no person bearing any likeness to the Chancellor. The Captain baffled all their inquiries; and it was only later that they discovered that Jeffreys had indeed been there, but finding the boat could not sail before morning, had gone upon another vessel for the night, and thereby nearly saved himself from his enemies and pursuers.

Nearly—but not quite. Chance, as some would call it; Providence and an outraged Maker, as we of Taunton maintain, decreed it otherwise.

Will, sorely grieved and disappointed, retired home at dark and went to bed as usual; but with the morning light restlessness came upon him, and he felt inaction impossible.

His host, the humble scrivener, was going about his daily duties, and Will walked with him. Their way led them through an unsavoury lane that was called Hope Alley, and lay hard by King Edward's Stair at Wapping. In passing down this alley they saw before them a sign hanging out, representing a Red Cow, which was the name of a pot-house much frequented by sailors. Will's glance travelling to this gaudy sign, suddenly encountered the gaze of a pair of rolling blood-shot eyes which seemed suddenly and strangely familiar. The next instant he had recognized, beneath the shade of a tarpaulin hat, the bloated visage of the terrible Judge last seen by him in the Assize Hall of Taunton.

Grasping the scrivener by the arm and whispering a few hurried words to him, Will hastened away for the guard; whilst the scrivener entered the house and the room, where the too reckless fugitive had adventured himself in order to indulge once more his intemperate love for strong drink, and found that worthy shrinking back into a corner, his hat pulled far over his eyes, his face hidden as much as he could hide it by a pint pot.

In a moment the house was surrounded by a hooting and yelling crowd. I have heard Will describe the scene a hundred times, and each time I seem to see it more plainly than the last—the cowering, craven coward now shivering and shrinking before men whom he had sworn at, raved at, cursed and brow-beaten, more cowed and terrified than the most miserable of his victims. And verily that crowd would have torn him limb from limb or ever the guards had come at him (for, contrary to the custom of an English mob, this one was bloodthirsty and furious to an extent which can better be imagined than described), had it not been for the action of the train-bands, who forced a way through the hooting mob and got the prisoner safe into a coach, though not before his clothes were torn half off his back, and he had been wounded by many a flying stone, and had shrieked aloud for mercy in his agony and terror.

That very day, after an interview with the Lord Mayor and by his own desire, he was carried to the Tower, but even so he barely escaped the fury of the populace; for when it was known that the coach contained this man so bitterly detested and feared, there were continual and determined attacks made upon it, and the bloated visage was seen from time to time appearing first at one window and then at another, whilst the miserable man clasped his hands and cried aloud for the mercy he never bestowed upon those who had implored it of him.

And thus he entered the Tower a miserable and despairing captive, only a little more than three years after that Bloody Assize with which his name will always be associated. Four months later he perished miserably, despised and hated by all men; and not even left in peace to die, but assailed by all sorts of malicious letters and even gifts which must have made his last days a hell upon earth to him. But enough of that bad man.

We of the West Country heard with stern satisfaction of his end, in the bright spring-tide and the happiness we were all feeling in the wise and just rule of our new Sovereigns. And the tale of how Will Wiseman was the instrument of his final capture, and thus was the means of avenging the miseries his hands had inflicted upon so many here, will always be a favourite one with young and old in Taunton Town.

Men remembered the prognostication of Mother Whale, and how she had prophesied an evil end for him, even as she had prophesied the exile of the tyrant monarch. It seemed, indeed, that in spite of all we had suffered, the Lord had been working on the side of virtue and freedom. The wicked King was disgraced and driven away; the yet more wicked Judge had died in the Tower.

THE END.

Lightning Source UK Ltd.
Milton Keynes UK
UKHW010701070820
367857UK00003B/777